THE WIZARD OF TIME

G. L. BREEDON

KOSMOSAIC BOOKS

Copyright © 2011 by G.L. Breedon
All rights reserved.
ISBN-10: 0983777705
ISBN-13: 978-0-9837777-0-0

For more information:
www.kosmosaicbooks.com

Thanks to my parents, for encouraging me to follow my dreams, no matter how long it might take.

Thanks to Andrea Clark, my constant first reader, for her lifelong friendship and diligent editing.

Thanks to my wife, Tsufit, for her boundless faith, her unceasing love, and her endless patience.

CHAPTER 1
THAT SINKING FEELING

Gabriel closed his eyes as the fist dug into his stomach, knocking the air from his lungs in a gust of breath and pain. He opened his eyes in time to see a second fist strike his chin. A blinding white light suffused his brain. His vision blurred as he saw another fist swinging for his face.

The bus swayed and the tires squealed as the brakes locked up. People screamed. He screamed. The bus hit the railing of the bridge. The boys beating him flew through the air as the bus tumbled over the railing, spinning as it fell. Gabriel spinning as it fell.

It must be a dream, he thought. It was too real.

The bus struck the water, the engine dragging it down into the river, the water rushing in, filling the bus as the screams echoed in the air until there was only water. Ice cold water filling his nose, filling his mouth, filling his throat, filling...

Gabriel woke from the dream, lurching up in bed, gasping, sputtering, and sucking for air as though water really were flowing down his throat and into his lungs against his will.

He hated dreams like that.

He had them sometimes. Dreams that felt more real than reality. Dreams where he saw and did things that felt like he was really seeing and doing them. But he knew they were dreams. He always knew. Because of the feeling. The feeling it was more real than his waking life. And he always knew something else as well — whatever happened in the dream would happen when he woke up. Not right after he opened his eyes, not in the first hour maybe, possibly not for a day or two, or even a week, but eventually it would happen.

So, Gabriel Salvador knew he was going to drown that day.

The first time it happened, he was five and he had dreamed he was falling out of a tree. The next day he had fallen out of the willow tree in the backyard. When he told his father about the dream, his

1

father had smiled and said it was what was known as a self-fulfilling prophecy. He dreamed he would fall out of the tree and then he had climbed the tree, remembered the dream, and was made so anxious by it that he had fallen. Gabriel didn't tell his father he hadn't remembered the dream until he saw the ground rushing up at him. He was lucky then. He only sprained his arm. But it happened again. And again. It couldn't be avoided. What he dreamed was going to happen.

Gabriel decided not to think about it. There was nothing he could do. If he stayed home from school, he might drown the next day. Or he might drown in the bathtub. Or it might rain for two days straight and he might drown in a flood. It didn't matter. But it didn't make him happy, either.

He climbed out of bed and looked at himself in the mirror above his dresser. He was tall and skinny for thirteen, his hair slightly wavy like his Jewish father's and dark black like his Guatemalan mother's. He looked like his father's child in the dim light of winter and his mother's in the sunny days of summer. Even his eyes seemed like a blend between his parents: deep brown with flecks of green. He wished one of his parents had been a fish. That might help.

He reached out to pluck his lucky pocket watch from the top of the dresser and paused. That was odd. Where was his lucky pocket watch? He had put it on the dresser the previous night before going out to practice catching fly balls with his dad in the back yard. Had it been there before he went to bed? He couldn't remember. Could it have fallen on the floor? Gabriel searched around the dresser and the room with no success. Where could it have gone? It seemed like a bad omen, losing your lucky pocket watch on the day you thought you were likely to die.

His father had given him the pocket watch on his thirteenth birthday, just as Gabriel's grandfather had given it to him when he had turned thirteen. His grandfather had inherited the watch in a foxhole during a battle in World War II when his best friend had thrown himself on a mortar to save his buddies' lives.

But there was no lucky watch to be found that morning no matter where Gabriel looked for it. He filled his pockets with the

2

usual things: coins, crumpled bills, a pack of gum, and a pocketknife and headed downstairs.

At breakfast his mother could sense his mood immediately. "Why the Glum Gus routine this morning?"

"Didn't sleep well," Gabriel said. He had learned long ago that telling his parents about his dreams never worked out. He didn't need any more lectures about over-active imaginations and he especially didn't need any more threats to see Dr. Wallace again. Gabriel didn't need a psychiatrist, he needed a hot breakfast. And a life jacket.

"Do I have to go today?" Gabriel asked. He knew the answer, but he figured he should try.

"Are you not feeling well?" his father asked.

"No, I'm fine." It was too late to start faking an illness. If he were going to go that route, he should have come down the stairs coughing. Besides, it didn't matter if he went or not. The dreams always came true.

"Then you have to go," his mother said.

"Is that boy still bothering you?" his father asked.

"No," Gabriel answered. "Not usually." Eddie Sloat was the neighborhood bully who had been pestering him for months.

"You should walk to school with Emily Baskin," his mother said. "You used to walk with her all the time."

"Emily hates me."

"That's ridiculous," his mother said. "Why would she possibly hate you?"

"Do you honestly think I understand why girls do any of the things they do?"

"Not to fear, Son," his father said with a grin. "Once they become women, their actions are wholly and completely comprehensible in every way. Why, I understand your mother better than I understand myself."

"That's odd," his mother said. "When boys turn to men they become completely obtuse. Your father surprises me every day with the things he says."

"I should go," Gabriel said, standing up. "Wouldn't want to be late." He kissed his mom and hugged his dad and started for the door.

"Walk with her."

"That's how I won your mother over. Ignoring her when she told me to go away."

Gabriel waved at his parents. If he couldn't figure out a way to let the dream happen without him drowning, it might be the last time he saw them.

"I love you both," he said as he closed the door.

***

The first raindrop exploded gently on Gabriel's face as he walked toward the school parking lot. He quickened his pace as a sheet of rain followed the lone raindrop. His best friends Tom and Harold laughed and rushed along with him and the rest of his class toward the waiting school bus. School was normally school, vastly boring daily drudgery, but today was a class field trip to the Museum of Natural History, so Gabriel was excited.

History was Gabriel's favorite subject. Baseball was the other. While Harold and Tom played other things, baseball was the only sport that had ever interested Gabriel. He suspected it was the history of the game that appealed to him — the way it had been woven into the character of the American psyche for over a century. Gabriel didn't think there would ever be a football player who held the same sort of mythological wonder as Babe Ruth or Mickey Mantle.

Stepping onto the bus, Gabriel wiped the rain from his face and looked around for a seat. Most of the seats were already taken. To his left he saw Emily Baskin. She looked up at him with a half-smile that quickly transformed into a scowl as he passed by her seat. Harold and Tom had already grabbed a seat, so Gabriel slipped into the seat across the aisle from them next to Larry, a sickly boy who was always sneezing. Something to do with allergies. Larry sneezed and wiped his nose on his jacket sleeve. How could you have allergies in a rainstorm, Gabriel wondered.

He groaned silently to himself as Eddie Sloat slid into the seat behind him and the bus rumbled into motion. Eddie was on the wrestling team and was forever wrestling smaller kids to the ground who had never even seen a wrestling match, twisting their arms, pushing their faces in the mud, and generally enjoying himself at their discomfort. Gabriel was one of his favorite targets, although Eddie had so far confined himself to verbal taunts and the occasional shoulder shove in the hallways.

Gabriel was skinny, but several inches taller than Eddie, so he had hoped to avoid any wrestling matches. Unfortunately, the thuggish red-headed boy bristled with animosity whenever Gabriel was around. Gabriel assumed it was because he was different. The only non-white kid in a small rural town. Although most of the kids accepted him for who he was, being different was enough for some people to hate you in a small town in 1980. It was certainly enough for Eddie.

Gabriel knew it was coming. It took no clairvoyance to see what would happen next. It was like it was scripted and he was just playing his part. It started with the finger snap to the back of his head. Gabriel didn't ignore it. His mother was always telling him never to start a fight, but to make sure he finished it if someone else did. His father was of the opinion that violence usually only led to more violence. Gabriel tried to walk a path somewhere between the two. Run when you could. Hit hard when you couldn't. Which is probably why he'd been able to avoid a fight with Eddie so far.

"Knock it off, Eddie," Gabriel said, whipping around and looking the other boy in the eyes.

"I didn't do anything," Eddie said with that gap-toothed grin of his.

Gabriel turned back around, but it wasn't long before the next finger snap came to the back of his head.

"Seriously, knock it off."

"It must be your imagination."

"I must have imagined you had enough of a brain to realize how stupid you're being." Not a great retort, but the best he could think of on short notice.

Then came the full-handed smack to the side of the head.

"If you want to fight, why don't you just fight?"

"I don't know what you're talking about."

"If you keep it up, Tom's going to kick your ass." That was Harold.

"I don't fight girls." That was Tom.

The fist came next. And then the pushing and the pulling and the yelling and the other fists. Some were Gabriel's landing on Eddie's face. Some were Eddie's landing on his. The bus was over the Tillet River Bridge by then. Gabriel was busy trying to punch Eddie's nose so he didn't have time to notice if the bus driver, Mrs. Hopper, was distracted. He thought he heard her voice somewhere in the din of shouting that erupted with the fight, but he wasn't sure. It didn't pay to listen to voices of authority when someone was punching you in the face.

So, maybe she was distracted. Maybe she turned the wheel when she was looking into the giant rearview mirror. Maybe she didn't see a car stop in front of her. Gabriel never knew. All he knew was the sudden fishtailing motion of the bus and then the squeal of metal against metal as the bus scraped along the guardrail of the bridge. And the screams. After the screams, it was hard to hear anything else. His own scream was particularly hard to hear over.

And then the bus was tumbling. Over the guardrail. Spinning as it fell. He could see the other students falling and twisting through the air, bouncing against seats and windows and the ceiling and the floor. He saw Tom's head hit a window. He saw Harold clutching at the leg of the seat. He saw Eddie, terror in his eyes and his mouth wide in mid-scream, slam his shoulder into the ceiling.

And he saw the water. The bus plunging toward it. Forty feet from bridge to river in long, panic-filled moments. Enough time to notice anything. A small eternity. And he had seen it all before.

The bus struck the water sideways and the motion within came to a jarring halt, bodies falling into the windows on the bottom. Some of the windows had been open. Others broke. The water began pouring in faster than Gabriel would have imagined possible. He was wedged under a body. Tom's body. Not moving. The blow to Tom's head must have knocked him unconscious. Gabriel could see Harold. Screaming. Everyone was still screaming.

"The door!" Gabriel screamed. He struggled up above the side of the seat and saw that the front door of the bus had been pushed open by the impact and water was rushing in. The entire bus would be flooded in seconds. He couldn't see Mrs. Hopper. Straining to push Tom's unconscious body off himself, he saw two kids struggling near the emergency door at the rear of the bus. It took a moment before he realized it was Emily Baskin and Eddie. Emily was struggling to get near the exit door and Eddie was trying to stop her.

"We have to get it open," Emily screamed.

"The water will come in," Eddie screamed back.

He probably can't swim, Gabriel thought. Gabriel hadn't been able to swim either until last spring. He hadn't wanted to learn, but his parents had insisted. It had been a mortifying experience. The only thirteen-year-old learning to swim with a class of seven and eight-year-olds. Apparently Gabriel had a higher tolerance level for mortification than most boys his age. He was glad he did. Otherwise, he might have been like poor Eddie; so afraid of drowning that he would try to stop the one person who could save him.

The water continued to flow into the interior of the bus from the windows and the front door. Emily continued to fight with Eddie near the emergency door at the rear. The water was up to their waists. People continued to scream. And Gabriel continued to struggle to get from underneath Tom.

He saw Eddie punch Emily in the face. Emily's head snapped back, but her legs never moved. She may have been a slender, geeky girl, but she knew how to take a punch. And she knew how to deliver one. Emily had six older brothers. Eddie saw the left hook, but he never noticed the right-handed haymaker that clocked him in the temple. Eddie collapsed with a splash into the ever-deepening water. Gabriel had just enough time to think that if it was going to be the last thing he saw, seeing Eddie Sloat being knocked out by Emily Baskin wasn't half bad.

Of course it didn't matter, Gabriel thought in a wave of despair. The rear emergency door only opened out. It would never budge until the water had already filled the interior of the bus. However, Emily didn't move to open the door. Instead, she reached down behind the rear seat and pulled free the large red fire extinguisher. *Why didn't I think of that?* Gabriel wondered as he continued to struggle with Tom's unconscious form.

Emily slammed the base of the fire extinguisher into the window of the exit door with all her strength. The window cracked. That was all. *Too bad*, Gabriel thought. Emily struck the window again. Nothing. She shouted in frustration and raised the fire extinguisher to strike again when the window suddenly imploded, a wall of water throwing her back into the bus. Gabriel barely had time to suck in a lung full of air before the water was over his head and the bus filled to capacity, sinking even faster than before.

Gabriel floated up to the opposite side of windows near the surface of the river as the bus swiftly sank to the bottom some fifteen feet below. The engine of the bus sank first, the rear falling more slowly. The bus rotated as it hit bottom, the ceiling becoming the floor. It was all Gabriel could do to keep his head straight and know which way was which. *Where was the door?*

He dragged Tom through the water, pulling him past the row of seats above their heads, struggling past kids panicking and drowning, past kids trying to swim for the exit door. Gabriel pushed people with one hand, pulling Tom with the other, using his feet to kick against anything he could use to reach the exit.

Someone before him had managed to open the door. Gabriel groped his way through the opening and looked around, seeing cloudy sky above the water fifteen feet over his head. He swam. He swam harder than he ever had before, the weight of Tom pulling him down, the small mouthful of air in his lungs burning to get out, stinging like acid in his chest. He could feel the weight of his clothes and shoes, his jacket making it harder to move his arms. He was getting closer. The water above his head was lighter. Brighter. Nearer.

He gasped for air, spitting water and wheezing. *I'm not going to drown today*, he thought as the rain beat down on his face. He grinned as he put his arm around Tom and began to swim for the shore. It wasn't far. Only thirty feet or so. He looked around as he swam and saw that he was not the only one swimming for the riverbank. Twenty or so of his fellow classmates paddled to safety. He could see Harold flailing his arms, trying to remember the strokes he must have learned when he was six like everyone else.

"Help me!" Gabriel shouted as he came to the shallow edge of the river. Harold struggled to reach them. Gabriel didn't even wait to get Tom all the way to the riverbank before turning him over, wrapping his arms around Tom's middle, and pulling repeatedly to empty the water from his stomach and lungs. Swinging Tom onto his back, Gabriel continued to push on his stomach to clear the water from his airway. Tom spit in Gabriel's face, his eyes fluttering open. Harold had reached them by then.

"Gabe," Tom said.

"You're okay now," Gabriel said.

"You saved me," Tom said with a weak laugh. "Just like Aquaman."

"There are still kids down there," Harold said, looking back at the river. The shimmering yellow form of the bus was easily visible beneath the gently flowing water.

"Stay here with Tom," Gabriel said as he looked into Harold's eyes. Harold could swim well enough to reach the shore once, but he would never make it twice.

"You can't go back down there!" Harold said, fear making his voice jump an octave.

"I'll be fine," Gabriel said, shrugging out of his jacket and kicking off his shoes. "My parents paid a lot of money so I'd be able to do stupid things like swim back down to sunken buses." He doubted that was what his mother had been thinking when she had insisted on the swimming classes.

He gave Tom a quick wave and then jumped back into the water, his legs kicking hard, his oddly long arms making for smooth, strong strokes that brought him to the middle of the river in hardly any time at all. His fellow students screamed, cried, shouted, and tried to swim for the shore. Gabriel looked down at the bus. He didn't see any motion, but he could see what looked like shadowy shapes that might be people. He sucked air in fast, let it out, and sucked it in again, filling his lungs. Then he dived.

He fought his body's natural inclination to float as he dove, his arms striking through the water in unison. It took a few seconds to reach the bottom of the river and the bus. A few seconds that allowed him to think. *What the hell am I doing?* He'd only learned to swim six months ago. Why was he the only one going back down? He'd been on the shore. The dream hadn't come true. Why tempt fate? And then he reached the bus and saw the two faces floating near the rear windows. That was why. Because you couldn't just let people die when you might be able to do something about it.

He edged around the emergency door and swam into the bus. There were more bodies than the two he had seen. They might be dead. Or maybe not. Five in all, he could see. He grabbed the one closest to the door. Emily. He thought she had gotten out. The fire extinguisher must have hit her when the window broke. Her open eyes stared right through him. He didn't look back for long. He grabbed her arm and hauled her toward the door, pushing her through and giving her a shove toward the surface. She moved upward. Not as fast as he had wanted. He hoped it was fast enough. He hoped someone above would get to her in time.

Looking back, he knew he couldn't save them all. Not all four that remained. He just couldn't hold his breath long enough. It wasn't possible. He could come back down. They might make it if he could come back down fast enough. He swam back into the bus and grabbed the arm of the next person he came to. *Perfect,* he thought. Just who he'd always imagined saving. Gabriel grimaced and pulled Eddie to the emergency door, pushing him through and giving him a shove toward the surface as he had with Emily.

Just enough, he thought. Just enough air. *One more and I'll go back up. Just one more,* he thought as he twisted around and swam back into the capsized bus once more. The next unconscious person he came to was Larry, the sickly boy who was always sneezing.

Larry's arm was wedged between the seat and the wall of the bus. Gabriel pulled on Larry's arm, but it was no good. Gabriel tried to pull at the seat. To bend it back just a little. Nothing. He pulled the seat with one hand and Larry's arm with the other. Harder. Harder. His lungs stung again. His vision was getting blurry. But he kept pulling. Then Larry's arm slipped free. Gabriel tugged at Larry and pulled him toward the emergency door. Then the world shifted.

The weight of the bus settling on the soft river bottom sent it tumbling again, lurching sideways once more. Gabriel spun with the bus as Larry's unconscious body fell on him, a shoulder pushing down into his stomach, forcing the air from his lungs in a burst.

Gabriel pushed and pulled at Larry's unconscious form, but it was no good. Larry was slight, hardly weighing a thing, but the angle of the seats kept him wedged against Gabriel.

He fought. He fought to move Larry's body. He fought to slide out from under him. He fought to hold what little air was left in his lungs. He fought to keep his vision straight. He fought the temptation to open his mouth. He fought as hard as he had ever fought for anything, but he couldn't stop himself. His body betrayed his will. His mouth slipped open and the bubbles of air flooded out. He tried to stop it. But it didn't last long. He pushed against Larry's body again. He knew it was a body now. Larry was dead. There was no saving him. No saving the others in the bus. No saving himself.

He held it as long as he could. Held the moment between breaths as long as he could. He knew how it would end. Just as it had ended in the dream. Maybe that was why he had come back down. Not to try to be a hero. Not because his conscience told him he should, but because of the dream. Because he knew the dream would be fulfilled no matter what he did.

He held on, hoping that someone would come down after him. One of the other students. Maybe a driver of a passing car. Someone. He held that un-breath and held it and held it and then before he knew it his mouth was open and he was sucking water into his lungs against his will. He willed his mouth to close, his lungs to expel the water, the spasms of his body to stop. He willed his eyes to stay open, his mind to stay clear, his vision to remain. He willed the blackness to stop. He willed his heart to start beating again. He willed his mind to remain conscious. He willed himself to remember his mother's face and the kiss she had given him. He willed himself to

11

remember his father's hug and his smile. He willed himself to remember who he was. He willed himself to remember his name. He willed himself to live.

And then Gabriel Salvador died.

CHAPTER 2
REBIRTH

Light.

Sounds.

Voices.

Was this death? Could you see lights and hear voices when you were dead? Was this the light at the end of a tunnel? No. The light seemed to come from everywhere. Could he see light without eyes? Did he still have eyes? Were his eyes open? Could he blink? The light winked out and back. He could blink. Could you blink when you were dead?

"He's coming around." A female voice. Soft and melodious.

"I hate this part." A male voice. Deep and resonant.

"Where?" That voice he recognized. That was Gabriel Salvador's voice. His voice. Could he have a voice if he were dead?

"You're safe," the female voice said. The room slowly came into focus and the lights did not seem as bright anymore. He lifted his head to the light and saw a large window. In front of the window stood a man and a woman. The man stood well over six feet tall, with a muscular build, deep black skin, and a wide, angular face with a hint of grey in his close-cut hair. He wore a necklace of shells around his neck. The woman was much smaller and much thinner, with olive-brown skin, piercing near-black eyes and a narrow face framed by a mane of deep gray hair. She wore a necklace with a small bluish teardrop-shaped glass pendant. Both wore white pants and white tunics. Could they be doctors?

"Everything will be okay," the man said.

"Am I dead?" Gabriel asked. Best to start with the most important question first.

"You were, and in some ways you are, but you aren't," the woman said.

"It's complicated," the man added. Dead but not dead. Yes, that sounded complicated.

"Where am I?" Gabriel asked. "Is this a hospital? Where are my parents? I have their work numbers on a laminated card in my pocket. My mom insisted. She likes to plan ahead."

"I hate this part," the man repeated.

"You're someplace safe," the woman said. That seemed…vague.

"My parents…?" Gabriel said.

"Your parents are fine," the man answered. That was vague as well. All this vagueness was beginning to make his head hurt.

"I want to see my parents," Gabriel said, trying to sound like he had the authority to demand what he wanted. He sat up a little. His head spun a bit, but it wasn't bad. He could see more of the room now. It clearly wasn't a hospital room. Not any hospital he'd ever seen. Not with walls of white painted stone.

"What's going on?" Gabriel said. "Why won't you tell me where I am? Why won't you let me see my parents? Who are you?" There was another question. One he didn't want the answer to. "What do you mean I was dead, but I'm not dead?"

"We will answer your questions," the woman said. "All of your questions. However, we have found that it is best not to head directly to the answers, but to come at them sideways. To sneak up on them, as it were. First come the introductions. My name is Sema and this is Ohin."

"I'm Gabriel."

"Yes, we know," said Ohin as he stroked his chin.

"Tell me, Gabriel," Sema asked, "did you know you were going to drown? Did you sense it in some way?"

Gabriel's eyes opened a little wider. How could they know? What was going on? "Yes," he replied. "I had a dream."

"And you had dreams like this often, didn't you," Ohin said. It wasn't a question.

"Yes," Gabriel answered. "My parents always think I'm making it up."

"But the things you see in your dreams always come true," Sema said.

14

"Yes," Gabriel said. "No matter what I do."

"But do they always come true exactly the way you dream them?" Ohin asked.

"No," Gabriel answered. "If I try to change them, the events change, but the result is the same."

"This is usually called precognition or clairvoyance," Sema said.

"It is a sign," Ohin added. "An indicator."

"Of what?" Gabriel asked.

"Of sensitivity," Sema said.

"Sensitivity to what?" Gabriel pressed.

"What do you think?" Ohin asked in return.

"What kind of game is this?" Gabriel asked. "Who are you?"

"Sensitivity to what?" Ohin repeated.

Gabriel didn't like this. No answers, just more questions. Questions he didn't like the answers to. And he knew the answer to the question. This wasn't the first time he had thought about the dreams and what they meant and why he had them. He'd asked this question himself. Many times. And he still didn't like the answer.

"Sensitivity to what?" Ohin said a third time, his voice gentle.

"To the flow of time," Gabriel said, staring into the deep brown eyes of the strange man before him.

"So you think you know what's going to happen in the future?" Sema asked.

"Sometimes," Gabriel said. "When I dream. When the dream feels more real than being awake."

"And do you believe that you see the future?" Ohin asked.

"Sometimes," Gabriel said.

"Sometimes you see the future or sometimes you believe it?" Sema asked.

"Sometimes I see the future," Gabriel said. "I always believe it."

"If you believe you can see the future, and you dreamed of yourself drowning," Ohin asked, "why did you swim back down to the bus when you were safe on the shore?"

"Because it wouldn't have changed anything," Gabriel said. "Even if I had stayed with Tom on the shore, it would have worked out that I was drowning some way. It always does."

"So you believe the future is immutable?" Ohin asked. "Fixed in stone."

"Not exactly," Gabriel replied. "It's flexible like the branch of a tree. You can bend it a little, but it always springs back to where it was. Just a little different, maybe."

"So you believe the future is set, but somewhat malleable?" Sema asked.

"Yes," Gabriel said. "That's what I said. What is this? Why are you asking me these questions?"

"Why don't you take a moment to think it through?" Ohin said.

"We've told you everything you need to know," Sema added.

Gabriel had been thinking it through. While one side of his mind answered Ohin and Sema's questions, the other side puzzled through all of the possibilities, examining all of the things he knew and looking for potential answers that would fit the circumstances. Why was he here with strangers? Why did they not look like doctors? Where were his parents? Why was this not a hospital? Why were they asking him questions about his dreams and seeing the future? How could they have known about his dreams about the future? How could they have known he had sensed he would drown? How could they have known that he swam back down to the bus? Why would they say that he had been dead? That he was dead, but in some ways, he wasn't?

"What year is this?" Gabriel asked. Best to ask a question when you fear you have the right answer. Particularly if the answer to your question might prove you wrong, and Gabriel desperately wanted to be wrong.

"Oh, he's quick," Sema said.

"It took me ten minutes," Ohin said.

"You haven't answered my question," Gabriel said, a hint of annoyance and fear finally reaching his voice.

"Because the answer will sound absurd without some explanation," Ohin said. "First, let me tell you that you are not in the time and place you were when you died."

"So I did die?" Gabriel asked. It had certainly felt like it when the water filled his lungs and his vision went black. Gabriel pushed the thought away.

"Yes," Sema said. "That was necessary, unfortunately."

"But I'm not dead now." Gabriel said. That seemed clear enough.

"Not from your perspective," Ohin said. Maybe not as clear as he thought.

"If I'm not dead from my perspective, from whose am I?" Gabriel asked.

"Think it through," Ohin said in a soft voice.

Gabriel was getting a little tired of being asked to think things through. "I'm dead to everyone in my time, aren't I?" he said. Ohin only nodded in response. "My parents. My sister. My friends. Everyone I knew. They all think I'm dead."

"You are dead in their time, Gabriel," Sema said. "You did drown in that bus. You did die."

"But then how can I be here?" Gabriel asked. "And how can they think I'm dead if there's no body? And don't tell me to think it through."

"If you knew the answer to that question without being told, I'd be lining up to be *your* apprentice," Ohin said. "You did die, but we took you from the bus the moment you expired. And your parents think you are dead because they buried a body that looked just like yours."

"I'll never see my parents again, will I?" Gabriel asked, tears beginning to push at the edges of his eyes. He knew the answer, but he had to ask.

"That you can think through, as well," Ohin said.

"If I went back to them," Gabriel said, thinking out loud, "that would change things. If I went back, time couldn't snap back to where it should be."

"Exactly," Sema said. "And what do you think would happen then?"

Good question, Gabriel thought. What happened when you changed time so badly it couldn't go back to the way it was supposed to be? Would time just change permanently? That didn't seem right. That didn't fit with the way he dreamed the future. If time couldn't change, either it was physically impossible for him to return to his parents, or doing so would result in something else. Something different.

"It would create two times," Gabriel said. "If I went back, it would change time and there would be two timelines, one where I was dead and one where I just appeared alive again."

"You are going to have your hands full, Ohin," Sema said.

"I am going to have the best apprentice the Council has seen in a hundred years," Ohin replied with a smile. "You are right, Gabriel. If you went back now, the Primary Continuum, the central timeline of the universe, would spilt. Your presence would be so radically different that the Primary Continuum could not absorb the change, and a bifurcation, a new branch of time, an alternate reality, would be created. A parallel universe where, as you said, you simply appeared."

"So why can't I do that?" Gabriel said. He was starting to get angry now. This wasn't fair at all. Whoever these people were, they should not be keeping him here when he could go home. "You brought me here, wherever here is, you can take me back. Who cares if there's a parallel universe where I'm alive? I think that would be a great universe. I'm sure my parents would be happy about it."

"What happens when a tree has too many branches?" Ohin asked.

"What happens when a branch has too many branches?" Sema added.

"And what happens if the branches reach too far from the main trunk of the tree?" Ohin continued.

Gabriel saw it in his mind. Branches reaching out too far, tilting the tree, the trunk splintering under the weight, breaking away, killing the tree. "The Primary Continuum is damaged by branches, isn't it? The more branches, the more dangerous it is to the entire timeline. So I can never go back." He felt the weight of the words sink into his heart. They had taken him just as he died so that his absence wouldn't change the main timeline. But why had they taken him in the first place? Why expend all that effort to save *his* life? Did he really want to know?

"You can move through time," Gabriel said, ignoring the questions in his head.

"Not me," Sema said. "Ohin is the one who can move through time. And take others with him."

"How?" Gabriel said. "How is that possible?"

"Magic," Ohin said.

"Seriously," Gabriel said. "How is it possible? Do you have a time machine?"

"I told you," Ohin said, "it's magic. All I have is my talisman." He touched the seashell necklace on his chest.

"There are many magics," Sema said. "There is magic to control matter and magic to control living things and magic to control energy. Mine is Soul Magic, which allows me to affect people's minds. And it is why you are far calmer than you might otherwise be."

"You're using magic on me?" Gabriel asked. It made no sense. Except that it did. Why was he so calm? Could there really be magic? Was this all a joke?

"Why do you think we have brought you through time to this place?" Ohin asked.

Gabriel knew the answer to the question. He just didn't want to say it out loud. Because it would sound too bizarre. Too impossible. "You took me because you think I can travel through time," Gabriel said.

"We don't think so," Sema said. "We know it."

"I can sense the power in you as easily as I sense it in myself," Ohin said. "You will be a Time Mage, Gabriel. That is why we have brought you here. To train you. Because we need you. We need all the Mages of Grace we can find. There is a war on, and we are losing. The War of Time and Magic. And if we do not succeed, the entirety of the Primary Continuum is at risk."

"Maybe we should explain that later," Sema said. "He is strong of heart and mind, but I can sense he is at the breaking point."

19

It was true. Gabriel did feel dizzy. Like he hadn't eaten in days. Like the room was spinning. "Where am I?" he said. "I need to know. When am I?"

"You are in England," Ohin said. "Or what will eventually become England. And if you sit up and look out the window, you'll have a better idea of when."

Gabriel forced himself into a full sitting position and looked past Ohin and Sema and through the slightly warped glass of the ancient window. Outside the window lay what seemed to be a cornfield, which might have made sense, but beyond that was something more difficult to explain. It was alive and nearly as tall as the tree it stood eating the leaves from. Four stout legs, a massive body, incredibly long tail, and a long, thick neck. There was no mistaking it. There was a dinosaur outside the window.

"That's…" Gabriel began. "That's…"

"That a Pelorosaurus," Sema said with a matter-of-fact tone.

"That's crazy," Gabriel said. "We must be seventy million years in the past."

"Nearly a hundred and twenty-five million," Ohin said. "It seems far, but time is really interrelational. Every moment is just as far from every other."

"Right," Gabriel said. "Of course. That makes perfect sense." Sema was right. He was at a breaking point. And he broke right past it. His eyes rolled up in his head and he passed out, falling back into the mattress of the bed.

"I hate this part," he heard Ohin say as everything went black.

CHAPTER 3
THE CASTLE

The birdlike creatures circled above, but never seemed to land. Or at least they were something that would one day evolve into birds. In millions of years.

Gabriel walked through the Upper Ward of Windsor Castle with Ohin. The Upper Ward was an inner courtyard of sorts. The castle was something else. Ohin had explained that it wasn't the real Windsor Castle. Well, it was *a* Windsor Castle, but not the one from the Primary Continuum. It had been snatched from an unstable branch of time in 1971 CE, just before the branch was severed from the Primary Continuum. It was fortunate timing, because a fire in 1992 had damaged more than a hundred rooms of the castle. Ohin said that it had required nearly fifty Time Mages working together to move the castle back into the far past of the Primary Continuum. Apparently you could move between alternate branches of reality and the Primary Continuum, but Ohin had not yet explained how. There was so much he hadn't explained.

This Windsor Castle was now the seat of the Grand Council of Magic. The stones of the castle had been altered with magic to degrade into ash if the Mages required it. A precaution, Ohin had said, in case something went terribly wrong. This way no archeologist in the future would ever dig up the remains of a one hundred twenty-five million-year-old castle. That was the sort of thing that created bifurcations, branches in time. It was the same reason the castle was placed so far in the past. Even if the presence of the castle somehow disturbed the dinosaurs outside its walls, it would be unlikely to create a bifurcation of the Primary Continuum since all the dinosaurs would go extinct around sixty-five million years BCE. Ohin had said that the castle had limited electricity, powered by a series of small

21

windmills outside the castle walls. Lighting also came from oil lamps, candles, and magic.

Gabriel tried not to think about too much of it. It was all very confusing. He had lain in bed for an entire day, contemplating it. Only after a good meal and a good night's sleep had he been allowed out of bed. Too much shock to the system to get up too soon, Sema said. Take things slowly, he was told. Try not to rush. Let your mind and body adjust. Adjust to being dead and then alive and being a Time Mage. Sure. That was easy. Just lie in bed and think about it all.

Sema had arrived the next morning for what she said would be their daily walk together. Mostly she asked him questions about his family. Letting him talk about his loss. He spoke about his mother, his father, and his sister. About missing them more than he had thought possible. About all the memories that flooded into his mind. Random memories. Like the rainy Saturday two years ago when his mother had made tomato soup and grilled cheese sandwiches, and they had all spent the afternoon together watching *The Philadelphia Story* on TV. It was his mother's favorite film. She loved Cary Grant. Memories like that. Sema informed him that his mother, father, and sister all lived long and happy lives. That made him feel better. Knowing they were happy somewhere in time.

When he asked, she told him that only three of his classmates had perished in the sunken bus that day. He had saved two lives. It was good to know that his death had made a difference.

He was in a much better mood by the time Ohin met them. As Sema departed, Gabriel wondered how much of his good mood was due to her magic and how much was the result of speaking aloud his deepest feelings. That could be pretty powerful magic of a different kind, he realized. But none of it really calmed his mind. And seeing the castle gave him more to think about. So much it felt overwhelming. Maybe they were right. Maybe he should have stayed in bed. Best to stick with things at hand. Things that he could think about one at a time.

"Why don't they ever land?" Gabriel asked, looking up at the leathery, winged creatures in the sky.

"There is an invisible barrier around the castle," Ohin explained. "It makes sure nothing gets near the castle and no one steps outside its grounds. Another security measure. The Council placed this castle far enough in the past so that it wouldn't be likely to affect the Primary Continuum, but there is no sense taking chances."

"And why Windsor Castle?" Gabriel asked, looking around the magnificent structure and its grounds one more time. It had been quite a shock to step from his room in the infirmary and into the courtyard to see the castle. He had recognized it immediately. He and his parents had taken a trip to London when he was eleven and he had spent hours dragging them around the castle and pouring over the guidebook for interesting bits of history. He loved the ghost stories in particular. King Henry VIII haunting the cloisters, the specter of Queen Elizabeth I in the Royal Library, the spirit of Herne the hunter and gamekeeper stalking the grounds with his wraithlike pack of dogs. He wondered if any of the ghosts had been brought back in time with the castle.

"The head of the Council, Elizabeth Palfrey, chose the castle," Ohin said. "I assume she wanted something that could house everyone. She was born in Victorian London, so maybe it felt comfortable."

It was certainly large enough. He supposed it needed to be. Hundreds of people lived in the castle. Although the Upper Ward was nearly empty at this time of the morning, he could see several people walking from one place to another on some sort of business. People from different times. Nearly all of them snatched at the moment of their deaths and brought here. People of all different ages, as well. Teenagers to elderly people. He was the youngest person he had seen. But he hadn't seen everyone. And the older people were older than they had been when they died.

Ohin had explained that Heart-Tree Magic, the magic of living things, helped them recover from the things that had killed them and kept them alive much longer. Ohin had said that he was nearly two hundred years old himself. It was difficult for Gabriel to get his mind around. People from throughout time bumping up against each other in a castle one hundred twenty-five million years in the past. People from every time period. Even people from the future. His future. They looked as though they had come from all over the world. Africans, Peruvians, Europeans, Chinese, Japanese, Samoans, everyone from everywhere. Some wore clothes from different time periods. Or they were clothed in variations on the simple tunic and slacks that Ohin wore.

It was almost too much to take in. But he wanted to take it in. At least part of him did. He had been given a second chance. He had been plucked back from death to be an apprentice Time Mage. It was too much to believe. He would learn to travel through time. To see places and things that others could only dream about. But no one had asked him. No one had given him a choice. Did he still have a choice? He would never see his parents again. Never see his friends. His sister. He was dead to them. What choice would he be given if he didn't want to become a Time Mage? He wondered if Ohin had felt this way when he had awoken from death to learn his fate.

"You're very quiet," Ohin said, placing his hands behind his back as he walked.

"What if I don't want this?" Gabriel asked. "What if I don't want to be a Time Mage? What if I don't want to travel through time and fight some war?"

"That is the moral quandary we are faced with every time we extract someone from the timeline," Ohin said.

"That isn't much of an answer," Gabriel said.

"No," Ohin replied. "There are no good answers. If you choose not to become an apprentice Time Mage, and you choose not to help in the war between the forces of Grace and Malignancy, then you will be given the opportunity to live out your life here in the castle. You might become one of the attendants, those who take care of the grounds and do the cooking. Or you could become a librarian or a museum scholar."

"So my choices are librarian or wizard of time," Gabriel said. "Will I go to school to learn magic?" Gabriel asked.

"A school for magic?" Ohin said, cocking his head to the side. "What an amusing idea. No. There are no schools here. Although your studies will continue. History especially. As for magic, all mages apprentice with a mentor, a skilled and superior mage. It will be my responsibility to train you, to teach you how magic works and how to move through time. And to teach you how to bear the responsibilities of being a mage, particularly a Time Mage."

"What sort of responsibilities are there?" Gabriel asked.

"The responsibility for the Primary Continuum, for one," Ohin answered. "And for the actions that we mages take within the Continuum and its branches. All of our actions have consequences. And we must accept the responsibility of our actions." It was sounding like being a Time Mage might not be as much fun as he initially imagined it to be.

"Will it just be you and me, or will there be other mages who I'll apprentice with?"

"You will apprentice with only me," Ohin said, "but you will join my unit. Mages are assigned to magic circles, teams of six that carry out missions together. Every team has a name. Our unit is called the Chimera Team."

"Why six?"

"There are six kinds of magic," Ohin said, "And each person can only accomplish one of them. So mages work together in teams of six."

"When do I begin?"

"We will begin soon," Ohin answered. "But there are introductions to make first." He gestured with his hand to where Sema walked back across the yard with a man and a girl.

"Oh," Gabriel said. They probably made you wait forever to get to the good stuff. Just like all teachers.

"Today you will meet the rest of the team," Ohin said. "Tomorrow you will travel through time."

Gabriel smiled at the thought of that. Traveling through time. Just a few days after being dead. It could make your head whirl if you thought about it too much. So much new information. So many extraordinary facts. So many wonders. And all coming so quickly. He felt like he had no time to breathe between revelations. But he had no more time to think about it because Sema was waving as she walked up with the man and girl.

Not a man and girl. While the one was a slender Hispanic girl, the other was an exceptionally tall Chinese woman. Not as tall as Ohin, but she stood at least six feet. Her long black hair was in a ponytail, which was why Gabriel had mistaken her gender at a distance. They wore the same white tunics Gabriel had seen most people in the castle wearing.

"Hello again, Gabriel," Sema said.

"Hello," Gabriel replied, smiling at Sema and the woman and girl.

"My name is Teresa," the girl said, extending her hand. She looked to be about fourteen and stood an inch or so taller than Gabriel. She had an oval face with a button nose and hazel brown eyes. He wondered what time she was from as he shook her hand. She had a powerful grip for a skinny teenage girl. The tall woman also extended her hand as she smiled.

"Welcome to the team," she said. "My name is Ling." While Teresa possessed the gangly energy of a young colt, Ling seemed all fluid symmetry and grace, her height and slender build combining to give the impression of a tiger at rest. She had high cheekbones and an almost masculine chin. He thought she might be in her late thirties. As she bent down to meet his eyes, he noticed she wore a Taoist yin-yang symbol dangling from a necklace.

"These are two more members of our team," Sema said. "You'll meet the others later today. Everyone plays a different, but essential role."

"Sema plays mother hen," Teresa said.

"Even to those of us who have been mothers ourselves," Ling added, her eyes narrowing as she grimaced.

"Well, you all need some mothering," Sema said, standing a bit straighter. "Someone has to look after all of you."

"That's supposed to be my job," Ohin said.

"Yes, but you're too nice about it," Sema said.

"So Ohin is in charge of the, what did you call it, the Crimean Team?" Gabriel asked.

"Chimera," Ohin said with a frown as Teresa giggled. "It's a Greek mythological creature with the heads of a lion, a goat, and a dragon. Each team chooses its name, as well as its leader. It is often the Time Mage, but not always."

"He doesn't want to hear all the boring rules of team organization," Teresa said. "He's a boy. He wants to see some magic. Like this." Teresa turned slightly to the side and raised her arms out before her, the palms of her hands facing the sky. In the blink of an eye, a lightning-blue ball of fire the size of a beach ball burst into existence above Teresa's hands.

Gabriel's eyes went wide and Teresa gave him a mischievous grin. He knew it must be true, since he stood in a castle with dinosaurs outside its walls, but until that moment, he hadn't been sure if he believed it. Now he believed. Magic was real.

CHAPTER 4
MAKING MAGIC

"If you're going to be a showoff," Ohin said, "you should at least explain how it works."

"Right," Teresa said as Gabriel blinked in wonder at the fireball floating before her. "First off, there are six kinds of magic." As she spoke, the fireball broke into six small balls of flame and assumed the shape of a hexagon floating in front of her. "First there's Fire Magic, which as you probably guessed, is my specialty. Each mage can only work with one kind of magic."

"Unless they are a True Mage," Ling interjected. "Then they can use all six forms of magic."

"But there are only six of them," Teresa said, "so that doesn't really apply to mages like you and me. As I was saying, before I was so rudely interrupted, there are six kinds of magic. Fire Magic, which is the best kind of magic if you ask me, although I doubt you will, because no one ever asks me what I think, controls energy. Any form of energy. Fire. Lightning. You name it. If there is energy to be magicked, I'm your gal. Then you have Wind Mages, like Ling, and they control the elemental forces of the universe. Such as…Such as. Hey, what are the forces of the universe, anyway? They sound really boring."

"You know very well what the forces of the universe are," Ling said, glaring slightly at Teresa's teasing. "They are the forces that allow the universe to function. Like magnetism and gravity." As Ling said the word 'gravity,' Teresa rose into the air and hovered there a foot and a half above the ground. Gabriel's jaw dropped open. He snapped it shut. He might be shocked and amazed, but there was no need to look like a bewildered bumpkin. Teresa smiled down at Ling.

"You're so easy to manipulate," Teresa said. "I wanted to be floating." Ling raised an eyebrow in skepticism and Teresa slowly rotated until she hung upside down, her ponytail pointing toward the grass, fireballs still suspended in the air before her hands. "And you cannot believe how much I love being upside-down."

"Ling," Sema said, a hint of disapproval in her voice. "What if she scorches the grass?" Gabriel looked over to see Ohin shaking his head. It seemed this sort of thing went on quite a bit.

"You know I never lose control of fire," Teresa said. At that, Ohin coughed and looked at her. "Well, except for that one time. How was I supposed to know the room was filled with explosives? No one told me. No one ever tells me anything. Besides, if something happens to the precious grass, Marcus can fix it."

"Marcus is one of the other team members," Ling said as she watched Teresa slowly spin back to the upright position and gently land on the lawn. "He is a Heart-Tree Mage, which means he has power over living things, like plants, animals, and humans. Heart-Tree Magic can heal and change living matter."

"And he can grow things," Teresa added, letting the fireballs fade away. "Like bodies that look exactly like ours, but aren't really alive. Very handy when you're plucking people out of time at the moment they die. Police like to have a body." Sema glared at Teresa in a way that suggested she was being rude or insensitive or both. Teresa ignored her.

"And inanimate matter," Ling said, pretending she hadn't been interrupted, "like rocks and metal, are controlled by Stone Magic,"

"Rajan is our Stone Mage," Teresa said. "I'm sure you'll meet him later. It'll be a pleasure. He'll tell you so himself."

"So you have Stone Magic for matter," Ling continued, "Heart-Tree Magic for life, Soul Magic for the mind, Fire Magic for energy, Wind Magic for the forces of the universe, and Time Magic for space and time. So, there you are. Magic in a clam shell."

"Nutshell," Teresa said with a giggle.

"Whatever," Ling said.

"But how does it work?" Gabriel said, looking from one face to another.

"How it works," Teresa sighed. "Boys love to know how it works. Never why."

"Magic works," Sema said, ignoring Teresa, "by focusing the mind on the fundamental nature of the universe and using the power of a talisman to concentrate and multiply that mental energy to alter the universe and perform one of the six kinds of magic."

"What kind of talisman?" Gabriel asked. He knew that a talisman was any kind of object that held personal or ritual significance. He noticed now that Teresa was wearing an ornately carved golden bracelet, just as Ling wore a yin-yang symbol at her neck, Sema a small teardrop glass pendant on a necklace, and Ohin had his seashells.

"A talisman can be anything," Ohin explained. "But it must be something that has the proper imprints."

"Imprints?" Gabriel asked.

"Every action leaves an imprint on the fundamental fabric of the universe," Ling explained. "These imprints stay with people or places or things."

"Imprints can be either positive, or negative, or neutral," Teresa added. "The greater the imprints, the more powerful the object or place becomes."

"An artifact is any object with strong imprints," Ohin said. "Imagine a sword that was used to kill hundreds of people. It would have strong negative imprints."

"Just as an object that was worn by someone who healed people would have strong positive imprints," Ling said.

"Mages have to use artifacts with strong imprints to perform magic," Gabriel said, making a connection he wasn't entirely sure of.

"Yes," Sema said. "Objects with negative imprints are called 'tainted' artifacts, while objects with positive imprints are called 'imbued' artifacts. A talisman is an artifact that has a special connection and meaning for a mage, lending it more power."

"But mages can only use either positive or negative imprints to perform magic," Gabriel said, seeing what that implied. "And that is why we're at war."

"You are correct," Ohin said. "A Grace Mage can only make use of positive imprints while a Malignancy Mage can only make use of negative imprints."

"We're the Grace Mages, in case you were wondering," Teresa said.

"Who are the Malignancy Mages?" Gabriel asked, unsure if he wanted to know.

"You'll run into them soon enough," Sema said. "Hopefully not before you are ready."

"He'll be ready," Ohin said, suddenly distracted as he turned to watch several people running across the courtyard. "He will be my apprentice, after all." Ohin squinted and looked at Sema, whose eyes had suddenly become unfocused as she looked upward. She seemed as though she were listening to some voice that no one else could hear. Gabriel saw more people running through the castle grounds now.

"We must go," Sema said, her eyes focusing on Ohin. "The Hiroshima outpost."

"Why don't the two of you show Gabriel around the castle?" Ohin suggested, his face grave. "It seems we have some business to attend to."

"It would be our pleasure," Ling said with a nod toward Gabriel. Sema took Ohin's arm and the two of them suddenly winked out of existence.

Teresa reached over and closed Gabriel's once again gaping mouth. "Probably jumped to the council chambers," she said by way of explanation. "You'll get used to it. You'll be able to do it yourself soon."

As Gabriel recovered from the shock of seeing Ohin and Sema disappear, the reason for their departure and the sudden activity of the castle coalesced in his mind. "There's been an attack?" he asked.

"You'll get used to that, too," Teresa said. "Happens all the time."

"It's nothing for you to worry about," Ling said, placing her hand on Gabriel's shoulder for reassurance. "Why don't we give you the grand tour?"

"Great idea," Teresa said. "I can show you all the places to hide when they need extra help in the kitchen."

"I'm sure you know all of them," Ling said with frown as she and Teresa led Gabriel across the Upper Ward courtyard.

Gabriel spent the rest of the afternoon getting a tour of the castle from Ling and Teresa. Construction on the castle had begun in the year 1350 CE, but it saw its largest expansion starting in 1824 when, for twelve years, the architect Jeffrey Wattville, commissioned by King George IV, brought the various buildings together with one vision. When it was finally completed, the castle covered some twenty-six acres.

The immense St. George's Chapel, although still used for various worships services, had been largely converted into a museum housing thousands and thousands of artifacts from every time and place imaginable throughout human history. Teresa mentioned the relics were necessary for time travel, but did not elaborate. Ohin would explain time travel, she said.

"Where do you both come from?" Gabriel asked as they walked along the wide hallway. "You both speak such perfect English."

"Thanks to this," Ling said, as she pulled a small crystal amulet on a chain around her neck from beneath her tunic. The crystal was oblong in shape, smoothly polished, with a milky white color. "This is a communication and concealment amulet."

"Soul Mages can make them," Teresa explained. "They create a psychic link between the person wearing it and everyone nearby. They translate language in our heads. And they can change the way we look so we blend in wherever we go." Teresa seemed to shimmer and then was suddenly wearing a long, blue, ornately milled Victorian dress. She winked at Gabriel and then shimmered again and was back in her white tunic and pants.

"So, it sounds to you like I'm speaking English," Ling said, "but actually I'm speaking Mandarin Chinese with the accent of a peasant fisherwoman near Shanghai in eighteen-sixty-nine, which is when I died giving birth to my fourth child."

"I'm sorry," Gabriel said, looking away. "I didn't mean to pry into your past."

"That's very sweet of you to say," Ling said, "but it has been nearly ten years since that day, and while I miss my husband and children, I miss them no more than anyone else who lives in this castle misses those they have had to leave behind. We get used to sharing our pasts. It helps."

"It hurts letting go of everyone I've ever known," Gabriel admitted, feeling the emotion of the statement catch in his throat.

"It sucks," Teresa said. "But there is one consolation."

"What's that?" Gabriel said, staring up into her eyes.

"Now we can do magic," Teresa said with a grin as she cupped her hands and a small ball of red flame leapt into existence above her palms. "And soon, you will be able to take yourself anywhere in time."

They walked back out to the Lower Ward courtyard and Ling left Teresa to continue the tour while she ran about some other business. Teresa gave a constant running commentary on the history of the castle and all of the things that had happened in the various buildings in the past, as well as all the things that had happened since she had lived there.

Gabriel listened as she talked and followed her finger as she pointed from one place to the next. As they walked, he found it harder and harder to pay attention and found himself once again thinking about his family. About walks with his sister, Kyla. About the last time he'd seen her. He thought about how she would never tease him again, or give him a book to read, or try to get him to eat her vegetables at family holidays so she could have more room for dessert. Gabriel suddenly realized that they had stopped walking and that Teresa had not spoken for some time.

"It'll get easier," Teresa said.

"Really?" Gabriel asked, looking away and rubbing his eye as though there were dust in it.

"It takes time," Teresa said. "I was born into a really large family. My grandparents loved kids. Lots of kids. They had seven, and each of their children had at least two kids. I had an older and a younger brother. And the whole family lived in the same neighborhood. We all spent most of our time at my grandparent's house. There was always somebody running through the kitchen, somebody making dinner, somebody breaking something, somebody fighting, somebody changing diapers, somebody laughing, somebody singing. Always something.

"Dinner was my favorite time. Everyone there all at once. All the voices all at once. My Grandfather and his big booming voice, swearing in Spanish for quiet and my mom insisting that everyone speak English at the dinner table. And my youngest brother wanting to know if it was okay to swear in English at the dinner table. I think the only thing that kept me sane when I came here is that there is always something going on. So many people all together like a big family. Ohin's not my dad, and Ling's not my mom, and Rajan isn't my big brother, but they're close enough. And after a while, they really grow on you. Even Rajan. He drives me crazy, but he's risked his life to save mine more than once. So, just be patient. It'll get easier."

"Thanks," Gabriel said. "I'll be fine."

"I know you will. Now let's see the tower where they used to keep the prisoners." She grabbed Gabriel's hand and pulled him into a run toward the tower across the courtyard.

CHAPTER 5
THE WATERLOO CHAMBER

Gabriel ate dinner that night in the Waterloo Chamber of Windsor Castle with Ohin, Sema, Ling, Teresa, and the two members of the team that he had not yet encountered: Marcus and Rajan. Originally a courtyard that had been roofed over during the restorations that began in 1824, the Waterloo Chamber was enormous. Paintings commemorating the battle of Waterloo in 1815 and the English triumph over Napoleon's invasion attempt lined the walls. The long and exceptionally large room provided plenty of space for hundreds of the castle inhabitants to dine together at one time.

The seven members of Ohin's team sat at one end of an incredibly long table that stretched the length of the room. They shared a blueberry pie that Sema served to each of them on small, ornate plates. The dinner had been magnificent. Big, thick slices of roast beef with small red potatoes baked in butter and rosemary. There had been string beans and peas and carrots and corn on the cob, all served on beautifully decorated china plates. The dinner conversation had ranged far and wide, but Gabriel had been able to learn where and when his new companions had come from.

Sema was from a successful merchant family in Istanbul at the height of the Ottoman Empire. She had married early and had a large family, being just as successful helping her husband mind the business as she was at minding the children. She had lived a long life and had been taken from the timeline in 1535 CE.

Ohin had been born into a Coptic Christian family in 425 CE in Aksum, or what would become known as Ethiopia. He had been a stonemason and had also married young, but died in his early twenties in a construction accident when a ceiling fell in on him. He was taken from the timeline shortly before his first child was born.

Gabriel felt boring and uninteresting compared with everyone else at the table.

"How are you enjoying your first meal in the castle, lad?" Marcus asked. "I always wanted to be invited to eat at Windsor Palace when I was a boy, and now I'd trade having hair again just to eat somewhere else for a change." Marcus had a real English accent. From England, not some psychically implanted translation from an amulet. He had been plucked from the timeline in 1763 CE, and he looked to be about sixty years old now. The way he had explained his death, it had been unclear whether he was a thief who had been killed for robbing an inn, or if he had been an innkeeper who was killed by a thief. He was a warm and gregarious man of medium height with bright hazel green eyes and a shiny, bald head.

"The meal is great," Gabriel answered, trying to swallow a bite of pie without chewing so he wouldn't be speaking with his mouth full. His mother was always chiding him about speaking with his mouth full at the table and while Sema didn't resemble his mother in any exterior manner, he suspected that he would get the same sort of reprimands from her. "I was wondering..."

"He's a wonder for wondering," Teresa said.

"You're a wonder for interrupting," Rajan said. Rajan was a handsome young Indian man with rich black hair and deep brown eyes. He had died in 1948 CE, in a wave of violence that rocked the region of Gujarat, along the border between the two newly divided countries of Pakistan and India, just a year after they had gained their independence from Great Britain. A book sat on the table next to him. Gabriel couldn't read the title, but he saw the name *Schopenhauer* on the spine.

"And who's keeping the conversation from moving forward now?" Teresa taunted.

"You were wondering?" Ohin said to Gabriel, ignoring the others. His deep voice carried over the table and beyond, cutting through the noise of hundreds of people eating.

"He's probably wondering if he can get reassigned to another crew," Marcus said.

"See," Teresa said, poking Rajan in the ribs, "even Marcus interrupts."

"I was wondering where all the food comes from," Gabriel said, jumping into the conversation before anyone could cut him off again. He suspected that getting a chance to speak at the table was going to be like getting a second helping: if you didn't take it, someone else would and fast.

"The Council maintains fields and livestock outside the castle walls," Ling said, stuffing a bite of blueberry pie in her mouth.

"The shield that protects the castle from interfering with the timeline here in the past extends nearly a mile in all directions," Ohin added.

"The climate doesn't allow for a terribly varied diet," Sema said, "but it is plentiful."

"And occasionally we manage to bring back delicacies that our stalwart cooks are unable to conjure up," Marcus said.

"Only when I don't catch you at it," Ohin said. "You know bringing things back before they are supposed to be destroyed can be risky."

"It is unlikely that a single barrel of ale is going to be missed by anyone in England," Marcus said. "Regardless of the time period it comes from."

"Was it an important artifact?" Gabriel asked, the sarcasm barely noticeable in his voice.

"The boy has it exactly," Marcus said. "They told me you were quick."

"Marcus thinks every barrel of ale is an important artifact," Rajan said.

"And flagon, and pint, and tea cup, if it has ale in it," Teresa added.

"Well, who knows what imprints a good aging barrel might have on it?" Marcus said.

"Maybe you should take one as a talisman," Ling said.

"Don't tempt him," Sema added.

"I just might," Marcus said in feigned defensiveness.

"I'd like to see you carry that around your neck," Teresa said with a giggle.

"You know he would if he could," Rajan said.

"You see the way of it now, don't you, young Gabriel?" Marcus said, the look in his eyes mixed equally between mischief and wounded pride. "They all turn on Old Marcus the first chance they get. He who heals them when they are sick. He who comforts them when they are low. And yet they would separate me from one of the few comforts I am allowed."

Everyone except Ohin laughed. Gabriel found himself laughing, as well. Even though he had only just met these people, Gabriel did find himself enjoying their company. Part of him wanted to be sullen and fume about his circumstance, but everyone's good-natured banter brought him out of the shell he wanted to climb into and curl up in. There would be time for the shell and the sullenness later that night. When he was alone. Right now, there were exciting new people to learn about and an exciting new life to uncover. That thought led him to what he seemed to do best today.

"So..." Gabriel began.

"Pay up," Teresa said to Rajan.

"You don't know what he's going to say," Rajan said.

"Yes, I do," Teresa said.

"I'll pay when you have proof," Rajan said.

"Who's paying for what?" Ohin asked

"Rajan and I have a bet about what questions Gabriel will ask next," Teresa said.

"To which, I insist that we hear the question before you pay me," Rajan.

"You're such a gallant loser," Teresa teased.

"So what is your question?" Ohin asked Gabriel.

"What do the Malignancy Mages want?" Gabriel asked, feeling his stomach tighten a bit as he realized that all eyes at the table were on him. "If we're fighting them in a war, what are we fighting over? How do we win?"

"See," Teresa said. "Pay up."

"That should hardly count," Rajan said, taking a rabbit's foot from his pocket and handing it to Teresa. "That was far more than one question."

"You're right, it's not fair." Teresa pocketed the rabbit's foot. "I feel terrible for you. Would you like to bet on how fast he learns to make a jump by himself?"

"Pass," Rajan said. "Only one rabbit's foot."

"Those are very good questions," Ohin said. "Especially in light of the attacks last week on the Hiroshima Outpost."

"Last week?" Gabriel said.

"Time travel," Teresa said.

"Last week for me," Ohin said. "I have been gone for nearly seven days in my personal timeline. To answer your question, the Malignancy Mages wish to control the Primary Continuum and all of the stable alternate branches of time."

"And to destroy the Great Barrier," Ling added.

"It depends on which one you run into," Teresa said. "They're a very confused bunch."

"What's a great barrier?" Gabriel asked, still trying to process the idea that Ohin had been away for a week in the last few hours.

"The Great Barrier of Probability," Ohin said. "Time travel is possible anywhere along the Primary Continuum until you come to the Great Barrier. Suddenly, for reasons we cannot explain, once you reach the year 2012 on October 28 at four forty-five in the afternoon Greenwich standard time, you can no longer travel forward in time. Nor has anyone ever traveled back from after that time."

"That doesn't make sense," Gabriel said. He hated math, but he loved science and he had spent hours reading books about space and astronomy. "Time moves at different rates depending on the mass nearby. It gets warped by gravity. So time moves slower on the sun than it does on Earth. Or you could travel really fast, like at the speed of light, and even if it only took you a few hours, it might be years enough to cross the barrier. Or what about other planets? A barrier like that couldn't exist. Especially not on other planets. It just doesn't make sense. Does it?"

"No, it doesn't make sense," Sema said. "It always gives me a headache thinking about it."

"Cross-dimensional synergistic probability matrix," Teresa said around a bite of blueberry pie.

"You are right that it doesn't make linear sense," Rajan said. "But that is why it is called the Great Barrier of Probability. It exists in all probable circumstances."

"We've approached it in every branching timeline we know of," Ohin said. "The result is always the same. The Barrier exists at the same relative instance in time everywhere in the universe and in all the branches of the Primary Continuum."

"The only way to cross it is to live through the time just before it," Marcus said. "But once it becomes four forty-six, there's no going back. Two Time Mages tried and were never heard from again."

"So who created this Great Barrier?" Gabriel asked, pressing for more information.

"We have no idea who created it," Ohin said. "Or why. Or even how it might be possible. We suspect a large circle of Time Mages created it. Mages can link their energy in a circle to multiply their power and we can only imagine that it must have taken a hundred or more Time Mages to accomplish something of this magnitude. As to why, we have no idea."

"Possibly to protect the past from something in the future," Rajan suggested.

"Or to protect the future from us," Ling said.

"How would it protect the future?" Gabriel asked even as the answer occurred to him. "Bifurcations! If the Great Barrier separated the past and future, no matter how many branches are created in the past, the future of the Primary Continuum after two thousand twelve will always be safe."

"That is one of the theories about The Great Barrier," Ohin said, looking Gabriel in the eyes with something the might have been pride. "And it is the one that most Time Mages subscribe to."

"But then what are the Malignancy Mages fighting for?" Gabriel asked. "How do they hope to control the Primary Continuum?"

"Any object, or place, or even person, can carry the imprints of positive or negative actions associated with it," Ling said. "And mages can draw power from those imprints just as they do with their personal talisman. All they need do is establish and maintain a connection with the object."

"For instance," Ohin said, "a battlefield can carry far more imprints, both negative and positive, than a sword or a dagger can. By establishing a connection to such a place or artifact, a mage can attain great power. Connections are made with magical artifacts called concatenate crystals."

"Like Hiroshima," Gabriel said. "That's what the outpost was protecting against."

"Exactly so," Marcus said, raising his glass with a smile. "And speaking of the outpost, when do we return to the field? Not that I haven't been enjoying our reprieve from the front lines, mind you." For emphasis, he emptied his glass in a single swallow, grinning at Sema, whose face had become set in a frown.

"Soon," Ohin said. "First, though, I want Gabriel to get a taste of time travel and at least a rudimentary feel for doing it himself."

"Fitting him for his time travel training wheels," Teresa said, amused with her metaphor. No one but Gabriel seemed to get the joke. "Like on a bicycle," she explained, with a sigh. Gabriel guessed that not all jokes translated through time, even with the help of the magical amulets around everyone's neck. He had one on a silver chain around his own neck now. Sema had made it for him. Gabriel pulled his mind away from the thoughts of the amulet and back to what Ohin was saying.

"Until we resume our missions," Ohin said, "everyone will maintain their training and study regimen. Gabriel will join us as time permits."

"Was that an intentional pun?" Teresa asked.

"What?" Ohin said.

"Oh, you're all hopeless," Teresa said, but she noticed Gabriel grinning at her and smiled back. Gabriel dug into the last piece of blueberry pie as the conversation continued to spin around him. He'd asked enough questions for one day and received far more answers than he really wanted. Answers that only led to more questions. Questions that he wasn't sure he really wanted the answers to. He decided that the best thing he could do just then was to continue stuffing his face with pie. There would be time for more questions later. There would always be time, Gabriel thought with a grin as he bit into the pie.

CHAPTER 6
READING THE STARS

Later that night, Gabriel sat on a bench at the edge of the Upper Ward courtyard looking up at the stars and wondering about his future. Sitting in the far past wondering about the future that would be his personal past, a past that he could go and see from a distance, but never again be a part of. His personal future was in no particular time and place. Everything was different now. Even the stars in the past were different, the position of the constellations changed completely by the slow processional tilt of the planet. He could still make out the belt of Orion, although it was not where he was accustomed to seeing it in the night sky.

He was glad to be alone. Someone had been with him nearly every moment since he had woken from death. Keeping him occupied. Showing him wonders and filling his head with facts. It was nice to have a moment to think about where he was and what it all meant. And to think about his family.

It occurred to Gabriel again that although he was the one who had died that day of the bus accident, in some ways, it was as if his parents had died instead. They were alive in their time, but he couldn't risk seeing them. Not really seeing them. He might be able to glimpse them from a distance someday, but he could never sit and talk to them. Never touch them. Never feel their arms around him. He felt the tears run down his cheeks as he thought about his parents. About his sister. About his friends. It was like the whole world had died and he alone had survived. They were gone and he still remained. And if what Ohin and Marcus said was true, he would remain for a very long time. He, who died first, would likely live longer than any of them.

He wiped the tears from him face. It felt good to let them out. To feel the pain of his loss. He knew these wouldn't be the last tears he'd shed for the loss of his parents and sister, but he felt a little better. And after all, he wasn't dead. He was alive. And more than alive. He was a Time Mage. Well, not yet. But he would be. And when he was...

The sound of someone walking along the fine gravel path encircling the courtyard reached his ears. Gabriel used the back of his white linen sleeve to wipe the rest of the tears from his cheeks. Looking up, he saw an elderly women approaching. She had short-cropped gray hair and pale gray eyes that complemented her alabaster skin. She was short, but not exceedingly so. It made her seem heavier than she was. She smiled as she approached.

"I see I am not the only one enjoying the stars this evening," she said in a crisp British accent. That meant she really was British. Gabriel had learned that when someone spoke using the amulet to translate for them, the voice he heard in his head was always in his own Midwestern late twentieth century accent. If they had a different accent, they were speaking English.

"I've never seen the stars so bright," Gabriel said.

"I'm not surprised, considering when you were born," the woman said. "You were taken from the late twentieth century, yes?"

"1980," Gabriel said. "I was born in 1967."

"A short time," the woman said. "Too short. Do you mind if I join you?"

"Sure," Gabriel said, sliding over on the bench to make room.

"My name is Elizabeth," she said, extending her hand. Gabriel shook her hand. Her skin was soft, but her grip was surprisingly firm. Now that she sat next to him, he noticed that she smelled like lavender. Then something occurred to him.

"You're Elizabeth Palfrey," Gabriel said, his eyes widening a little. "You're the head of the Council."

"Found out," Elizabeth said with a wink. "I had hoped for a little anonymity for a while. I so rarely find any these days. Unless I'm traveling. I wanted to come and meet for myself the newest member of our little community."

"Thank you," Gabriel said. "That's very kind of you."

"Piffle," Elizabeth said. "It's totally self-serving, I assure you. Hardly anything I do is just to be polite. There is always a second intent, hidden or otherwise. The unfortunate side effect of being mistress of the manor."

"You don't seem to like being in charge," Gabriel said, stating what seemed obvious before realizing that it might be rude to do so.

"Very discerning," Elizabeth said. "No, I am not particularly fond of being the head of the Council, but someone has to do it, and the best qualified person has gone off to search for the meaning of her existence and the other possible candidate refuses to accept the mantle, so that leaves me.

"In all honesty, between the two of us, I'd much rather be spending my days on a beach with a good book. I know the perfect beach. A little Greek island called Samos. There is a beautiful town there. Lovely people. Amazing food. Epicurus lived there until he was eighteen. I met him once. Not what I expected. But we do not always get to choose the life we wish to lead, as I'm sure you are coming to realize all too well."

"Tell me about it," Gabriel said with a sigh.

"I just did. Honestly, twentieth century English phrases make little sense to me. So many of them seem redundant."

"I just meant that I understand," Gabriel said.

"Well of course you do." Elizabeth placed her hand on his arm and looked him in the eyes. "It does lessen. The weight of it. The weight of letting go, at least. As the years pass, it becomes easier to accept. The pain becomes simply an old ache. Familiar. Almost comforting."

"Does the rest of it get any easier?" Gabriel asked.

"Unfortunately, no," Elizabeth said, looking up at the stars. "The war goes on and on. Friends are lost. New friends appear. Battles are won. Battles lost. But there is always The War. It's always been like that, though. Even before magic. It's always a struggle between those who want to claim power and use it for their own selfish ends and those who stand up to them. The same story again and again all throughout history."

"May I ask you a question?" Gabriel said.

"Certainly," Elizabeth replied, looking back down from the stars to Gabriel's eyes. "I hear you have some very good questions."

"Can the war ever end?" Gabriel asked. It was another of the questions he wasn't sure he wanted answered but felt compelled to ask.

"Oh, if I thought the war couldn't be won, I'd be off in a cave like Nefferati," Elizabeth said with a laugh.

"Nefferati?" Gabriel said.

"She's one of the other two True Grace Mages. She's a very remarkable woman, which is saying something coming from me. I'm rather remarkable myself. She is the oldest mage, True or otherwise. She was born on the banks of the Euphrates around 3500 BCE and claims to be nearly seven hundred years old, but I suspect she's lying about her age. She's eight hundred, if she's a day. I was her apprentice many, *many* years ago. Plucked me out of the timeline herself. Taught me nearly everything I know. About magic. About leadership. About life. She is my best and closest friend." Elizabeth was silent for a moment. Gabriel could tell by the look on her face and the tone of her voice that she had not meant to reveal that last bit of information. She clearly missed the elder woman a great deal. Gabriel suspected she missed Nefferati more than she admitted even to herself. She sighed and looked at Gabriel. "I've become maudlin."

"What about the third True Grace Mage?" Gabriel asked, thinking to distract Elizabeth from her sudden dark mood.

"Akikane," Elizabeth said. "Young by my standards. Only three hundred years old or so. You'll like him. Everyone likes him. I suspect there are Malignancy Mages who like him. He lived in Feudal Japan in the fourteenth century and was born into a family of warriors and spent the first years of his life as a samurai. Then he had an epiphany. I'm sure he will tell you about it. He tells everyone about it. He destroyed his sword and became a Buddhist monk. At least for a time. Then he forged a new sword. One that he only ever used in the defense of others, and never to kill."

"And what about the Malignancy Mages?" Gabriel asked.

"We believe there are several hundred, which would leave us fairly evenly matched. But they are not as well organized as we are.

As you probably know, there are three Malignant True Mages. The oldest of them is Kumaradevi. She was a princess who lived in India around 300 BCE. She is nearly as powerful as she is old and she is almost five hundred years old. She gave me this." Elizabeth pulled back the edge of her tunic and revealed a deep red scar along the edge of her collar bone. "She was very unhappy with me. I killed her husband. Tall man. Very pretty. But I digress.

"The second True Malignancy Mage is named Vicaquirao," Elizabeth said. "He was a general in the Incan Empire in the mid-1400s. A wicked piece of work, that one. He's nearly four hundred years old. And clever. Too clever by half. Although no one has heard from him in nearly twenty of our years, which is suspicious. Some suspect that he has been killed by Apollyon, but I don't believe it."

"Apollyon?" Gabriel asked.

"It's not his true name, of course," Elizabeth said, "but he thinks it makes him sound important. His real name is Cyril. The third True Malignancy Mage. He is also the youngest, merely one hundred fifty, but the most dangerous, in my opinion. He actually has a philosophy, a rationale for the destruction he wreaks. It sounds like a hodgepodge of Nietzsche and Nazism, but it draws him a large number of followers. Moreover, he knows how to lead, damn him.

"He was Vicaquirao's apprentice once. Vicaquirao found him in ancient Greece, during the time of Alexander the Great. Around 310 BCE. He was a soldier in Alexander's army. We don't know exactly when, but Vicaquirao educated him over a number of years to be his protégé."

"That's all six," Elizabeth concluded with a stifled yawn. "There can be only three True Grace Mages and three True Malignancy Mages. Nefferati made that prophecy herself. Although part of it has yet to be fulfilled."

Gabriel yawned, quickly slapping his fist over his mouth.

"Tired?" Elizabeth asked. "I don't blame you. I could do with a bit of rest myself. What I could really use is a vacation." She reached into a pocket and withdrew a small coin as she stood up. She handed it to Gabriel. "Here. In case you need a vacation sometime. Sleep well."

"Thank you." Gabriel stared down at the coin and saw it was from ancient Greece. He wondered what Time Mages did on holiday. And why Councilwoman Elizabeth had given it to him. How could the coin lead to a vacation? Was he supposed to pay for it with the coin? When he looked up to ask her, Gabriel saw she was gone. Typical, he thought to himself. More questions.

CHAPTER 7
THE TIME MACHINE

The next morning, as instructed, Gabriel stood on the balcony at the top of the Clock Tower promptly at seven o'clock, looking out over the grounds and the fields beyond the castle, watching the sun slowly ascend in the sky. Actually, Gabriel was early. Half an hour early. Only the sheer emotional exhaustion of the long and incredible day before had made it possible for him to fall asleep. Nevertheless, he had awoken with the first hint of sunlight, his mind filled with thoughts about time travel and magic. He had grabbed a quick bite of eggs and bacon in the Waterloo Chamber as soon as the cooks started serving breakfast, then he headed straight for the tower.

He didn't know if Ohin would be early, but he struck Gabriel as the sort of man one didn't keep waiting. As he watched the clock, Gabriel remembered Teresa telling him that there were over four hundred fifty clocks spread throughout the castle. There was even a man whose job it was to maintain and repair all the clocks. Teresa had said it was a job with little time off. She had thought that was funny. Gabriel laughed more at her pouting about him not laughing than at the joke itself. Looking down from the castle clock as it struck seven, Gabriel saw Ohin arrive.

"Good morning, Gabriel," Ohin said as he stepped onto the balcony of the tower with a book in his hand.

"Morning," Gabriel said, trying to still the tumbling of his stomach. Maybe eggs hadn't been such a good idea.

"Are you ready for your first lesson?" Ohin asked.

"Not really," Gabriel said, speaking quite literally from his gut, "but if I think about it too long I might freak out."

"Well, we would not want that," Ohin said. "Our first lesson will be a simple one. We will use a relic to travel to several times where that relic existed. Nothing complicated." As though traveling through time wasn't complicated, Gabriel thought. "First, you will need to change the way you are dressed."

Even as he spoke, Ohin's clothes shimmered in the sun and suddenly he wore a tweed suit with vest and tie. Gabriel thought it looked Victorian, from the late 19th century. "Now, focus your mind on what I am wearing and try something similar for yourself." Gabriel stared at Ohin's clothes and focused on the concealment amulet hanging around his neck. He felt the connection with it in his mind and the air around his body shimmered. Suddenly he was wearing an exact duplicate of the suit Ohin wore.

"What about money?" Gabriel asked.

"We don't normally use currency," Ohin said. "Since we try to interact with people as little as possible. However, the castle can make excellent forgeries of nearly any currency we might need for a mission. Now for the relic." He held up the book so that the cover was visible. Gabriel's face broke into a wide grin as he laughed. He hadn't thought Ohin had a sense of humor.

"H.G. Wells's *The Time Machine*?" Gabriel asked.

"Always good to start the day with a little irony," Ohin said, patting the book lightly. "To travel to a particular time and place, a Time Mage must have an object from that time and place. Something that has either been made by human hands, or was once alive, like a bone or a fossil. We call the objects we use to travel through time relics."

"The St. George's Chapel," Gabriel said as something clicked in his mind. "That's why there are so many antiques from throughout history in the chapel."

"Exactly," Ohin said. "But you can only travel in time and space to where that object has been. This relic is a first edition of Mr. Wells's novel, published in London in 1895. So, we can use the book you hold to travel to England, but only to places and times where the book resided. That is why we collect so many relics in the chapel." It made a strange kind of sense, Gabriel thought. It also made sense of the Greek coin that Councilwoman Elizabeth gave him the night before.

"Now, tell me what you can sense, if anything, from the book. Here, have a seat." Ohin indicated a small stone bench behind them. As they sat down, Gabriel took the novel from Ohin's hand and held it gently in his own. He wasn't sure what he was supposed to be looking for, or what he was supposed to feel. Mostly he felt silly.

"I don't feel anything," Gabriel said.

"Relax your mind," Ohin said. "Close your eyes and watch your breath." Gabriel did as instructed. "Don't try to think about anything. Don't try not to think. Just watch your breath. If a thought fills your mind, just let it go as you exhale. Still your mind."

Gabriel watched his breathing. This was familiar to him, at least. His mother had started meditating nearly four years ago after reading one of her New Age books and going to a seminar at the local library. She had insisted on teaching Gabriel how to meditate, as well. Mostly, Gabriel suspected, because his father had shown so little interest. Gabriel had taken to it quickly and often joined his mother in an evening meditation after dinner. In the autumn and winter, at least. Spring meant baseball and summer meant longer nights for playing baseball. Gabriel didn't have trouble choosing between meditation and baseball. That was no choice at all.

Sitting on the Clock Tower bench with Ohin, Gabriel was suddenly grateful to his mother for her insistence that he join her on all those nights of meditating. At first, he could not keep the thoughts from racing through his mind, but as he noticed his attention drifting, he let the thoughts go as he exhaled and refocused his mind on his breath.

After a few minutes, he began to feel more relaxed. More at peace. After about ten minutes of meditating on his breath, he sensed something different. Not a thought. Not a feeling. He wasn't sure what it was. It was like trying to remember an event based on the momentary sniff of a once-recognizable fragrance. A feeling he knew but had never felt before. Strange and familiar at the same time. Then it came to him and he knew what it was and why he recognized it. It was the feeling he had in his dreams of the future. The feeling that would linger with him for moments after waking from the dream. It made him feel fearful and powerful and lightheaded all at once. He slowly breathed the feelings of anxiety out.

Leather chair. Book cases lining the walls. A small table. A glass of wine. A fireplace, the flames leaping up into the chimney. On the chair. A book.

Gabriel opened his eyes. "I saw a room."

"Really," Ohin said, a quizzical look on his brow. "What room?"

"I don't know. There was a bookcase and a fireplace. And a leather chair. And this book was on the chair. *The Time Machine* was on the chair." Gabriel held the old novel up in his hands.

"Curious," Ohin said. "I was expecting you'd report more of a tingling feeling, not a full placement vision."

"That was one of the places the novel has been, wasn't it?" Gabriel asked, already knowing the answer.

"Yes," Ohin said. "That room was where the book resided for the first ten years of its existence. It is very unusual that you were able to see it so clearly. And so far back. And so soon. It took me a week to gain my first time-sight of a relic. And even then I could only press back a few years of its existence."

"I felt something odd at first," Gabriel said. "Like what I feel when I have dreams that come true. Will I still have dreams like that?"

"Probably not," Ohin said. "Once out of the timeline of The Primary Continuum, your time-sense, which is that feeling you described, is usually useless for prediction. Unless you are back in a specific time for a long enough span of years. There are exceptions. Nefferati for one. But she is very old, and the power did not come back to her for a long time. However, you will be able to sense the flow of time around people and things in the places you travel.

"Well, now that you have found a destination, why don't we try a quick visit? But first, one last alteration to our appearance." Ohin shimmered again, suddenly appearing as a Caucasian man instead of an African, his skin a pinkish white rather than dark chocolate. Gabriel gaped. Ohin still looked like himself, only not at all.

"We don't want to appear out of place if we are seen," Ohin said.

"You just look so odd," Gabriel said before he realized what he meant and what he had said didn't resemble each other at all. Any more than this Ohin resembled the real one.

"You'll get used to seeing yourself look different," Ohin said. "However, I can adjust the attunement of the amulet so that anyone with another amulet will see me more normally, while everyone else will see me as you do now." Ohin shimmered again, suddenly himself, still dressed in a Victorian suit. After a few moments of instruction, Gabriel made a similar modification to the color of his skin that anyone seeing him might experience.

"Hand me the book," Ohin said. "But keep your hand on it." Gabriel did as told. Ohin used one hand to share the book with Gabriel and placed his other hand on Gabriel's shoulder. "In order to take someone or something through time with you, it is best to touch them. There are exceptions, but they are best tried only by powerful and experienced Time Mages.

"Also, a Time Mage can learn to ghost the movement of another Time Mage through time, to follow them to their destination, even without the use of a relic. That is for another lesson. For now, still your mind again and focus on the book. Try to bring back that time-sense vision of the room with the fireplace and the chair. I am going to move us through time to that place. I want you to pay attention and try to sense what it is I do. Do not watch with your eyes. Just be. There is only you and me and the book and that room."

Everything around them went dark and Gabriel felt his stomach turning inside out even as a knife pierced his brain. There was something else, too. A sense of power. Power within himself. No, power outside himself. No, a power that was ever-present, of which he was merely one manifestation. Just as suddenly as the blackness came, blinding white light suffused him and Ohin and the book. Everything bled a brilliant white light. Then they stood in front of the fireplace, the leather chair nearby, the bookcases surrounding them. Only the book wasn't on the chair, and there was no wine glass, and no fire in the fireplace. Gabriel looked around.

"Wow," was all he could say.

"Exactly," Ohin said.

53

"But the fire is out," Gabriel said, looking around as he let go of the old book.

"I moved us to a different day," Ohin said. "One when I sensed there was no one in the house."

"You could sense that?" Gabriel said with amazement.

"Yes," Ohin said. "As you approach a particular time, you will be able to sense what is different from one day to the next, how one hour differs from another, one minute from the last. Now, tell me what you sensed."

"Between the darkness and the blinding white light there was a power," Gabriel said. His heart quickened thinking about it. "I can't describe it exactly, but I could sense this power bending and warping around me and through me. And a pain in my head like a headache, only worse."

"The pain in your head will subside a little with each journey," Ohin said. "It is your brain struggling to process things it was never intended to experience. The power you felt was the energy of an imbued artifact interacting with the fundamental energy of the universe, guided by my own subtle energies."

"Magic."

"Yes."

"We're really in London in 1895," Gabriel said, staring out the window. Outside the sun was high in the sky and people walked along the sidewalks, horse drawn carriages and flatbed wagons rumbling down the street.

"Of course we are," Ohin said. "Now let's see if you can guide us to some other when and where." Ohin held the novel out to Gabriel, who placed his hand on the worn cover of the book. Gabriel felt Ohin rest a hand on his shoulder as he closed his eyes and he tried to clear his mind.

"This time," Ohin said, "I want you to not only hold a sense of place and time from the book, but sense the energy of my talisman." Gabriel felt Ohin place the necklace of seashells on top of the book so that his hand touched both. It was easier now to perceive the flow of the book's passage through time. Maybe his time-sense was developing. Maybe Ohin was helping him. Either way, as he focused his attention on the book, he could see moments from where it had been and who had been near it.

One seemed clearer than the others did. He wasn't sure when in time the moment was, but there was a beach and a woman was reading the book beneath the shade of a large umbrella, its wooden stake stuffed firmly into the sand. He held that image in his mind even as he reached out to try and sense the imprinted energy of Ohin's talisman necklace of seashells.

"When you have a place and time clearly in mind," Ohin whispered, "hold it as you focus on the power of the necklace. The necklace is like a magnifying glass for your own magical energy. Feel the power within you. Feel the power of the imprints of the necklace. Focus your mind and bring those two sources of energy together. And when you hold them together, focus your will upon that image of where and when you want to go."

Blackness descended, and then blinding white light seared through his brain. When it ceased, Gabriel opened his eyes to see that he stood on a beach several hundred feet away from the water, near an overhanging bank of long grass. A woman sat near the water reading a book under an umbrella. She wore a full bathing suit of black with a bit of skirt around the waist. He thought he might have seen something like it in an old movie that took place in the 1920s. Ohin laughed. Gabriel looked up to see a wide, white-toothed smile spread across his mentor's face.

"What'd I do wrong?" Gabriel asked, trying to figure out what the source of Ohin's amusement might be.

"Wrong!" Ohin said. "Who said anything about wrong? That was brilliant." He slapped Gabriel on the back. Ohin's clothes shimmered and he suddenly wore loose cotton pants, a white cotton shirt, and suspenders.

"Really?" Gabriel asked. He focused on the amulet at his neck for a moment and his appearance changed, as well.

"Yes," Ohin said. "I didn't bring us here, you did. One second I'm talking to you, sensing how you're manipulating the energy, and the next thing we're standing here."

"So I did it right?" Gabriel asked.

"Not just right," Ohin said. "Perfect. You even moved us away from the book so we wouldn't pop into someone's view." That was true now that Gabriel thought back. He had sensed the presence of the woman and willed himself to move away from it. "I've never heard of something like it before," Ohin said.

"What do you mean?" Gabriel asked.

"No one has ever made a second jump all on their own," Ohin said. "It usually takes weeks for an apprentice to learn how to jump under their own power. Sometimes months. You must be a prodigy."

Gabriel didn't know what to say. All he could think to do was smile back at Ohin and laugh along. Him. A prodigy. Of Time Magic. That was too crazy to think about. And wonderful. He couldn't wait to tell…Well, the people he really wanted to tell he couldn't. Even if he could find them in time, he couldn't talk to them. But he could tell Teresa. And Sema and Ling. And Marcus and Rajan. He could tell them.

"Well," Ohin said, "now that you've done it once, let's see if it was a fluke. This time, I want to see if you can take us to a particular moment in time. I happen to know that on August 7th in 1960, this book was in the satchel of a young man watching the movie version of the novel at his local theater. See if you can take us there."

Gabriel nodded and brought his attention back to the book and the necklace of seashells. He could not sense a distinct day or year, but the image of a movie theater flashed through his mind. Moments later, at least moments from their perspective, Gabriel and Ohin stood at the back of the balcony of a large movie theater. He recognized the movie projected on the screen immediately. Director and producer, George Pal's adaptation of *The Time Machine*. He had stayed up late one Saturday night a year ago and watched it with his father. His father was an even bigger fan of science fiction than he was. It made him smile to remember it. He also smiled because he had just made his second jump through time alone and gotten it right. He grinned up at Ohin, who grinned back.

They jumped back and forth along the Continuum three more times. First to 1968 in San Francisco when the book was in the pocket of a young hippie dancing in Golden Gate Park. Then back to

1943 when it was in the knapsack of a pilot getting ready to take off for a bombing run across the English Channel. And finally to a bookstore shelf in Manhattan in 2006. The last thing Ohin showed Gabriel was how to move through space, jumping from one end of an empty aisle of books to the other. A Time Mage, Ohin explained, could move through any distance of space as long as they could see where they were going or if they had been in a particular place before.

As they stood together in the back of the bookstore, Ohin placed a hand on Gabriel's shoulder. "I think that is enough for our first lesson. Why don't you see if you can take us back to the castle?" Ohin pulled a small orange-brown rock from his pocket. It was a piece of amber. A thought occurred to Gabriel as he looked at the dragonfly suspended within it.

"How does the council keep the castle safe from the Malignancy Mages?" Gabriel asked. "Can't they find it with a piece of amber like this or some other relic?"

"The castle is protected by layers of magic," Ohin said. "A piece of amber or a relic from that time by itself is not sufficient to reach it. Only a Time Mage who has been there can sense it. You should be able to sense the time placement of the castle when you scan the piece of amber. "

Gabriel started to reach for the amber fossil that would lead them back through time to the castle and stopped. There was something else he needed do first. Somewhere and some when he needed to go. If an object could be used to travel anywhere in time it had been, maybe a person could do the same thing. Maybe he could act as his own relic. He reached within and sought with his time-sense for the moment he was looking for, examining his own body as he had the copy of *The Time Machine*.

"I need to get something first," Gabriel said.

"That would be…" Ohin started to say, but the pitch-black darkness, followed by the blinding white light, cut off his words.

They stood in Gabriel's bedroom.

"…Unwise," Ohin said, finishing his thought that had been interrupted by decades in one moment. Gabriel's room looked just as it always did. The small desk, the unmade bed, the bookcase, the stack of comic books and magazines, the baseball and glove on a chair. It was night and the room was dark, but the light of the moon cast enough of a glow through the windows for them to see. Gabriel walked over to the dresser.

"This is your house, isn't it?" Ohin asked in a whisper.

"Yes," Gabriel said. He could hear voices, now that he took the time to notice. He had arrived exactly when he wanted to. The voices he heard were his parents and his own. He was downstairs having dinner with his parents. His previous self. The self of a few days ago. Gabriel had taken himself and Ohin to the night before he had the dream about drowning.

"We always feel most comfortable in our own time," Ohin said, the tone of his voice blending both anger and understanding, "but you know the risks. It is too dangerous to be here, especially in this house."

"I needed to get this," Gabriel said, picking up an aged and dented silver pocket watch from the dresser and holding it by the chain for Ohin to see. The pocket watch spun on the end of the chain, reflecting moonlight around the room.

"Taking something from this time and place could create a bifurcation," Ohin said. "If it is missed or needed for some future action, the result will be a new branch away from the Continuum."

"I already took it," Gabriel said, realizing that didn't necessarily make sense to Ohin. "I mean when I looked for it the morning...the morning I drowned, when I looked for it, I couldn't find it. Anywhere. I know I put it on the dresser when I came home. When the me downstairs came home an hour ago. So I must have come through time to take it."

"Do you remember seeing it before you went to bed?" Ohin asked, curious.

"No," Gabriel said. "I never even looked at the dresser that night. Tonight."

Ohin looked at the pocket watch and then reached out his hand and held it a moment. "This is a greatly imbued artifact. The imprints on it are very strong."

"It was my grandfather's," Gabriel said. "It was given to him by a friend, a soldier in World War Two who died saving my grandfather and four other men. It was my good luck charm."

"And now it is your talisman," Ohin said, his voice a deep whisper.

"I remembered I couldn't find it and I suddenly realized why," Gabriel said. "I should have said something, but I was afraid you wouldn't let me come here to get it." Gabriel could feel the imprints of the pocket watch now that he knew what to look for and was impressed to find that the simple heirloom handed down from his grandfather was nearly as powerful as the imbued seashells that Ohin used as a talisman.

"You need to learn to trust me," Ohin said. "And me to trust you. You made the right choice coming here, but next time, give me some warning."

"Sorry, it won't happen again." He looked up at Ohin in the dim light. He didn't like the idea of disappointing Ohin. "I'm ready to try and take us back to the castle now."

"We should do something first," Ohin said, clasping a firm hand on Gabriel's shoulder.

A moment of blackness and blinding white and they stood outside the kitchen window looking in on his previous self and his parents having dinner. The tears rolled down Gabriel's cheeks before he even felt them in his eyes. He saw his mother laughing at something his father had said. A story about their marriage, Gabriel remembered. How Gabriel's father had gone out shopping for a baby crib and had come home with a camping tent instead. Gabriel's grandfather had shouted, "What's your boy gonna sleep in, an orange crate?" He could see himself laugh, as well. And his father's wide grin as he retold the often-told family tale. Gabriel felt his face break into a smile as he watched through the window. So much happiness, so much pain, all bound up together in the same moment.

"I want to go home," Gabriel said, extending his hand.

"I wanted you to see this now, so you wouldn't be tempted to see it later on your own," Ohin said as he placed the small chunk of amber in Gabriel's upturned palm.

"I know," Gabriel replied as he closed his eyes, holding the amber fossil in one hand and the pocket watch in the other. He felt the energy and imprints of the pocket watch as easily as he felt Ohin's hand on his shoulder.

"Make sure you return us after we left," Ohin said. "Arriving too early could be...awkward."

"Right," Gabriel said. "Avoid bifurcations. We should get t-shirts made."

An instant later all was blackness then whiteness, then they stood on the balcony of the Clock Tower of Windsor Castle one hundred twenty-five million years in the past. Gabriel looked up at the clock and saw from the placement of the minute hand that they had been gone less than an hour.

"Excellent execution," Ohin said. "You've done better than I could possibly have hoped. I have never heard of an apprentice Time Mage learning so quickly. I'm very proud of you." Ohin ruffled Gabriel's hair.

Gabriel wiped the last of the tears from his eyes. He made Ohin proud on the first lesson. If he could never make his parents proud of him again, and he couldn't without creating a dangerous new branch of time, then making Ohin proud would do just fine.

CHAPTER 8
DINNER TIME

The day was long. Filled with hour after hour of new and interesting things. Ohin and Gabriel returned in time to join the other members of the team for their morning training session. Ohin briefly described Gabriel's amazing accomplishments to the others as they gathered on the grass of the Upper Ward. Gabriel felt the heat rising on his face while Ohin spoke.

"I guess you're not the only prodigy," Rajan said to Teresa.

"You're a prodigy?" Gabriel asked.

"I have a knack for Fire Magic," Teresa said, wrinkling her nose in embarrassment.

"And before she joined us here, she was a math prodigy," Rajan said. "Already in her second year of a physics degree."

"Math is harder than magic," Teresa said. "But I've never done anything as impressive as making a time jump on my first try." At Teresa's sunny smile, Gabriel found himself experiencing an uncomfortable warmth all over again. For a moment, he wasn't sure if it was from her words or her smile, which was enchanting as it lit up her face.

After being congratulated by the others, the training began. The entire day was a training session of one sort or another, but it always began with defensive arts lessons led by Marcus and Ling. Gabriel was surprised to find that Marcus turned out to have as innate a skill in combat as he did with healing. Just another irony of his life, as he said. Gabriel was not entirely surprised to find that Ling was even more formidable, at least with her bare hands. Gabriel wondered aloud how a fisherman's wife had learned to hit so hard and so fast. She explained her father had been more than a fisherman. More than that, she didn't explain.

The Council felt it was important for each member of a team to be able to defend themselves without the use of magic, in case they were trapped in a time and place where they had no access to an imbued artifact. The sessions began with unarmed combat taught by Ling and then moved to the use of different weapons throughout the history of the world, from knives and daggers, to swords and spears, and even to more modern weapons, as taught by Marcus. Magical training followed the defensive arts training.

For Gabriel's first lesson, they learned to weave magic together and fight other mages in combat. One team would be pitted against another in the gardens beneath the North Terrace, just outside the castle walls proper. Gabriel learned how to accurately project himself and others through space so that he could his help fellow teammates when under attack. The team members practiced fighting one-on-one with magic, as well.

The power of the magical conjuring was reduced for safety's sake, but Gabriel still ended up with singed eyebrows from dodging Teresa's fireballs too slowly and bruises from failing to jump through space before Rajan rippled the lawn like a carpet, tossing Gabriel into the air to flail and fall on his backside. It didn't help that he was still occasionally distracted by the sight of a gigantic, long-necked dinosaur in the distance. How were you supposed to concentrate with dinosaurs roaming around?

After a brief lunch, they spent the rest of the day studying in the library. History. Geographical history, biological history, cultures around the planet, languages, customs, cities, famous people, important battles and wars, significant works of art, architecture and literature. The Council liked the teams to have a background in the history of the places their missions took them to, but Ohin insisted that his team have a knowledge of every time and place, because one never knew what might go wrong and where they might end up.

They paid special attention to the dress and look of peoples from each place and time throughout the world. The magical amulets they all wore could only conceal them properly if they had a correct image of what to look like already in their minds. And even though the amulet would let them speak with anyone, what to say and how to phrase it was equally important. Gabriel began to suspect that he would need to study harder now that he was finally free from school than he ever had while he was in one.

By the end of the day, Gabriel was exhausted. And starving. Dinner couldn't come fast enough. When it did, it was just as mouth-watering as the night before. And the conversation between his new friends just as lively.

"If it had been a snake, it would have bit him," Ling said, referring to Rajan and an artifact that he had somehow misplaced.

"If it had been a snake, he would have eaten it," Teresa added. "Rajan will eat anything."

"What's wrong with snake meat?" Rajan asked. "As long as you season it properly."

"I can't understand how a boy brought up in a culture of culinary delights such as India could have such an insensitive palate," Marcus said.

"I can't understand how an old man from England could claim to know anything about food at all," Rajan retorted.

"Ah," Marcus said in mock seriousness. "Point taken. Unless it's fried."

"I'll grant you fish and chips," Rajan said, "but that's as far as it goes. If you want real fried food, you go to the South of the States."

"I hardly think so," Ling said. "The Chinese were frying food while the Europeans were still eating meat raw."

"Ah, I love steak tartare," Marcus said, licking his lips.

"With a raw egg and capers," Rajan agreed.

"What is it?" Gabriel asked.

"Raw ground meat," Teresa said.

"Barbaric," Ling said with visible distaste.

"Raw meat with raw egg," Gabriel said. "That's gross."

"One culture's disgusting is another culture's delectable," Sema said.

"For an example of that, just look at Rajan," Teresa said. "I hear that Medieval Germanic girl, Brigit, thinks he's quite tasty."

"People like sweet, not sour," Rajan said, visibly embarrassed. "Or so I heard Lord Edward say the other day." Now it was Teresa's turn to be embarrassed. Gabriel didn't know who Bridget or Lord Edward were, but had a pretty good idea of what Teresa and Rajan thought of them.

"I have something else for us to talk about," Ohin said, speaking for the first time since finishing his meal. "Something we're all hungry for." A silence fell over the table as all eyes turned to Ohin.

"We have a new mission?" Teresa asked.

"Yes," Ohin said.

"About bloody time," Marcus said.

"What's the mission?" Rajan asked.

"Am I included?" Gabriel asked.

"You are most definitely included," Ohin said, settling his gaze on Gabriel. "This mission was chosen with you in mind. After the display of your talents this morning, the Council wants me to accelerate your training."

"Is that wise?" Sema asked, glancing at Gabriel with a look of concern.

"We can only hope so," Ohin said. "The operation is not particularly dangerous, but it will be educational for our young Time Mage."

"What is the mission?" Rajan asked a second time, raising his voice a little.

"Severing the link to a crystal," Ohin said. "Yesterday, Vladimir's team salvaged a concatenate crystal from the Hiroshima outpost. It is the first of a linked chain, so we do not know how many more crystals it is connected to.

"However, when Vladimir severed the link between the first crystal and its tainted artifact, he was able to sense the time and location of the next artifact in the chain, linked through the second crystal." Gabriel hadn't realized that such a thing was possible and he suspected by the way Ohin was speaking in his direction that the information was being recited mostly for his own benefit. "Our mission will be to locate the second artifact and sever the link to its crystal. And if possible, determine what might be the next artifact in the chain."

"What's the artifact, and where are we going?" Ling asked.

"The artifact is an Aztec sacrificial dagger," Ohin said. "While you were studying this afternoon, I spent some time with Chimalli and Vladimir trying to pinpoint where the dagger is. We suspect it is one of the daggers used during the reconsecration of the Great Temple of Tenochtitlan in 1487."

"That was before the Spanish Conquistadors, wasn't it?" Teresa asked. "Does Manuel know anything about it?"

"Yes, it was," Ohin said. "And Manuel knows a little from his time there later, but unfortunately, Manuel is on a mission right now. However, Chimalli's time period was also close to that of the dagger, so he will be helping us to prepare for the mission and will accompany us as a guide."

"Who's Chimalli?" Gabriel asked. "And who is Manuel?"

"Manuel is an Earth mage," Sema said. "He was one of the Spanish soldiers who landed with Hernán Cortéz in 1519, and he witnessed some of the sacrifices."

"And the slaughters that came afterward," Teresa added.

"Some of our hands are less clean from our previous lives than others," Rajan said.

"Not mine," Marcus said, raising his hands before him. "I have lily white hands and a heart pure as the driven snow."

"Don't look now, but a dog's been lifting his leg on that snow," Rajan said.

"Manuel, like many of us, did things before coming here that are regrettable," Sema said. "He is a perfectly nice gentleman."

"Exactly the point I was trying to make," Marcus said.

"Chimalli is a Wind Mage," Ohin said, steering the conversation back where he wanted it. "He was an Aztec laborer. He knows the city and the temple and will help us learn about the history and culture before we make the jump."

"How much time do we have to prepare?" Ling asked.

"Not long," Ohin said. "The Council wants to act quickly, before the Malignancy Mage with the third crystal in the chain learns what happened to the first crystal and can sever the link to the second crystal. If we are quick about it, we may be able to sever all the links in the chain before the Malignancy Mages notice anything. So, as much as I don't relish the idea, we will make the jump tomorrow morning."

"So soon?" asked Marcus, sounding slightly concerned. "We normally have a few days to prepare."

"I know," Ohin said. "But we must act quickly, and the Council feels that while we may be a little unprepared, we have the collective experience to make the operation a success without any significant risk."

"We don't all have the experience," Gabriel said, noticing everyone was looking at him.

"And that's why you are going along," Ohin said. "The only way to learn how to sever the link between a tainted artifact and a concatenate crystal is to see it done. I suggest you all stop by the library this evening and refresh yourselves on Aztec culture and history before getting to bed early. Tomorrow should not be a taxing day, but we all know how plans can change."

"Truer words were never spoken," Marcus said, almost sounding glum.

"Our plans never go the way they're supposed to," Teresa said to Gabriel with a chipper smile.

"But our missions always succeed," Ling said, glowering at Teresa.

"And no other team can say the same," Sema added with yet another look toward Gabriel.

"Yes," Rajan said. "But not because of the plans."

"There's a bad omen for you," Marcus said. "Teresa and Rajan agreeing on something."

"I, for one, don't believe in omens," Ohin said, calling everyone's attention to himself with the depth of his voice. "I do believe in all of you. However, Teresa and Rajan are correct; our plans always do seem to go astray, regardless of how well things end, so much so that I often wonder why we bother making a plan at all. Nevertheless, since we do have a plan, we will stick to it until it seems wise not to. Besides, now that Gabriel is bringing his considerable talents to our fold, maybe our plans will go perfectly from now on."

"A toast to Gabriel," Marcus said, raising his glass. Marcus loved to toast at any possible provocation, but the smile on his face led Gabriel to suspect that his motivation for this toast was more genuine than usual. The others raised their glasses together, Gabriel bringing his up last to meet theirs. Then they drank in unison, Gabriel sipping his raspberry juice.

"May he bring us as much luck as he brings talent," Ling said.

"Our very own good luck charm," Teresa said with a laugh as she sipped from her glass.

"Does that mean I get the rabbit's foot back?" Rajan asked.

"You know, you're almost cute when you're absurd like that," Teresa said to Rajan.

Everyone laughed and Gabriel took a second small sip of his juice, wondering what tomorrow would be like and wondering if he would be able to sleep for thinking of it. Between the large meal, the extra-long day, and the two hours after dinner spent with the others in the library looking up books on the Aztec civilization, Gabriel had no trouble falling asleep that night.

CHAPTER 9
TEMPLO MAYOR

Breakfast was short, but filling. Gabriel felt too nervous at first to do more than pick at his food, but under Sema's continuous admonishments that a mission through time was no place for an empty stomach, he finally managed to eat a pancake and two large sausages. The others didn't seem to be feeling any of the anxiety that plagued Gabriel's stomach. He wondered if he would keep his breakfast down. He certainly hoped so. He couldn't imagine anything more embarrassing than puking all over his companions on his first mission.

The banter between the others took its usual form, with Teresa teasing Rajan, Marcus teasing everyone, Sema trying to mother them into better behavior, Ling grousing about too much noise at the breakfast table, while Ohin remained sternly silent and watchful. It was all moving too fast, Gabriel thought to himself.

Only a few days ago he would have been sitting in English class with his friends. He had been an average kid living an average life in 1980. Yesterday he was jumping back and forth through time with a man born in Africa over 1500 years before he was. A man who could bend time around himself like others would wrap a blanket around themselves. And Gabriel had done the same. And today he was going to be jumping from millions of years in the past to an Aztec city in 1487 CE to find a sacrificial dagger. It made his head and his stomach reel. Sema must have sensed his inner turmoil.

"You don't have to go if you don't feel ready for it," Sema said, leaning over so that only Gabriel could hear her voice. "You are very young, and this is much earlier in the training for a mission than usual."

"I'm okay," Gabriel whispered back. "I'll have to go on a mission sometime, and this one sounds easy."

"They all sound easy," Sema said. She frowned, realizing that her statement was not exactly reassuring. "You'll be perfectly safe with all of us around you."

"Oh, I'm not worried about that," Gabriel said, suddenly realizing it was true. "I'm more worried about making a mistake."

"I can't imagine that will happen," Sema said with a gentle pat on the arm.

After breakfast they gathered outside in the Horseshoe Cloister to listen to Chimalli tell them a little more about the Aztec Civilization. He was of obvious Mesoamerican decent: handsome, with short-cut grey hair, the features of his face sharp, his cheekbones high. His eyes shone with the same intelligence and humor he displayed when speaking.

"As you probably know," Chimalli said, "my people are the Nahua, and in the Nahuatl language Azteca means 'the people of Aztlan,' which is what we called our portion of the world. Although some believe it refers as much to a mythical place as to the lands where the Nahua people thrived and built what would later be called the Aztec civilization."

Gabriel had read something similar the night before. He had also learned that Chimalli's name meant 'shield' in the Nahuatl language. Ling had said this was fortunate since he might shield them from their ignorance. Even though they had spent hours studying in the library the night before, Gabriel felt he had only scratched the surface of Aztec history. Normally a team would have days to prepare for an operation and make sure they knew its history before they traveled.

"As Ohin told you," Chimalli continued, "we believe a Malignancy Mage has made a connection between a concatenate crystal and an Aztec sacrificial dagger, and we suspect that link was made shortly after the reconsecration of the Great Temple of Tenochtitlan, or the Templo Mayor, as it is known in Spanish, in 1487 CE. Tenochtitlan is the capital city of the Aztec empire built on an island in Lake Texcoco. As you hopefully learned from your hasty studies, the reconsecration took place during the reign of King Ahuitzotl. The Aztec kings were known as the *tlatoani*, or 'Great Speakers,' of their people. The supreme leader Ahuitzotl took p after his brother Tizoc died mysteriously. There are those who believe that Ahuitzotl had his brother poisoned so he could assume the throne.

"One of Ahuitzotl's first acts was to expand the Great Temple, building over the previous temple to create one even larger. Just as other kings had done before. The reconsecration of the Great Temple took place the year after King Ahuitzotl came to power."

"I lived twenty years before this time," Chimalli said, "but I have a good idea of what happened during that period from meeting with others who lived through it and from at least one visit there myself. The moment we will be traveling to is at the end of four days of the reconsecration of the Templo Mayor. Over the course of those four days, at least ten thousand people were sacrificed to the Aztec gods at temples throughout the city. There are some estimates that suggest as many as eighty thousand died in those four days."

Gabriel read about humans sacrifices the night before, but he still couldn't get his mind around a number that large. Over ten thousand people killed by having their hearts ripped from their chests with obsidian and flint daggers, only to have their bodies tossed down the side of the temple to pile at the bottom where their heads would be cut off and placed upon skull racks. It bothered him deeply, and he hoped that he wouldn't be seeing any of it. He wondered how Chimalli could be so calm about it.

"That is a lot of people being sacrificed in a short period of time," Chimalli said. "That is more than might have been sacrificed in an entire year." He paused for a moment and looked at those around the courtyard. "Any questions?"

Gabriel looked at the faces of the others. No one said a word. The thought of the sacrifices seemed to have silenced everyone.

"So why are we sitting around like a pile of rocks?" Marcus said. "This isn't Stonehenge. Let's find this bloody dagger and be done with it. If we're quick about it, we can be back in time for lunch."

"We can always be back in time for lunch," Gabriel said, feeling good about the mission and meeting Chimalli

"Figure of speech, lad," Marcus said with a grin.

70

"Is everyone ready?" Ohin said. There were nods all around as everyone stood up. "Prepare your appearance." Ohin shimmered and suddenly wore thin leather sandals, a loincloth, and a *tilma*, a three-cornered cloak of rough spun cotton. Gabriel focused his mind on the concealment amulet around his neck, the air shimmering around him as he matched Ohin's attire. The other men suddenly appeared to be wearing the same sort of clothes while the women wore simple dresses and sleeveless shirts. They all looked like themselves, but he knew that anyone who saw them would think they looked like Chimalli, a native Nahua. From the quality of their clothes, they would be taken as nobles if someone saw them. Only nobles wore clothes made from cotton. Common citizens wore clothes fashioned from the coarse fibers of the maguey plant, a cactus-like plant that grows throughout the region.

They gathered into a tight circle holding hands. As long as there was a chain of people touching, they would all be safely swept along with Ohin when he made the jump through time.

"Is anyone not ready to go?" Ohin asked.

"Last chance to use the bathroom," Teresa said with a smirk. Gabriel laughed, but no one said anything. Ohin took a shard of pottery from his pocket and held it in his hand. Gabriel knew that the shard was from Tenochtitlan and that while it would get them to the right place, Ohin would need to navigate carefully to put them near the time of the four days of sacrifice for the temple. Gabriel stood to Ohin's right, holding Teresa's hand. Sema held Ohin's left hand and he gestured for Gabriel to take his right. As he did so, Gabriel could sense the shard of pottery, and an image of a great city came to his mind.

"We go," Ohin said simply. The sun was gone, blackness sweeping around them, the cloisters disappearing, and then everything was a brilliant white.

They stood in the center of a broad, earth-packed street in the middle of a massive city, looking up at an enormous stone pyramid nearly two hundred feet tall. Two sets of wide steps, over a hundred stairs each, led to the flat top of the pyramid where two box-like shrines capped the structure. Although they were nearly half a mile away, Gabriel could make out people at the top of the Templo Mayor, the great pyramid. And something rolling down the steps. And something piled at the bottom.

Gabriel gasped. The sacrifices were happening now.

"Too early," Chimalli said.

"Obviously," Teresa said with distaste.

"One moment," Ohin said as the darkness came again, followed by the brilliant white light.

When the white light faded, they stood in the same spot, but it was nighttime. Torches illuminated the temple, and lights from oil lamps glowed throughout the city. The half-moon in the sky above draped the city in a ghostly blanket of pale light.

"We are a few days later," Ohin said, letting go of Gabriel's hand. Everyone in the circle did the same. "From what I can sense, the dagger is still at the temple. In the shrine at the top of the stairs." Ohin began to walk toward the Great Temple.

Although there were two hundred thousand citizens living in the city, few people were on the streets at night. Those few employed by the city to sweep the streets clean each night were the exception. Gabriel was not worried about the people they passed. Not only would the magical amulets make them appear to be noble residents of the city, but as long as Sema was nearby, her Soul Magic would ensure that no one would notice their passing.

As they walked along the street, Gabriel marveled at the architectural brilliance of the city's planners and builders. The streets were uniformly straight, laid out on a grid of smaller lanes crossing four wider main avenues. These four avenues led to the heart of the city, to the sacred plaza of temples and the Great Temple in particular. As they walked, Gabriel could see a grid of canals that crossed the streets. Long strips of floating fields called *chinampas* bordered the canals. Corn, vegetables, and flowers filled the fields, each about the width of a street.

The buildings of the city were made of adobe, some with thatched roofs. The homes each had two stone chimneys, smoke drifting up from many of them. Other larger buildings must have belonged to merchants or the wealthy. The city was divided into four districts by the main avenues. Each district was further divided into neighborhoods called *calpulli*, which were dominated by collections of families and merchants.

Gabriel could see other pyramids at the city center, some large and wide, some small and narrow. Each had its own purpose. Different pyramids for different gods. Down one canal he could see the water of Lake Texcoco that the island city was built upon. Down another street he could see a market plaza, empty at night. It was a beautiful city. So beautiful that Gabriel had trouble comprehending it. How could you be so smart as to build a city this incredible and think that killing thousands of people a year was a remotely intelligent thing to do?

However, by all accounts, even though the Aztec people felt driven to conquer and expand their empire by blood, they were also a well-ordered and industrious society. They believed in hard work, respect for authority, and performing one's duty. They even had schools where children learned history, dancing, and the rules of Aztec society, a society and a city that were alive and pulsing with creativity, but one also marked by constant death and destruction. It was a knot of ironies that Gabriel struggled to untangle.

Within a few minutes, they passed through the *snake wall*, a large stone wall surrounding the city center and adorned with serpent heads. The city center was entirely paved and Gabriel saw a courtyard where the Aztecs played *tlachtli*, a game in which players battled to pass a rubber ball through a stone circle using their hips. Not surprisingly, the losers were often sacrificed to the gods. Beyond the ball court, Gabriel could see the palace of the king. Several pyramids, in addition to the Great Temple, sat at the heart of the city. The smaller temple in front of the Templo Mayor was that of Quetzalcoatl, the wind and sky god, often depicted as a feathered serpent.

As they approached the foot of the Templo Mayor, Gabriel could see that the bodies had been cleared away, some to be eaten, he seemed to remember. He pushed that out of his mind. Two guards with spears stood at the base of the temple stairs, but they did not seem to notice anyone walking past them. There was also a large stone carving of a woman with her head, arms, and legs chopped off. The *Coyolxauhqui Stone*. Coyolxauhqui was an Aztec moon goddess and the stone depicted the method of sacrifice. Gabriel wondered why it was her image when the sanctuaries at the top were dedicated to Huitzilopochtli, the Aztec god of the sun and war, and Tlaloc, the god of rain and fertility. Although there were no bodies, there were plenty of heads. Thousands adorned the skull racks that surrounded the base of the temple. He had been trying to ignore them by staring at the carved Coyolxauhqui Stone.

"Do we have to walk past all of those?" Gabriel asked, indicating the rows of severed heads.

"Never mind the heads," Marcus said, looking at Ohin. "Are you going to make us walk up all those stairs?"

"I have no intention of making you do either," Ohin said as he came to a stop. Gabriel's time-sense told him what was coming, but the others seemed to be expecting it as well. The blackness surrounded them, the white light came, and then they stood on the flat top of the pyramid. Gabriel looked around. Everyone was there. He wondered how many people Ohin could take through space without touching them. It must take a great deal of power and experience. He also wondered how long it would take before he could manage it.

Two guards stood at the top of the temple. Between them burned a large fire near a stone altar where the victims of the sacrifices would be held down by the priests as their hearts were cut out of their chests. The guards both briefly moved their heads in the direction of the mages, but Sema touched the glass pendant at her neck and they turned away in unison, lying down where they stood and falling asleep.

"The dagger is in there," Ohin said, pointing to one of the stone sanctuaries on the top of the temple. "The sanctuary of Huitzilopochtli, the sun god." The two sanctuaries had angular walls and flat roofs so they almost looked like miniature pyramids themselves. The one on the right was covered in red and black paint and decorated with human skulls. This was the sanctuary of the sun god, Huitzilopochtli. The sanctuary on the left belonged to the rain god, Tlaloc, and was painted in blue in white.

"They aren't the only tainted artifacts in there," Sema said. Gabriel tried to sense the dagger and any other artifacts, but he couldn't. That too must come with experience and power, he thought. However, he did feel something. Something strong. Then he realized what it was.

"The entire temple is imprinted, isn't it?" Gabriel said as they walked behind Ohin to the sanctuary of Huitzilopochtli.

"Yes," Teresa said. "Any place with this much murder would have to be."

"But then why don't the Malignancy Mages connect the crystals to the temple, or to other places?"

"Sometimes they do," Ling answered. "But a temple is much easier to track down than a dagger."

"This temple has been connected to and severed from at least six times that I know of," Chimalli added.

"Gabriel and Chimalli, inside with me," Ohin said. "The rest of you stand guard. Teresa, if you would join us to provide some light, please. Leave any relics or artifacts, besides your talismans, outside with Rajan. They can interfere with the severing process."

"Sure," Teresa said, handing Rajan a small statue and the rabbit's foot from a pocket of her dress as she stepped into the sanctuary. Suddenly a warm glow came through the doorway. Gabriel, Ohin, and Chimalli handed Rajan their relics.

When they stepped into the sanctuary, they saw that Teresa had created four tiny balls of fire which floated in the corners of the small stone chamber. The back of the room held a stone idol of Huitzilopochtli, the walls painted with murals depicting stories of the god's exploits and the many sacrifices to him. In the center of the room was a small stone hearth for fires to burn sacrificial offerings. Along one wall was a low stone table with various ritual implements laid out across it, such as clay bowls, polished skulls, and five sacrificial daggers. Three of the daggers had long black edges of chipped obsidian that Gabriel knew were sharper than most steel blades, while two were fashioned from flint. The daggers had different handles, each carved from jade in the shape of an animal, such as a jaguar, a snake, or a bird. Gabriel could clearly sense the imprints of the daggers now.

"So the Malignancy Mages connect to the imprints of the dagger with a contaminant crystal?" Gabriel asked. Teresa giggled behind him

"A concatenate crystal," Ohin corrected him in a gentle tone. "Like this one." Ohin pulled a miniature crystal globe from his pocket and handed it to Gabriel. The crystal was a small, two inch wide ball of milky white glass. "Concatenate means 'to link in a chain.' That is an inactive crystal, waiting to be linked. A Time Mage can link the imprints of an artifact or a place to the crystal. Crystals can also be linked together."

"The more links in the chain," Chimalli added, "the more powerful the magic you can perform."

"Up to seven," Ohin said. "No chain of concatenate crystals can have more than seven links."

"Chrono-quantum entanglement degradation," Teresa said, almost absentmindedly from the back of the room.

"Can you sense which dagger has been linked to a crystal?" Ohin asked.

As Gabriel reached out with his magic-sense to the daggers, his eyes widened a bit and he looked up to Ohin.

"All of the daggers have been linked to a crystal," Gabriel said.

"Someone has been very busy," Chimalli said.

"And someone else will be busy now," Ohin said. "I'll sever the first one, the one we came for, and then Gabriel can try his hand at one of the others." Ohin choose a dagger from those on the table and carried it to the far side of the room, away from the other ritual objects. Gabriel followed him.

"Now watch closely. With your magic-sense, not your eyes."

Gabriel calmed his mind and focused on the obsidian dagger in Ohin's hands. He could sense the tendril that connected it to a Malignancy Mage's concatenate crystal, stretching through time and space, linking the two objects together. He could also sense the magical energy rising in Ohin, focused through the necklace of seashells hanging on his chest. Gabriel felt the magical energy leap out from Ohin and surround the dagger in a tight sphere. He could sense the thread connecting the dagger to the malignant concatenate crystal flickering around the blade, trying to find a way through the shield of magical energy that Ohin had encased it in. Then Gabriel sensed the thread connected to the imprints of the dagger begin to fade. Then it was gone. Ohin released the shield of magical energy around the dagger and looked at Gabriel.

"Do you think you can do that?"

"I think so," Gabriel answered, wondering how difficult it would be to duplicate the magic Ohin had performed. Chimalli handed Gabriel another dagger from the table. Gabriel stilled his mind and focused on the magical energy within himself as he took out his grandfather's pocket watch.

He focused the energy, allowing it to build before reaching out to the imprints of the pocket watch. Then he extended his magic-sense and felt for the thread connecting the dagger of chipped and polished volcanic glass to a concatenate crystal somewhere in time. As he felt the thread, he willed the magical energy flowing through him to surround the dagger in a shield of magical power. The magical space-time thread from the dagger winked out of existence, and the glass of the dagger blade cracked in half with a loud pop. Gabriel winced and looked up at Ohin.

"Next time, a little less magical energy," Ohin said with a frown.

"Too much energy and you might damage the object you're trying to sever," Chimalli said as he grinned at Gabriel.

"He's trying to be the Superman of Time Mages," Teresa said. "He doesn't know his own strength."

"Why don't you try another one?" Ohin said. "This time try to sever the connection gently. Like you were snipping a rose bud from the stem. Not as though you were trying to cut it off with an axe."

Gabriel took a deep breath, straightened his shoulders and tried again. He realized that even though the concatenate crystal that the dagger was connected to might be anywhere in time, severing the connection between them did not require all that much magical energy. It was more like trying to smother a candle flame by placing a snuffer over it, rather than blasting it with a fire extinguisher. When he had finished, he looked to see Ohin smiling again.

"That's more like it," Ohin said. "Now why don't you replace Rajan on watch? We'll need him to repair this broken blade so there will be no chance of a bifurcation of time taking place. I will finish the other two daggers. You can enjoy the view."

"It's a lovely view," Chimalli said, his voice a mix of sadness and irony. "When I lived here, few people saw the view from the top of the temple and lived to tell about it."

"Just try not to look at the heads on racks at the bottom," Teresa said from the corner. "Spoils the view."

"Right," Gabriel said, "I won't look down." He stepped out of the sanctuary to the top of the temple pyramid. Sema, Marcus, Ling, and Rajan stood silently at the four corners of the pyramid watching the sky and the city for any possible disturbance. It was unlikely that Malignancy Mages would appear, but there was no need to take chances. The others nodded silently to Gabriel as he stepped over to Rajan.

"How's it going inside?" Rajan asked.

"I broke one of the daggers," Gabriel admitted, his voice cracking with embarrassment.

"Bit of a butter fingers, are you?" Rajan said.

"I didn't drop it," Gabriel said, a bit defensively. "I accidentally used too much magical energy when I severed the connection and it shattered."

"I guess you don't know your own strength," Rajan said.

"That's what Teresa said," Gabriel replied.

"Well, great minds think alike, and so do ours. Don't tell her I said that. I'll go see to the dagger. Just keep an eye out for anything unusual."

"Like standing at the top of an Aztec temple in the middle of the fifteenth century isn't unusual," Gabriel said.

"You know what I mean," Rajan said. "Keep an eye out for magic. And hold these." Rajan handed Gabriel the small pouch with the artifacts he had collected from Teresa, Ohin, Chimalli, and Gabriel. As Rajan walked into the sanctuary, Gabriel looked in the pouch and saw, among other things, the shard of pottery Ohin had used to travel back to the temple and the small chunk of amber with the dragonfly suspended in it that would take them back to the Windsor Castle in the Cretaceous Period one hundred twenty-five million years ago. He put the pouch in his pocket.

Gabriel stood where Rajan had looked out over the Aztec city. Lights from oil lamps, small fires, and torches dotted the cityscape, the moon reflecting off the lake surrounding the stone metropolis. Fires burned at the tops of the other temples, giving the city an even greater sense of size.

Gabriel marveled. It really was stunning. The organization, the planning, the execution of the design, and all accomplished without a single piece of modern machinery. He wondered what the reaction of the first Spanish soldiers must have been. He thought about finding Manuel when he got back to the castle and asking him.

Then he noticed something that felt like magic. Not from the city spread out before him, but from behind him. From the temple sanctuary where Ohin was. Something not quite right. Something that his time-sense said was all wrong. As he looked back at the sanctuary doorway there came a flash of red light.

He ran toward the sanctuary entrance even as the light faded away. Sema, Marcus, and Ling had seen the light, if not felt the surge of magical energy. He didn't think they could have sensed the disturbance of space-time the way he had. At the doorway, he found the sanctuary empty. Ohin, Chimalli, Teresa, and Rajan were gone. Sema reached the sanctuary as Gabriel stepped inside.

"What's happened?" Sema said as she walked past Gabriel. The small fireballs Teresa had set floating in the corners of the sanctuary had vanished. Only dim moonlight illuminated the chamber.

"There was some disturbance in the fabric of space-time," Gabriel said. "I could feel it even from outside."

"A trap," Marcus said from behind. "A bloody trap."

"Maybe something went wrong with severing the connection to the dagger," Sema said.

"Tǎoyàn de! Ohin would never leave without us," Ling stated as she pulled a hand-cranked flashlight from a pocket in her dress.

Gabriel heard a click, and the white light of the flashlight flicked around the room. It looked just as he had left it.

"He couldn't travel anywhere," Gabriel said, pulling the chunk of amber from the pouch in his pocket to show them. "I've still got his relic that leads back to the castle."

"How many blades were there?" Marcus said as he pointed to the stone table with the sacrificial daggers. Ling swung the light of the flashlight to the low set table.

"Five," Gabriel said, seeing that there were now only four.

"It was a trap," Sema said.

"How?" Gabriel asked.

"I don't know how it works," Ling replied, "but I know that relics and artifacts can be enchanted to take someone through time against their will."

"But then where are they?" Gabriel asked.

"They could be any place in time that dagger was," Marcus said.

"We need to get back to the castle," Ling said. "You'll have to take us, Gabriel."

"No," Marcus said. "Not back to the castle. Not yet."

"Why the hell not?" Ling growled.

"Because this trap wasn't likely to be random," Sema said.

"Someone at the castle has turned colors," Marcus said.

"Then where the hell do we go?" Ling said, anger making her face flush.

"There's something happening outside," Gabriel said before Marcus or Sema could answer Ling's question. "Someone is traveling through time." He could feel it clearly now. They ran for the door in unison.

They rushed out of the temple top sanctuary, each scanning the city and the temple. Gabriel saw a cluster of four people standing at the base of the temple stairs. He knew they were mages even at a distance. He could feel the magical energy they held. His hopes rose for a moment, imaging that the Council had sent a rescue party. The magical energy felt different. Odd. Unlike the energy he was used to sensing. Then he realized it was because these were not mages sent by the Council to take them back to the castle. These were Malignancy Mages.

"Him," Sema said.

"I should have bloody known," Marcus cursed.

"Jiànhuò!" Ling spat.

One person stepped forward from the four. All were dressed in black, but this one was taller than the others were. He had long black hair and, although Gabriel could not see him perfectly, he knew by description who stood at the bottom of the temple; it sent a cold chill down to his stomach. "Apollyon," he said in a whisper.

In unison Ling, Sema, and Marcus extended their arms. One of the men grabbed his head and crumpled to the ground, another pitched back through the air, and a third went rigid and was suddenly immobile. Gabriel knew his companions were casting magic at the Malignancy Mages below, but Apollyon seemed unaffected.

Suddenly he stood at the top of the temple only a few feet before them. Gabriel and the others staggered back. It happened so quickly, Gabriel barely sensed the distortion of space-time before Apollyon completed his jump. He stared at them with contemptuous dark eyes. Gabriel could see now that he was an extremely handsome man, of Greek descent, with sharp features and an even sharper intelligence radiating from his eyes.

"Pitiful," Apollyon said. "How is your newest Time Mage to learn with such shoddy examples? Allow me to instruct him." Apollyon raised his hand and a crimson fireball the size of a watermelon burst into existence and leapt directly toward Gabriel. His first impulse was to jump through space, and he reached for the magic energy within him, but he was too new to magic, and there was no time to jump through space to safety, no time to duck; there was barely time to raise his hands. Somehow he did. He raised his hands as he reached for the magic within.

The fireball stopped just before it hit him, hovering, frozen in midair before his open palms. It didn't make sense, and he could see the look of shock and surprise on Apollyon's face, but Gabriel didn't wait for explanations. He focused his will on the fireball, and it shot back through the air toward Apollyon. The black-clad man was so surprised by the turn of events that the fireball burst around him. While Apollyon was stunned and stumbled back down the steps of the pyramid, Gabriel could see that the impact of the fireball had little other effect. He felt hands on his shoulders as Marcus pressed a stone with a small, round hole carved in one side into his right hand.

"Take us now!" Marcus said. "Make the jump, Boy, while there's still time."

CHAPTER 10
ST. FILLAN'S STONES

Gabriel didn't wait to ask questions. It didn't matter where and when they jumped to, as long as it was far away from Apollyon. Gabriel reached out with his time-sense toward the stone. An image filled his mind of a hut and a forest and green hills. He willed his magical energy through the pocket watch and toward that place in time. Then the blackness encircled them, the white light filling everything, and they suddenly stood in the little field at the edge of the forest that Gabriel had seen.

"Jump again, Gabriel," Sema said.

"Before he can follow," Ling hissed.

Gabriel knew they were right. A True Mage with Apollyon's power could sense the distortions in the fabric of space-time and follow them to their destination even without a relic. The only way to lose him was to make repeated time jumps.

Gabriel used the stone in his hand again and jumped. And jumped again. And again. The stone did not seem to have moved much in space. It was always the same low mountains in the background, the same streams, the same lake, the same green hills and sparse forests. Sometimes a house became visible for a moment, sometimes a cluster of homes that indicated a town, sometimes nothing but a field of low grass with grazing sheep. Gabriel felt safe when he saw the sheep for some reason and stopped there.

"Do you think that's enough?" he asked, looking around. He noticed the others had reverted to their white tunics and pants. He looked down and saw that he had unconsciously done the same.

"I doubt anyone could follow those jumps," Marcus said, catching his breath.

"My head is spinning," Ling muttered as she staggered away.

"Very well done, Gabriel," Sema said, patting him on the shoulder with one hand while pressing the heel of the other to her temple.

"Where are we?" Gabriel asked, holding up the stone as he looked around at the flock of sheep wandering away over the dark green hillside.

"Scotland," Marcus said, taking the stone back from Gabriel. "Glen Dochart. Home of Saint Fillan and his healing stones. This one is my talisman."

Gabriel found that all three mages were staring at him. "What?" he said, unsure of why he was the focus of attention.

"You stopped that fireball, lad," Marcus said. "Do you know what that means?"

"Not really," Gabriel said. "It was just a fluke. I wanted to duck or use magic to jump away, but there wasn't time."

"Mages can only use one kind of magic," Sema said. "A Time Mage can't wield fire."

"And you threw that fireball back at Apollyon without even moving your arms," Ling said.

"I just did it without thinking," Gabriel said.

"Which is probably why no one noticed before," Sema said.

"The boy's so strong in Time Magic, who would think to look?" Marcus said. "Even if they did believe."

"Believe what?" Gabriel said.

"The prophecy," Ling said. "The damn prophecy."

"I don't understand what you're talking about," Gabriel said, looking from face to face and trying to figure out if he had done something wrong. Why else would they seem so concerned?

"You caught and then threw a fireball," Marcus said. "Only one kind of mage could do that, lad."

"A True Mage," Sema said.

"I can't be a True Mage," Gabriel said. "There are only six True Mages."

"Yes," Ling said. "One for each magic."

"Three for the forces of Grace and three for the forces of Malignancy," Sema added.

"But the Prophecy speaks of a Seventh True Mage," Marcus said.

"One who is different," Ling added.

"One who is unique," Sema said.

"One who can use both kinds of imprints," Marcus said. "One who can stand between the forces of Grace and Malignancy and wield them both."

Gabriel said nothing, his mind a flurry of thoughts, a windstorm raging inside his head. He was a True Mage. That's what they had said. That's what catching the fireball meant. He could use all six magics. He would be a True Mage like Councilwoman Elizabeth, and Akikane, and Nefferati.

But he was more than that. If what they said was true, he could also use tainted artifacts, objects with negative imprints, like the True Mages of Malignancy. Like Apollyon. The windstorm picked up speed and the world seemed to spin. His knees buckled and he sat down in the short grass. Ling and Sema knelt down beside him, placing a hand on either shoulder to steady him. Marcus looked down at him, his face a mask of seriousness, but his eyes gentle.

"Do you know what this means, lad?" Marcus asked.

"I can use all magics and any artifact," Gabriel said.

"If the prophecy is true," Ling said.

"That's easy enough to verify," Sema said.

"That's not what I meant," Marcus said. "The boy needs to know."

"Know what?" Gabriel asked. What could be worse than being half Malignancy Mage?

"Apollyon saw you," Sema said. "He'll know what you are."

"Being able to use both Grace and Malignant imprints makes you very special," Ling said.

"Don't try to soften it for him," Marcus said, looking Gabriel directly in the eyes. "You'll be hunted, boy. The Council will love you, oh yes, they'll fawn over you like a prize peacock, but they won't be the only ones who'll want your favor. You're valuable, boy. Grace magic in one hand, Malignant magic in the other. Your power could tip the balance. Could end the war. One way or the other. And Apollyon knows it. He'll be looking for you now. Searching."

"I'd never help the Malignancy Mages," Gabriel said, fighting the icy feeling in his stomach, letting the anger well up in his voice.

"We would never think that you would," Sema said.

"But if Apollyon gets a hold of you, he'll try to persuade you," Ling said.

"And he is a powerful Soul Mage," Sema said. "He can be persuasive even to those who hate him. And he has other methods, as well."

"If he can't win you over to his side," Marcus said, "he'll try to kill you."

"Great," Gabriel said, his anger evaporating, overtaken by the icy fear in his stomach. "I think I'd like to go back to the bus at the bottom of the river now."

"There's no point in frightening him needlessly," Sema said, glaring at Marcus.

"I said Apollyon would try to kill him," Marcus said. "I didn't say he would. Hell, we'd all lay down our lives to protect the Seventh True Mage. The whole castle would."

That didn't make Gabriel feel any better. He was no longer helping fight a war between wizards; he was at the center of it. His actions might not only endanger himself, but all of the Grace Mages and the Council, and with them, the whole of the Continuum. The windstorm in his head stopped. All the trees of his mind had already blown down. He could barely think. He focused on his breath. He had to see. He took out his pocket watch. He looked down at his hands; one closed around the watch, the other open, palm up. He reached for the magic within and focused it through the pocket watch, willing the image in his mind into existence. A small ball of mandarin-colored fire appeared, floating above his hands.

"Teresa's going to be so jealous," Ling said. "It took her a whole hour to manage that."

"The lad is a quick study," Marcus said.

"He'll need to be," Sema said.

Gabriel let the flame wink out, but held on to the pocket watch. It was true. At least part of it.

"We should go back to the castle," Ling said. "Maybe we can contact Councilwoman Elizabeth or Akikane before anyone sees us."

"It might be too risky," Sema said. "The spy at the castle may not know about Gabriel."

"We can't sit on our asses here in Scotland," Ling said, her temper rising again.

"We need a plan," Sema said, forcing authority into her voice.

"Those always work so well for us," Marcus said, reaching out a hand and helping Gabriel to his feet.

"We need to find Ohin and the others first," Gabriel said. "They may be hurt. We can't wait for the castle to send out a rescue party."

"I agree," Marcus said.

"We don't even know where in time or space they got thrown by that booby-trapped dagger," Ling said. "They could be anywhere."

"I don't think so," Gabriel said. "One of the daggers was gone, so I think they were thrown somewhere along the timeline of the dagger. Which means they're probably near the temple somewhere in time."

"That makes sense," Sema said, sounding reassuring, "But we don't know when."

"If we can go back to just after the trap was sprung," Gabriel said, "I might be able to sense the time stream they followed and track them to their destination."

"You're very gifted for your age," Ling said, "But even I know that takes a great deal of power for a mage."

"And we would have to travel to a time after we left," Sema added. "A time where we were sure that Apollyon would be gone, as well."

"Ten minutes should be enough," Gabriel said.

"I'm no Time Mage," Marcus interjected, "But ten minutes is a mighty long time after the magic of the jump is enacted. No offense, lad, but I doubt even Ohin would be able to sense the time stream that long after."

"If it could be sensed," Ling said, "Apollyon would have been able to follow us."

"Every jump makes it harder to follow," Gabriel said. "As long as Ohin didn't jump again, we could find him."

"Gabriel," Sema said, placing a hand on his cheek. "You're just not strong enough to work this kind of magic."

"Not by myself," Gabriel said. "Not with just my pocket watch."

"Not with all our artifacts," Ling interrupted.

"But if what you say is true," Gabriel said, "I'd have access to all the imprints and power I need to track the time stream and follow Ohin."

"You can't do that," Sema said. "It might be dangerous."

"The daggers," Marcus said. "They might still not be enough power, though."

"Not the daggers," Gabriel said, taking Sema's hand. "The temple."

The others were silent a moment. They knew he was right. The imprints on the temple were enormous. Far greater than all of their artifacts combined. It held all the negative imprints accumulated through decades of human sacrifice. He could only tap that power if he really was the Seventh True Mage. If he did, he would be touching the very darkness that he was trying to fight.

"It is a plan," Ling said.

"And it just might work," Marcus said.

"It's too dangerous," Sema said. "We don't even know for certain that he can use negative imprints."

"You're right," Gabriel said. "We need to find a tainted artifact so I can test it."

"That's madness," Sema said. "You need more study before attempting something of that nature."

"And who's going to teach me?" Gabriel said, feeling defiant. "You can teach me Soul Magic, and Ling can teach me Wind Magic, and Marcus can show me Heart-Tree Magic, but none of you can teach me how to use a tainted artifact. I'm going to have to learn it on my own. I don't like the other alternative." He could see by their reactions they knew he was thinking about Apollyon.

"Just because you can use tainted artifacts, doesn't mean you should," Sema said. "You don't know what it will do to you."

"Sema has a point," Ling said. "From all we know, use of tainted objects affects the mind of the user. They're called Malignant Mages for a reason."

"Exactly my point," Sema said, raising her voice.

"I understand that it's dangerous," Gabriel said, "but we have to try."

"We could go back to the castle first," Sema said. "There are more experienced mages who could find Ohin."

"It's my responsibility," Gabriel said. "I'm his apprentice."

"It's not your fault," Sema said.

"I don't think that it is," Gabriel replied, his voice getting firmer as he spoke. "But it's still my responsibility. And since I'm the only Time Mage here, we're going where I say we go."

A deep silence fell over them. Gabriel could tell by the look on Sema's face that he had just crossed some invisible line. Her eyes narrowed, but she didn't speak.

"You've been spending altogether too much time with Teresa," Ling said with a scowl. "Her poor attitude has rubbed off on you."

"The lad has a point that is hard to argue with," Marcus said. "He's our ticket home."

Sema still had not said anything. Gabriel held her stare. He knew he had affronted her, that as the eldest in the group and the one with the most experience, he should have deferred to her judgment, but in his heart, he knew he was right to try to find Ohin as quickly as possible. He no longer felt that he could trust anyone at the castle.

Sema licked her lips and squinted. *"Do you think I could not make you take us back to the castle?"* he heard a voice say in his head. It was Sema's voice, but her lips had not moved. His eyes widened. He reached out for the magic within himself and focused it through the pocket watch still in his hand.

"You could try." He thought the words as clearly as he could. Sema's eyes now widened. She cocked her head slightly, and then, surprisingly, she laughed. Before he knew what happened, Sema had grabbed Gabriel and pulled him into a powerfully strong embrace.

He was confused, but happy. He found himself smiling and hugging her back.

"No wonder you want to find your teacher so badly," Sema said. "You're just as stubborn as he is."

"What was that all about?" Ling asked, looking the two with curiosity.

"A private discussion," Sema said.

"Wonderful," Marcus said, clearly seeing what had happened. "Now they'll be whispering about us all right in front of our faces. Trading quips with their lips sealed."

"I do not stoop to such behavior," Sema said. She looked at Gabriel. "I'm sorry. I should not have threatened you."

"Neither should I," Gabriel said. "I'm sorry as well."

"Now that we're all sorry to one degree or another," Ling said, "Let's move our asses and get this job done."

"We need to find a tainted object first," Gabriel said.

"Where along the timeline of the stone did you drop us, I mean, set us down?" Marcus asked. "Near the beginning, the middle, or at the end?"

"Near the beginning, I think," Gabriel said.

"Good," Marcus said. He shimmered and suddenly he wore a kilt and a billowy, white cotton shirt. "I know exactly where to find what we need." Gabriel looked to Ling and Sema and saw that they suddenly wore long peasant dresses one might find on an 8th century Scottish woman. Gabriel frowned. Ever since his mother's inspired choice of a costume on his ninth Halloween, he had hated kilts.

"Marcus, don't be absurd," Sema said. "Kilts weren't introduced to Scotland until the end of the 16th century."

"Are you positive?" Marcus asked, seeming confused.

"You of all people should know," Ling said.

"Yes, but the lad doesn't know," Marcus sighed as he frowned. "Wanted to see how long I could get him to wear it." Marcus switched his attire to simple wool pants and long, rough-spun cotton shirt. Gabriel breathed a sigh of relief. "This way. It's not far."

"Good one, Marcus," Gabriel said with a grin. "I'll remember that if we come across a lonely keg of ale."

"Ah, you can't hold a small joke against me," Marcus said as he led them up a steep hill. They all laughed. Gabriel wondered what he would see at the top of the hill and where Marcus was taking them. What tainted object would they find? And what would happen when he tried to use it?

CHAPTER 11
THE SEVENTH TRUE MAGE

"Here's where it helps to know your history," Marcus said, pointing to the small stone abbey by a large pool of water. "St. Fillan brought Christianity from the monastery of St. Columba on the Scottish island of Iona into the Breadelane, all through Glen Dochart, and as far as Killin." The names made little sense to Gabriel, but he assumed they referred to the places he could see from the top of the hill where they stood. "Now, this was in the 8th century CE, round about the middle. The dates are a bit foggy, but we know he died in the year 777.

"However, we're not so concerned with St. Fillan himself as with what he left behind. His healing powers were renowned, and it wasn't long after his death before he was canonized and made a saint. That abbey down there is named for him. And in the year 1306, Robert the Bruce, the first king of Scotland, was defeated at Methven and retreated to St. Fillan's abbey, where the abbot at the time gave him shelter. It was here that Bruce would see the relic of St. Fillan's left arm, which he would later credit with his defeat of the British. The upshot being the abbey was well-funded under Bruce's reign."

"I agree the history is fascinating," Ling said with impatience. "But how the hell does it help us?"

"Well," Marcus said, "we see the abbey here, and all we need to do is travel forward in time until Bruce and his men arrive to take shelter."

"And then we find a sword," Sema said.

"Sword, axe, dagger, well-used cudgel," Marcus replied. "It doesn't really matter. They'll all be tainted."

"Right," Gabriel said as they all started down the hill. As they got closer, they could see a monk tending some plants in a small garden and a boy feeding chickens on the far side of the abbey.

Neither noticed them. Gabriel reached out with his magic-sense and could feel Sema casting magic over their minds. He couldn't grasp exactly what she was doing, but he understood the effect. The mages walking down the hill would seem invisible to those below. Unless someone saw them that Sema did not notice.

Gabriel sensed the magic could only work on a mind that Sema was aware of. He wondered how many minds she could affect at once. He also wondered how long it would take him to learn to do the same. It seemed that his earlier attempt at Soul Magic, of speaking to Sema without words, had been a bit of luck. While he appeared to have a natural talent for sensing the fabric of space-time, sensing mind energy felt much more difficult.

When they reached the abbey, Gabriel took out his pocket watch. He placed his other hand on the wall of the abbey and raised his arm holding the pocket watch. Sema placed her hand on his.

"The abbey isn't large enough to house Bruce and all his men," Marcus said, "so I'd look for a time when there were a large number of soldiers camped outside."

"And night time would be best," Sema said. "No need to draw attention to ourselves before I can convince people we don't exist."

"Okay," Gabriel said. He reached out with his time-sense to the abbey. He could feel it stretching back and forward in time. Not in a line, actually. More like moments layered on top of one another, but holding the same space. Images flicked through his mind, all seeming very much alike. Day and night, spring and summer, fall and winter, the abbey in disrepair, and new walls added. People in the yard and on the hills. People in the abbey. Weddings. Seasonal celebrations.

Then an image slipped past. One a bit different. Many men. And he could see soldiers. He focused on it. That had to be it. "Hold on," he said to the others as the blackness surrounded them. The blazing white light followed and soon they stood in the same place, soldiers camped about, small fires burning here and there to give light to the moonless night.

Marcus looked around and took his hand back. "Well done, lad," he whispered. "1306 on the mark."

With Sema helping him to avoid notice, Gabriel walked into the army camp in search of a tainted weapon. He knew the one he wanted. It didn't take long for Gabriel to locate Robert the Bruce's tent among those spread around the grounds of the abbey. It was the only one with guards posted outside. Gabriel paid close attention with his magic-sense as Sema caused the guards' minds to cloud with sleep. Quickly slipping inside the tent, Gabriel immediately saw the weapon he was looking for: the battle sword of Robert the Bruce. It was heavier than he expected. He had to use all his strength just to hold it up. A double-handed, double-bladed sword, it was nearly as long as he was tall.

Sliding his hand into his pocket to touch his watch, Gabriel held Sema's arm as he jumped through space. Blackness and a brilliant white light and they stood next to Ling and Marcus at the edge of the abbey in the shadows.

"Couldn't find a bigger sword?" Ling asked, staring at the blade Gabriel struggled with.

"I thought it might be easier to use," Gabriel said, laying the sword down in the grass beside the abbey wall.

"I doubt even Robert the Bruce finds it easy to use," Marcus said as he knelt down beside the sword. Sema and Ling also knelt down as Gabriel slowly drew the long sword from its sheath and placed it across his folded legs. The well-polished blade glittered in the reflected light of the Scottish campfires.

"Something simple," Sema said, seriousness filling her voice.

"Nothing fancy, lad," Marcus added.

"See if you can make this stone float in the air," Ling suggested as she placed a fist-sized rock in front of him. From the tone of her voice and the look in her eyes, Gabriel suspected she was curious to see how well he might perform Wind Magic. "Reach out to and try to sense the force of gravity that holds it down. When you feel it, will it to avoid the stone, and then you'll be able to hold the stone in a cradle of the gravity that doesn't touch it."

"Okay," Gabriel said, looking down at the sword. He handed Marcus his pocket watch and placed his hands on the sword. He could sense the imprints immediately, but that did not surprise him.

He had been able to sense the imprints of the sacrificial daggers, as well.

The sword was filled with negative imprints. Robert the Bruce might have been fighting for a just cause, for the freedom of his people to choose their own king, but the sword he swung in battle had taken many lives. Each death had left a subtle energy imprint on the blade.

He reached within himself for his own magical energy and as he held it, focused his mind and will upon the sword. Gabriel felt a wave of nausea wash over him as he reached out to the sword. It wasn't like reaching out to the pocket watch. The imprints of the watch filled him with a sense of warmth and power that reminded him of standing in the sun at noon on a summer's day.

The power of the sword felt very different — a cold ocean with massive waves crashing down, threatening to crush and suck him into its depths. While he felt like he was guiding the energy of the imprints in the watch when he used it, it felt like he needed to struggle to control the imprints of the sword. Like they wanted to lash out, and he would need to force them to take the shape he wanted.

He paused a moment and extended the unseen senses of his mind to feel for the gravity that held the stone before him pressed into the dew-damp grass. He was surprised to realize that he could sense the force of the gravity. He felt like a fish that had suddenly realized it was swimming in water. The presence of gravity was such a constant he had never noticed it. Now that he did, he could feel how it enveloped the stone. How the stone too had a weak gravity emanating from it, as well. How he did also. How everything with mass did.

As he focused his magical energy through the sword and began to will the gravity holding the stone to bend around it, he felt the nausea again. Bile reached up to the back of his throat and he nearly retched. He focused his mind and willed the gravity to avoid the stone. He blinked in surprise as the stone slowly rose from the ground and began to hover ten inches in the air. Ling had been correct. If he willed the gravity to avoid the stone, he could cradle it and move it.

He pushed the stone toward Ling with his mind. Ling swore in Chinese. He didn't know what she said, but she sounded afraid. Sema's amulets didn't always translate swear words. Gabriel let the stone drop back to the ground and released the magical energy of the sword. He was happy to be free of it. He turned to his three companions. They all had the same look in their eyes: a mixture of fear and awe.

"That settles that," Ling said as she spat on the ground.

"How do you feel?" Sema asked. "I sensed a great deal of discomfort."

"It's not pleasant," Gabriel said, "but I'm okay."

"What does it feel like?" Marcus asked. "Using a tainted artifact?"

Gabriel thought for a moment. "Like dropping a piece of gum on the floor of the boys' bathroom and being forced to eat it."

"Thank you for that image," Marcus said with distaste.

"Now we know," Ling said, looking at Marcus and Sema. "You are the Seventh True Mage." She looked Gabriel in the eyes. She seemed wary and Gabriel realized why. This was the closest any of them had come to sitting peacefully with a Malignancy Mage. Was that what he was? Wasn't he more than that?

"If I'm not a Grace Mage and I'm not a Malignancy Mage, what am I?" Gabriel said. It was a worry that had been growing more palpable every moment since he had touched the tainted power of the sword.

"You're something special," Ling said, the features of her face softening. She must have sensed the distress she had elicited in Gabriel and reached out to place both hands on his shoulders. "You are something unique, Gabriel. Something that has never existed. And people will fear you."

"Both on the sides of Grace and Malignancy," Marcus added.

"But we will not fear you," Sema said.

"We'll be right there with you," Ling agreed. "We'll help you through this. Help you figure out how to be what you are."

"And how to use your powers wisely," Sema said.

"Because there will be those who simply want to use you," Marcus added. "Apollyon will be one, but you'll find plenty at the castle ready to treat you like a shiny new weapon to be tested in battle."

"So you stick with us," Ling said, her eyes sharp and serious, "and we'll watch your back."

Gabriel could feel a tightness growing on his throat and he coughed before it could move to his eyes. He realized now the feeling that had been eating at the back of his mind and churning his stomach since they had told him what catching the fireball back at the temple meant. It was fear. Fear that he would become something he didn't want to be. Fear that he might already be that thing. But Ling didn't think so. And neither did Sema or Marcus. They didn't see some evil mage in the making. They saw something in him that they trusted. And he trusted them. So, he would trust himself as well. Even if doing so was as frightening as facing Apollyon.

"Thank you," Gabriel said. "Now let's go back and find Ohin and the others."

"Right," Marcus said, patting Gabriel on the back and standing up. "But first you might best put that sword back before the King of the Scots wakes up and finds it missing."

Gabriel stood up and Marcus helped him re-sheath the sword. "I'll be right back," he said as he took his pocket watch from Marcus. He could have used the energy-tainted sword to jump back to the tent, but Gabriel had already made one clear decision: he would only use tainted artifacts when it was absolutely necessary. A moment later, he stood in the tent again. He placed the sword where it had been and was back at the side of the abbey a moment after that. He was getting better at jumping through space. It hardly took him any time at all to manage it now.

The others were waiting. They each raised a hand, stacking them one upon the other. Gabriel placed his hands on either side of his companion's palms, one holding the Aztec pottery shard and the other holding his pocket watch.

"No closer than ten minutes after we left," Sema cautioned. "We don't know how long Apollyon may have lingered."

"Everyone stay alert," Marcus said. "We don't know what we may find."

"If we can't stay alert heading back to a fight with Apollyon, we should retire now," Ling with a hint of agitation. "Jump already. Let's get this over with."

CHAPTER 12
TWINS IN TIME

Gabriel didn't waste time responding to Ling. He reached out to the pottery shard with his time-sense and felt his way to the correct moment, a moment just shortly after he had left the top of the Aztec temple. Blackness and white light followed swiftly, and suddenly they stood in the middle the wide avenue where they had first arrived in Tenochtitlan.

He was surprised for a moment, and then he remembered that a Time Mage could only use a relic to move to places it had been while it was originally in the timeline of history. This was as close to the temple as the shard had ever been. He looked up the avenue at the Great Temple. There was no sign that there had been a magical battle at its pinnacle. The city still seemed mostly asleep.

"I'll take us to the top of the temple," Gabriel said, his hands still holding those of his companions. He looked at the temple top. He could see it clearly and knew it from memory. A swirl of blackness and blinding white and a moment later they stood on it, staring down at the city. The first thing he noticed was that the two guards were still asleep. That was good. Thanks to Sema's Soul Magic, they had slept through the earlier battle. He saw that the others had reassumed the guise of Aztec locals, so he focused on the amulet at his neck and did the same.

They each broke the contact of their hands and moved in unison toward the sanctuary where Ohin and the others had disappeared. Gabriel found the inside of the sanctuary just as he had left it. He couldn't tell how long it had been since the explosion of magic had sent Ohin and the others through time, but he didn't think it was more than ten minutes.

"Let's get on with it," Marcus said, taking up a station at the entrance of the sanctuary.

"Yes," Sema said. "We'd best hurry."

"Before that bastard Apollyon shows his ugly face," Ling said.

Gabriel placed the pocket watch and the pottery shard in his pocket and raised his left hand to touch the slanted wall of sanctuary. Reaching out with his time-sense, he sought the faded tendrils of the time-jump that had forcibly thrown Ohin and the others away through time. He could sense nothing, but he hadn't expected to. He would need the added magical power of the temple to amplify the remaining signs of the time jump.

He stilled his mind and focused the energy within himself before reaching out to the imprints of the temple. The imprints of the temple were far greater than anything he had touched previously. He had sensed them distantly before. Ohin had explained that buildings and places did not feel the same way as smaller objects did. Something as large and as old as the temple permeated the surrounding space with its imprints to the point where it became like background noise, like the many voices in a crowd creating a wall of sound. It was for this reason that Ohin had been able to block out any interference from the temple's imprints when he had been attempting to sever the connections between the sacrificial daggers and the concatenate crystals.

When Gabriel reached out for the power of the tainted imprints of the temple, he was nearly overwhelmed. He staggered slightly. Concerned, Ling put her hand out to steady him. "I'm all right. It's a little overwhelming, is all," he told her.

"Remember to breathe," Sema said from behind him.

He took a deep breath and focused his own magical energy into that of the temple, feeling it magnified beyond anything he had experienced before. The sickening taint of the negative imprints churned his stomach, but the power he held was immense. He used that power to focus on the slender threads of the time-trail that lingered after Ohin's forced jump. He could sense them now. He willed them to take shape in his mind. He could feel them like fragments of a shattered glass spread across the room. However, try as he might, he could not make them take shape, could not make them take an intelligible form. He strained, but no image flickered into his mind. Frustrated and nearly ready to vomit from the psychic stench of the temple's tainted imprints, Gabriel released the connection.

"I can't find it," Gabriel said, letting his arm fall to his side. "It's been too long. Even with all the power of the temple's negative imprints, I can't get a clear image of where they went."

"We should leave," Marcus said, stepping over to join Gabriel. "Now."

"Maybe if I moved just a few minutes closer to the jump," Gabriel said, "I might be able to sense the time-threads."

"Minutes closer to Apollyon, you mean," Ling said.

"Marcus is right," Sema said. "We should leave now. If not back to the castle, at least someplace safe."

"The boy is correct," a voice from the doorway said. "Even I could not sense the threads of time at this distance from the event." Gabriel knew the voice, even though he had heard it only once. He spun to see Apollyon striding through the doorway. Sema instantly stepped in front of Gabriel to shield him, but he could easily see around her as Apollyon raised his hand.

"Do not be senseless," Apollyon said, his voice deep and resonant. As he stepped out of the doorway, another man entered. One who looked exactly like Apollyon. Gabriel blinked in confusion and he heard Ling gasp. "We thought you might return."

"Xiéè!" Ling shouted. "Abomination!"

"Worse than that," Marcus said.

"No need for insults," the duplicate Apollyon said with a silky smile.

Gabriel reached for the power of the temple's imprints, but they slid away from him. He tried again, but he could not touch them this time.

"So you have learned to taste of the dark power," the first Apollyon said. "Apparently your teachers failed to mention that only one mage at a time may hold the imprints of an artifact."

"I am a much more learned instructor," the second Apollyon said.

"Jump away, Gabriel!" Sema said.

101

"Gabriel," the first Apollyon said. "A perfect name for the Seventh True Mage."

"The boy cannot jump," the second Apollyon said. "He has no relic at hand."

It was true. While the pocket watch, chunk of amber, and pottery shard were still in his pocket, he was not yet adept enough to make a time jump without actually touching them. And he could not use the temple itself as an artifact while Apollyon held its imprints. Moreover, he could not just leave Sema, Ling, and Marcus behind.

"Which one of you is the real one?" Marcus asked, his voice dripping with contempt.

"Maybe neither of us is," the first Apollyon said.

"You can't have him," Ling said, clenching her jaw. "You'll have to kill us to first."

"Do you honestly think that will be difficult?" the second Apollyon said.

"And then the boy will have to watch you die," said the first Apollyon.

"Much better if you simply stand aside," the second Apollyon added.

Gabriel suddenly noticed that while Marcus called him 'boy' all the time, it didn't bother him, but instead felt affectionate, like a term of endearment. When Apollyon uttered the word, however, it filled Gabriel with loathing and anger. He wasn't sure why there were two Apollyons, but he could guess. It had to mean that Apollyon was making copies of himself by creating bifurcations. How that could be done, he wasn't certain, but what better way to create an army of loyal and powerful Malignancy Mages? The reason they were there was clear. They wanted him. He would be extremely valuable to them even if only as a hostage.

How could he get them all away?

"It's okay," Gabriel said. "I'll go." As he stepped forward, he placed his left foot so that it touched Ling's right.

"No!" Sema said and turned to him.

"The boy is as smart as he is gifted," the first Apollyon said.

"He knows this can end only one way," the second one said.

"You have to promise to leave them alone and I'll go with you," Gabriel said, staring at the two Apollyons.

"You can't do that, lad," Marcus said, grabbing Gabriel's shoulder.

"You can't trust them," Ling said. "He only tells lies and if there are two of them, then that's twice as many lies."

"I won't allow it," Sema said, her cheeks flushed with anger.

"It'll be okay," Gabriel said as he gently raised his hand to calm her. He laid his hand on her neck, his fingers touching the glass pendant of her talisman. "I'll go with him," he said as he reached for the magic energy within himself even as he threw the full power of his time-sense into Sema's pendant and focused his magical energy through her talisman. The blackness followed only a moment later. Lightning flashed around him, from one of the twin Apollyons he assumed, but then the white light filled all of existence and when it ceased, he stood in a large plaza, the moon full in the sky above. He looked around quickly.

Venice, he thought. He knew it from pictures his sister had shown him of her summer spent hiking through Europe. This was the Piazza San Marco, or St. Mark's Square, as it was known in English. St. Mark's Cathedral at one end. The canals behind the Doge's Palace. The square tower of the St. Mark's Campanile, rising over three hundred feet into the night sky. He saw a few people at the periphery of the piazza and felt Sema's Soul Magic turning their attention away.

"Jump again, lad," he heard Marcus say, and he was already beginning to do so when suddenly the four of them were thrown apart by an invisible force, and Gabriel felt something odd about the fabric of space-time. A wall erected between him and the fabric of time and space within the Continuum. He knew what it was from a description Ohin had given him. A space-time seal. A shield that would prevent time travel.

Gabriel looked around to see that a least one of the Apollyons had been able to track him through time. He was too far from Sema and the others to make another jump even if he could manage to break Apollyon's space-time seal.

Before he had time to think any further, the fighting began. Ling and Sema raised their arms toward Apollyon simultaneously as Marcus clenched his fists at his waist. Apollyon raised one hand toward them all and squinted his eyes slightly. Gabriel could feel the flow of magic passing between his fellow mages and he was amazed not only at the power Sema, Marcus, and Ling wielded, but the ease with which Apollyon was holding them off.

"It is a shame you have such pitiful teachers," Apollyon said. "I will be sure to better your instruction." He flicked the open hand of the lowered arm and suddenly Ling was hurtling through the air.

"No!" Sema screamed, but no sooner had the sound begun to leave her voice than she and Marcus were lifted off their feet and thrown together.

Gabriel watched in horror as Ling crashed into the side of the Campanile tower with such a force that he could see a crack form along the outer wall of the structure. Ling fell to the ground thirty feet below, her body limp and lifeless.

Gabriel ran toward Sema and Marcus, thrusting his hand into his pocket and grasping at his grandfather's silver watch. He could feel the rage within him as he ran. He wanted kill Apollyon. Wanted to engulf him in flame and destroy him. But he knew that was impossible. He knew that he was not nearly strong enough or experienced enough to defeat Apollyon in combat. But he might be able to distract him.

As he ran, he reached his arm out and a stream of fireballs erupted into the air, shooting forth from his palm and flying toward Apollyon. They were not large, but they were plentiful and the only offensive magic Gabriel knew. He could sense Sema and Marcus hurling magic at Apollyon with redoubled effort. It was not enough to defeat Apollyon, but it was enough to momentarily divert his attention.

Even as the fireballs sped toward Apollyon, Gabriel felt a flicker in the space-time seal. The fireballs winked out of existence, but it didn't matter. By then Gabriel had reached Sema and Marcus. As he ran, his hand grasping for the watch had found something in his pocket he had entirely forgotten about. Something he reached out to with his time-sense as he threw his arms around Sema and Marcus. The blackness flowed around them and the white light flooded his existence as he heard Apollyon yell in rage, trying to re-establish the space-time seal.

Then they were on a beach, the white sands beneath them, the ocean rolling out beyond them for miles, white plaster-covered houses dotting the hillside. And then the blackness and the white light again. And again. And again. He kept jumping. Moving anywhere and everywhere the coin in his pocket had ever been. He would glimpse the scene only long enough to focus and jump again. A dock yard at a Greek port. An ancient city that he could not name. An open field of olive trees. A battlefield. An island again. Over and over, new places.

Finally, he felt Sema squeezing his arm and Marcus shouting. They came to rest on a deserted stretch of beach, a small Greek town in the distance. He knew the town. Samos. The Greek town that Councilwoman Elizabeth had told him about when she gave him the coin in the Upper Ward courtyard only a few nights past. He unclenched his right hand in his pocket and released the watch and the coin. Sema and Marcus knelt on the sand as they had in St. Mark's Square moments ago.

"Ling!" Gabriel said in a strangled shout as he sank to the ground between Marcus and Sema. She placed her arms around him. He could feel her body shaking from the sobs of her tears.

"She's gone, lad," Marcus said, placing his hand gently on Gabriel's shoulder.

"We have to go back," Gabriel said, tears streaming down his face. "She might still be alive."

"She died the moment she struck the tower," Marcus said, his eyes also filled with tears. "I could feel the life go out of her even from where we were."

"But you could save her," Gabriel sobbed. "You're a Heart-Tree Mage. You could bring her back. You brought me back."

"It's different, Gabriel," Marcus said.

"Even if he could," Sema said, wiping the tears from her eyes. "Apollyon is still back there. And the other one could join him. We were very fortunate you were able to save us."

"Which was too damn risky, boy," Marcus said, his voice stern. "You get this through that thick skull of yours right now. We are all expendable if it means saving you."

"You should have jumped alone if you knew you could," Sema said. "Marcus is right. You are far more important than any other mage or any number of mages."

"I couldn't," Gabriel said, tears still filling his eyes. "Apollyon placed a space-time seal around me as soon as he found us. It was only by distracting him that we escaped." He paused for a moment, looking between the elder mages. "And I'm not more important than Ling."

"You are," Sema said. "And Ling knew that."

"She died knowing she was protecting someone special," Marcus said, kicking at a newspaper that had been lying on the piazza bricks and had gotten sucked through time with them. "Someone important."

"She died because of me," Gabriel said.

"No, she died because of that bastard, Apollyon, and his new twin," Marcus spat. "And he'll pay for that. They both will."

"Apollyon is creating bifurcations in time to make copies of himself, isn't he?" Gabriel said, desperate to talk about anything other than Ling's death.

"He must be," Sema agreed. "But it's terribly dangerous and wicked."

"Describes Apollyon to the letter," Marcus said, glancing at the Venetian newspaper and frowning.

"But how could he do it?" Gabriel asked, his breathing starting to return to normal. He could hear the ocean waves gently crashing along the shoreline. It helped calm him.

"He would have to go back to a point when he was living normally in the timeline," Sema said. "Apollyon is one of the few mages trained before being plucked from the timeline at his death."

"Elizabeth said that Vicaquirao trained him," Gabriel remembered aloud.

"Yes," Marcus said. "He was a fully trained True Mage before he left the timeline permanently to battle Grace Mages. He must have picked a time in his past when he was nearly fully trained and created a bifurcation, a branch at that time."

"Then he would need to enter that new branch and bring himself back," Sema said.

"And now he is making an army of twins," Gabriel said, imagining what that would look like.

"I suspect it's more than that," Sema said. "In the same way that one can connect the energy of an artifact to a concatenate crystal and then link several crystals together, True Mages can connect their power over space and time. It is not easy, and takes a great deal of training. Elizabeth told me she once did this with Nefferati. It might be easier with a twin created from a bifurcation. If Apollyon can connect with copies of himself, it would be like having a series of extremely powerful concatenate crystals all linked together and able to draw power from each other."

"Apollyon was never going to spare us and let his secret out," Marcus said. "And the Council surely needs to learn of this. There are probably only two or three copies of him so far, or you would never have been able break a space-time seal he held, but he could be making more even at this moment."

"What about Ling?" Gabriel said, standing up and facing Sema and Marcus.

"She died trying to give you time to bring us here," Sema said.

"And where are we?" Marcus said, looking around. Gabriel could sense that they were both trying to change the subject.

"Samos," Gabriel said. "It's a Greek island. Councilwoman Elizabeth gave me the coin the other night when we talked."

"Samos," Marcus said looking around. "I should have guessed."

"You'll be safe here," Gabriel said, stepping back from the other two.

"Gabriel, you must give it up," Sema said. "There is nothing you can do."

107

"Maybe there was a bifurcation created because of us," Gabriel said. "Because of the magic."

"I don't think so," Sema said. "I was very intentionally clouding the minds of the few people who were still out that night, and I only wavered for a moment."

"You'd know," Marcus said. "You'd have felt it, if anyone could."

"I didn't feel anything," Gabriel said, thinking back to those few seconds of fighting in the piazza.

"I didn't think so," Marcus said, picking up the newspaper. He handed it to Gabriel.

"I can't read it," Gabriel said, staring at the Italian prose. While the amulet at his neck could translate spoken words by making a psychic connection with the listener and the speaker, it could do nothing for written language. For that, one needed study.

"Just look at the date," Marcus said, pointing to the corner of the newspaper cover. It read July 11, 1902.

"So?" Gabriel said.

"Ah," Sema said, seeing the date and seeming to collapse a bit more into the ground. "There really is nothing that can be done."

"I don't understand," Gabriel said.

"July 11, 1902," Marcus said. "The Campanile, the tower that Ling was thrown into, collapsed at 9:45am on July 14th, three days later."

"History records that a crack in the tower appeared a few days before the tower collapsed," Sema said.

"But what about Ling's body?" Gabriel asked. "Wouldn't someone notice it? Wouldn't that create a bifurcation?"

"Not necessarily," Sema said. "There were many people who threw themselves from the tower. Her clothes are nondescript for a reason. No one can use the amulet, except a mage. The changes might be slight enough that the Continuum simply absorbs them."

"We could at least go back for her body," Gabriel said.

"And if she was always the cause of the crack in the tower and its collapse," Marcus said, "then there would be no branching in time because this is the way the Continuum was supposed to happen. And her body is supposed to be there."

"And it would be too great a risk," Sema said. "Apollyon, or one of his twins, might wait there for you to do just that."

"You're right," Gabriel said, looking at them both in turn as he slipped his right hand into his pocket. "I know you're right. Everything you say makes sense."

"Of course it does," Sema said, her voice soothing.

"But I don't care," Gabriel said. "I'm sorry." He reached out his left hand and Sema's glass Venetian pendant flew from her neck, the chain breaking with a loud snap.

"No!" Marcus shouted and he scrambled to his feet trying to reach Gabriel.

Gabriel held the pendant firmly in his hand. The look on Sema's face was one of shock and horror. Gabriel winced as he reached out to the pendant with his time-sense. Staring at Sema, he felt as though he had just slapped his grandmother. As though he had committed a vile and unforgivable sin. But it was nothing compared with the sin he had in mind to commit.

"You'll be safe here," he repeated as Marcus lunged and the blackness enveloped Gabriel's world.

CHAPTER 13
THE WRONG THING TO DO

When the white light faded, Gabriel stood beside a Venetian canal two blocks from St. Mark's Square. Then he felt it. The shift in the fabric of space-time that told him his older self had arrived in the piazza with Sema, Ling, and Marcus. The ripple of space-time indicating Apollyon's arrival came next. He could vaguely sense the space-time seal Apollyon had created. It was too localized to affect him two blocks away. At least he hoped so. Gabriel didn't have long if his plan was going to work.

Looking down the canal, Gabriel saw a number of gondolas and small boats. There were not many, but there might be enough. There were few people on the streets this time of night. He didn't think any of them had noticed him suddenly pop into existence, which was what he had hoped. He had only seconds and not many of those. He needed to do something significant. Faintly he could sense the magic energy from the piazza. He hoped that Apollyon would be too distracted by Gabriel's older self to notice what he did next.

Clasping the pocket watch in his hand, he raised his arm toward the canal and focused his mind and will, trying to make a burst of magical energy that would be too quick to attract Apollyon's attention two blocks away. The water of the canal rose up in a wave, the gondolas and boats washing onto the street. The people in the boats screamed and the few Venetians on the street yelled and leapt back to safety. Gabriel wondered if it had been enough. He reached out with his time-sense. Was it there? Had it happened? Would he know what it felt like to be sure he had done what he needed to?

There. Something like a bending of the fabric of space-time, a sharp rip that seemed to break off in a new direction. Then it felt normal, or almost normal, as though he were looking in a mirror while looking at a second mirror. That must be it. It had to be. He

110

had created a bifurcation, a new branch of time at just the moment before Ling died. And she would die soon if he didn't act quickly.

He reached out again with his time-sense. He knew where he needed to go. He focused his own magical energy through the pocket watch and willed himself to that place. The blackness and brilliant white lasted only a moment and then he was two blocks away, standing behind a pillar at the Doge's Palace, right near the tower of St. Mark's Campanile.

He heard a scream and turned to see Ling flying through the air, hurtling toward the tower. He had not released his magical energy and, focusing it again through the pocket watch, he concentrated his will on the force of gravity and the energy of motion and the movement of the air, creating a cushion of wind between Ling and the tower wall. And then she struck. He hoped that his cushion had been enough.

He could see as she fell, limp as a rag doll, that the force of the impact had still created a crack in the wall of the Campanile.

He watched her fall, trying to time it perfectly, so quickly Apollyon would not notice. Sema was screaming now. Again, Gabriel willed a burst of air and a reversal of gravity just as Ling neared the ground. Her body paused slightly before striking the earth, and then he released it. Ling hit the ground with a thud. He could see his older self across the piazza, running toward Apollyon hurling fireballs. Gabriel knew this was his chance.

He was still far enough away not to be affected by the space-time seal, but he could feel it flicker and waver as Apollyon focused his attention elsewhere. Gabriel grabbed the coin from his pocket. Reaching out with his time-sense, he willed himself to move to Ling's side. Blackness and whiteness and he was kneeling beside her, his hand reaching out to her head, and then blackness and whiteness again, and he was jumping through time.

There was a strange feeling as he moved back, like turning around a tight corner, and he realized it was the movement back from the alternate branch of reality he had created to the normal sense of space-time within the Primary Continuum. It passed quickly and the hillside in Greece materialized. He did not wait, he jumped again. And again and again, pausing only for moments as each Greek scenery materialized and then was washed away by blackness and brilliant white light. After a dozen jumps, he felt safe.

They were on a beach. The same beach. He could see the small town in the distance, spreading along the shore and up into the hillside. He could sense that it was later than when he had left Sema and Marcus. The sun was lower in the sky. It was late afternoon. Several hours had passed from their perspective. He looked around, but his attention was drawn downward as he heard Ling moan. She reached up and held his hand. She was hurt. Badly. He could see the whole left side of her body beginning to bruise. He wondered how many bones were broken. She was bleeding from her scalp, as well.

"You're okay," Gabriel said to her, stroking her hair, pulling it back to see how deep the cut on her head was. "You're going to be okay."

"What happened?" Ling struggled to whisper. "Where are we?"

"You're safe," Gabriel said. "We're all safe." He looked around frantically for Marcus and Sema. Where could they be? There in the distance, walking along the water. Could that be them? He looked down at Ling. She didn't look like she could make another jump.

"I have to get Marcus," Gabriel said. "I'll be right back."

"Don't leave me," Ling croaked, feebly squeezing his hand.

"I'll be right back," Gabriel said, pulling his hand free from Ling's as she moaned. He stood up, reaching for his space-time sense and then suddenly he stood before Marcus and Sema as they came to a halt beside the water.

"Gabriel," Sema shouted and flung her arms around him. "We thought…"

"Hours, boy!" Marcus said. "You've been gone hours. We thought the worst."

"I'm fine," Gabriel said as he pulled back from Sema. He could see tears in her eyes. "There's no time. Ling needs you, Marcus." Sema and Marcus had no time for more than a brief exchange of shocked expressions before Gabriel placed his hands on their shoulders.

A moment later, they were a mile down the beach standing over Ling. She looked up at them and smiled weakly. "I don't feel so good," she said and passed out. The three quickly knelt beside her. Marcus took out St. Fillan's stone and placed his other hand on Ling's stomach. He concentrated for a moment and then spoke.

"Broken bones, internal bleeding, a ruptured spleen, massive concussion. She's in a bad way."

"Will she live?" Gabriel asked, his voice filled with desperation. It was all for nothing if she wouldn't live. She had to live.

"I'll do my best," Marcus said. "I can keep her stable for now. But it will take time to heal her proper."

"The tide will be up soon," Sema said, looking out at the ocean as each gentle crash of waves came a little closer.

"Those trees over there," Gabriel said. "Will that be enough shelter?"

"Yes," Marcus said, "but we can't jump there. She's in no condition for it."

"I can carry her," Gabriel said as he reached within and focused his energy through the pocket watch and willed the gravity to bend around Ling. She slowly rose a few inches in the air and floated there. She moaned again. Gabriel began walking her through the air over to the small stand of cypress trees at the edge of the beach. Sema and Marcus followed silently.

As they walked, Gabriel handed Sema her glass pendant. She took it wordlessly. Under the wide branches of the trees, Gabriel gently lowered Ling to a small patch of thin grass. Marcus knelt beside her again, this time clasping the ancient healing stone artifact in both hands as he held them above Ling, slowly moving them from one part of her damaged body to another.

Gabriel didn't know what to do, so he sat on the sand beside Ling and tried to focus on what Marcus was doing, how he was reaching out with Heart-Tree Magic and slowly healing Ling's body. She moaned and moved occasionally as Marcus worked, but she did not regain consciousness. It took Gabriel a few minutes to realize that Sema was also reaching out to Ling with Soul Magic, keeping her unconscious throughout Marcus's healing.

He saw fishermen in boats near the shore, but they did not seem to notice the mages. Sema again, he assumed. As time went on and Gabriel concentrated more, he could sense the ways that Marcus was manipulating Ling's life-energy. Bones were being set back right and mended together. The internal bleeding stopped and Ling's spleen seemed to begin functioning again. The blood vessels in Ling's brain contracted and her concussion disappeared. An hour later, Marcus finally stopped. Sweat dripped from his bald head and ran down his face. He sat back and leaned against the thin trunk of the nearest tree, slumping with exhaustion.

"She'll recover," Marcus finally said after a long pause. "But she needs rest. She should have at least the night to recover before we try a jump. A jump would be a tricky thing in her state."

"I've made sure she will sleep until morning," Sema said. "But we should try to find some shelter for the night."

"I can look down the beach," Gabriel said.

"I'll go with you," Sema said, but she made no move to stand. She and Marcus stared at Gabriel. He avoided their gaze. The silence stretched on. Gabriel didn't want to be the first to speak. What was there to say? He knew what he had done. But as he watched Ling sleeping in the wild grass, he could not feel that that what he had done was wrong. Risky, yes. Impetuous, certainly. But how could it be wrong when she was alive and safe with them?

Finally, Sema spoke. "We understand why you did it," she said, speaking slowly as though choosing her words carefully. Gabriel sensed her anger at what he had done, as well as her relief that he had succeeded. "But I do not think you understand the implications."

"It's not that we are not grateful to have Ling back," Marcus said, wiping his brow with the back of his hand. "But what you have done has placed us all in even greater jeopardy than before."

"I assume you created a bifurcation," Sema said, "but tell us exactly what you did." Gabriel took a deep breath and then carefully recounted his rescue of Ling. What he had done and how. He had wanted to simply snatch Ling without creating a bifurcation, a new branch of time, but since he knew that Marcus had sensed her death, taking her before she could die in the Primary Continuum would have created a bifurcation anyway. One that Apollyon was more likely to notice. Gabriel finished recounting his actions and waited. There was more silence. When Sema spoke, she sounded weary.

"You have a good heart, Gabriel," Sema said, "but you must learn to think with your head as well. Do you not see that you have created another reality where there is a second Sema, a second Marcus, and yet one more Apollyon?"

"To hell with another Apollyon," Marcus said, spitting into the sand. "He's created another one of him. You've created a second Seventh True Mage who can use the powers of both Grace and Malignancy."

"You have given Apollyon exactly what he would hope for," Sema said.

"But it was the best I could do," Gabriel said, feeling defensive and sickened. He had known he was creating a new reality, but he hadn't really taken the time to think through the implications of doing it. By doubling back on his personal timeline, as well as that of Sema, Marcus, Ling, and Apollyon, he had created doubles of all of them when he had formed the bifurcation. He had known that a new reality meant new versions of himself and the others, but he hadn't stopped to think through what that would mean. What it would mean to him. What it would mean to the war. What it would mean for Apollyon and what it would mean for the other Gabriel, the one he had created by splitting the reality of the Primary Continuum.

"The best thing you could have done would have been to do nothing," Marcus said, his voice more gentle.

"There is only one course of action open to us now," Sema said. "We must return to the castle and inform them of what you have done and then the branch of time you created must be severed. It must be cut at the root. The very moment you created it."

"That will insure the other versions of us are trapped in the severed branch," Marcus said. "If the cut is made at the same moment as the branch was created, there will be no chance of anyone crossing back. Wait a moment too long after the branch was created, and the other Apollyon could take the other you backward into the Primary Continuum."

Gabriel considered this in silence for a moment. "They will all die," he said. "All of them will cease to exist."

"Maybe," Sema said. "Most likely, even. I don't claim to understand it all, Teresa might be able to explain it, but even if the branch manages to survive being severed and does not immediately collapse, that could potentially be worse than if it simply winked out of existence. We have no way of knowing what horrors could arise in such a reality."

"What can I do?" Gabriel said.

"For now, nothing," Sema said. "Help me find a place for Ling to pass the night."

They left Marcus with Ling beneath the trees and walked along the beach away from the town. The sun was nearing the horizon. It would set in another hour or so. They walked in silence for a long while.

"I'm sorry I took your necklace," Gabriel said finally. He had been thinking about the look on Sema's face when her pendent had flown into his hand.

"You did what you thought was right," Sema said quietly. She was silent for a while before she spoke again. "You saved Ling, but at a terrible price. What you did was unforgivable to the Council, but I can't say that a part of me isn't glad you did it. A large part. But if you should ever be faced with such a choice again, no matter who it is, especially if it is me, you must not repeat your actions."

"I won't," Gabriel said. He wondered if that was a promise he could keep. They walked in silence again for several minutes.

"When I was a girl," Sema said, breaking the silence, "not much younger than you, I stole some fruit from a vendor in the local market in Istanbul. My family was poor, and we had been eating scraps and begging for weeks. I showed my mother the fruit and she questioned me about where it had come from. I lied and said I had found it. But I could never lie to my mother. She was very sad when I told her the truth.

"When my father found what I had done, he marched me back to the fruit vendor and made me confess. The vendor was stern, but fair. He accepted the fruit I returned without comment, but I had eaten some dates and these I would have to pay for. So every day from then on, I went to work for the fruit vendor. Once I had repaid the cost of the dates, he kept me on. Eventually, I married his youngest son and we opened our own fruit stand. Ultimately, we had children and prospered to become one of the most successful merchant families in the city."

Gabriel said nothing. He wasn't sure what he should say.

"Do you see why I am telling you this?" Sema asked, looking down at him.

"Well, because…" Gabriel began and then decided on the truth. "Not really."

"Because even if we have done things that we know are wrong," Sema said, "if we set them right, if we make amends, then sometimes the end can turn out for the better." She said no more and Gabriel added no words to hers. He hoped his actions worked out for the better, as well.

After about a mile, Gabriel spotted a cave in the rocky hillside near the beach. It was far enough away from the shoreline and high enough in the rocks to avoid the tide, although it seemed a very precarious climb to get up to it. Gabriel jumped them to the entrance of the cave and they peered inside. It was small and filled with the bones of some long dead animal, but it would do.

Gabriel stepped back, stilled his mind, and gathered his magical energy, focusing it through the pocket watch and willing gravity and the wind to do as he wished, causing a gust of air to burst into and out of the cave, cleaning it as best as possible. Sema nodded and took his hand.

A moment later, they stood beside Marcus. Gabriel used his magic to float Ling along as they walked down the beach together toward the cave. The sun was nearly down, and there seemed little likelihood of people spotting them. When they reached the place where they could see the cave, Gabriel took Marcus by magic to the entrance and then went back down to Ling, guiding her gently up toward Marcus. Then he took Sema's hand and jumped through space to join them.

Gabriel gathered some wood and started a small fire using magic. The air had begun to cool as the sun went down. Sema suggested that the two of them take a quick trip to the small town down the beach and see if they could procure some supplies.

Leaving Marcus to tend to Ling, Gabriel and Sema jumped instantly to a point a hundred yards down the beach from the edge of the town. As they walked into the town, Gabriel could see people heading home for the night. The town was not large. Maybe a few hundred people in all. By the looks of their dress and the manner of the tools they carried, Gabriel suspected that they were far in the past. Sema thought it must be nearly 300 BCE or more. They both used their amulets to change their appearance and blend in.

"Now watch closely," Sema said. "You may need to do this yourself one day."

Sema walked over to where a fruit vendor packed his goods away for the night. He didn't seem to notice them at all. Gabriel could sense the way Sema deflected the man's attention from recognizing he saw them. She took a small canvas sack from near the pile of fruit and began filling it. Gabriel watched as the man helpfully opened a sack of pears he had just closed so that she could take some.

Gabriel reached out with his consciousness and could feel how Sema had made the suggestion to the man's mind. Then they were walking along the street again. Sema performed a similar magic twice more, a man sorting his fish by the last light of the setting sun put two of the largest aside. Gabriel picked up the fish without notice. Next came a bottle of wine from the owner of a shop who brought it to the door and left it on the stoop as they passed by. Gabriel could tell that the suggestion had not been specific. Sema had simply planted the idea that someone might need whatever could be provided and spared.

Suddenly, a small boy of eight or so came running across the street carrying a large melon that was clearly too big for him. He had bright eyes and grinned widely as he struggled to get the melon to what seemed to be his house. Sema laughed as she watched the boy. Once the boy was in the house, they continued on their way. Within a few minutes, they had enough for dinner, breakfast, and maybe even lunch: dates, olives, bread, and grapes. They had even procured two small blankets of thickly woven wool.

"This is how a Soul Mage goes shopping," Sema said, looking down at Gabriel, his arms full of the bounty she had acquired.

"But what if someone needed these things?" Gabriel said. "Couldn't it create a bifurcation?"

"If they were items in short supply or likely to be missed," Sema said. "The key is to acquire things that are plentiful so there is some other object to replace them. If there had been only two fish, we would be a little hungrier tonight as I could not have taken them without risking it creating a bifurcation when the person who was supposed to eat the fish could not."

Gabriel nodded. Small changes. They turned a corner and Sema placed her hand on his shoulder. He took this as a cue to jump back to the cave and reached out with his space-time sense to find it. A second later, they stood beside the fire Gabriel had made. Marcus looked up with a tired smile.

"I was hoping you'd think of some wine," he said as he licked his lips.

"Even I am tempted to drink after this day," Sema said, setting the bottles down near the fire. "It seemed cruel to deny you something so small."

They set about making some dinner, debating whether waking Ling to partake of the food would help her condition. After carefully checking her vital signs, Marcus decided that she needed rest more than nourishment. Gabriel helped clean the fish and cut some fruit with a dagger that Marcus slipped effortlessly from his sleeve. Marcus roasted the fish, skewered by sticks, over the fire, and they ate while watching the stars come out in the sky.

"Epicurus would have been proud," Marcus said of the meal as he licked his fingers.

"I think we saw him in the town," Sema said.

"When?" Gabriel asked.

"That small boy who ran in front of us with that oversized melon," Sema said. "I'd recognize those eyes anywhere."

"Councilwoman Elizabeth said that Epicurus lived on this island when he was young," Gabriel said.

"He'll leave in about ten years to begin his studies," Sema said.

"So you've met him before?" Gabriel asked.

"In a manner of speaking," Marcus said. "It was in an alternate branch of time. We spent a day together, later in his life."

"You don't get a chance to meet many famous people with the work we do," Sema said. "There's too much risk of creating bifurcations. So you tend to remember the ones you do meet close-up."

"Particularly if they are handsome Greek men with pretty eyes," Marcus said, casting Sema a teasing glance. Gabriel thought he could see Sema blushing, but it might have been the warm light of the fire. "This night, the fire, the cave, it reminds of a night I spent years ago hiding from the Queen's Guard. They were looking for a man who had been robbing noblemen along the main road from London to Cambridge, and he bore an unfortunate resemblance to me. I had a great deal more hair then. It was not an easy time. The poets were far more romantic about it." Marcus cleared his throat and recited:

"The wind was a torrent of darkness upon the gusty trees,
The moon was a ghostly galleon tossed upon cloudy seas,
The road was a ribbon of moonlight looping the purple moor,
And the highwayman came riding,
Riding, riding,
The highwayman came riding, up to the old inn door.

"Of course, Alfred Noyce was born a good one hundred twenty years later, so what did he know? No young Bess for me. Just tending to a companion who had the bad luck of catching a crossbow bolt in his leg. He was always catching some manner of armament. Had more scars than freckles, which says something for a redheaded Irishman. Donovan. Great drinker and a better singer. He had a voice like warm whiskey. Clumsy as a drunken ox in a tea shop, though. I thought for certain his moans would bring the Queen's hounds down upon us, but by sunrise he was back to cursing and bragging about a new scar, and drinking the last of the brandy. That was a fine night."

"It sounds terrifying," Gabriel said, staring at the wide grin on Marcus's face.

"Oh, it was," Marcus said. "But it ended well. That's what makes a fine night. If the sunrise finds you still alive when you thought you'd be dead."

"This night is fine," Sema said, catching Marcus's gaze and holding it.

"Yes, and the company isn't bad, either," Marcus added with a laugh. "This cave isn't much, but it at least we'll be comfortable tonight."

"Particularly Ling," Sema said.

Comfortable? Gabriel cocked his head as he looked up at the stars. Why did that sound familiar? What was that nagging feeling at the back of his mind? Like there was a word on the tip of his tongue that he couldn't remember. Like he had left the house and forgotten something. Something he would remember only as he was too far away to go back. Go back. Back to where? Back home? Ah, yes. That was it. Comfortable.

"I know where Ohin is," Gabriel said in a voice so loud it startled Sema and Marcus, who had both started to doze. "I know where he is and I can take us there."

CHAPTER 14
LOST AND FOUND

The following morning, Gabriel was the last to wake. He stepped out of the cave, blinking with the sudden shift from sleep as much as from the light of the sun, now well above the horizon. Ling sat at the edge of the rocks eating a slice of cantaloupe. Gabriel could see Sema and Marcus walking at the water's edge along the beach. Ling looked up at him, but said nothing. She took another bite of the melon, sucking the juice from the rind. Gabriel sat down beside her.

From the look of the remains encircling her, Ling had eaten at least two melons, all the remaining olives, the leftover fish from the night before, and half a loaf of bread. She threw down the well-chewed rind of melon and wiped the juice from her mouth with the back of her sleeve. Teresa had said once that Ling's name meant 'delicate' in Chinese. She cleared her throat, spat, and looked at him. Gabriel wondered if the name had been intentionally ironic on the part of her parents.

"You put Sema and Marcus in one hell of a tight spot," Ling growled. "When you risked your damn fool life to save them, they felt indebted to you."

"But…" Gabriel began.

"But they were responsible for you," Ling said. "You are still only an apprentice, and it is not your place to question the decisions of those who are in charge of the mission, particularly when they have far more experience than you may ever have. Do you think I like every decision Ohin makes? Well, I don't. But I follow orders. Why? Because he knows what he's doing and he's in charge. Get this through that rock you call a brain right now, this is a war, and people die in wars, and if you don't follow orders, more people will die."

"I know that."

"Well, you certainly don't act like it," Ling said, her voice filled with anger. "What the hell were you thinking, anyway?"

"I thought…"

"I was dead. I was already dead."

"But…"

"Do you know what you've done? Do you what we have to do now?"

"I know. I just…"

"Do you think Ohin would have gone back for you? Do you think he would have gone back for any of us?"

"I don't know. I…"

"Well, he wouldn't have," Ling shouted and turned toward the water and the sunrise. She was silent finally and so was Gabriel. He didn't know what reaction he had expected from Ling, but this wasn't how he had imagined things would go at all.

"He wouldn't have," Ling said again. "None of them would have. But you did." She stared at Gabriel. "Why would you do that? You barely even know me. Barely even know any of us. Why risk yourself for Sema and Marcus? Why risk so much to save me?"

Gabriel didn't have to think about it. "Because it seemed like the right thing to do. Because I like you." And then he spoke aloud what had been his real motivation. The one he had been afraid to admit to himself. "Because you're all the family I have now."

Ling moved with the same swiftness and fluidity as she did when fighting, and Gabriel found himself with her arms locked around him in a powerful motherly hug. His head felt like a clay pot trapped in a vice as she pressed him to her chest and held on. He could feel her sobbing. Feel the tears on his neck. And it brought tears to his own eyes. After a long minute, she let go of him and clasped both hands on either side of his head, staring at him fiercely.

"Damn you!" Ling said, her eyes blazing, struggling to speak as though the air in her chest could not rise to become words. She let go of Gabriel and seemed to collapse in on herself. When she spoke, it was in a near-whisper. "My first child, my son Win, he died of fever. We were a fishing family. He caught a chill one day. Too long in the rain. My husband Gu blamed himself. The boy was only ten. Old

123

enough to fish, but not in the rain for that long. I blamed my husband.

"Win died after a week of chills and sweats. He couldn't eat anything. And then he died. And I blamed myself then. Because I couldn't save him. I would have done anything to save him. Anything. No matter what the cost." She fell silent again. When she looked up into his eyes she spoke loud and clear. "Thank you. Thank you for my life. Thank you for saving me, Dìdi Érzi." Ling grinned and Gabriel grinned back. "Do it again, though, and I'll bust your head." She rustled his hair.

"But if I did it again…"

"Don't argue with me. I'm no pushover like Sema and Marcus." Gabriel's head reeled trying to contemplate that statement as Ling offered him the last slice of melon. "Sorry. I ate everything. I'm starving. I could eat a horse. And I love horses. Beautiful creatures. But I'd eat one whole. Raw."

"I'd settle for eggs and bacon," Gabriel said.

"And a goat cheese and mushroom omelet," Ling said. "Marcus said you know how to find Ohin."

"I think I know where he is."

"Then let's find him and get back to the castle," Ling said. "If we time it right, we can arrive for brunch."

Sema and Marcus came back a few minutes later.

"Everything been said that needed to be said?" Sema asked.

"Yes," Gabriel said.

"I made my views clear," Ling said.

"She has a way of saying thank you that you'll not likely forget soon," Marcus said, rubbing his elbow. "Damn near broke my arm."

"You startled me," Ling said. "I thought I was dead. Again."

"And this was the face you thought you'd see in heaven," Marcus said. "I'm flattered."

"Who says I thought I was in heaven?" Ling said, tossing a fish bone at Marcus.

"You'd think you'd have more gratitude," Marcus said with feigned indignation.

"I'm just annoyed that I was finally in Venice again and didn't get to see the Gallerie Dell'Accademia," Ling said. "We were blocks from one of my favorite museums and all I saw were the bricks of the Campanile. The best part of traveling through time is seeing art I've never seen before."

"If Ling is well enough, we should go," Sema said.

"She's healthy as a bear," Marcus said. "And she'll be hungry like a bear for a few days, but that's not so different from usual." Another fish bone flew past his head.

"You're sure you know how to find Ohin?" Sema asked.

"Positive," Gabriel said. "Ohin told me that we always feel more comfortable in our own time. But the temple at Tenochtitlan was built much later than his time, so I'm sure that whatever time he ended up in, he would travel to my time to wait for us."

"And you're sure Ohin will think of all this?" Marcus asked.

"Pretty sure," Gabriel said.

"No one has a better idea," Ling said.

"But what year do you think he will he go to in your time?" Sema asked.

"Ohin isn't the sort to sit on his rump waiting for years for us to show up," Marcus said.

"Well," Gabriel said, "I was taken from the timeline in 1980, but the temple was only just being excavated then. So I'm guessing he'll use the Coyolxauhqui Stone at the base of the temple."

"It was rediscovered in 1978," Marcus said.

"So it might have been in a museum when I left the timeline," Gabriel said.

"That's good," Marcus said. "At least they'll be comfortable. Teresa is always complaining about the lack of air conditioning in the castle."

"Let us go, then," Sema said, extending her hand between the others. Ling and Marcus placed their hands on hers. Gabriel reached into his pocket and withdrew the watch and the shard of Aztec pottery. They would need to go back to the temple at a time when the Coyolxauhqui Stone was still there and then use it to find Ohin.

125

He placed his hands around theirs and stilled his mind, searching out a time when the city of Tenochtitlan was not busy, a time at night, a time when they would attract little notice. He found an image in his mind as he used his time-sense to probe the pottery shard. Focusing the energy within him through the pocket watch, blackness surrounded them, and the white light soon washed over everything.

They stood in a different part of the city. It even looked like a different city under the moonlight of the night sky above. It took Gabriel a moment to realize why. Tenochtitlan was in ruins. Not ancient ruins. Recent ruins. Buildings and temples shattered. Streets deserted. Houses gutted by fire. One of them was probably the last place the piece of pottery he used to travel through time had been whole as a vase. Looking around, he could see what remained of the Templo Mayor a quarter mile away.

"After the Spanish conquest of the city," Ling said. "1521."

"Weren't the most tolerant lot, were they?" Marcus said as he surveyed the destruction.

"Spain was the birthplace of the Inquisition," Sema said, a certain bitterness in her voice.

"We should go," Ling said and headed toward the temple. Gabriel and the others followed, using their amulets to alter their appearance. As he walked along the ruined street, he remembered his feelings of disgust for the practices of the Aztecs. The wars to gain captives for sacrifice. The huge numbers of victims. Here and there he passed what could only be bodies still rotting in the streets, others floating, bloated, in the canals. This was just as disgusting. How many times would he see this throughout his time travels? Violence leading to violence. Death bringing more death. It made him tired, and he had only just woken from a full night's sleep.

As they walked, Gabriel tried to remember from his studies the series of events that had led to this. This was the time of king Moctezuma II, sometimes called Montezuma. He was the second king named Moctezuma. Moctezuma II had been considered a living god, and it had been forbidden for citizens to look upon his face under penalty of death. He had been extremely powerful, but also extremely religious.

Like most Aztecs of the time, he was convinced of the truth of his myths, both those that commanded his people to provide blood sacrifice to satiate the gods, as well as those that told of how the god Quetzalcoatl would return from the waters of the ocean to the east. So when Hernán Cortéz, the Spanish explorer and *Conquistador*, arrived in 1519 on the eastern coast of what would one day be called Mexico, Moctezuma II and many of his people believed it was the return of Quetzalcoatl. The fulfillment of prophecy. It was really the arrival of 530 soldiers in Spanish ships. By August 15th of 1521, the city had fallen, and the Spanish Conquistadors were the new rulers of what remained of the Aztec empire.

As they reached the base of the temple a few minutes later, Gabriel reflected that there wasn't much left of the Aztec empire for the Spanish Conquistadors to rule. Although they had seen a few Spanish soldiers and a pair of priests, and even a few remaining Aztecs, no one had so much as glanced in their direction. At the base of the Templo Mayor, the Great Temple, sat the Coyolxauhqui Stone, blackened by the soot of fire, but still intact.

Gabriel placed his hand upon it, and the others placed theirs upon his shoulder. He reached out with his time-sense toward the enormous carved stone and tried to feel his way forward, or what would be forward if time were straight like an arrow. It was more like being in a spherical room filled with millions of tiny windows, each one leading to a time and place where the Coyolxauhqui Stone had been. He searched and found images of the stone buried beneath rubble and earth. That was no good. It would be most unfortunate to jump into a future where they would be buried alive. If he had been using a fragment of the stone from a future date, he would have been able to move them a short distance away, but by using the stone while still within the natural flow of the Continuum, he would need to stay in contact with it.

He continued to search for the right place. There it was. An image of the stone unearthed in the middle of a city block. Darkness and whiteness followed, one after the other.

They stood in Mexico City near an excavation that looked like it had recently been a construction site. Streetlights provided illumination from the distance. Two policemen stood nearby talking quietly and smoking cigarettes. They turned at the sound of Gabriel and his companions climbing out of the pit that the Coyolxauhqui Stone still sat in. Sema raised a hand to them and the policemen turned back to their conversation.

Marcus was the first to the top of the slight pile of earth and rubble. He helped Sema and Ling on to the stone-paved plaza as Gabriel clambered up to join them. He could see the Torre Latinoamericana building rising straight into the night sky. Nearby the silhouettes of the Mexico City Cathedral and the Sagrario Metropolitano church beside it filled the sky. He remembered the names from his brief study of Mexican history back at the castle.

"What next?" Ling asked.

"Well," Gabriel said, "I'm guessing that Ohin will try to go to the exact date that I was taken from the timeline. Which is probably about two years from now. So, we need to find a place where he would wait during that day and we can spot him."

"It will probably be close to the temple," Sema said.

"We'll need to find a way to check the dates," Marcus added.

"A news stand," Gabriel said. "If we find a news stand, I can use it as a relic, and we should be able to see the date on newspapers."

"It's worth a try," Ling said. "It's better than waiting here for two years."

They walked out of the construction and excavation site into the city proper. As they walked, they used the concealment amulets to shift their appearance to that of late 20th century tourists. This meant jeans and branded t-shirts. It felt odd to be walking through essentially the same city some five hundred years later. It was incredible to see how the city had changed from its origins. It made him feel out of place even though he was essentially back in his own time.

Gabriel wondered if it would always feel like this. Like he did not quite belong anywhere or any when. Maybe that was why Councilwoman Elizabeth had insisted on placing the castle so far in the past. Because it could only feel like home if it was distant enough from the lives the inhabitants had lived.

"Over there," Marcus said, pointing to a little tobacco shop. "They'll sell papers there in the morning."

"Perfect," Gabriel said. "We can stand out of the way beside the building and if anyone sees us, we won't be popping into existence in the middle of the street." They stepped over to the little tobacco shop and took positions where they could see the street. Marcus looked longingly through the shop window at a box of cigars.

"Do you know how long it has been since I had a really good cigar?" Marcus said, more to himself than anyone else.

"The smoking physician," Sema said. "The greatest irony."

"I'm not saying I want one," Marcus said. "Just that I miss them."

"No one made you give up cigars," Ling said.

"No, but I can't stand the looks I get from certain puritans," Marcus said. Sema made a noise that sounded like a cough, but carried more implications.

"Ready?" Gabriel said, ignoring the others. He wanted to find Ohin as soon as possible. Then he could confess what he had done and get it over with. He knew Ohin would be unhappy, and he wanted to get that moment of feeling like he had disappointed his mentor behind him. Gabriel leaned his back against the wall of the shop as Sema and Marcus stood on either side of him, hands on his shoulders. Ling stood in front of him, turning to the side so she could see the entrance to the little tobacco shop. She placed her hand on his shoulder.

Gabriel reached out with his time-sense and saw in his mind's eye a moment when there were daily papers stacked in front of the shop for sale. Whiteness followed blackness, and they slid to that moment in time. People hurried along the sidewalks and the streets were filled with noisy traffic, but Gabriel could feel Sema extending something that felt like a bubble of Soul Magic, deflecting interest from them.

"April, 1979," Ling said.

"We're looking for September 17th, 1980," Gabriel said, focusing his time-sense on the wall of the tobacco shop again. A

129

moment later, they stood in the same place on another day. It was later in the afternoon this time and raining.

"Close," Marcus said, wiping the rain from the top of his bald head. "August 2nd." Gabriel reached out again trying to gauge how far a few weeks would be. He didn't know when Ohin might be waiting for them, so he tried to place them in the early morning of the 17th. The sun crept above the tops of the buildings to the east when they emerged from the blinding whiteness of the time jump.

"Seventeenth," Ling said.

"Now all we have to do is hope Ohin stayed near the temple," Sema said. "I don't know how we'll find him in the city otherwise."

They walked back along the street the way they had come just moments ago. Or nearly two years ago from another perspective. They found that the excavation had made significant progress. The outlines of the Templo Mayor were visible again, although the Coyolxauhqui Stone was missing, moved by then to some museum or university archeology facility. They walked around the area surrounding the excavation site, but saw no one they recognized.

"You should be able to sense them," Sema said. "Mages can sense magical ability. That's how Ohin found you. Just passed you on the street by accident."

"Reach out with your magic-sense," Marcus said. "A mage can sense their own breed of magic easier than others."

"And since you can conjure all six magics," Ling said, "you should be able to feel something."

Stopping and standing still, Gabriel closed his eyes. He stilled his mind and tried to reach out and feel any magical energy that might be nearby. He could sense Marcus, Sema, and Ling beside him, each radiating a slightly different form of magical energy, like different hues of light. However, that was all. Maybe Ohin and the others were too far away. Maybe he was wrong. Maybe Ohin was in some other place and time.

"Nothing," Gabriel said.

"Then we keep walking," Marcus said.

They walked a great deal that morning. Up and down the streets near the temple excavation site. They walked through the Plaza

Manuel Gamio, past the Cathedral Metropolitana, past the Placio National, and around and around, circling the streets nearby the temple site again and again.

Finally, by mid-afternoon, they were too hungry to go on. While Marcus and Ling waited at an unobtrusive street corner, Gabriel helped Sema procure some food for lunch. Following Sema's example, and focusing his magical energy through the pocket watch, he found it relatively easy to place a mental suggestion in the mind of a street vendor to prepare a few tacos and set them aside. He also found another street vendor open to the silent suggestion of placing several bottles of lime Jarritos where Gabriel could grab them.

A few minutes later, the four mages sat on a stone bench, eating a meal amidst the noise and bustle of the city while they watched the excavation site. As Gabriel took a long swig of the Mexican soda, he felt something tickle the back of his brain. Then the tickle became a poke.

"Someone has just moved through time near here," Gabriel said. Reaching out with his time-sense as well as his magic-sense, he looked back at the Plaza Manuel Gamio in front of the cathedral. "Over there," he said, leaping to his feet, leaving the soda bottle on the curb and pulling the watch out of his pants pocket as he headed for the plaza.

The others were right behind him as he quickly walked along the street. He knew it must be them now. He could sense the magical energy of a Time Mage. And the other energies he sensed were those of Fire and Earth Magic. However, he only sensed the energy of three mages, and that worried him. Something must have happened.

As they came around the corner of the street and got a clear view of the plaza, it was obvious Chimalli was missing. Ohin, Teresa, and Rajan walked away from the side of the cathedral and into the open plaza. Somehow, Rajan had a book in his hand. Ohin must have used the cathedral itself as a relic to move through time.

Teresa spotted them first and waved. Gabriel waved back. He wanted to run to them, but didn't know how effective Sema's Soul Magic protection would be and he didn't want to risk any mistakes just then. The two groups of mages walked slowly toward one another, meeting in an empty corner of the plaza. As they met, Teresa threw her arms around Gabriel and hugged him tight.

"See, I told you he'd figure it out," Teresa said as she released Gabriel and they turned to the others.

"It's good to see you again," Rajan said. "Do you still have the pouch?" Gabriel handed Rajan the pouch with their relics and talismans in it. Rajan pulled the rabbit's foot from the pouch and handed it to Teresa, who extended her hand and smiled. Gabriel wanted to smile, as well, but he knew what was coming. Everyone exchanged embraces and congratulations, Ohin patting Gabriel on the shoulder.

"I knew you would figure out how to find us," Ohin said.

"I thought it through," Gabriel said.

"Where's Chimalli?" Sema asked, searching Ohin's eyes.

"Chimalli is dead," Ohin said, his voice becoming cold. "He was killed by the trap that was set on the dagger." Gabriel had known it was coming, but was shocked nonetheless. He had not known Chimalli long, but he had liked the elderly mage.

"Chimalli betrayed us," Rajan said, his eyes cold with anger.

"They were holding his wife," Teresa said.

"I can't believe Chimalli would betray us," Marcus said.

"He admitted it just before he died," Rajan said.

"But why?" Gabriel asked.

"And who had his wife?" Sema added.

"Apollyon," Ohin said as though he were saying a curse. "He created a bifurcation so that he could capture Chimalli's wife."

"Everyone knew how much Chimalli missed his wife," Marcus said. "It was all the man talked about with a drink in him."

"But it wouldn't really be his wife," Sema said.

"To Chimalli, it was the same," Rajan said.

"Apollyon was torturing her," Teresa said. "He must have created at least two bifurcations because Chimalli said the first thing Apollyon did was present him with her head."

"He said Apollyon told him that more heads of his wife would follow unless Chimalli helped him," Ohin said. "He knew the dagger was booby-trapped to create a warp in time and then explode."

"To his credit, he placed himself between Ohin and the blade at the last moment," Rajan said. "And fortunately the dagger was not originally from the temple, so we won't need to replace it."

"He did save my life," Ohin said. "I can almost forgive him because of that."

"I can't," Rajan said. "He should have gone to the Council. The Council could have helped him."

"I doubt the Council could stop Apollyon from creating as many copies of Chimalli's wife as he wanted for torturing," Teresa said.

"We assumed there was a spy when Apollyon appeared at the temple," Sema said.

"Likely more than one," Ohin said.

"It was Gabriel who saved us," Marcus said.

"Yes," Sema added.

"Indeed," Ohin said. "Then we can be very proud of my new apprentice."

"No, you can't," Gabriel said. He had been dreading this, but it would be best to get it over with. Like any truly painful thing, it was better behind you than in front of you. "I've done something that you will not be proud of."

"But he thought he was doing the right thing," Marcus said.

"It is really my responsibility," Sema said. "I was the senior member of the team at the time, and it is my fault that it happened."

"The boy didn't understand," Marcus said. "And who can blame him."

Ohin stared at Gabriel in stern silence, his eyes probing his young apprentice. He glanced at Sema and Marcus. Then at Ling. Ling would not meet his eyes and remained as silent as she had been since they were all reunited. "What have you done?" Ohin demanded.

Gabriel nearly quailed at the tone of Ohin's voice. He swallowed, his throat suddenly dry. "I created a bifurcation."

"To save me," Ling quickly added.

He told Ohin everything. About the fireball, about being a True Mage, about their escape to Scotland, about returning to the Aztec temple and finding Apollyon waiting, jumping to Venice, Ling's death, and the escape to ancient Greece.

Then came the hard part. Telling how he had stolen Sema's pendant from her neck and gone back to save Ling. How he created a bifurcation with copies of both himself and Apollyon in it, as well as Sema and Marcus. Ohin was silent while Gabriel finished telling the story. They were all silent. Ohin looked at Gabriel and Ling. They both met his gaze this time.

"I know what I've done," Gabriel said. "I understand what it means and what needs to be done now."

"What needs to be done now," Ohin said, "is to inform the Council." He fell silent again. He continued to stare into Gabriel's eyes. Gabriel could not break away from his gaze. Doing so would seem like another form of failure. A failure to accept responsibility for his actions. No one spoke.

Finally, Ohin sighed. "I cannot tell you how happy I am to have Ling back with us." He placed his hand on Ling's shoulder. "Her loss would have been nearly too much to bear. But we would have borne it. As we will bear the loss of any of us. None of us is so important that we can risk the stability of the entire Continuum for one of our lives. You, as the Seventh True Mage, may be the exception to that rule, but not the rest of us.

"What you have done was risky, selfish, shortsighted, and incredibly dangerous. More than that, you may have succeeded in giving Apollyon the one thing he will truly desire now. You. We will speak of this further. For now, we will go back to the castle and report to the Council. They will most likely charge us with the task of severing the branch of time you created. You will not only need to be there, you will assist with the process. Now that you know how to make a new world, you must learn how to end it. And how to bear the burden of it. You have the amber?"

Gabriel looked to Rajan, who dug into the small leather pouch for the chunk of amber with the imbedded dragonfly that would lead them back to the castle. He handed it to Ohin. No one spoke as each one extended a hand to the center of the group, Ohin placing his palms on either side of the stacked hands. Gabriel stared at the others' hands. He could not look them in the eyes. Their silence told him enough of what they thought of his actions. But what did his own silence tell him?

He had not tried to justify his actions to Ohin. He had not told him his motivations at the time. What he had felt in his heart. Why he had thought it was the right thing to do even though it was forbidden. And Ohin had not asked. Gabriel didn't suspect that the Council would ask these questions, either. He wondered what their punishment would be. These thoughts flooded his mind and threatened to overwhelm him as the familiar blackness surrounded them, and the blazing white light, which he was beginning to even enjoy, washed them away from the late 20th century Mexico City and left them standing in the Lower Ward of the castle once again.

CHAPTER 15
THE SWORD OF UNMAKING

A thick fog of silence hung over Gabriel and his teammates as they walked back through the castle courtyards to the living quarters in the apartments surrounding the Upper Ward. Ohin told Gabriel to wait for word from him in Gabriel's quarters and walked toward the Round Tower and the Council chambers. Teresa looked over her shoulder to watch Ohin go.

"Now that Mr. Responsibility has left," Teresa said when Ohin finally stepped out of earshot, "I'd simply like to say that, I, for one, could not be happier that Gabriel saved Ling. Even if it does mean he may have upset the balance of power in the Continuum, which might result in the destruction of everything the Council has been trying to prevent for six hundred years." She turned to Ling with a playful smile. "See, I do like you."

Ling tried to laugh, but it came out sounding too much like the beginning of a sob. Teresa put her arm around Ling as they walked.

"We're all glad you're back," Rajan added. "I'm sure the Council will go easy on you."

"What choice do they have?" Teresa said. "He's the Seventh True Mage. The golden egg. The great prize. The hope of ages and all that crap. If they try to give you any grief, threaten to go on strike."

"Don't give the boy any ideas," Marcus said.

"Yes," Sema added. "He has plenty of ideas of his own."

"Ignore them," Teresa said, giving Gabriel a hug as the group parted ways, each heading for their own apartment. "I think you did a great job for your first mission." She kissed him on the check and Gabriel felt an unfamiliar flush of warmth well up within his chest. However, his thoughts were already too confused to be even more confused by any complicated thoughts about Teresa. He breathed deep to clear his head.

"Thank you," Gabriel whispered. He watched them head for their own apartments, Sema and Marcus in the state apartment wing, and Ling, Rajan, and Teresa in the private apartment wing. Gabriel headed to his room in what had been the visitor wing of apartments. He was lucky to have his own room because he was still new. Apprentices were expected to share rooms, but this rule was lifted for the first month of residence at the castle to give each new mage time to adjust to their new life and the loss of their old one.

Gabriel undressed and took a hot shower. He let the water run over his head, down his face and along his back. He always did his best thinking while in the shower. The water gently cascading along his body seemed to relax and unlock parts of his mind that were harder to access when he was dry.

He found himself thinking about the future. His personal future. What did it mean for him to be the Seventh True Mage? He had only just begun to accept the idea of being a Time Mage. What would it mean to be one of only seven people who could use all six magics? Moreover, what would he become if he could access the power of both imbued and tainted artifacts? Had Teresa been right? Was he too important to the war to punish too severely? Was he so important the Council would try to use him like some new and dangerous chess piece able to mimic the movements of all the other pieces? Did he have a destiny? What did it mean that he was the fulfillment of a prophecy? Did he still have control over his destiny, whatever it might be? Did he really have any choices left?

He had chosen to go back and risk the stability of the Primary Continuum to save Ling. Had that really been the right choice? What would happen to all those people cut off from the Primary Continuum when the Council severed the branch of alternate time he had created? What would happen to the other version of himself?

The water began to run cold before Gabriel came up with an answer to even one of his questions. He got out of the shower, dried off, and changed into a new set of cotton tunic and pants. He chose the black set this time. He wasn't sure why. Maybe because it made him more noticeably different. As different as he felt. He had just finished slipping on the matching black cotton shoes when a knock came at his door. It was Ohin.

"I need to speak with you," Ohin said. "Inside would be best."

Gabriel showed Ohin in and sat on his bed. Ohin eased himself onto a slender wooden chair far too small for his large frame. They were both silent for a moment. Gabriel wasn't sure what was coming next, but he didn't want to risk getting in more trouble by opening his mouth before he understood the consequences. Finally Ohin spoke.

"The Council held an emergency session."

"I don't even get to make a statement to the Council?" So much for keeping a closed mouth, he thought to himself.

"No statement was needed," Ohin said. "The Council has chosen to be lenient. You clearly knew that creating a new branch of time to save Ling was a violation of Council laws, but you are also a very new apprentice under great duress. You will make restitution for your actions by helping Akikane to sever this new branch of time from the Primary Continuum."

"That's it?" Gabriel said with a sigh of relief.

"It's no light punishment," Ohin snapped. "You will watch as a world of people you brought into existence are snuffed out for all eternity."

Gabriel swallowed as Ohin's words sunk into his heart. His real fear came to his lips. "I thought they might kick me out."

"Kick out the Seventh True Mage?" Ohin asked with a frown. "Impossible. They need you too much. So much so, that we have all been sworn to secrecy regarding your true nature. We know the Malignancy Mages have spies among us. You must not reveal yourself to be the Seventh True Mage until it is safe to do so."

"When do we sever the branch I made?" Gabriel asked.

"Soon," Ohin said. "Akikane has requested to meet you first. He will be one of your teachers now. To help you in becoming a True Mage. He'll call for you when he's ready. Until then, remain in your room." Ohin held Gabriel's gaze for a moment. There was a great deal said in that silent stare. Gabriel had to struggle both to keep his eyes locked with Ohin's and to keep back the tears that seemed ready to burst forth. It did not help that Ohin's eyes revealed a heart in great struggle.

The elder Time Mage seemed torn between disappointment in Gabriel's actions and gratitude for saving Ling's life, much the way that Gabriel's heart seemed torn between guilt and pride. Ohin sighed and silently stood. Without saying a word, he left the room, closing the door firmly behind him.

After Ohin left, Gabriel had intended to meditate or study. Anything to take his mind off the events of the past few days. Anything to keep his thoughts from fixating on the events that were to come. Sitting at the small desk, staring out his window onto the fields and forests beyond, he found he couldn't concentrate. Looking across the room at the bed, he realized how tired he was, even though he had awoken only a few hours before. Lying down on the bed, he told himself that he would just rest his eyes.

The knock on the door woke him. And a voice. Rajan's voice.

"Akikane wants to see you."

Gabriel looked at the clock. He couldn't remember what time it had been when he had dozed off, but the sun was now considerably lower in the sky. Shaking his head to clear the sleep, he went to answer the door.

"Decided on a little siesta, did you?" Rajan said, standing in the doorway holding a book in his hand, as usual. "Akikane wants to see you."

"Do you know what for?" Gabriel asked, closing the door to his room and following Rajan down the hall.

"Do you honestly think anyone tells me anything?" Rajan asked. "I was sent to fetch you like a pail of water."

"Why you?" Gabriel asked as they left the old visitor wing and headed for the old state apartments across the Upper Ward courtyard.

"I volunteered. I wanted to talk to you."

"What about?" Gabriel asked.

"I wanted to tell you what the others won't."

"Tell me what?" Gabriel asked, fearing from Rajan's words that the others of the team were secretly harboring resentment at his actions.

"The truth," Rajan said. "They are not really angry at you. They are angry at themselves."

"I don't understand," Gabriel said.

"You did exactly the right thing, for exactly the wrong reasons," Rajan said. "And those reasons would have kept everyone else from doing what you did. You risked the entire Continuum to save one life, to save Ling. They are all glad that you did so, and now they are angry with themselves for caring more about Ling than about the entire Continuum. And the reverse, as well. In their heads they know you were wrong, but in their hearts they want to believe you were right."

They walked in silence as they crossed the courtyard. Rajan led Gabriel through the corridors of the state apartments to Akikane's suite. Finally, Gabriel could resist no longer. "What about you? What do you think?"

"I only hope I have the courage to ignore the rules in a crisis like the one you faced," Rajan said, a hard look in his eye. "What's the point of saving the world if all the decent people are dead at the end? In here."

Rajan opened a door and ushered Gabriel into a large room filled with light and the sound of combat. The same ornately paneled wood so common throughout the castle lined the walls, but the room had been renovated to resemble a Japanese dojo, with padded floors and wood-framed rice paper screens. Japanese ink paintings adorned the walls, bamboo and bonsai plants placed to catch the light from the large windows.

In the middle of the space, a small Japanese man with closely trimmed gray hair fought five men and three women with wooden swords. Akikane and his students. They were all barefoot and dressed in simple white uniforms. Akikane held a long wooden sword in his right hand and a shorter one in his left. The students surrounding him held only one sword each as they wove in and out of a constant series of attacks.

Akikane moved through them like smoke flowing around trees, deflecting attacks and delivering unblocked strikes in return. Gabriel had never seen someone move so fast. It seemed impossible how fast he moved. He appeared to know when a blade was going to move toward him before its owner did. The fight was exhilarating to watch, but puzzling. Gabriel noticed that some of the students moved with almost the same speed and grace as Akikane himself. The True Mage glanced up at Gabriel with a smile. Suddenly, a blur of motion flickered around the room and all eight students were lying on the floor.

Akikane held his swords at the ready for a moment and then lowered them with a bow to his opponents. The students struggled to their feet and bowed in return. As they straightened up, Gabriel could see them rubbing their arms, legs, backs, and heads. Places that had come into contact with Akikane's swords.

"Good, good," Akikane said and smiled. "Much improvement."

"Yes," said a tall blond man as he rubbed his head. "We lasted nearly a minute longer."

"More importantly," Akikane said, "you and Marie came very close to actually hitting me." One of the women smiled and Gabriel guessed that she must the one Akikane had singled out. Akikane looked across the room at Gabriel. "Now I must attend to another student. Out, out. Same time tomorrow. We will work with blindfolds." Akikane handed his wooden swords to one of the students and waved his hands at them as though shooing small birds out of the room.

Gabriel turned around to say goodbye to Rajan and discovered he was already gone. Gabriel had been so engrossed in watching the swordfight, he had not noticed Rajan depart. The last student to leave closed the door, and Gabriel found himself alone with Akikane, who stood in the center of the room, his face beaming with a nearly beatific glow. Gabriel had never seen someone who looked so completely happy and at ease with himself. Moreover, the elderly man seemed hardly winded after the fight with his students. Gabriel felt unsure of what to expect, so he said the only thing he could think of.

141

"Rajan said you wanted to see me."

"Yes, yes," Akikane said, striding across the room and grasping Gabriel by the shoulders. His hands seemed incredibly strong, but his grip was merely firm, not painful. "I wanted to meet you before we begin out little adventure together."

"Adventure?" Gabriel said, wondering if he was referring to Gabriel becoming his student.

"To sever the branch of time you created," Akikane said. "We will leave in a few minutes."

"So soon?" Gabriel asked. For mages who could control time, they all seemed to want things done as soon as possible.

"Yes, yes," Akikane said. "There is no choice." He walked over to one side of the room where several swords hung on the wall. Gabriel noticed that the opposite wall featured a large statue of the Buddha and a shrine. Gabriel followed Akikane to the wall of swords as the elder mage spoke. "The branch must be severed within thirty-seven hours of its creation. Preferably by the hand that created it."

"Why thirty-seven hours?" Gabriel asked.

"Who knows, who know?" Akikane said with a wide grin. "There are people who like to make theories to explain it, but I prefer to think that it is simply the way it is. Why is the universe here at all? Why is time travel even possible? Why is the speed of light exactly what it is, never slower or faster? Some people question too much. It is as it is."

"I still don't understand," Gabriel said, trying to get it straight in his head. "If the branch is created, then it exists already in the future. What do thirty-seven hours have to do with it?"

"The branch of time you created only exists as a potentiality," Akikane said. "After thirty-seven hours, that potentiality will collapse into a reality. For thirty-seven hours of relative time, time as you experience it after creating the branch, the alternate timeline exists only as potential. Like a gift box that has been not yet been unwrapped. Until it is unwrapped, there could be many things in the box. But once it is opened and you see it, the potential becomes reality."

"So if we sever the branch I created right after the moment of its creation," Gabriel said, thinking it through as he spoke, "the doubles of myself and Apollyon and Sema and Marcus won't just cease to exist, it will be like they never existed at all."

"Exactly, exactly," Akikane said, poking Gabriel in the chest for emphasis. "Very bright."

"And if we waited longer than thirty-seven hours," Gabriel said, "then the branch I created would become a new reality and Apollyon could escape from it with the other version of me."

"Yes, yes," Akikane said. "This would be unfortunate." Gabriel thought that was more than a little bit of an understatement.

"But I took Ling out of that branch," Gabriel said. "If we sever the branch before it becomes a reality, what happens to her? Does she just disappear?" The idea chilled him. To have caused all this trouble to save Ling, only to have her fade away.

"No, no," Akikane said, grinning again. "Taking her from the branch of time you created and bringing her into the Primary Continuum collapsed her state of potential being into a state of actual being. Potential became reality."

"That's good," Gabriel said, sighing with relief. Something occurred to him as he thought about the new branch of time. Something unsettling. "Sir," Gabriel began. He wasn't sure how to address the True Mage, but using his first name seemed ill-mannered, considering his age and his experience. "Why is Apollyon creating branches of time to double himself if he could just go and pluck himself from branches that already exist? And if he could do that, can't he find another branch where I already exist and take that version of me?"

"Good questions, good questions," Akikane said. "The reason is simple. Only one version of a person can be realized as a mage. No matter how many branches of time might have a version of you living in them, only one can ever become a mage. Once that potentiality is realized, it can never be realized again. As with much about magic, we do not know why."

"You mean if I die," Gabriel said, "There will never be another Seventh True Mage?"

"Exactly, exactly," Akikane said. "Unless you have made a double of yourself in a branch that is allowed to collapse from potentiality to reality. This is why Apollyon is creating copies of himself from the Primary Continuum. Making branches around a time when he was already a mage."

"How many copies has he made?" Gabriel asked. "How many is he trying to make?"

"Too many, too many," Akikane said. "I suspect he will be looking to make a hundred and eight copies of himself."

"A hundred and eight," Gabriel said with surprise. "So many?"

"Oh yes, oh yes," Akikane said. "To break through The Great Barrier will require more magical power than has ever been assembled before. Except maybe to create it. And a hundred and eight is a special number. Very special. Many cultures consider it a significant number. Hindu. Buddhist. Many others. Now, a test." Akikane pointed at the wall of swords. "I have a blade I use for pruning bad branches. Can you tell me which one it is?"

Gabriel looked at the wall of swords. Twenty-one swords lined the wall, each resting horizontally on a pair of wooden brackets. In the center, stacked one atop the other, sat seven long swords. On either side of the long swords sat a row of seven shorter swords. The long swords had blades nearly three feet long, while the blades of the shorter swords ranged from a foot-and-a-half to two feet in length.

"The long swords are called daito-katana, and the short swords are called shoto-wakizashi," Akikane said. "But can you tell me which one is the sword we will use today?"

Gabriel centered his mind and extended his magic-sense, feeling the imprints of the blades. Several of the blades had no imprints at all. He wondered if they were ceremonial rather than practical swords. From one of the longer swords and one of the shorter, he could sense deep negative imprints. He wondered why Akikane would keep such tainted swords. The rest of the swords had positive imprints, and Gabriel remembered the story Councilwoman Elizabeth had told him, of how Akikane had use a sword defensively without ever taking a life with its blade. It was clear which of the swords that was. The one at the top of the wall.

"That one," Gabriel said, pointing at the sword resting on the wall seven feet above the floor.

"Very good, very good" Akikane said, smiling his gentle smile again. "Can you get it for me?" There was no ladder, no steps, and no stool, so Gabriel reached into his pocket and clasped his hand around the silver pocket watch, reaching for the magical energy within himself. A second later, the sheathed sword rose out of the wooden arms that cradled it. Gabriel focused his mind and the sword flew toward him a little faster than he had intended. He tried to raise his left hand to catch the flying blade and would surely have been struck in the face had Akikane's hand not flicked forward and snatched the sword at the last possible moment.

"Good, good," Akikane said. "A little less thinking next time. Too much thinking leads to too much magic. Magic is like salt. Always use just the right amount. Not too much, not too little."

"I haven't had much practice," Gabriel said.

"Slowly, slowly," Akikane said. "Each day you will be a little better than the last." He unsheathed the sword so that Gabriel could examine the blade. "This I call my Sword of Unmaking. I only ever use it now to sever a branch of time."

"Is this the sword you used when you stopped being a monk?" Gabriel asked as he examined the edge of the sword's blade. It looked sharp enough to sever a branch of time.

"Yes, yes," Akikane said, resheathing the sword. "But I never stopped being a monk. Once you take the vows, they are for life. Even if your life changes the way you must live them. I was a warrior long before I was a monk. And I was a monk for many years. Many peaceful years. But they were years of peace only for me. There came a day when I could no longer sit and meditate while other warriors were taking innocent lives.

"There was a village near the monastery that came under attack by bandits. I was there in the village square when they came, swords drawn and demanding food and money. I had come to beg for rice for the temple. One man stood up to the bandits. A simple farmer selling his vegetables. They killed him and his daughter. As I watched their bodies fall to the ground, I realized that my vow of nonviolence could not have been intended to be a vow of non-action. It was then I took up the sword again. And left the monastery.

"A monastery is no place for a monk with a sword. There is no good place for a monk with a sword. Except in battle." Akikane paused as he stared at the sword in his hand. His smile faded slightly. Just for a moment. Then it was back, and he was beaming at Gabriel. "Now we should go. Ohin is waiting. There is work to be done."

Gabriel followed Akikane to the door. As he left the room, he asked the question that had been on his mind since he entered it. "Will you teach me to fight with a sword? Like I saw earlier?"

"To be sure, to be sure," Akikane said, placing his arm around Gabriel's shoulders as they walked. "But the sword is the least of what I will teach you." He handed Gabriel the Sword of Unmaking as they walked, and Gabriel held it gently in his hands, like something alive that must be treated with great respect. It felt right to hold it. It felt very right.

When they met Ohin in the Lower Ward courtyard, Gabriel was surprised to see the entire team assembled. "You're all going?" he asked.

"We're like your bodyguards now," Teresa said with her usual broad grin. "We go wherever you go from now on. Rajan's on bathroom duty."

"I think he can manage that alone," Rajan said, raising his eyebrow at Teresa. Sema patted Gabriel's shoulder, Marcus rustled his hair, and Ling slugged him in the arm. The usual greetings.

"I'll wait for you here," Ling said.

"You're not going?" Gabriel asked.

"Too dangerous," Ling said.

"Potential dysphasic reality collapse," Teresa said. Gabriel cocked his head in silent question.

"Get too close to the place where you made the branch while it's severed and I might wink out of existence," Ling said.

"Unstable probability determinates," Teresa said.

"Unsafe," Marcus added.

"Unwise," Sema said.

"Unlikely," Ling said, clearly unhappy to be left behind.

"Unbelievable," Rajan said with a frown at Ling's stubbornness.

"The plan," Ohin said loudly, gathering everyone's attention, "is simple." Teresa rolled her eyes. Ohin pretended not to notice, but Akikane smiled at her with his gloriously peaceful smile, and she fidgeted with her hands in embarrassment. "Gabriel will take us back to the moment just before he created the alternate branch of time. Hopefully close enough so that we can see the exact moment he created the bifurcation. At that moment, Akikane will sever the new branch of time from the Primary Continuum. There should be nothing for anyone else to do except watch."

"Wish we got jobs like this more often," Marcus whispered to no one in particular. Akikane beamed at him and Marcus coughed.

"Sema," Ohin said, nodding toward her. Sema stepped forward and handed Gabriel the Venetian glass pendant she normally wore as a talisman. He noticed a string of prayer beads wrapped around her wrist as a replacement.

"I will expect this back," Sema said as Gabriel took the pendant.

"Of course," Gabriel said, looking around as everyone formed a circle around him and placed a hand on his shoulder.

"When you are ready, Gabriel," Ohin said, his voice calm enough to help ease Gabriel's nerves. "I will lend my power to yours for the jump. It is a large group to jump at once."

Gabriel nodded as he took his pocket watch out and held it together with the glass pendant. He reached for the magical energy within himself and focused it through the pocket watch as he opened his time-sense to the glass pendant, searching for just the right moment. A moment memorable, but just slightly different from the last time he had experienced it. He could feel Ohin's magical energy blending with his own. Then blackness surrounded them and the familiar white light washed everything out of existence.

They stood on a street at night in Venice. The same street where he had created the bifurcation of time to save Ling. The canal was there, just as before, but they stood farther along it. He felt the hands of his companions leave his shoulders. Everyone stepped into the shadows just as Gabriel saw his previous self appear down the street.

147

"Soon," he said, pointing to his earlier self at the end of the street. He could feel the bend of the space-time fabric as the even older version of himself must have appeared in St. Marks Piazza two blocks away with the other, original versions of Sema, Ling and Marcus. Akikane stepped up beside Gabriel and withdrew the sword.

"Here, here," Akikane said. "Hold the hilt with me. I will show you how it is done." Gabriel took hold of the hilt of the sword even as he watched the older version of himself raise his hand and the water of the canal explode. He could sense the fabric of space-time twist and rip away. He also sensed the flow of time slow down. He realized that Akikane was helping him, reaching out to him with Soul Magic and assisting him to better observe what the elder True Mage was about to do.

Gabriel could almost see the rip in the fabric of space-time now, he felt it so clearly. And he could also feel the power that Akikane channeled through the Sword of Unmaking. Only when he had touched the tainted imprints of the Aztec temple had he felt more power.

While that power had been like swallowing a barrel of thick, crude oil, this was like ingesting the purest of spring waters. As he extended his time-sense, he could feel Akikane focusing that power, like brilliant sunlight through a magnifying glass, on a very specific portion of the fabric of space-time. Not a portion really, not a location, not a place, not even a moment, but an aspect of its being, a point of potentiality. Gabriel could feel that point, that facet of space-time possibility beginning to form, beginning to branch away from the stability and seeming solidness of the Primary Continuum. In some ways, it was like looking through a portal, a doorway to another dimension of yet unrealized reality, another world, another possible timeline.

Just at the point where its being began to become, began to be realized, Akikane unleashed a focused burst of magical power, and like a sharpened blade sliding through a slender thread, the alternate branch of time was gone, the portal slipped shut and the world beyond it was no more. The world that might have existed there had vanished, and all the potential people of that world were snuffed out in an instant, an alternate version of himself included. No wonder Akikane called it the Sword of Unmaking.

Gabriel realized he was still staring at the blade. He looked up. They were firmly in the Primary Continuum, the scene as it had been when they arrived. A few people walking the streets on either side of the canal. Two gondolas and a small boat slowly gliding through the water. His previous self was gone now, as that reality had dissolved with the severing of the alternate branch of time. Gabriel looked back to see Akikane smiling yet again.

"Good, good," Akikane said. "Clean cut. Very fine."

"Well done," Ohin said, placing a gentle hand on Gabriel's shoulder.

"What now?" Gabriel asked.

"We wait," Ohin said. "We need to wait for the events in the piazza to play out."

"For you to rescue us," Sema said as she looked at Marcus.

"For Apollyon to leave," Akikane said.

Gabriel heard other words between those that had been spoken. To wait for Ling to die again, he thought. As he extended his magic-sense, he could feel the fight going on in the piazza two blocks away. If he focused intently, he could almost discern the type of magic being used. The Wind Magic Apollyon used to hurl Ling into St. Mark's Campanile. The Fire Magic he used while running toward Sema and Marcus.

Gabriel looked up at Sema and Marcus, standing beside the canal with him, glad they were here with him now. He knew from their faces they could sense the magic, even if he didn't think they could tell which beyond their own form of magic was being used. And then the sense of Time Magic as the fabric of space-time warped slightly, and the previous version of himself jumped away with Sema and Marcus. He felt the fabric of space-time warp again, only a fraction of a second later, and he knew that Apollyon was gone.

"It's safe now," Gabriel said, wanting to speak before anyone else, to make sure they knew he was paying attention to what had happened.

149

"Yes," Ohin said. "I'll take us back." Everyone reached out a hand, placing them on Ohin's broad shoulders as he removed a piece of amber from his pocket. A moment of blackness and whiteness and they stood in the Lower Ward Courtyard again. Ling leapt up from a bench and ran over to them.

"You're still here," Marcus said with a sigh of relief.

"Of course she is," Teresa said. "I told you there was nothing to worry about. Cross-temporal stability quotient. You're feeling solid, aren't you?" Teresa tried to poke Ling with her finger, but Ling caught it and held it firmly, making a noise that sounded like a growl. "Hardly any risk at all of her disappearing. Even for a few minutes." Teresa pulled her finger free from Ling's hand with a grin.

"Did everything go as planned?" Ling asked, looking at Akikane, Ohin, and Gabriel.

"For once," Rajan said.

"Everything has been set right," Ohin said. "The alternate branch will never be."

"But you will," Akikane said, eyes twinkling peacefully. "You will."

"I think we should celebrate over dinner," Rajan said.

"How surprising," Teresa said. "Rajan wants to eat."

"And wine," Marcus said. "I know the perfect bottle to open for a celebration."

"And Marcus wants to drink," Sema said. "Again, how surprising."

"That is a good idea," Ohin said. "We need to discuss the next steps and the next mission."

"We need to find the place where Apollyon is making his copies," Gabriel said, assuming that was the next step.

"Yes, yes," Akikane said, beaming as he walked toward the Waterloo Chamber across the castle grounds in the state apartments. "And to do that, we will need to find Nefferati."

The statement left Gabriel so stunned he stood rooted to the spot while the others walked away. Ling gave him a push in the middle of the back. He stumbled forward to catch up with the group, Ling at his side.

"Nefferati?" Gabriel asked, not knowing what else to say.

"Ohin says she is the only one with enough experience to locate the place in time that Apollyon is using to make his duplicates," Ling said. "It will be hidden with powerful magic."

"Right," Gabriel said, wondering just how powerful Nefferati was if True Mages like Akikane and Elizabeth could not find the spot in time where Apollyon was hiding his illicit activities. They walked on in silence behind the others for a moment. Then Ling rustled his hair and laughed.

"What?" Gabriel said, wondering at the source of her amusement.

"It's funny," Ling said. "When I first met you, I figured you'd be a troublemaker. From further up the timeline than nearly everyone. An annoying know-it-all making my life difficult."

"I wonder who you could be talking about," Gabriel said, looking ahead to see that Teresa was too far away to hear their conversation.

"Exactly," Ling said, following his line of sight. "She's like a daughter in that way. I had two daughters back before all this, as well as my son. She's like a combination of both of them in one. They never listened to me, either. But you. You listen to everything everyone says, you're sweet and polite, and even manage to be modest about being the fulfillment of the prophecy. Humble about being the Seventh True Mage. And yet you cause more trouble than anyone!" Ling laughed again and slugged him in the arm as they walked. From her, this was like being showered with hugs and kisses, and Gabriel felt his cheeks grow hot as he smiled back.

CHAPTER 16
THE BEST LAID PLANS

Dinner that night was the usual affair: scrumptious food, plenty of wine, at least for the adults, boisterous banter from Marcus, Teresa, and Rajan, and cordial conversation among Sema, Ling, and Ohin. Gabriel felt happy for the first time in days. He noticed the rabbit's foot switch hands between Teresa and Rajan again and asked a question that he had been wondering about for some time.

"What happens if you lose a bet and you don't have the rabbit's foot to hand over?"

"Why don't you make a bet and find out?" Teresa said with a look of innocence.

"Don't take the bait, lad," Marcus said.

"I think I'll pass," Gabriel said.

"Not a betting man?" Rajan asked.

"I think I've gambled enough lately," Gabriel said, and the others laughed.

After dinner, Gabriel took a nighttime walk with Ling and Sema through the castle grounds. They walked several paces behind him, talking between themselves. Gabriel had wanted some time alone to think things through and clear his head, but Sema and Ling had volunteered to go with him. When he had suggested he might want to be by himself, they had seemed oddly deaf. Apparently he was to have bodyguards even within the castle walls. At least for the time being. Until it was known who the spy was. Or spies.

He was desperate to try more magic, to practice with Fire Magic or Wind Magic, but he had been cautioned not to try any magic that might reveal his status as a True Mage until it was known by everyone in the castle.

He walked through the grounds, staring up at the stars in the sky above, wondering what his future would hold. He seemed to spend a lot of time doing that lately. Wondering what would come next. Stopping Apollyon from making more copies of himself was the first mission, but what would come after that? Would he even be allowed on any missions? Councilwoman Elizabeth had been of the opinion that he should not be risking his life even on the mission to find Apollyon's secret branch of time where he copied himself. She felt that he was too valuable to jeopardize in such an endeavor.

Akikane had apparently been insistent that his new apprentice train to the fullest extent possible. Gabriel was thankful for that. He had no idea what dangers he might face, but being the Seventh True Mage probably meant he would face more than most, and it would be best to have as much training and experience as possible. It had helped that Akikane made it clear that he would personally accompany Gabriel on this mission.

Figuring that if he couldn't practice magic out in the open, he could at least practice it in his room, Gabriel decided to say good night to Ling and Sema. They insisted on accompanying him to his quarters. As they bid him goodnight, Sema gave him a light kiss on the forehead and Ling gave him a wink and whack on the arm. In his room, alone for the first time in hours, Gabriel practiced making fireballs fly around his quarters, making several books that Ohin had brought him levitate at the same time, trying to swirl them around in a controlled dance of paper and light. When one of the books collided with one of the fireballs and burst into flame, Gabriel released his concentration. The burning book fell to the floor, along with the others, as the fireballs winked out of existence.

Staring at the book as it burned, Gabriel tried to think of what to do. How could he use magic to put the fire out? The flame from the book grew larger and began to threaten the faded Persian rug. He was about to grab a glass of water from his dresser when something occurred to him.

Focusing his mind again, he concentrated on making the flame smaller and smaller until it finally flickered out. He picked up the book as he used magic to open the window and air out the room. Many of the pages at the beginning were beyond recovery, but most of the latter half of the book was still legible. He looked at the title.

Flames from Nowhere: An Apprentice Guide to Fire Magic. Gabriel laughed as he went to bed. Maybe Teresa would tell him what the front of the book had said. At least the most interesting part, the advanced Fire Magic, was still readable.

Before breakfast the next morning, Gabriel met Ohin at a bench in the courtyard of the Upper Ward. Ohin had asked him to be there when the sun came up. Gabriel wasn't sure why people who could control time needed to get up so early, but he didn't complain. It had never done him any good to complain to his mother about what time he needed to get up, and he doubted that Ohin would be any more flexible than his mother had been.

Gabriel sat down next to Ohin.

"Morning," Gabriel said.

"Good Morning," Ohin said, handing Gabriel a small leather-bound book. For a second, Gabriel thought the book was a copy of the one he had burnt the night before and wondered how Ohin had known, and wondered even more so if he was in trouble for damaging a book from the castle library. Then he read the title. *A Time Traveler's Pocket Guide to History, Third Edition,* edited by one William Mackel. Gabriel paged through the book. It had a detailed timeline in the front and sections with illustrated entries in chronological order, as well as a section at the back with names and places arranged alphabetically. It was small, but incredibly detailed. Idly, Gabriel realized there must be a printing press somewhere in the castle to be making all these specialized books.

"Thank you," Gabriel said, looking from the book to Ohin.

"You're welcome," Ohin said. "I thought it might be helpful until your studies of history are complete. I kept it in my pocket for years while I was an apprentice."

"I have trouble imagining you as an apprentice," Gabriel said, flipping through the pages of the book again.

"I was an apprentice for a long time," Ohin said with a sigh. "More than once. Before I was plucked from the timeline, I was a stonemason, and I apprenticed with my master for ten years. They were hard years, filled with long hours and backbreaking work, but good years, as well. He was a kind teacher, patient with a slow learner, and forgiving of mistakes. I was an orphan and he and his wife were like the family I had never known. She used to bake spiced-honey bread and serve it with fresh cream from goat's milk. I miss the taste of that.

"It was a long apprenticeship, but not one where I learned to read. You are lucky to have been taken from a place and time when reading was common. I came from a land with a written language, but a long oral tradition. The written language was called Ge'ez, but an apprentice stonemason had little time for learning to read. It took a great deal of effort to learn English, which Councilwoman Elizabeth has established as the common language for the castle. At first, it was actually easier for me to memorize the book from someone reading it to me than to read it myself."

"You memorized this whole book?" Gabriel said, his eyes widening.

"That and many others," Ohin said. "It's not that hard once you learn how. People in your time had gotten lazy about using their memory, but for a time traveler, it is essential to have a powerful recall. While that little book will slip in your pocket, you cannot hope to carry all the books with all the knowledge you are likely to need."

"I have a pretty good memory for names and dates," Gabriel said, sliding the book into one of the deep pockets on the side of his pants. It was a perfect fit.

"I'm sure you do," Ohin said. "And I'll help you to improve it. I have something else for you." Ohin handed Gabriel a small piece of amber. Gabriel held it up to the light and could see a beetle suspended in the orange-brown fossilized tree resin. "This relic is yours to keep. It will allow you to make your way back to the castle in the event of an emergency. I want you to keep it on you at all times."

"Thanks," Gabriel said. It felt like someone had given him a key to the castle.

"Follow me," Ohin said as he stood.

"Where to?" Gabriel asked, sliding the amber-encrusted beetle into his pocket as he stood.

"To see about finding Nefferati," Ohin said.

Gabriel followed Ohin through the grounds to the state apartments and a large wooden door that led to what used to be called the King's Drawing Room. Ohin knocked and Gabriel heard Councilwoman Elizabeth's voice beckon them to enter.

Councilwoman Elizabeth's office was decorated much the way Gabriel had imagined. It looked like the sitting room of British royalty. A white marble fireplace sat behind a large gilded desk of elm in the middle of the room, a large oriental carpet covered the wooden floor, and paintings by Peter Paul Rubens decorated the walls. Ling had mentioned the painting of *St. George and the Dragon* as being one of her favorites in the castle. Now that he could see it, Gabriel understood why she liked it. It exuded an extremely attractive sense of power and purpose. Several large leather chairs surrounded a low, ornately carved wooden table. A silver tea service sat on the table with four delicately made china teacups. Elizabeth and Akikane sat in two of the leather chairs.

"Thank you for joining us," Elizabeth said, pouring tea into two of the empty cups.

"Thank you for inviting us," Ohin said as he made a slight bow and took a seat. Not knowing what was expected of him, Gabriel imitated Ohin's bow and sat next to him. Akikane gave Gabriel one of his characteristically beatific smiles. Gabriel couldn't help but smile back.

"After some considerable effort," Elizabeth said, "Akikane and I have been able to locate the time and place of Nefferati's retreat." She held up a stone arrowhead. "She left me this to find her in the event she was needed."

"Without Nefferati, we have little hope of finding where Apollyon is making his bifurcations to twin himself," Ohin said

"The magic that cloaks the branches is too strong," Elizabeth said.

"Even for us," Akikane said. "Even for us."

"But we believe Nefferati may be able to sense where the branches are being made," Elizabeth said. "A Time Mage, or a True Mage, can use a relic to scan through history and sense disturbances in the Primary Continuum. In a similar way, we used this arrowhead to discover where Nefferati has sequestered herself."

"Where is she?" Gabriel asked.

"Neolithic China," Ohin said.

"Which is where you will be going," Elizabeth added.

"I will accompany you," Akikane said.

"You aren't going?" Gabriel asked Elizabeth, surprised that she would not want to see her old teacher.

"That might prove to be unhelpful," Elizabeth said.

"Most unhelpful, most unhelpful," Akikane said.

"When Nefferati departed the castle," Elizabeth said, seeming to choose her words carefully, "we were not on the best of terms." Ohin made a noise that sounded like an abortive snort of laugher. Elizabeth shot him a glance, and he cleared his throat.

"If you don't mind my asking," Gabriel said, "why did Nefferati leave?"

"That is Councilwomen Nefferati to you," Elizabeth said. "The boy sits quiet like a mouse and only opens his mouth to ask the one question I don't want to answer," she continued, speaking to no one in particular.

"I'm sorry," Gabriel said. "I didn't mean to be rude."

"It's not rude at all," Elizabeth said. "If you're going to meet her, you should understand why she left. And sending you will be our best hope of ensuring her cooperation."

"Why wouldn't she want to help?" Gabriel asked.

"She left the Council and the castle because she wanted no more part in the war," Elizabeth said. "She said she could not live with the actions she felt she had no choice but to take, and so she went away. When she departed, we had words." Elizabeth did not attempt to elaborate on what those words might have been, but Gabriel assumed that if she wasn't going to accompany them to find Nefferati, the words probably had not been pleasant.

"But how can I convince her to help?" Gabriel asked.

"Because of the prophecy," Ohin said.

"Nefferati is the one who made the prophecy of the Seventh True Mage," Elizabeth said. "Meeting you may convince her that it is time to return to the Council and the war."

"We hope, we hope," Akikane said.

Silence surrounded them for a moment. Ohin broke it by standing up. "We should meet the others for breakfast," he said. "Then we will leave."

"I will meet you in an hour by the Great Oak," Akikane said, standing.

"And I will await your return with good news," Elizabeth said, remaining seated.

Gabriel found it hard to concentrate on breakfast. He couldn't think of food when he knew that in less than an hour he would be meeting the most famous mage of all. He found himself staring around the Waterloo Chamber absentmindedly instead of eating his porridge.

"I wonder what she'll look like," Teresa said, taking a bite of an apple muffin.

"Old," Marcus said, buttering his second slice of bread.

"Will she help, though?" Rajan said around a mouthful of eggs.

"Of course she will," Sema said, taking a sip of her favorite Turkish coffee.

"She damn well better," Ling added, biting hard into a cranberry scone.

"More important than what she will do, is what we must do," Ohin said, wiping his chin with a napkin. "I want to make sure that two of us are close to Gabriel at all times."

"How close?" Gabriel asked. He was beginning to resent being treated like a fragile child.

"As close as possible," Ohin said, staring Gabriel down. "Councilman Akikane will be joining us, and I doubt we will have anything to worry about with Nefferati present, as well, but I want everyone to spread out and assume defensive positions when we arrive."

Which is exactly what they did twenty minutes later when they met Akikane in the Horseshoe Cloister and he took them through time to the edge of a clearing in the middle of northwestern China just south of a place that would one day be called Beijing, somewhere near the year 12,000 BCE. Gabriel stared at a small hut in the center of a clearing of low grass. Marcus moved to the right, Sema to the rear, and Ling left, making sure the clearing was safe. Rajan and Teresa stayed near Gabriel while Akikane and Ohin strode toward the hut.

A gentle breeze rustled through the wild grass of the quiet clearing, the sun high and hot in the cloudless blue sky above. Gabriel guessed it must be midsummer. Marcus and Ling moved to the edges, circling to the back of the hut as Ohin stepped up to the wooden door. He paused a moment and then knocked. There was no reply. He took a moment to look through a small window at the side of the hut.

"Empty," he said.

"Nothing in the back," Marcus said as he and Ling reappeared from behind the hut.

"Just a table, a goat, and a few chickens," Ling added.

"Where could she be?" Akikane wondered aloud. "Where could she be?"

"Picking berries," a sharp, low voice said from the edge of the forest. A tall, thin African woman with a halo of near-white hair stepped from the trees, branches rustling around her. She wore a simple gray cotton dress and carried a bucket of red berries. She crossed the grass in long graceful strides, ignoring the party of mages as she walked behind the hut and disappeared around the back. Everyone looked around at each other in confusion. Except Akikane.

"Same, same," Akikane said. "Nothing changes." Akikane walked around the hut and the others followed.

When Gabriel came around the edge of the hut, he saw the woman who he assumed must be Nefferati sitting on a stump at the head of long, crudely hewn wooden table pouring small red berries from a simple wooden bucket into a shallow clay bowl.

"Don't just stand there with your mouths open drawing flies," Nefferati said, "sit down and have some berries." She popped one into her mouth.

Slowly, Gabriel and the others sat on the benches around the table, each reaching into the clay dish and drawing out a berry. Gabriel sat between Rajan and Teresa at the far end of the table.

"Now," Nefferati said, "let's skip the usual polite manure about how happy everyone is to meet me and get to the point. Why are you here, Akikane? And since when do you need an entourage?"

"We are here because we need your help," Akikane said. He still smiled, but it seemed strained for the first time since Gabriel had met him.

"Really," Nefferati said. "And here I thought you came for the berries."

"This is Ohin and his team," Akikane said, gesturing to those seated around the table. "Marcus, Rajan, Gabriel, Teresa, Ling, and Sema."

"Names I will soon forget," Nefferati said.

"Not likely, not likely," Akikane said.

"What are you playing at, Akikane?" Nefferati said as she snatched a handful of berries from the bowl.

"Apollyon," Ohin said, interjecting himself into the conversation.

"What about him?" Nefferati said. "Not my problem. He's the Council's problem now. Speaking of which, where's my famous apprentice? Couldn't find the time to call?"

"She has a council to run," Akikane said.

"Too busy, my bony butt," Nefferati said.

"Apollyon is making copies of himself with bifurcations," Ohin said. He kept his eyes on Nefferati. She eyed him back.

"Interesting," she said finally. "But how is that my business?"

"We are having trouble locating the point in the timeline where Apollyon is creating the branches," Akikane said.

"And you thought to drag the old woman out of her hole to help," Nefferati said.

"We hoped, we hoped," Akikane said.

"Your war, your business," Nefferati said. "Berries are my business now."

"Things have changed," Akikane said.

160

"Same Council, same ideas, same war," Nefferati said. "Nothing changes."

"The Seventh True Mage has been revealed," Ohin said. Nefferati raised her eyebrows and stared at Ohin.

"True, true," Akikane said when Nefferati looked to him.

"Who? Where?" Nefferati asked.

"Him," Ohin said, gesturing toward Gabriel. Gabriel met Nefferati's gaze as she snorted.

"A boy!" Nefferati said.

"The Seventh True Mage, even so," Akikane said.

Nefferati fell silent as she stared at Gabriel. All other eyes were on her, but she didn't seem to notice. "What's Apollyon playing at, making copies of himself?" she said finally.

"We believe he is trying to acquire the power to destroy The Great Barrier," Ohin said.

"Hmmm," was all Nefferati said.

"Will you help us?" Akikane said. "The entire Continuum is at stake."

"That's what they always say when they want something," Nefferati said. "The Council," she added, clarifying what she meant. "I'll think about it. I want to talk to the boy first."

"Of course, of course," Akikane said.

"Alone," Nefferati said. She still stared at Gabriel. He tried to stare back, to match her gaze, but eventually he broke away to look at his teacher. Ohin nodded to him, and Nefferati stood up.

"Nothing to fear, boy," she said as she saw the nervous look on his face. "I'm not a cannibal, just an old woman. Give me your arm. I know a nice deer path we can follow." Gabriel looked behind him at the table of his companions. Akikane was smiling, as ever, while Ohin squinted, whether from concern or the sun, Gabriel could not tell. Marcus gave an encouraging nod of his head, and Teresa gave him a thumbs-up gesture. He took Nefferati's arm and followed her into the forest.

They walked along a thin dirt path that meandered through the trees. The scent of pine filled Gabriel's nostrils and reminded him of his grandparent's farm. They had planted pine trees along the edge of the fields, and his grandmother and he would collect the pine needles each Autumn to boil them down for homemade cough syrup. Although she appeared as old as his grandmother, her face wrinkled and sun-worn, there was nothing remotely grandmotherly about Nefferati.

"Where did they find you?" Nefferati asked, pulling a branch aside so they could pass.

"In 1980," Gabriel answered, assuming she was referring to the time more so than the place.

"Close to the Barrier, then. How old are you?"

"I'm thirteen-and-a-half," Gabriel answered.

"A man in some cultures."

"I suppose."

"And Ohin?"

"My teacher. For Time Magic."

"And you've been trained in the other magics, have you?"

"Not yet. Akikane is going to be my primary teacher. And the rest of the team will help."

"The serial repeater and that slack-jawed lot sitting around the table? Fat lot of good they'll be, teaching you magic."

"They've done well so far," Gabriel said with a slightly defensive tone. Whatever had made Nefferati unhappy all those years ago seemed to have kept her unhappy.

"And who's teaching you to use the dark imprints?" Nefferati said.

"No one. I don't want to use dark magic," Gabriel said, remembering what it felt like to touch the imprints of the Scottish sword and the Aztec pyramid.

"I suppose Queen Elizabeth supports this foolish notion," Nefferati said with derision.

"We haven't actually discussed it," Gabriel said. "I made the decision on my own."

"How the hell do you expect to fulfill the prophecy of the Seventh True Mage if you don't use dark magic?" Nefferati asked.

"I thought I had fulfilled the prophecy," Gabriel said.

"Only the first part, boy," Nefferati said. "The easiest part." Nefferati glanced behind them. "Do you have a talisman yet?"

"Yes," Gabriel said, looking behind. He wondered what was living in the forest they walked through. Were there people nearby? It seemed unlikely, but it would be just his luck to run across some ancient Neolithic Chinese hunting party and inadvertently create a new timeline.

"Let me see it," Nefferati said, holding out her hand. Gabriel dug in his pocket and retrieved the silver watch, placing it in Nefferati's outstretched palm. She looked at it and sniffed. "Is that it? No others? Nothing hidden in your sock for emergencies?"

"No," Gabriel said, realizing as she spoke that it might not be such a bad idea to keep a spare Talisman handy. Sema, at least, had more than one talisman.

"Good," Nefferati said taking one more glance behind them at the path leading back to the hut. They had walked nearly half a mile while they talked, and Gabriel could not even see the hut through the trees any more. As he looked back from the trail behind them, he saw Akikane standing in the path ahead. Nefferati saw him as well.

"Release the boy," Akikane said, drawing his sword from the sheath strapped to his waist in one silent and elegant motion.

"You always were the quickest one of the lot," Nefferati said, taking a small coin from a pocket of her dress. "But not quick enough." Then the all-too-familiar blackness surrounded Nefferati and Gabriel and her hand clutched at his arm like a vise. Gabriel didn't understand what was happening. He barely had time to struggle when the whiteness overtook everything.

They stood in a field near an ocean. Gabriel tried to break free of Nefferati's grip, but it was useless. She was incredibly strong for someone so aged. The blackness followed swiftly by the whiteness again, and they stood outside a ruined castle. Nefferati jumped again. And again. Gabriel lost count and began to get dizzy. It was much more difficult to make repeated jumps as a tagalong rather than as the Time Mage doing the jumping. Finally, they came to a stop in the middle of another forest. The trees were thicker this time. And taller. Oak and hickory, Gabriel thought as he looked around. It seemed like it must be midday, but very little light fell through the canopy of the trees.

"What's going on?" Gabriel shouted as he finally broke free of Nefferati's gasp. He stepped back several paces as she released him. "What are you doing? We didn't come to hurt you!"

Nefferati laughed. Then her body began to morph, her skin changing color, the shape of her face altering, her hair becoming long and straight and night-deep black. Gabriel stared in shock. Several seconds later, he was looking at an Indian woman nearly half a head shorter than the woman she had been a second before. She had a thin face with a strong jawline and deep set eyes. She smiled ominously at him. "They could not hurt me if they tried," the woman said, her dark brown eyes filled with a mixture of contempt and pleasure. "I wonder how that old Japanese fool figured it out. No matter. He will not be able to follow us where we go next."

"I'm not going anywhere with you," Gabriel said, beginning to suspect the full implications of what had just happened and exactly how much danger he was in. "I know who you are."

"Well, at least they've taught you that much," the woman said. "But your education will be under my supervision from now on."

"What do you want?" Gabriel asked.

"I have what I want," the woman said. "And it is time we were gone."

"I won't go with you," Gabriel said.

"Oh, I think you'll do exactly as I say," the woman said. "Now sleep." She waved her hand before her, and Gabriel felt his eyes flutter and his mind fade to blackness.

CHAPTER 17
PALACE OF ~~LIGHT~~ DARKNESS

The fog of sleep slowly dissipated, gradually replaced by greater and greater clarity until one thought finally managed to solidify in Gabriel's mind.

Kumaradevi.

That thought brought him to full consciousness in an instant. He kept his eyes closed and pretended to still be sleeping, listening for any sign of where he might be and what might have happened to him. He was lying on his back in a bed, it seemed, with a heavy blanket drawn up to his chin. The glow on the back of his eyelids told him there was light entering from somewhere, possibly a window. He could hear nothing except his own breathing, which had quickened its pace considerably since he regained his senses.

He opened his eyes. What he saw was not at all what he had expected.

He was in an enormous four-poster bed with soft pale sheets and a thick down comforter with a black and red design of seven intersecting swords embroidered on it. Sitting up, he saw a window letting light into the room, its long velvet drapes cast aside. There were several windows, in fact, for the room was large and opulently furnished.

Climbing from the bed, he examined the room more closely. A large mahogany desk and two huge leather chairs sat beside a small couch and a low table. Near this sat a dining table with a wooden top and slender, ornately carved stone legs. On top of the table lay a silver serving tray with several plates topped with silver covers. A crystal pitcher of water rested beside the tray with a crystal goblet. Behind the table, near the far wall, sat a large copper tub for bathing. On the wall opposite the windows were two tall and well-polished oak dressers between which stood an enormous walnut armoire.

165

Wide and intricately woven rugs with abstract and repetitious patterns covered the stone floor and long tapestries depicting colossal and violent battles draped the walls. There was a lone door, carved from a single piece of wood with large iron bands bolted across it for reinforcement. The inside of the door had no handle and no hinges. Gabriel wasn't getting out until someone came for him. But getting out of where? Where was he?

As he looked down, he realized that he wore black silk pajamas. His clothes had been taken. His chunk of amber, his only way home. He got up and went to the armoire, opening the carved wooden doors wide. Inside were several sets of clothes, all identical. Black pants and black shirts with a red symbol of a sword woven into the chest. And several thick, wool jackets with the red sword sewn on the right breast. The floor of the armoire had three pairs of black leather shoes. He opened the drawers of the dressers. Underclothes and socks were all he found. There was no sign of the pocket watch or piece of amber that could take him back to the castle or the book that Ohin had given him, *The Time Traveler's Pocket Guide to History*. He had hoped they might leave him the book. If it had been printed at the castle, it might have been able to take him back there.

With a sudden flash of thought, he placed his hand to his neck and found the amulet still there. Surely the amulet had been made at the castle. He pulled it out and his hopes evaporated. It was not the same amulet. This one was a piece of flat, circular obsidian. He had nothing to link him back to the castle. And Kumaradevi had his pocket watch. If he managed to retrieve the pocket watch, could he use it to escape? It was just one small question among far too many larger ones. Where was he? What had happened to the real Nefferati? What did Kumaradevi want with him? What would happen next?

He was thankful when his stomach rumbled to voice its unhappiness at being empty. It distracted him from his thoughts. He walked over to the dining table and lifted the edge of the silver cover from the large china plate. Underneath sat an omelet with bacon and fried potatoes. Under the silver cover of a smaller plate, he found a large, thick-cut piece of toasted wheat bread. Beside the plate sat a glass jar with some sort of dark berry jam and a small silver spoon.

Gabriel's stomach growled again. Looking up from the plate of food, he realized the one thing he had not done, the one place he had not looked. He went to the nearest window.

The sight through the window filled him with despair. He was in a tower of some sort in the middle of a large and sprawling palace. Looking down, he could see that the window of his tower chamber resided at least two hundred feet above the palace buildings below. He thought about cutting the drapes and tying them together to create a rope, but there was no way to open the window. He would have to break the thick and heavily leaded glass to escape through the window. It was a possibility, but one that would have to wait for a later time.

Staring out the window again, he tried to get a sense of when and where he might be. The palace was like none he had ever seen in any book. The buildings were of gray and black granite blocks of various sizes and shapes. If the walls of his room were any indication of the masonry used to construct the rest of the palace, the blocks fit together without the benefit of mortar. It reminded him of the construction of Incan stone masonry he had read about, but the style and design of the buildings was wholly different from any he was familiar with.

All of the buildings were built to a scale that implied giants might be housed within, although he could see people walking along the wide internal streets of the palace. The shorter buildings had a circular shape with domed roofs, while the taller buildings were composed of different-sized square blocks, welded together at the seams. From another window, Gabriel could glimpse the edge of what might have been a pyramid of some sort. Beyond the palace, a city of short and squalid buildings spread out for miles. The city was a complete contrast to the palace in every way. The palace was haunting in its stark, colossal design while buildings made from scraps of wood, mud, stone, and grass lined the city. It looked like a good stiff wind could blow the city away at any moment.

Gabriel sighed, his fears and suspicions overwhelming him for a moment. If he was right, he was very far from home. Very far indeed. And it wouldn't matter if he had his pocket watch at all. His stomach rumbled again. He looked back to the table with the breakfast that had been prepared for him. At least his captor wanted him to be well fed and comfortable. He tried not to think about his captor. Not just yet. Not until he had eaten. And it would be best to dress before eating. Who knew what might happen after breakfast?

Dressing took little time. There was no choice in what to wear. He pulled on a tightly tailored black wool jacket and slipped on his black leather shoes, idly wondering how his captor had known his sizes so well. His clothes and shoes fit perfectly. That could not be simple chance. How long had he been asleep? How much had they known about him before his kidnapping? How much more did they know about him now?

Before eating, he moved the serving tray to the opposite side of the table so that he could see the door. He didn't want to spend his time thinking about what might come through the door while his back was to it. This way he could face the door as he considered his predicament and try to remember as much as he could about Kumaradevi. He knew she had been an Indian princess of some sort. That she was dangerous. But what else?

He realized that she was right about one thing at least; his education under the Council's guidance had been woefully incomplete. But then again, he doubted that Councilwoman Elizabeth or Akikane or anyone else on the Council could have anticipated this. Or could they? Only his team and the council knew that he was the Seventh True Mage. Was it possible that one of the Council members was a spy for Kumaradevi? Or maybe an assistant to one of the council members. The only other possibilities were the members of his team, and he refused to believe that any of them could have sold him out for any reason.

As he finished the last bite of his omelet, there came a soft knock at the door. It didn't strike him as coincidence, and he quickly scanned the room for places where someone might be able to spy on him through a peephole. There were too many likely spots, and he had no time to consider the question as the door opened. Gabriel pushed the chair back from the table and stood up. It might be a good idea to be on his feet. Just in case.

A young woman in a long, rough-spun, brown wool dress entered with her head bowed. The first thing Gabriel noticed was her bare feet. The second was the thick iron collar that she wore. It fit snugly around her neck, and Gabriel could see where it had chafed her dark brown skin raw. She kept her eyes down as she entered and did not look up until she stopped a few feet away from him. She had deep blue eyes, which contrasted with her dark black hair. She had smooth skin and a narrow nose, but her eyes seemed tired, and her hunched shoulders gave her a fearful look. Although she had looked up, she did not meet his eyes.

"I am Pishara," the woman said with a curtsy. "I am to be your server."

Gabriel looked at Pishara for a moment and then past her to the open door. Beyond the doorway lay a corridor filled with shadows. Something else was out there. Someone else. He could sense it. Now might not be the best time to make a run for it. "What does that mean?" Gabriel asked, wondering if she had come to take the empty plates away.

"I am to be your servant here in the palace," Pishara said. "If you have need of anything, I will provide it for you."

"I had a piece of amber with a beetle trapped in it inside in my pocket," Gabriel said.

"That you may not have," Pishara said. "Are you finished with your meal?"

"Yes," Gabriel said, stepping from behind the table.

"Was it to your liking?" Pishara asked.

"It was very good," Gabriel said, wondering where this conversation might head.

"And you rested well?" Pishara asked.

"Fine," Gabriel said. "Slept like a baby."

"That is good," Pishara said, almost smiling. "Now it is time I take you to see the Empress." Gabriel had a very good idea who the Empress was. "You will follow me." Pishara walked to the door, not bothering to see if Gabriel would follow. He wondered just what sort of servant she was. The sort who could give him orders as well as bring him breakfast, he guessed.

Following Pishara out the door of his room, he discovered that he had been right, there were people in the corridor. Two very large and pale men wearing leather and mail armor and holding long metal spears stood on either side of the doorway. One reached out and closed the door, but otherwise neither acknowledged his presence.

The corridor darkened immediately, but a dim light glowed ahead, and Gabriel followed the silhouette of Pishara toward it. The source of the light was another corridor where two more men stood. These men were dressed in clothes much like his own. The taller one had deep black hair and a red flame embroidered on his left jacket breast, while the shorter one had reddish hair and a red circle on his left jacket breast. They caught Gabriel's eye with a look of contempt, but fell in step, without a word, behind him and Pishara. She led them to a flight of spiral stairs that seemed to go down forever.

"This is Viktor and Seamus," Pishara said, indicating the men who followed them with a raised hand. "They will be your bodyguards. To protect you." To make sure he didn't escape was more like it.

Gabriel followed her around and around and down and down the stairs for several minutes before they reached what he assumed was the ground level. While he wasn't winded, he wasn't looking forward to climbing those stairs to get back to his room. Then it dawned on him that he might never see that comfortable room again. That was a thought best pushed aside, which is exactly what he did.

Pishara led Gabriel and his guards through corridor after corridor, some wide, some slender, some lined with paintings and tapestries, some lined with windows that looked out over the rest of the palace. Finally, they arrived before two enormous bronze-clad doors that rose some thirty feet above the floor. On either side of the doors stood four guards with spears. They looked much like the men outside his tower cell. They stared straight ahead with a look that implied instant death for anyone who was not supposed to enter.

The redheaded guard to Gabriel's right extended his hand and the huge doors swung slowly open. As the doors glided inward, Gabriel felt gently with his magic-sense and realized that the redheaded guard was a Wind Mage. A Malignancy Wind Mage. That explained the dagger on his belt. Probably his talisman, Gabriel thought. The red circle on his jacket must mark him as a Wind Mage. The red flame embroidered on the other guard's jacket probably meant he was a Fire Mage. These were good things to know. Things he might be able to use later. At least he would know what a mage was without having to probe them with his magic-sense.

As the doors continued to swing open, Pishara led the way into a room so large that Gabriel had trouble believing his eyes. Gigantic stone pilasters set into the granite walls and a long row of free-standing columns supported a vaulted ceiling some one hundred fifty feet above. Between the pilasters stood thin windows that rose from twenty feet above the floor nearly all the way to the roof. Ornamentation of gold and silver decorated the stone of the walls and the support columns. Chandeliers hung from the ceiling, each with a thousand candles burning, casting a warm glow to the room. The stone floor was a continuous mosaic of different-colored granite stones, making a pattern of seven swords crossing at the hilt.

Statues lined the walls of the room, although Gabriel could not figure out what they were supposed to represent. Each was more grotesque than the last and it took him a moment to realize that they depicted humans in various states of agony. He let his eyes slide away from the statues and settle on the center of the room. At the far end of the chamber, some two hundred feet from the door, was a raised dais with an enormous chair of what seemed to be polished white marble. In the throne chair sat Kumaradevi. Hundreds of men and women dressed in black wool jackets lined the audience chamber, each with one knee touching the floor, their heads bowed.

Kumaradevi looked resplendent in a long, flowing gown of crimson silk with black trim. She seemed relaxed and radiant, her left hand hanging languidly over the arm of the throne, her eyes shining with a brightness that amplified the elegant features of her face. A necklace of seven concatenate crystals strung together with a fine web of gold rested on her collarbone. Gabriel guessed that each of those seven crystals linked to a separate chain of six more crystals. The necklace represented forty-nine crystals — an unbelievable store of tainted and malignant magical power. She looked smug and satisfied, but something about her spoke of hunger to Gabriel. A hunger for something he was supposed to provide.

As they reached the base of the throne, Pishara and the two guards quickly knelt and bowed their heads. Now that he was closer to it, Gabriel realized why the throne looked so much like ivory from a distance. Kumaradevi sat upon a throne made of human skulls and bones, cut and fitted together like some intricate jigsaw puzzle, polished to a pearly white sheen.

"You must kneel," Pishara whispered from beside him

Gabriel looked at the throne and Kumaradevi seated upon it, staring down at him with a wicked smile, and made a decision: he would not kneel.

As he stood there the smile faded from Kumaradevi's face, and her eyes changed from wide and joyous to narrow and angry.

"Why do you not kneel before your Empress?" Kumaradevi said, the anger of her face flickering away to be replaced with a charming gaze.

He knew it was the wrong thing to say, but for some reason he couldn't help himself, and even as he spoke the words, he knew he would regret them.

"Because I am the Seventh True Mage, and you are not."

The pain seared into his head like a white-hot blade driven into his skull. He tried to cry out, but the sound caught in his throat. He tried to bring his hands to his head, but they would not move. His arms were as frozen as his voice. He knew through the blinding pain that there was only one movement his body could make. Only one action that would stop the pain. Tears filled in his eyes, and he felt them running down his face, but it didn't matter. The pain became so intense that he could no longer see the throne room or Kumaradevi or anything else. He knew what would stop the pain. Knew what would make it cease immediately. But he didn't do it. He wouldn't do it. He could feel the pain beginning to peak, and he knew he would pass out in a matter of moments.

"You are a very stubborn little boy." He heard the words in his mind, echoing like a foghorn in a giant cave. *"You seem to think you still have a choice in obeying me. Let me show you how many choices you have."*

Gabriel felt a pressure through the pain. A pressure on his shoulders, pushing him down. He struggled against it, but his legs were no longer his own. His right leg bent and his left even more so as the pressure on his shoulders pushed him to the ground. Kneeling on one leg, the pressure continued to press at him, forcing him to bow his head in imitation of the hundreds of others behind him.

"That is better," Kumaradevi said. "We would not want people to think you were ungrateful for your rescue."

The pain vanished as quickly as it had come, but Gabriel still could not move, even to raise his head. The same invisible force that had pushed him to his knee still held him in place. Seething at Kumaradevi's words as much as her actions, he found he could speak.

"I am most grateful for my rescue," Gabriel said, staring at the granite mosaic at his feet and knowing he was again about to say something he would probably regret. "One day, I will be sure to reward you for it so you will know my gratitude."

Gabriel felt his head pulled back by the invisible force until he stared at Kumaradevi's face. It was a beautiful face, he thought. The only pleasant thing about her. He noticed that those beside him looked up at her. Kumaradevi ignored his words as she spoke.

"It is with great pleasure I present to you the Seventh True Mage, Gabriel Salvador," Kumaradevi said, her voice ringing unnaturally loud through the cavernous audience chamber. "The forces of darkness have been allied against us for centuries, but now, with the power of the Seventh True Mage at our side, we shall once again reach forth from our sanctuary of light and claim that which has been denied us for so long. Soon, once his training is complete, we shall free ourselves from the shackles that the so-called Council of the Continuum has placed upon us, and we shall destroy the usurper and his mindless minions, and we will take our rightful place as the ruler, the Empress of All Time." The assembly behind him raised their voices in a cheer. Gabriel stayed silent. He wondered what sort of world considered the Council a force of darkness and Kumaradevi the embodiment of light.

"You have all served the Empire with great skill and devotion," Kumaradevi said, "and when we have taken the Continuum, you will have your reward of the spoils. There will be hundreds of worlds like this one created, and those of you who please the Empire will have your kingdoms there." Another cheer arose from the assembly of mages, and Gabriel felt his stomach turn to ice. Hundreds of worlds like this? And she planned to use him to accomplish it? And if he resisted? He brought his mind back to the present as Kumaradevi spoke again.

"When our champion, the Seventh True Mage, the Destroyer of Worlds, the Breaker of Time, has brought us our victory, all those who have opposed us shall suffer for their crimes. Just as others, who once opposed us, suffer now." As she spoke, Kumaradevi raised her eyes toward the ceiling of the chamber. Gabriel followed her gaze upward. A gasp of shock escaped his lungs. He had not noticed it when he entered the chamber, his eyes distracted by too many things, but near the chandeliers hovered a woman encased in a sphere of flickering yellow and red electric bolts of light. She looked frozen, as though suspended in motion. Suspended in the act of screaming. Suspended in agony.

Nefferati.

Gabriel's mind reeled. He had wondered what might have happened to the real Nefferati. She had been captured to become a display piece for Kumaradevi's palace. A reminder to all who came to seek audience with her of what became of her enemies. At least she was still alive, Gabriel thought. He doubted that Kumaradevi would have killed Nefferati when she could keep the Grace Mage alive in anguish. As Gabriel brought his gaze back down to meet Kumaradevi's eyes, something she had said gave him almost as much discomfort as having seen Nefferati dangling in the air above. She had called him the Destroyer of Worlds. The Breaker of Time.

That could not be good.

"Our day is upon us," Kumaradevi said. "Our victory is at hand. Now we prepare for the Great Battle." She rose from the throne and glided down the steps to the floor of the audience chamber. The cheers continued, but no one rose to their feet as she passed.

Everyone stayed kneeling. Gabriel found himself dragged to his feet by the invisible force of Kumaradevi's magic after she had walked past him. He heard her voice in his mind. *"Follow me."* He felt an invisible hand push him forward, and he followed her down the long black carpet, through the audience chamber. Glancing behind, he saw that Pishara and his guards followed.

As Kumaradevi exited the audience chamber, several servants in long gray robes stepped behind her. A man carrying a small stack of books joined a woman holding a tray with goblets of wine, followed by a thin man holding a tray of cheeses, breads, and fruits. Beside him walked another woman carrying a small table with paper and pen. Behind all of them all walked a woman holding a bowl of water and a small towel. Apparently, Kumaradevi believed in having her needs met at any moment wherever she went. And she liked supplication wherever she went as well. No matter who they passed, each and every person dropped to one knee and bowed their head.

She led the procession through the main corridor and down another, up three flights of stairs, and through a wide courtyard filled with small gnarled trees and tall statues similar to the ones he had seen before, looking like half-human creatures twisted in pain. Past the courtyard, they came upon a wide stone terrace with a marble railing carved to resemble a snake writhing atop a string of sword tips. The terrace held a raised platform and a throne chair similar to the one in the audience chamber. Carved from a solid piece of granite, this one resembled a mass of human bodies bent beneath a great weight. Gabriel ignored the throne as he stepped up beside Kumaradevi at the railing.

"Behold the Palace of Light," Kumaradevi said, spreading her arms wide to indicate the size and opulence of the palace grounds. The balcony offered a good view of the rest of the palace. Gabriel could see hundreds of buildings, dozens of courtyards and gardens, and the pyramid temple he had glimpsed earlier from his room. He could also see a building that looked like a coliseum and a smaller arena directly below the terrace that looked like it was used for fighting. As he saw what filled the arena, he could not help but jump back from the railing in surprise. Kumaradevi laughed and pushed him forward again.

"Is...is that..." Gabriel stuttered. "Is that a dragon?"

"What does it look like?" Kumaradevi said.

"It looks like a dragon," Gabriel said.

"Then I suppose it is," Kumaradevi said.

"How is that possible?" Gabriel asked as he stared at the dragon. It must have been nearly a hundred and twenty feet long and thirty feet tall at the shoulders with a neck that stretched well beyond that. Its leathery wings clung tight to its blue and green-scaled body, held close like a cloak wrapped against a chill. It swung its head around, and Gabriel could see that its eyes were glazed and milky. The way it moved made him realize that it was blind. He looked more closely at the dragon's scales and the way it shuffled slowly, dragging tree-thick chains connected to huge metal shackles around its legs. Gabriel suspected that the dragon was very old.

"It is possible," Kumaradevi said, "because I made it possible. I see your magical education has been limited to say the least. I will teach you, in due time, how to create dragons if you wish. It is not all that hard. Once you find the proper beasts to alter and blend together. They are marvelous creatures, if fashioned properly. Difficult to keep fed, but wonderful to watch in battle."

Gabriel tore his eyes away from the dragon and noticed for the first time that people stood in the sunken stone arena. Three people tied to large wooden stakes with kindling wood piled to their chests. Gags filled their mouths, but their eyes were not covered. The woman bound between the two men could not look at the dragon, keeping her head turned completely to the side. In contrast, the men on either side of her could not take their eyes off the beast, their heads weaving back and forth with every movement of the dragon's long neck, large mouth, and man-sized teeth. The three looked thin and bruised. It seemed they had been starved and beaten for weeks.

Gabriel found his stomach suddenly queasy and his legs weak. He did not have to be told what was coming next. He looked away from the scene below as Kumaradevi's voice drew his attention.

"Your insolence today was unacceptable," Kumaradevi said with a hard look in her eye, "but I blame myself. It was not properly explained to you how to behave in my royal presence. You were uninformed. So, I will inform you now of how you must behave. And to drive the lesson home, I will show you what happens to those who displease me." She gave Gabriel a sparkling smile. She might have been offering to make him cookies from the way her lips curled. "You will always kneel upon greeting my royal presence, in the audience chamber or anywhere else. You will speak only when given leave to do so, and you will stand only when I request it of you. As you are to be my apprentice, when we are not in formal situations, you need not be so formal. However, you will request permission to approach me and to speak to me. When you address me, it will always be as Empress, or Your Royal Highness, or Your Grace. Is that clear?"

"Yes," Gabriel said. "Your Grace." He tried to keep his face neutral, but it was a struggle. He had never really felt hatred for anyone before, but he was beginning to feel something hot and unpleasant burn in his heart for Kumaradevi.

"Now then," Kumaradevi continued, "violation of these very simple principles will be punished. Severely. Below us, you can see three people who have displeased me. I want you to watch what happens to them."

"May I ask a question, Your Grace?" Gabriel said. He wanted to proceed cautiously.

"You may," Kumaradevi replied, tilting her head with curiosity.

"What did they do to displease Your Grace?" Gabriel asked.

Kumaradevi's eyes narrowed, but she replied. "That man on the end, he disobeyed a direct war command to slaughter a village. He seemed to think that sparing the village was the noble thing to do. When I want nobility, I will order it. The woman was caught trying to poison my food. While we are True Mages, even we can fall prey to poison if it is the right kind. I forced her to eat poison herself for the past month. A slow poison. Very painful. But she seems likely to die soon, and I know for a fact that she fears dragons more than anything else. Her family was killed by dragons when she was a child.

177

She still has the burns along her back from her escape. She'll soon have burns on the front to match.

"The other man was a great disappointment to me. I had charged him personally with increasing the imprints of a certain sword, and he used that blade to defend a woman and her child from his own men. It completely warped the imprints of light and contaminated them with darkness." Gabriel knew that by darkness she meant positive imprints of Grace. The men were being killed for showing compassion, and the woman for trying to put an end to the horror of Kumaradevi's world.

"Empress," Gabriel began, "would it not be more fitting to suspend these traitors in time the way you have Nefferati?" They might remain trapped in a moment of agony for years, but they would be alive when Kumaradevi was defeated. And he already nurtured a strong seed of determination to see Kumaradevi defeated.

"How did you know Nefferati was held in time stasis?" Kumaradevi asked.

"I could sense it," Gabriel said. "Your Grace." He was trying desperately to remember to add that sickening phrase whenever he spoke.

"Really?" Kumaradevi said. "I'm surprised, given the paucity of your education to date. But to answer your question, if I imprisoned every slave, soldier, and servant who displeased and betrayed me in a time-stasis bubble, I would have the entire palace lit up like a bonfire."

"May I ask, Your Grace, why you have imprisoned Nefferati rather than killing her?" Gabriel said. Maybe he could postpone the execution long enough for him to think of a reason for Kumaradevi not to kill the people tied to the stakes below.

"I imprisoned her because she does not deserve death," Kumaradevi said.

"What did she do to displease Your Grace?" Gabriel asked.

"She killed my son, for one," Kumaradevi said, her voice suddenly filled with bitterness. Gabriel had not expected this, and he could see the anger rising in her eyes as she thought of it.

"I am sorry to hear that, Your Grace," Gabriel said. "You must have loved your son very much to be so wrathful." He could barely imagine Kumaradevi loving anyone, but he supposed that she could be as possessive about people as she was about things. Kumaradevi opened her mouth as though to respond to Gabriel's sentiments, but closed it instead. "May I ask where we are in time, Your Grace?" Gabriel said quickly, hoping to change the subject.

"We are in a world of my creating," Kumaradevi said. "In a branch of time I have made and altered to suit my purposes. It is hidden by magic more powerful than you can imagine, so you need not bother wondering if your friends on the Council will find you. And you need not worry your head with fancies of escape because there are only a handful artifacts still remaining in this world that also exist in the Primary Continuum. As your precious Ohin may have told you, one can only jump between the Primary Continuum and an alternate branch of reality with artifacts that exist in both. So, unless you happen upon a fossil of great age, you will be going where I tell you and when. Now, we will cease this pointless distraction and proceed with the act you so obviously dread."

Raising her hand, lightning leapt forth from Kumaradevi's palm and crackled through the air, striking the dragon in the center of its scaled brow. The dragon roared with pain, its bellow echoing throughout the palace grounds as it belched a stream of coral-colored fire across the arena, engulfing the prisoners in flame. Gabriel looked away, but Kumaradevi grabbed his jaw in her slender hand and forced him to face the arena. He closed his eyes, but the screams of the prisoners were as bad as what he had seen.

"Open your eyes and look," Kumaradevi growled. "Look and see what disobedience will bring. While I will not burn you at a stake, I will make branches and branches of time to bring versions of your loved ones here, your mother and father and sister, and I will roast as many of them as it takes to ensure your obedience. Now open your eyes, or you will be dining on the charred carcasses of those three traitors for a month. And do not doubt that I can make you chew and swallow."

Gabriel opened his eyes, and he looked, and he listened, and he let the flame of hatred in his heart fill him to burn as brightly as the dragon flames sweeping the arena below, consuming everything in their path, just as he hoped his anger would one day consume Kumaradevi. As he glanced aside, he saw Pishara give him a quick look of sympathy that swiftly faded behind a mask of indifference.

CHAPTER 18
BATTLES AND HONORS

Hours later, Gabriel still seethed in silence, following Kumaradevi through the palace from one errand to another. She was a tyrannical ruler, to be sure, but not indolent about it. She personally attended to many of the details that could easily have been delegated to a lesser functionary. It was hours before Gabriel realized why the Empress was so involved in the minutia of running her kingdom: She did not trust anyone else to make the decisions that needed to be made. Whether that was because she had no room for trust in her heart, or because the people who ran her Empire were untrustworthy, Gabriel was not sure. Either way, it was a weakness he could exploit, given time. And it looked as though he would have plenty of time. He could think of no way to jump away from this world of horrors. He was trapped in a bizarre circus where everything was reversed, the clowns bringing tears instead of mirth, the audience suffering instead of laughing.

Finally, when it seemed there were no more documents to sign, no more servants to upbraid, no more soldiers to punish with lashes of a whip, no more engineers to chastise for failure to complete construction of buildings on time, Kumaradevi made an announcement.

"I am hungry," she said, her voice imperious as ever. "How would you like to see a dragon in battle?"

It took Gabriel a moment to realize that she spoke to him and another second to stop himself from saying what he really wanted to say and frame what he hoped was the proper response. "If it would please you, Your Grace."

"Then we shall see how my nations fare in the War of the Colors," Kumaradevi said as the familiar blackness wrapped around her, Gabriel, and all of the attendants. When the whiteness bled away,

181

Gabriel found himself standing on a hilltop overlooking a wide-open plain between a mountain range and a forest. In the valley below battled two armies, one with deep red banners, red armor, and red shields battling another army similarly colored in dark green.

Gabriel could hear the cries of the men even from where they stood on the hilltop nearly a mile away. In the sky above, he could see four dragons clashing in combat, a man strapped to the back of each. The colors of the dragons, like the men, matched the army they defended — two crimson and two green. The beasts snapped at each other as they flew past, diving to strafe the troops of the opposing side with jets of molten hot flame. Even in his darkest dreams, Gabriel had never imagined such a scene of devastation and horror was possible.

Disgusted, he looked away to see Kumaradevi walking toward a large tent, open on all four sides. A meal of various meats and vegetables lay on a long wooden table beneath the canvas canopy. He walked away from the edge of the hillside and joined Kumaradevi at the table. Two men joined them, one clothed in blood red armor and the other in deepest emerald green. Everyone waited until Kumaradevi had been helped into her seat by her attendants before taking their places at the table. Gabriel sat beside Kumaradevi.

The servants quickly filled Kumaradevi's plate. No one made a move to touch the food on the table. Gabriel kept his hands in his lap. He knew instinctively that his survival, if not the survival of everyone he cared about, would depend upon him watching and learning quickly. Kumaradevi ate in silence, smiling at those around the table as they averted their eyes. Finally, when her plates had been removed, the servants stepped forward to serve the meal, placing sliced roast beef and potatoes upon Gabriel's plate, along with some green things that he hoped were vegetables.

As those around the table ate, Kumaradevi allowed the two generals to boast of their strategy and what each assured her would be the imminent success of their respective army. "I certainly hope one of you is successful soon," she said with what might have been a laugh. "I grow weary of this stalemate, and I am sorely tempted to bring the Indigo Army into the fray and force a conclusion."

Both generals protested that such an action, while surely her prerogative, was wholly unnecessary. Each man vowed to bring the other to heel before her next visit. She said nothing, but graced them each with a smile. Gabriel couldn't smile. He knew these armies were slaughtering each other so Kumaradevi could link more concatenate crystals to the battlefields and weapons and increase her power.

She smiled at the generals once more and then, without warning, she suddenly swept her arms wide and a swift billow of blackness engulfed the table. A burst of white followed and Gabriel, Pishara, and the attendants stood in what Gabriel assumed were Kumaradevi's personal suites. A series of large rooms, one set for dining, another for sitting, another that seemed to be a library, a fourth that had a large desk in the middle of it, and another with a massive mahogany bed seemingly carved from a single piece of wood.

Kumaradevi swept down the hallway connecting the various rooms and stepped into the writing room. Three men and three women waited for her there, standing at attention. Gabriel got the impression they had been standing in the room for a considerably long time. As he followed Kumaradevi into the room, he noticed the insignias emblazoned on the breasts of the six people standing there. Each one was different. The flame for Fire Magic, a solid red circle for Wind Magic, a tree growing out of a heart for Heart-Tree Magic, an open circle with three wavy lines inside for Earth Magic, a red eye with the center left black, to represent the pupil, for what Gabriel guessed was Soul Magic, and an infinity symbol for Time Magic. He knew who these people were, but Kumaradevi confirmed it as she turned and spoke to him.

"These are your new tutors," Kumaradevi said, raising her hand to indicate the six black-clad mages. "They will be instructing you in the various magics and how to use them. When you have exhausted their knowledge, I will find more knowledgeable instructors to train you." She pointed to a tall man with the Time Magic symbol who might have been Indian or Pakistani. "This is Malik," Kumaradevi said. "He will teach you Time Magic." She continued around the room. The petite Thai woman, Malee, would teach him Fire Magic.

Heinz, the broad shouldered German, Earth Magic. Wind Magic would be taught by the sharp faced Korean woman, Jin. Heart-Tree Magic, by the bone-thin African woman, Malawi. Finally Bob, the slightly overweight American, would teach him Soul Magic. It was like his team from the castle seen through a funhouse mirror. While none of them met Kumaradevi's gaze, they each stared at him. It gave him an unpleasant feeling in his gut.

"You will begin your training tomorrow in the arena," Kumaradevi said. "It should be clean by then. You will afford each of your instructors the same courtesy you extend me. If they are unhappy with your performance, I will be unhappy with your performance, and I trust I have made it clear that my happiness is your paramount concern. Tonight you will join me for a state dinner in your honor. Now, go and change into something more befitting the occasion." With a wave of her hand she dismissed him. Gabriel did not wait for a second dismissal.

"Thank you, Empress," Gabriel said as he bowed from the waist. He spun smartly on his heel and followed Pishara out the door, trailed in turn by his two bodyguards, Viktor and Seamus. The door closed behind them, though no hand touched it. As he followed Pishara down the hallway and out into the corridor beyond Kumaradevi's apartments, he tried, as he had all day, to make a mental map of the palace. It would be important to know where things were and how to get to them if he was ever to have any hope of escaping.

Following Pishara, he realized it would be knowledge long in coming. He was already lost, confused by the constant twists and turns of the corridors and the stairs that led up only to lead down again. The palace seemed designed to frustrate easy navigation. Gabriel did not have to wonder whether this was accidental.

When they finally came to the spiral staircase that he knew would lead them to his tower prison, he was almost relieved. At least he had a sense of where he was. The climb up the stairs took much longer than the walk down had earlier that day. By the time they reached the top, Gabriel was well winded, although neither Pishara nor his two bodyguards seemed to be breathing heavily. The two guards still stood on either side of the door to his room. The door to the room was open, but Gabriel could see three large steel bars in brackets bolted to the wall. Each one could slide over to block the door closed. His only hope to escape from the room would have to be through the windows. He wondered how long it would take him to learn to fly and how long it would take to steal an artifact strong enough to manage it.

As he entered the room, he saw that the large copper tub in the corner had been filled with water. Apparently, someone had drawn him a bath. He couldn't imagine anyone bringing water up those long stairs in buckets, so there must be pipes of some sort in the palace tower. He made a mental note to try to find out where they were. Every little bit of knowledge about the palace could prove useful for an escape.

"You will bathe," Pishara said. "You will find a long coat in the armoire. I will return for you in one hour to escort you to dinner." She bowed slightly before pulling the door closed as she left. He could hear the three steel bars swinging into place.

Gabriel collapsed into one of the leather chairs, exhausted. Not from the climb or the day's events, but from the emotional impact of all that he had seen and heard. He was a prisoner in an alternate world so vile and disgusting that it was hard to comprehend the magnitude of the suffering taking place every moment throughout the land, solely for the purpose of tainting more artifacts and places with negative imprints so that Kumaradevi could amass more power.

Frustrated with himself for letting despair grip him so tightly, Gabriel got up and began to check the room again. Maybe there was something he had missed. Something he could eventually use to escape. There was a small closet hidden behind a tapestry he had missed earlier. It turned out to be a privy. Unfortunately, the stone chute that carried the waste straight down was too small to possibly fit in. He sighed as he realized he had been momentarily excited by the idea of escaping through the sewers.

He took the opportunity to relieve the pressure in his bladder and then continued to examine the room. There was little more he had not noticed that morning. He discovered another small closet hidden behind a tapestry. It was a simple wash room with a small sink and a copper pipe that descended along the wall from the ceiling. At least he knew where the water came from. And if it came from the ceiling, then maybe the top of the tower held a water cistern that could be ruptured to create a diversion at some point. Everything was a potential component of an escape plan.

He examined the windows again, just because it made him feel he was being thorough, but they had no hinges, and he doubted they could be opened without breaking them, which would surely bring the guards. If he could secretly get his hands on an artifact, he could overpower the guards, but where to get an artifact that would not be missed? Maybe he could steal one from one of his tutors. He sighed. Any artifact that went missing in the palace would immediately draw suspicion to him. Realizing there was nothing else he could do, he stripped off his clothes and slid into the tub.

The water was still very warm and must have been near scalding when first poured into the copper basin. He could see a drain at the front of the tub, but did not see how the water could have been heated. Then he remembered where he was. A palace filled with mages. A bar of honey-scented soap sat on the lip of the tub, and he scrubbed himself as he mulled over the twin thoughts that consumed him: where to find an artifact, and how to escape. As he rinsed off, he remembered something that Ohin had said back at the castle. Just thinking of him and the rest of the team, how much he had grown accustomed to them, how much he had come to care for them, nearly drove the idea that had blossomed in his mind straight out of it.

Clenching his teeth and wiping what might have been soap from his eyes, he tried to remember exactly what he had been told. An artifact could gain imprints by close proximity or use by a person taking actions that were either negative, like killing someone, or positive, like saving someone's life. However, an artifact could also be intentionally imbued with imprints by concentrating one's mind and will upon it. This was essentially how prayer beads became imbued with positive imprints, priests and monks praying and meditating over the beads. If he could find some innocuous object, one that no one would suspect if he carried it with him, he could intentionally imbue it with enough imprints to use as a talisman. Of course it could take years, but a least it was a plan. He would have to be cautious, however.

While a Malignancy Mage could tell that an artifact had been imprinted from a short distance, they would have to touch it to know that it was imbued with positive imprints. It would need to be something common, but something he could keep in the open. He was almost certain his room would be regularly searched while he was away from it. However, if he found the right object, he might be able to leave it in the room while he was gone. As long as the room was not searched by a Malignancy Mage, or as long as that mage didn't touch every object, he might get away with it. But what object?

And if he could get out of the castle, how could he get back to the Primary Continuum? Kumaradevi had said that only a few artifacts still existed in both worlds. He would need to find out what and where at least one of them was and when he could get access to it. And then another thought occurred to him, one that made him place his hands on his head in despair. He couldn't just leave the palace alone. If he did find a way to escape, he would have to find a way to release Nefferati, as well. If he was found missing, Kumaradevi might kill Nefferati to ensure that a rescue party from the Council could not free her. His escape could be a long time in coming. Unless he could think of something brilliant.

A knock on the door brought him back from his reveries.

"Are you ready?" he heard Pishara say from the other side of the door.

"Almost," Gabriel called out, grabbing a nearby towel and wrapping it around himself as he ran to the dresser.

"Would you like some help dressing?" Pishara said as he heard the steel bars outside the door sliding open.

"No," he said, hastily drying himself with one hand has he pulled clothes from the dresser. He managed to get his pants on before Pishara entered.

"You are tardy," Pishara said. "We will need to walk quickly to arrive at the dinner on time. It is unwise to make the Empress wait."

"Right," Gabriel said pulling on a boot. "Sorry. I dozed off in the tub."

"You must gain more stamina," Pishara said. "You will need it in the coming days."

Pishara led Gabriel through the labyrinthine corridors of the castle to the great dining hall. An impossibly long table filled the center of the opulently decorated room. The guests for dinner were already present. Nearly a hundred men and women in black lined the table, each wearing the red insignias that denoted their status and rank as mages in Kumaradevi's forces. Along the center of the table sat a wide variety of foods on large silver trays. A roasted boar, a large apple in its tusked mouth, roasted ducks, various vegetables, stacks of breads and cheeses, bowls of fruit, and bottles of wine. The food seemed to go on and on. An attendant showed Gabriel to his place just as Kumaradevi arrived. He waited until Kumaradevi had been seated by her attendants before taking the one remaining seat to her left.

As at the lunch earlier that day, Kumaradevi ate first and alone. The table remained silent as her attendants sliced a piece of boar for her and cut it into small pieces. She poked at them causally with her fork, delicately placing them in her mouth and chewing with a wide smile for Gabriel. She seemed immensely pleased. That was good, Gabriel thought. *The happier she is, the less she is likely to notice me.*

When she had finished eating, Kumaradevi spoke. "This meal is to consecrate a covenant between our royal person and the person of the Seventh True Mage, who is very lucky we have rescued him from his servitude at the hands of the Dark Mages of the Council of Night. Gabriel will be our servant, our first among servants, our right hand in the battle to end all battles, our sword, our shield, and our champion. With this food, we all enter into this covenant. You shall serve him, he shall serve me, and I shall serve the greater calling. Now, eat your fill, and remember that each bite symbolizes the contract that binds us together. Each sip of wine a symbol of your commitment. Your flesh is my flesh. My will is your desire. My victory shall be your victory."

She raised her glass and all those at the table raised theirs in response. Gabriel held his high. The men and women along the table smiled back as deeply as Kumaradevi smiled at them, but Gabriel could see a few glance at him with looks in their eyes that were anything but signs of servitude or pleasure. Kumaradevi took a long swallow of wine and placed the goblet on the table.

"Let the feast begin," she said in a melodious voice that echoed throughout the dining hall.

Gabriel looked down as a servant placed a slice of roasted boar on his plate. He thought of Kumaradevi's words and all he had seen since she had brought him to her world. He had never felt less like eating.

CHAPTER 19
LESSONS IN ~~LIGHT~~ DARKNESS

That night, after the endless dinner finally concluded and Pishara escorted him back to his rooms, Gabriel lay in bed thinking about how he could find an artifact to imbue with positive imprints. He needed to think of something that would take his mind off the horrors he had seen throughout the day. And the longer he could think about the artifact, the longer he could postpone sleep, because he knew what sort of nightmares waited for him when he closed his eyes.

Artifacts.

He considered the amulet at his neck, but it was already an enchanted artifact forged by a Malignancy Mage. Trying to imbue it would be unwise. Besides, he would need something that he could hide in plain sight in his chamber. It would need to be something he could be seen to hold, in case someone entered the room unexpectedly. And it would be best if they saw what they expected to see.

Why hadn't he thought of that? He looked around the room to see if there was something there he might use. A small pewter candleholder sat next to his bed. He could even reach his hand out to touch it with his head on the pillow. If someone came in, it would look like he had fallen asleep with his arm over the bed. He reached his hand out and placed his fingers on the base of the candleholder. It felt cool to the touch. It had a dish-like base to catch the fallen wax and a looped handle to make it easier to carry. He slid his index finger through the handle loop.

He had his artifact. Now, how to imbue it? He had received no instructions on imbuing artifacts. Like all other aspects of his magical education, this area lagged. Ling, or was it Teresa…He smiled inwardly thinking about them…One of them had said you needed to use your conscious will to intentionally imbue an artifact.

He closed his eyes and tried to calm his mind with the meditative techniques his mother and then Ohin had taught him. It took a while, the images of the day's events fighting to displace his focus on his breath.

Many minutes later, with his mind stilled, he felt within himself for his subtle energy and as he grasped it, he filled his mind with thoughts of love and compassion, willing this mix of mind and energy to enter the candleholder. For nearly twenty minutes, he concentrated his mind on the energy within himself, focusing it and guiding it into the candleholder. Finally, he had to stop. He was dozing off. And to be honest, he wasn't even sure if what he was doing was working. He tried to use his magic-sense to determine if the candleholder had acquired any imprints, but if they were present, he felt too exhausted to sense them. He blew out the candle and rolled over. He fell asleep within moments, dreaming nightmares of nightmares within the nightmare he was living.

He woke to a knock on the door.

Pishara entered the room carrying a silver tray with covered plates and a small oil lamp. She placed it on the table as Gabriel sat up. The smell of bacon wafted through the air and Gabriel's stomach groaned. Darkness still clung to the windows.

"What time is it?" Gabriel asked, getting to his feet.

"Time for you to begin your day," Pishara said. "Your tutors will be waiting for you in the training arena at sunrise. You will eat now. Dress quickly. I will return shortly." Pishara bowed slightly and walked from the room, closing the door as she left. Gabriel splashed some water on his face from a basin on a table in the corner of the room. Drying his face, he sat down at the dining table and lifted the silver cover from the plate. Eggs, bacon, fresh sliced strawberries. Better than he had expected. He wolfed the food down and then changed into his now standard black clothes.

Pishara knocked and entered shortly after he had pulled his boots on. She said nothing, gesturing him to follow, so he did so in silence. She led him back down the stairs and through the corridors of the palace. Gabriel tried to guess which turn would be next, which led to the arena. He found he was right less than half the time.

He noticed that palace servants and soldiers they passed all gave them a wide berth, stepping to the sides of the halls, servants stopping and bowing their heads, soldiers staring straight ahead, and the few mages they encountered looking at him with a mixture of distain and sometimes outright hatred. Gabriel assumed it was because he was Kumaradevi's favorite pet now and that meant there would be fewer opportunities for any of them to become her pet. He would have gladly traded places with them. When Pishara delivered him to the training arena, he saw no evidence of the previous day's execution. His six tutors waited for him in the sunken, sand-covered pit.

"You will need this," Pishara said as she removed a dagger from her pocket and handed it to Gabriel. Gabriel held it in his hand. The sheath was fashioned of hardened leather and the handle of simple serrated wood for a better grip. He slid the blade out slightly, touching the blackened steel. He didn't need to be told that it held numerous negative imprints. He could sense them even before he touched it.

"Thank you," Gabriel said.

"I am told that it has slit the throats of over a hundred men, women, and children," Pishara said, her voice betraying no emotion. He wondered how she really felt about Kumaradevi and her palace and her world, but he knew better than to ask. He wasn't sure he wanted to hear the answer, even if it was the truth.

"It will be your talisman today," Pishara said. Gabriel wondered how much she knew about magic and why she was the one to hand him the dagger.

Pishara motioned for him to descend the stone steps that curved along the arena wall and to the floor below, but she did not follow him. As he walked down the steps, he noticed another mage standing along the top of the arena walls. His insignia identified him as a Time Mage. Gabriel probed the dagger and was surprised to find that it was not nearly as powerful as his pocket watch. Great. His first lesson and already he was being hobbled. As Gabriel stepped into the arena floor, Malik strode forward.

"You are the Empress's new pet," Malik said, "so we will train you like one." Gabriel almost laughed at the mention of the word 'pet,' but he knew that would be the wrong way to start the day. No sense giving them the idea that the pet might be mocking them. "Do you know how to use that?" Malik said as he looked at the dagger in Gabriel's hand.

"Yes," Gabriel said, he hands tightening on the dagger instinctively.

"Good," Malik said. "Then we begin." Before Gabriel could blink Malik had disappeared and Gabriel felt a boot in his back trusting him forward to the ground. Wiping the sand from his face, he looked up to see Malik grinning. "Too slow. Maybe you are not awake yet. Maybe you need something to stimulate you." Malik nodded to Malee, the Thai Fire Mage. A moment later, the ground around Gabriel exploded with bolts of lightning.

Gabriel leapt to his feet, reaching for the magic within and focusing it through the blade, the taste of its imprints on his mind like thick black oil over sweet, ripe fruit. He tried to jump through space to the top of the arena, to get a better view and assess the situation, and honestly, to get as far as possible from the Dark Mages. He flickered at the top of the arena wall and found himself back where he had been, standing in the sand. A space-time seal. If he hadn't been so distracted he would have sensed it. The ground beneath his feet welled up and erupted, throwing him through the air. He landed on his shoulder and heard a popping noise as he dropped the dagger.

"You cannot jump out of the arena," Malik said in a booming voice. Gabriel now knew why a Time Mage stood on the arena walls. "And you must never drop your talisman." The talisman flew through the air and struck Gabriel in the stomach as he sat up. He groaned as the air rushed out of him. As he scrambled to his feet, he tried to wipe the tears of pain from his eyes without letting his tormentors see. He saw Heinz laughing as he stood up. For the first time he noticed Kumaradevi seated on her viewing throne on the balcony above. He turned his eyes away from her and focused on the six mages spread out around him. His arm hung uselessly from his shoulder, the pain making it nearly impossible to keep from crying out. However, he knew that would not be a useful thing to do.

"I think his shoulder is dislocated, Malawi," Heinz said. "Maybe you should help him with that."

"Certainly," Malawi said, "Maybe you could assist me." A pain that made the pain in his shoulder seem like a gentle caress suddenly racked Gabriel's body. He felt his shoulder pop back into place, but the pain did not end. He felt his body go rigid, his breath becoming quick and short and then he did cry out. He screamed, the pain seeming to grow with the volume of his voice. Then he felt himself being lifted in the air and hung upside down.

"Enough," Malik said, and Gabriel fell six feet to the ground. He managed to tuck himself into the fall and roll to avoid injury this time. "He doesn't seem to know how to defend himself. Your previous instructors were very poor indeed."

"Seventh True Mage, my ass," Bob the fat American said.

Gabriel knew he needed to do something, anything, to fend them off for a little while. Pretending to struggle to his feet again, he reached for the magical power within and focused it through the dagger. A windstorm of sand erupted from the floor of the arena, a whirling tornado trapped in the circular stone walls. A bolt of lightning struck out for him, but he was no longer where he had been standing. He appeared behind Malawi and as he focused again, she flew through the air, smashing into Heinz. Another bolt of lightning struck near where he stood, but he already stood across the arena again, balls of fire erupting from his hands to join the vortex of sand spinning through the air. He felt Malik appear next to him, but he jumped again and again as Malik followed, swinging his fist at Gabriel's head.

Gabriel focused the next time he jumped, and Malik flew into the wall of the arena. A lightning bolt from Jin's hand burst toward him, and he caught it in his own hand, a blaze of light connecting them for a moment, then he flew backwards, falling in the sand. He jumped through space even as he fell, coming to stand behind Jin and focusing his Wind Magic to throw her through the air. Then his head split in two by the pain that suddenly tormented it, like a knife twisting deep into the frontal lobe of his brain.

"Pretty good, boy," Bob the Soul Mage said, "but not good enough." The wind storm collapsed, sand falling to the ground as the other mages got to their feet. Gabriel struggled against the pain in his head, but like the bolt of lightning that had been too strong for him, he couldn't resist it, falling to his knees. The dagger he had been given simply wasn't powerful enough. He noticed now that the bright spheres that each of the Dark Mages wore at their necks were not amulets. They all wore a concatenate crystal, each likely linked to one of Kumaradevi's battlefields. They each had access to far more magical power than he could muster. As the pain ceased, he fell backward to sit on the ground.

"Better than I thought you could do," Malik said, "but not well enough. On your feet. Let us see how you defend against simultaneous attack."

The rest of the morning was more of the same. Gabriel being attacked by several vastly more knowledgeable mages with far more powerful talismans, trying to defend himself, or simply trying to evade their attacks. Lunch was a simple meal of meat, bread, and cheese served in a plaza above the training arena. Gabriel noticed that his meal looked considerably less appetizing that that of his *tutors*.

The afternoon was reserved for one-on-one instruction. He trained with Malik, who taught him how to slow his perception of time in battle. This mostly involved Malik entertaining himself by whacking Gabriel with a wooded staff while jumping from position to position around him. During the one-on-one sessions, Gabriel was forbidden from using any magic other than the one he was being taught. He was only allowed to use multiple magics when facing multiple opponents. Although he was tempted to violate this stricture, he refrained from doing so out of fear that the punishment for infraction might be worse than the training itself.

By dinner, he was more bruised and exhausted than he had ever been in his life. Most annoying, the dagger was taken from him each time he left the arena, so there was no chance for using his powers to heal himself, much less escape. Dinner that night was served in the main dining hall, where all evening meals were held. Although Gabriel sat at Kumaradevi's side as usual, she did not speak to him. She carried on conversations with others at the table, but he was invisible to her. No one else spoke to him, either. He ate in silence, and was happy for it. He also noticed that the attendants served him the smallest, worst portions of everything at the table. Apparently, his performance in the arena dictated the quality and quantity of the food he might receive.

That night in his chamber, he rubbed his shoulder as he concentrated on imbuing the candleholder with positive imprints. He lasted only a few minutes before collapsing in the sheets, which were noticeably less soft. He dreamt of fighting shadow-clad warriors each holding swords while he brandished a butter knife.

He woke to Pishara bringing him a bowl of cold porridge. He grimaced as he ate it, dressed, and followed her to the arena where the day unfolded very much like the day before. The day after that was similar, and the day after that and so on for week after week, the only variation being the quality of the food he earned and the artifact that he could use as a talisman. Some days it was the dagger, other days a sword, one day an axe, but they were never as powerfully imprinted as his pocket watch. If he performed well, his reward was an edible meal. If he did badly, he received some manner of indigestible gruel on his plate.

He took solace in the knowledge that after nearly six weeks, the imprints of the candleholder were nearly half as strong as the talismans he practiced with each day. He calculated that if he could manage to continue to imbue the candleholder for six months, it would be nearly powerful enough to use in an escape attempt. However, an escape looked less and less likely each day. As he had continued probing his chamber for possible flaws he could take advantage of, he had discovered that the walls, door, and windows were reinforced with magic. It would take a great deal of magical power to break out of his room. That meant attempting escape outside of his chamber and that would be very difficult as Pishara and his two guards followed him everywhere.

He lay in bed each night going over various options and possible plans. It helped buoy his spirits and keep his mind off the torments of the day. He made a strict rule with himself that he would never let the Dark Mages see him cry while he suffered at their hands. No matter what they did, he would not let them see a tear on his face.

However, alone at night in the darkness, he could not stop the tears from coming, could not hold them back. He felt helpless while in the arena, and he was just as helpless in the bed at night, but at least he could admit his fears for a few minutes. The strain of holding his fear at bay all through the day, day after day, felt like a balloon resting on the tip of a knife. Like he would burst and disintegrate at any moment. But the tears helped. They calmed him. And gave him enough clarity of mind to continue imbuing the candleholder.

The near impossibility of escape, and the steady daily abuse at the hands his instructors, left him in an almost constant state of depression. Pishara stayed with him one morning as he tried to force himself to eat the cold and hardened oatmeal she had brought him for breakfast. He had been knocked unconscious the day before, and this was his *reward*.

"You are no longer making progress," Pishara said quietly. Gabriel raised his head as he smashed the tasteless oat paste into his mouth and swallowed. It was odd enough for her to have stayed, but even more unusual for her to speak of his training. She rarely said anything that was not an explanation or an order.

"I'm doing the best I can with the talismans they give me," Gabriel said, his voice angry as he glared at her. How could she possibly understand what he faced every day in that infernal arena?

"You must try harder," Pishara said, "or they will have no respect for you. And if they do not respect you…" She let the rest of the sentence fall away. He knew what the unspoken words implied. If he could not make them respect him, the abuse would only continue and likely worsen. He needed them to see him as the Seventh True Mage instead of an apprentice-pet to be bullied and beaten.

"They each have linked concatenate crystals," Gabriel said, putting his spoon down forcefully. "If I had one of those, I could beat them." It was true, he thought. If he had one of the crystals, he could best them. But he knew better than to ask Malik for one. And in a way, he was thankful not to have one. It unsettled him enough to touch the tainted imprints of the talismans Pishara gave him. He did not want to think about the wave of revulsion that would flood him if he linked his mind through a concatenate crystal to one of Kumaradevi's battlefields.

"That is unfortunate for you," Pishara said, almost sounding like she cared. "There are whispers that you are not what you have been said to be."

"Hand me a talisman with Grace imprints, and I'll prove it," Gabriel said, his voice as bitter as the taste in his mouth. Pishara said nothing in response. She smiled slightly and bowed her head toward the door, indicating for him to follow her to his lessons. Gabriel pushed the chair away from the table, stood, and followed her out the door.

It had taken him a few days to realize it at first, but Pishara never took him to the training arena the same way twice in a row. There were dozens of ways to navigate through the palace corridors from the tower to the arena, and she choose a different one each morning and each night. But after so many weeks, Gabriel was confident he knew where he was and how to get where he wanted to be in the palace if he needed to. He knew the way to the coliseum where he attended violent games with Kumaradevi twice a week and the paths to the temple where helpless villagers were sacrificed to the Empress, who Gabriel had discovered was worshiped like a god by the people of the Kumaradevi's world. Naturally, she demanded sacrifices to bestow her *grace*.

He pushed away the thoughts of his mental map of the palace and his plans for escape as they came to the top of the arena stairs. As usual, Pishara handed him his talisman for the day. It was a sword again, but not one he had held before and he sensed something different about it at once. As she laid it in his hand, he knew immediately that this was a very unusual sword. It held imprints of both grace and malignancy. Pishara said nothing to him, only bowed her head, and walked away. As he walked down the stairs, Gabriel examined the sword. It had a leather-and-wood sheath and a leather-

198

wrapped handle. Pulling it slightly from the scabbard, he examined the double-edged blade. As he stepped into the arena, he unsheathed the blade entirely, holding the sword up in the early morning sun, watching the light play along its polished surface. He knew what sword this was.

"The boy bares his steel today," Heinz said with a laugh.

"He must mean to challenge us," Malik said. "We have apparently been too easy on him."

"Then we should show him the respect of honoring that challenge," Jin said with a wicked laugh.

Gabriel looked up and for the first time in nearly two months of captivity and cruelty, he grinned. He reached into himself for his magical power and focused it into the sword, the sword once wielded by the man he had seen executed the first day of his confinement. The sword used to defend the innocent as well as to kill. The sword that was at once tainted and imbued.

A lightning bolt from Malee struck the wall behind him, but he already stood on the other side of the arena. He risked a quick glance at the balcony above before jumping through space again to another spot by the walls. The balcony was empty, as he had hoped. Kumaradevi had given up watching his training after the third day, and he did not want her to witness what he was planning to do for fear it might arouse her suspicions of him, if not outright jealousy.

As he jumped through space yet again, fireballs and a small sandstorm erupting where he had been standing, he felt Bob the Soul Mage's assault. With the power of the sword's dual imprints, he easily rebuffed the attack. In fact, the strength of the sword surprised him. The man killed for imbuing it with positive imprints must have been working at it for nearly as long as he had been killing people to give it tainted imprints. Because of the double imprints, the sword would have been nearly useless in the hands of either a Grace of Malignancy mage, but as Gabriel had suspected, he could wield both of the sword's imprints simultaneously to focus and amplify his own magical energy.

He jumped through space yet again and felt Malik trying to impose a space-time seal. Gabriel had been shielded enough times to know what to do now that he had the power, and he found it easy to dissolve the space-time seal and jump again, this time to the exact center of the arena. For what he had in mind, it would be best to be in the middle of his opponents. The ones behind him would think they had an advantage because he could not see them, but weeks of practice had helped him hone his space-time sense to discern where someone was regardless of whether or not he could see them. And what he had in mind required his *tutors* to think they had the upper hand.

Of course, he could not do what he really wanted to do, even though the sword was clearly powerful enough to accomplish it. He needed to defeat the Dark Mages completely, to gain their respect through their own submission, but he could not defeat them so badly as to make Kumaradevi fear him. The more she feared his power and abilities, the less likely she was to leave him alive.

"You are finally learning a little," Malik said, his voice betraying his annoyance at Gabriel having deflected his magic. "I think it is time for you to have a real lesson!"

Gabriel was expecting it, hoping for it, in fact, but the power of the simultaneous attack of all six mages focusing the full strength of their concatenate crystals upon him took him by surprise nonetheless. Focusing all of his will into the sword, he held the various magics at bay. The ground beneath his feet trembled, but did not move, regardless of how much Heinz cursed and swore.

The invisible force field of gravity Jin tried to use to throw him through the air instead flowed around him like water around a stone. The space-time seal that Malik attempted to place on him crumbled. Malik tried to jump behind Gabriel, only to find himself locked in a space-time seal. Gabriel easily deflected American Bob's Soul Magic attempts to cause him pain and create hallucinations. He felt his body begin to weaken, but immediately it grew stronger as Malawi's dark Heart-Tree Magic came undone.

This all happened in a matter of seconds and a second later, the six Dark Mages went rigid, their heads snapping back as Gabriel raised the sword above his head, focusing the entirety of his will upon the multiple magics he commanded. A moment later the Dark

Mage's mouths opened in synchronous screams as some invisible pain gripped their minds.

Gabriel's lungs exploded with a yell as he struggled to control the powers he had unleashed. The air burst alive with a blaze of lightning bolts, the ground swayed and rippled like water, the six mages, still ramrod straight, rose into the air and began to spin in place as the sand of the arena swept up into a funnel cloud rising up and beyond the top of the circular walls. Then with an enormous burst of light, the six Dark Mages flew back like leaves caught in a mighty wind and struck the curved wall of the arena, falling limply to the ground, sand raining down everywhere. Everywhere except where Gabriel stood, slowly lowering the sword to his side, holding it casually in one hand.

The Dark Mages lay upon the ground barely conscious. Gabriel looked up to the single Time Mage at the top of the arena wall. The man looked panic-stricken. Gabriel realized that he could easily break any space-time seal the man might create. He could escape the arena now if he wished. The Dark Mage looking down at him seemed to have realized the same thing. He stood frozen, like a rabbit hoping to escape the notice of a nearby wolf. Gabriel looked back down at the six Dark Mages scattered on the ground around him. Some of them tried to stand up, but had little success. Gabriel opened his left hand, and the sword sheath flew to it. Slowly, he resheathed the blade.

"I think our lesson is over for today," Gabriel said, letting his anger and contempt fill his voice fully for the first time since his captivity in the palace began. "I wouldn't want to wear you out." Turning away from them, ignoring them as though they were too insignificant to be a threat, he jumped through space to the top of the stairs. Pishara and his bodyguards awaited him. They had seen everything. The guards looked wary, concerned Gabriel might continue to take his vengeance out on them. They backed away as Gabriel approached.

"Thank you," Gabriel said, softly so that the guards could neither see nor hear him as he handed Pishara the sword.

"I cannot imagine what for," Pishara said quietly as she smiled and bowed her head. "What would you like to do now that your lessons have ended early?"

"I want to have a real breakfast," Gabriel said, beginning to feel good for the first time in nearly two months as he imagined his victory meal. "Eggs, bacon, fried potatoes, and pancakes with fresh berries and lots of syrup."

"I believe that can be arranged," Pishara said. "Please follow me." She led him back into the palace. He had breakfast on a balcony overlooking a grand garden. It was the best meal he could remember having in a long, long time. It reminded him of the meals in the Waterloo Chamber back in Windsor Castle. His Windsor Castle. He offered for Pishara to join him, but she demurred, insisting that the meal was his and well earned.

"They will respect you now," she said as he ate. His guards kept a good distance from him after his display in the arena.

"As long as I have that sword," Gabriel said.

"That can be arranged," Pishara said, with her usual smile and bow. A messenger arrived shortly thereafter and handed a note to Pishara. She read it quickly and then folded it and placed it in her pocket. "Your meal is finished. The Empress wishes to see you immediately. She is headed to the audience chamber. We will meet her on the way." Gabriel felt suddenly deflated, the excitement and exhilaration of his victory evaporating like rubbing alcohol in the sun.

He wiped his lips with his napkin as he stood up, trying to hold on to the flavor of the food and the moment just passed, hoping they would not both turn sour. Silently, he followed Pishara back into the palace proper.

As they walked through the corridors of the palace, Gabriel tried to calm his breathing, his body, and his mind. He felt like some invisible demon chased him, his legs weak and unsteady, his stomach churning the recently eaten breakfast, and his breath catching in his throat, unable to make it all the way down into his lungs. Kumaradevi had certainly heard about his defeat of the six Dark Mages, his so-called *tutors*. What if she had learned about the sword he had used? What would she do? Would she punish him? Or worse yet, would he be forced to watch some version of his mother or father being punished for his actions? How would she respond to what he had done and how could he convince her that it would not happen again? He had been impetuous. He hadn't thought it through. Displaying too much power had been dangerous. But he had so wanted to give back to the Dark Mages who had tormented him for nearly two months just a little of their own vile medicine. He smiled despite his worries. He had certainly given Malik and the others a lesson they would not soon forget. And it had felt good to wield that much magical power.

Another worry crossed his mind. Had the use of the tainted imprints begun to change him? Had they begun to alter who he was and what he might do? Had the constant embrace of evil contaminated him? Had he been absorbing some of their effects? Could that happen?

It had felt very good to smash the Dark Mages against the arena walls. It had felt good to let his anger explode and lash out at those who had abused him. But would it stop there? What would happen if he began to enjoy the feeling of the power and anger as much as Kumaradevi did? Maybe that was her plan all along. Maybe she told Pishara to give him the sword with the mixed imprints. There were too many questions again and too many worries. Gabriel barely managed to get his breathing calmed before Kumaradevi strode across a wide garden courtyard.

As they approached, Gabriel sank to his knee and bowed his head in unison with Pishara and his guards. Kumaradevi barely slowed as she said, "Follow me."

"Yes, Empress," Gabriel said, rising quickly to his feet and walking behind Kumaradevi and her entourage of attendants.

"At my side," Kumaradevi said, and Gabriel quickened his pace to walk next to her. "I hear that you have taken to declaring the hours of your instruction."

Gabriel wasn't sure how to respond, so he went for the middle ground between truth and apology as he said, "Only this morning, Your Grace."

Kumaradevi favored him with a smile. Gabriel almost smiled back in response, it was so glowing. It was the first smile she had offered him since his initial day of imprisonment. "I am pleased that you have finally begun to show the potential I had hoped you possessed," she said as they walked down another corridor. "As a reward, this afternoon you will accompany me to a special audience with the eight kings of my empire. Now that you have begun to show some promise, I want to make sure that my subjects are familiar with you."

"Thank you, Empress," Gabriel said, stifling a sigh of relief. He wasn't going to be punished. He should have known. Kumaradevi always rewarded conquest.

"Tomorrow you will be given new tutors," Kumaradevi continued. "Tutors who will have two concatenate crystals rather than one. You will be granted one crystal to use for training. Your old tutors will become your servants. You must learn to be a lord, and a lord must have servants. They will see to washing your clothes and sheets from now on. Pishara will continue to bring your food, however. It might not do to trust them with your meals."

Gabriel closed his gaping mouth. Again, he should have known. He began to see the glimmers of an escape plan. If he defeated enough tutors, he might be trusted enough to be given freer reign of the palace. Freedom that could lead to escape. How many tutors and how many years might that take? He had no time to consider these thoughts. They had reached the audience chamber.

"The kings will arrive shortly," Kumaradevi said, the enormous doors seeming to open of their own volition as she waved her hand before them. "The royal person must always be seen on the throne when her subjects enter the chamber. This way they are more aware that it is *they* who come to *me*. Possibly, I shall make them crawl the length of the chamber. That always helps them remember their place. Sometimes kings begin to believe they are more than pawns."

A loud crash erupted behind them, shaking the room and sending vibrations along the floor and up Gabriel's legs. He spun on his feet to see that the enormous chamber doors had been slammed closed. He glanced at Kumaradevi and saw that she was just as surprised as he was by the closing of the doors.

"What is the meaning of this?" Kumaradevi shouted at her attendants, her face contorted with rage.

"I have come to settle the check for my stay," a voice said, ringing throughout the chamber so loudly that Gabriel threw his hands over his ears instinctively as he looked around for the source of the voice. A woman's voice. A voice he remembered.

"No!" Kumaradevi screamed, and Gabriel followed her gaze back around to the carved throne of bones at the front of the chamber. There on the throne sat Nefferati, holding a small crystal, cupped gently in her hands.

"The bill is due," Nefferati said, her voice still echoing throughout the chamber like a clap of thunder, "and I intend to pay in full."

Kumaradevi raised her hands, and Gabriel could feel the power she began to focus through the seven concatenate crystals around her neck, but before she could fully grasp that power, an enormous explosion of light filled the chamber and he flew through the air. As he landed, he rolled and came to his feet in a crouch. He had received plenty of practice recovering from explosions in the last few weeks. Kumaradevi and the others did not recover so quickly. In fact, he and Kumaradevi were the only ones to get to their feet. The others seemed unconscious. Without thinking, Gabriel scanned the unconscious forms looking for Pishara. He didn't know what would happen next, but he did not think she deserved to be trapped here in the middle of a battle.

Nefferati walked down the central aisle of the audience chamber now, and as Kumaradevi brushed disheveled hair from her face, the room erupted in bolts of lightning and fireballs. Stones fell from the ceiling and rose from the floors. The windows exploded, and shards of glass flew through the air like a mad flock of glittering birds.

Gabriel spun and ran. He heard Kumaradevi screaming behind him as he dashed down the aisle, trying to stay low and avoid the flying glass, leaping this way and that to avoid stones as they burst forth from the floor or came crashing down from above. He could hear Nefferati shouting curses, swearing in a rage of anger that had been kept boiling for years while she had been trapped in Kumaradevi's prison of warped space-time. As he ran, he noticed a man running beside him. As Gabriel looked, his heart constricted in his chest and he nearly stumbled. Apollyon.

"Come with me," Apollyon said, reaching out his arm. "To safety."

Gabriel did not hesitate, he ran for his life, ignoring the falling stones and the flying glass, running as fast as he could, away from Apollyon.

"Well, it was worth a try," Gabriel heard Apollyon say behind him. Then he flew backward through the air, his mind falling into darkness, into sleep. His last conscious thought was to wonder why Apollyon's hands seemed so gentle when they gripped him about the shoulders.

CHAPTER 20
OUT OF THE FIRE AND INTO...

The sound of birds chirping.

Insects buzzing through the air nearby.

A soft breeze caressing his face.

A gentle swaying motion that seemed to rock in time with his breath.

Gabriel was awake, but he did not want to open his eyes. Once he opened his eyes, it would begin. It would begin all over again. His captivity. This time at the hands of a man he feared as much, if not more than Kumaradevi. He had fallen from the frying pan to the fire to the jaws of the wolf. But his captivity wouldn't really begin until he opened his eyes. Until then he could pretend he was somewhere safe. Somewhere like the castle. Or his old house. He could pretend he was lying on the grass in the backyard, dozing beneath the twin hickory trees that draped their branches over the back of the house.

"Ah, good, you are awake," a man's voice said. It was a lighter voice, not the gravelly voice of Apollyon that Gabriel had expected.

Gabriel opened his eyes and saw a brown-skinned man with close-cropped gray hair and dark brown eyes setting a tray with tea down on a small wooden table. The man was not tall, barely taller than Pishara, only a little taller than Gabriel. The man smiled as he poured two cups of tea and sat in one of two wicker chairs. Gabriel looked around his surroundings. He was lying in a hammock, which explained the gentle swaying motion he had felt. The hammock hung from the support posts of a spacious wooden porch that wrapped around a large log cabin.

As he rotated his head, Gabriel saw that the cabin sat on the wide plateau of a mountain. A long valley, surrounded by deep green a forest of pine trees, spread out below the mountain range. The sky above was a vast azure blue, spotted here and there with small white clouds. He wondered where he was. Moving slowly, he eased himself around in the hammock and lowered his feet to the floor. The man with the gray hair was smiling at him again. He was handsome, but the smile wasn't like Kumaradevi's smiles had always been. This man seemed genuinely happy. But happy at some success or because of someone else's suffering? That was the question. Gabriel stood up from the hammock and walked over to the empty wicker chair.

"Sit," the man said. "Please."

Gabriel sat down, keeping his back straight and avoiding the cup of tea. He noticed that his aches and pains were gone. So too were the bruises on his arms. Someone must have healed him while he slept. He also noticed now that the serving tray held two sandwiches and a cup of blueberries. His stomach gave a grumble, but he ignored the food. He wondered how long he had been unconscious for his stomach to be so empty. He had eaten only a few minutes before accompanying Kumaradevi to the audience chamber, the thought of which brought back other thoughts as well.

"Where is Apollyon?" Gabriel said, trying to keep his voice calm.

"Nowhere near here, thankfully," the man said.

"But I saw him in the throne room," Gabriel said. "He took me."

"You saw what you were intended to see," the man said. "What others were intended to see. Especially our beautiful friend with the fondness for thrones made of her enemies' bones."

Gabriel was confused. "If Apollyon didn't capture me from Kumaradevi, who did?"

"A very good question," the man said with a wide grin. "Why do you not see if you can puzzle it out?"

Gabriel looked around the porch of the cabin again. There was no one else in sight, and he could see no signs of others being present. He thought about his captor as he looked at him. Was this the man who had rescued him from Kumaradevi? And would he now be this man's prisoner instead? The man wasn't from the Council, that was fairly certain, or Gabriel would be back at the castle. He clearly had no love for Kumaradevi and didn't seem too fond of Apollyon, either. That narrowed down the possibilities considerably.

"Vicaquirao," Gabriel said, knowing that the man who sat across from him was the one he'd named.

"Very good," Vicaquirao said. "I had heard you were quick-minded. I am glad to see it is true."

"You freed Nefferati," Gabriel said.

"I needed a distraction," Vicaquirao said. "What better way to keep Kumaradevi busy than to release her ancient nemesis?"

"What do you want with me?" Gabriel said, deciding to get to the point of this conversation as he grabbed a half sandwich and took a bite. Vicaquirao wasn't about to poison him, and he would need a full stomach and a clear head to face this particular adversary.

"What do I want?" Vicaquirao said, sounding as though he were musing about the question for the first time. "I want the same thing all the others want, Gabriel. I want to use you to accomplish my own goals. I do not just want to make you my pawn. I want to make you my knight, my bishop, and my rook, all rolled into one."

"I'm not going to be anyone's pawn," Gabriel said. "Or any other piece on the board."

"You already are," Vicaquirao said, with a hint of sadness in his voice. "The Council intends to use you to destroy Apollyon and Kumaradevi, and myself if they knew I was still around. Apollyon wants to use you to destroy The Great Barrier and help him gain control of the entire Continuum. And Kumaradevi would use you to destroy the Council and Apollyon as well. You see, no matter who holds your hand, they will all put a sword in it and point you where they want you to go."

"The Council isn't trying to make me do anything." Gabriel said. He knew it was a lie as he said it.

"They will not make you do anything," Vicaquirao said. "They will appeal to your better nature and convince you it was your idea."

"And how do you want to use me?" Gabriel said, putting the remainder of his sandwich back on the plate. He had lost his appetite.

"If I told you that, it would spoil the surprise," Vicaquirao said, suddenly smiling again. "Rest assured that no harm will come to you

209

while you are in my care. Let me simply say that while Kumaradevi sees the battle, and Apollyon sees the war, and the Council sees the end of the war, I see the war after the war, and the war after that."

"If you're not going to tell me how you plan to use me," Gabriel said, "then you can at least tell me what you really want. The Council wants to protect the Primary Continuum, Kumaradevi and Apollyon want to rule it. What do you want?"

"Two things," Vicaquirao said, "and I am hoping they are not mutually exclusive. Can you guess what the first is? How much has the Council told you about me?"

Gabriel thought about the second question and realized he knew the answer to the first. "You want revenge," Gabriel said, suspecting for the first time that he might have an inkling of Vicaquirao's plans.

"A dish best served with your enemy's head on a platter," Vicaquirao said. "Yes, I want revenge. There are few things that really upset me, but trying to kill me is one of them."

"Why did Apollyon try to kill you?" Gabriel asked, hoping he could gain some useful information that he might be able to use later to his advantage.

"Why does any boy rebel against his father?" Vicaquirao said with a rhetorical tone.

"I don't understand," Gabriel said. "You weren't his father. Apollyon was born in Macedonia in 300 BCE."

"Which is where I found him trailing behind Alexander's army hoping one day to be a soldier," Vicaquirao said. "Of course he went by the name Cyril then. I saw him for what he was immediately, but I decided not to jump ahead in his timeline and try to pluck him out at his death. He was young at the time, only 13, and I felt an affinity for him. I had been a young boy once wishing to be a soldier. I thought that if I took him from time to time and trained him I would gain his loyalty. I would enchant his memory when I put him back in the timeline, moments after I had taken him. He only knew he was a True Mage when he was with me.

"When I finally took him from the timeline at the moment of his death, he was already fully trained. Eventually, he saw me as just as great a threat to himself as the Council. Which I still take as an insult.

210

I am far more dangerous than the Council will ever be." Gabriel found himself inclined to believe Vicaquirao when he smiled as he did just then. "And so he tried to kill me. I will not bore you with the details. Suffice it to say, I found it expedient to appear to be dead for some time."

"So," Gabriel said, hoping Vicaquirao was telling him the truth and would continue to, "you want revenge against Apollyon. What else do you want?"

"To be honest," Vicaquirao said, "I would be happy to be left alone."

"What do you mean?" Gabriel asked.

"Just what I said," Vicaquirao said. "I was never interested in dominating the Primary Continuum or destroying The Great Barrier. What would be the point? I am already more powerful than most gods in any mythology. And who wants to be in charge of all that? What a nuisance. You have seen Kumaradevi, running from meeting to meeting. And the Council. I'm sure you've seen them at work. Late nights and long hours, for what? To rule? I have no interest in ruling. Quick way to put yourself in the way of someone else who wants power. No, I would just like to be left alone to sit in my little world and do as I please."

"Then why kidnap me?" Gabriel asked.

"I prefer to think of it as a rescue," Vicaquirao said, taking another sip of tea. "Allow me simply to say that I would not have brought you here if I did not think it would benefit me."

"So this is an alternate reality, this place?" Gabriel said, gesturing slightly to indicate the mountains and the forest valley.

"Not so brutal and barbaric as Kumaradevi's world," Vicaquirao said, "but just as well hidden. I have eliminated all but a handful of artifacts that might exist in this world and the Primary Continuum, but other than that, I largely leave this world to its own devices."

"You mean you don't try to milk it for malignant imprints?" Gabriel said.

"What would the need be?" Vicaquirao said. "I assure you, human beings are sufficiently cruel and evil on their own. They need

211

no encouragement from me. I stay out of the way and let the world run as it will."

"But you still link concatenate crystals to the artifacts and places that people taint with their actions," Gabriel said, his tone accusatory.

"Of course I do," Vicaquirao said. "Why let all that power go to waste?"

"Because of what they are and how they were made," Gabriel said, thinking about all the times he had been forced to touch the tainted imprints of various artifacts in order to defend himself in the arena of Kumaradevi's palace.

"I am a Dark Mage," Vicaquirao said, his tone sounding defensive for the first time. "I gain my magical power from dark imprints. That is the way of the universe. I did not make it such, and I have no control over it. Do you think I chose to be a Dark Mage? You have the luxury of choosing the imprints you use, but the rest of us, every other mage in existence, must use the imprints we are drawn to."

"You can always choose not to use magic," Gabriel said.

"True," Vicaquirao said, his smile returning. "But that is a choice open to all of us, even you. No one forced you to use dark imprints to defend yourself in that arena. You choose to use them."

"That was different," Gabriel said, his cheeks flushing. "I was being attacked."

"If you were really a man of your convictions, you would have turned the other cheek," Vicaquirao said.

"They would have killed me," Gabriel said, feeling now much like he had in that arena: beset upon from all sides.

"Do you really think Kumaradevi would have killed the Seventh True Mage?" Vicaquirao asked. "At the very most she would have held you in stasis like Nefferati. She might even have chosen to ransom you for someone else she could use more easily. No, the truth is, you have not yet realized what you are and what you mean to the balance of the Continuum. There is a reason you are able to use both dark and light imprints. Look at the history of any timeline in any reality and as long as humans are present, there is always a struggle between darkness and light, between grace and malignancy.

You are at the very center of that struggle. And that means you have more choices than anyone else. It also means that your choices are more important than anyone else's."

Gabriel was silent. It was too much to think about all at once. Vicaquirao was right. He did have a choice. He didn't have to use malignant imprints. He didn't even have to use grace imprints. He could choose not to use magic at all. But what would the result of that choice be? And if he did choose to use magic could he really avoid using tainted imprints? Could he say no to malignant imprints if using them meant the difference between people living and dying? Could he say no to using malignant imprints that had their source in the suffering of others if it meant he could use those imprints to stop someone else from being made to suffer? What if he had the chance to destroy Kumaradevi's rule, but could only do so by using artifacts with malignant imprints? Could he justify that?

It was a choice that no one on the Council would ever have to make. It was a choice that only he would ever be faced with. Could he justify the choices he had made already? Would he make the same choices again? And then he saw it. Why Vicaquirao wanted him.

"You want to control my choices," Gabriel said, blinking with the sudden clarity of the statement.

"Not control them," Vicaquirao said, smiling wider than ever, "merely influence them. They will always be your choices. But if I can have a say in how you make those choices, at least as loud a voice as the Council, then maybe the Continuum will be able to remain whole."

"What do you mean, remain whole?" Gabriel asked. "What's wrong with the Continuum?"

"They have not told you?" Vicaquirao asked. "Even Kumaradevi was afraid to speak of it."

"Who hasn't told me what?" Gabriel asked, feeling once again like everyone was keeping him in the dark about things he should have been told of from the start.

"The prophecy," Vicaquirao said. "No one has told you the prophecy, have they?"

"They told me the prophecy spoke of a Seventh True Mage who could use both positive and negative imprints," Gabriel said, trying to remember if he had been told anything else. What had Kumaradevi called him the first day?

Vicaquirao leaned back in his chair and recited:

"He shall come without warning
And leave without sign.
His coming shall mark the dawn of the endless night.
He shall walk among them, but be not of them.
He shall bestride the night and day.
Twilight shall be his world,
And all lands shall be his domain.
He shall pick of both trees
And eat of all fruits
He shall plant new seeds
And harvest new crops
He shall be the Breaker of Time
And the Destroyer of Worlds
And all things shall hang in his balance
Until he is no more and yet is again."

Gabriel was silent, the words ringing in his head like the bells of a cathedral all sounding at once. The words were not entirely clear, but one thing was. He was far more dangerous than he had imagined. More dangerous to everyone.

"You can hardly blame them for not telling you," Vicaquirao said. "I am sure they only wanted to spare you the trauma of wondering every night if you would be the undoing of the entire Continuum."

"How could I?" Gabriel asked. "I'm just a kid."

"Today you are a youth," Vicaquirao laughed, "and you are already as powerful as six mages at once. In a few years, maybe ten, maybe five, you will become the most powerful mage that has ever existed. Assuming you live that long."

"Assuming Kumaradevi or Apollyon or you don't kill me," Gabriel said, his tone defiant.

"If I wanted you dead, you would be," Vicaquirao said. "You are not seeing the full picture. All things have their place, their purpose. I know what mine is. You will need to discover what yours is. I cannot show you that. Neither can the Council. You are on your own. The most any of us can do is try to influence your final decisions. For instance, the Council would destroy Kumaradevi's world if they could find it, but would you? Would you condemn all those innocent lives to sudden nonexistence because of Kumaradevi's cruelty? How many lives will you end to save the stability of the Primary Continuum?"

Gabriel thought about the world he had created when he had saved Ling and how he had helped Akikane sever and destroy it to keep another version of himself from being created. This brought a question to his mind.

"Why didn't Kumaradevi create an alternate reality with me in it and double me the way Apollyon is doubling himself?" Gabriel asked.

"For the same reason she does not double herself," Vicaquirao said. "She trusts no one, not even a double of herself. Now stop avoiding my question."

"I will destroy only the worlds that I absolutely must," Gabriel said, making it a promise and a pledge to himself as he voiced the words.

"A good enough answer for now," Vicaquirao said, standing up and stretching. "I think tomorrow I shall show you something that will help clarify the choices you will need to make in the future. For now, feel free to wander around the grounds. Please do not be foolish enough to try and flee. I can find you wherever you go. And you cannot get far in this terrain. Dinner will be at sun down."

With that, Vicaquirao made a slight bow and walked back into the main room of the cabin. Gabriel watched him go, but lost sight of him as Vicaquirao moved deeper into the shadows of the house. Not knowing what else to do, Gabriel got up and walked down the steps of the porch. Running away would probably be futile, but at least he could take a walk and clear his head.

Gabriel strolled down the grassy slope of the hill the cabin sat on. He soon came to a path that led into the woods. As he walked, he

215

tried to consider his options. Did he have any options? He could run now, but to where? How far could he get on foot? Vicaquirao was right. The landscape was much too formidable for an escape. He was trapped here until he could think of something. He would have to start planning an escape from scratch. He would need to find a new object to begin imbuing and hope for clues from Vicaquirao that would tell him how to escape from this world and get back to the Primary Continuum. For the moment, however, he could do nothing. Which left him little to occupy his thoughts other than his conversation with Vicaquirao.

How much of what Vicaquirao had said could he trust? How much should he believe? Gabriel had the distinct feeling that Vicaquirao had not lied to him, but had phrased his arguments in such a way as to sway Gabriel's thinking closer to his own. He had admitted that he wanted to influence Gabriel's choices. Which was ironic, as Gabriel hadn't had any real choices lately, not since he had been plucked from that bus at the bottom of the river. Or was that true?

He had choices. He could have chosen to become a castle servant rather than a mage. He could have refused to go on missions. If he had, he might never have been revealed as the Seventh True Mage. And he was the only one who made the choice to save Ling. Vicaquirao was right. Gabriel had even made choices while held captive by Kumaradevi. He might not have been able to refuse training without risking the lives of his parents, but he could have failed at it instead of succeeding. He could make that choice now. He could refuse to help Vicaquirao with his plans, whatever they really were. But how would he know that he wasn't making exactly the choice Vicaquirao wanted him to? Did Vicaquirao truly want to be left alone after he had achieved his revenge? Somehow Gabriel couldn't really imagine it.

The path Gabriel had been walking along came out of the forest and deposited him back in the clearing, well down the hill from the cabin. He looked at the sky and saw the sun slipping behind the western mountains. As he walked back to the cabin, he wondered what mountains these were. It looked like Colorado. Maybe these were some alternate-reality version of the Rocky Mountains. If he knew where in the world he was, it would help him know where to go when he had imbued an object enough to jump somewhere.

Even before he entered the cabin, his mouth started to water from the smell of the food. Stepping through the door, the smell of garlic, onions, and a tangy hint of tomatoes filled his nostrils. The cabin had a large open design, with a kitchen on one side, a dining area in the middle and a living room in the back. A set of wide, rough-hewn stairs led up to the second floor. The first thing to grab Gabriel's attention was the presence of light bulbs. Electric light bulbs.

"You have electricity," Gabriel said as though he'd never seen it before. It had been a long while since he'd seen an electric light bulb. Kumaradevi's world had only oil lamps, candles, and torches for light.

"Yes," Vicaquirao said. "I believe in the creature comforts. There is a solar power array on the backside of the roof. This little world of mine is not anywhere near that level of technology yet, but I detest the way oil lamps and candles stain the ceilings. And electric lamps have a warm, soothing glow that is difficult to achieve with magic glow bulbs. Have a seat. Dinner will be up shortly."

Gabriel took a seat at a long dining table of thick cut oak planks lacquered and polished to a high sheen. Two glasses of red wine, an open bottle, simple glazed clay plates, and a wooden bowl with salad sat on the table.

As Gabriel pulled his chair in and placed his napkin on his lap, Vicaquirao entered from the kitchen carrying a tray containing a large bowl of steaming linguine and a smaller bowl with tomato sauce. The tray also contained a basket overflowing with thick-cut, garlic-topped slices of bread. Gabriel's stomach rumbled as he began to lick his lips in anticipation. Until he remembered something. This was his favorite meal. Right down to the cherry tomatoes in the salad. Had the meal been made by anyone else he might have chalked it up to coincidence, but not with Vicaquirao. And why had Vicaquirao made the meal himself? Were there really no servants? Or were they hidden?

"You made dinner yourself?" Gabriel said as Vicaquirao sat down.

"I love to cook," Vicaquirao said. "I hope you enjoy it."

"You don't have any servants?" Gabriel asked.

"No," Vicaquirao said. "I prefer solitude. Fewer chances for betrayal. It is just you and me. So you will do the dishes."

Vicaquirao served Gabriel the pasta and sauce, placing a small portion of salad on the side of his plate and handing him a piece of garlic bread. When he had served himself, he raised his glass of wine. Gabriel did the same. He was very conscious of the choice.

"To the future," Vicaquirao said. Gabriel touched his glass to Vicaquirao's and took a sip. It was very good, but it went straight to his head. He decided to avoid any more of it until he had a full stomach. He would need his wits about him to have dinner with Vicaquirao.

"It's very good," Gabriel said, between bites of linguini. It was always best to compliment the chef, especially when he was the jailer.

"Thank you," Vicaquirao said. He had still not given any hint as to how he knew this was Gabriel's favorite meal. Gabriel could only think of one possible explanation. Vicaquirao had spent some spying on him in the Primary Continuum before his near-death there. Which meant Vicaquirao might know as much about Gabriel as he knew about himself.

He could see that Vicaquirao would be a much more difficult adversary than Kumaradevi had ever been. She was cunning, but in a cruel and crude fashion compared to Vicaquirao. It would be best to try to steer the conversation in directions that might he might use himself, Gabriel thought, before Vicaquirao could steer them elsewhere.

"I was wondering something," Gabriel said as he took another piece of garlic bread from the basket. "When I was brought to Kumaradevi's world, did that create a bifurcation? Does she now have two worlds to rule?"

"Interesting and perceptive question," Vicaquirao said, taking a sip of wine. "The simple answer is no, your presence did not create a new bifurcation."

"But what happens to the people in the future of a branch that has its past changed?" Gabriel asked. "Do they suddenly forget things that have happened? Do they suddenly cease to exist?"

"Essentially, yes," Vicaquirao said. "A change in the past of an alternate reality could mean that someone is not born or that someone does not meet their future spouse. The potentiality of the branch will reorganize to accommodate this new reality. Therefore, people will cease to exist or forget what they had known. Unless the alteration to the branch is too large to allow its reality to reorganize, in which case a new branch will be formed."

"And that new branch will be even less stable and have an even more flexible reality," Gabriel said, seeing it in his head like an endlessly tall tree of ever-branching possibilities.

"Exactly," Vicaquirao said. "Very astute. You really are as bright as everyone says." Gabriel felt his face warming and hated himself for it. That was the danger of Vicaquirao. He was so likable that the things he did and said almost seemed reasonable. Gabriel took a sip of wine to cover his face and tried to focus on the fact that he was a prisoner of the man sitting across the table.

The rest of the meal passed in idle conversation, Gabriel trying his best to glean any information he could with obscure questions. He had hoped that his original line of questioning would have given him some more information about Vicaquirao's world, but the older mage proved very adept at being informative while revealing nothing useful. After dinner, Gabriel washed the dishes and set them to dry on a wooden rack near the sink. When he had finished, he returned to the main living area to find Vicaquirao reading in a large leather chair near a fire.

"I think I'll go to bed," Gabriel said.

"A wise idea," Vicaquirao said, looking up from the book. Gabriel tried to get a look at the author, but could only see a title that said *Thus Spake Zarathustra*. "You will find your room on the right at the end of the hall upstairs. The bathroom is across from it, if you wish to shower. We will leave early tomorrow after breakfast. I have something I want to show you, and I like to get an early start. You should be used to that. I will wake you at dawn. And please, do not try to imbue any of the things you might find in your room. I will know of it if you do. Your bedside lamp is a little more cumbersome than a candleholder in any case.

"Beside your bed, you will also find your copy of *The Time Traveler's Pocket Guide to History*. Your study of history was sorely neglected under Kumaradevi's tutelage. I will not be so lax. Do not bother trying to use it as a means to travel back to the castle. The time shield that prevents the castle from falling permanently into the timeline of the Primary Continuum also prevents any objects created there from being used as relics for time travel. It is just a book. It will not take you from this cabin. Besides which, we will not be staying in any one place for very long. Make yourself comfortable in my homes and in my presence, but do not try to leave without my permission. While your time with me will be far more comfortable than it was with Kumaradevi, you no more want to cross me than you would her."

Vicaquirao paused a moment to make sure his words had been heard. Gabriel said nothing in response.

"Good. We understand each other. Sleep well."

Gabriel chose to say nothing. Instead, he climbed the stairs, walking down the hall to his room at the end. A large bed covered in a patchwork quilt of colored squares sat near the window. There was a closet, a dresser, a small desk against a window, and a table near the bed with an electric lamp. The dresser and closet held clothes similar to those that would have hung in his closet back in his bedroom at his parent's house. Gabriel suspected Vicaquirao was trying to make him feel comfortable.

On the bedside table, Gabriel found his copy of *The Time Traveler's Pocket Guide to History*. He sat on the bed and picked up the book. He flipped through the pages in the moonlight, not bothering to flick on the lamp. He had missed the book. It was like being reunited with an old friend. With all of his friends. The book was the only real connection to the castle and his life there.

Setting the book back on the nightstand, Gabriel lay down on the bed and stared at the darkened ceiling. Turning his head to look through the window, he could see the stars in the sky above the mountains. How had Vicaquirao known about the imbued candleholder? And more importantly, how much more did he know about Gabriel? And how had he come to have Gabriel's copy of *The Time Traveler's Pocket Guide to History*? Could it really be the same book? Gabriel had little time to contemplate these questions as sleep took hold of his thoughts and cast them into a dream world, a deserted island, shadows and shapes following him along the beach and into the jungle.

CHAPTER 21
GRACE AND ATROCITY

Gabriel woke to a knock on the door. As he raised his head, he saw Vicaquirao entering with a wooden tray that held a bowl of fruit, a cup of tea, and a slice of toasted bread with a thin slab of butter melting in the middle of it. A dim light filtered through the window. He sighed. He hated getting up early.

"A light breakfast," Vicaquirao said. "Eat and shower and meet me downstairs in half an hour. And I assure you, the sheets are clean." Vicaquirao smiled and walked back down the hall.

Gabriel realized he had slept in his clothes on top of the quilt all night. He started to wonder what his dreams had been about, but his dreams had been unpleasant for so long that he had no real desire to relive them.

Gabriel ate, showered, and dressed exactly as instructed. As much as Vicaquirao liked to talk about choices, Gabriel realized that his were very limited. He dressed in a pair of faded jeans and a blue t-shirt covered by a long sleeve flannel shirt. Sliding on a pair of sneakers, he stuffed *The Time Traveler's Pocket Guide to History* into his back pocket, picked up the serving tray, and carried it downstairs. Through the windows, he saw Vicaquirao sitting in a chair on the porch. Setting the tray in the kitchen, he joined Vicaquirao outside.

"Good," Vicaquirao said. "You look well rested. We have a bit of traveling to do today. There are some things I want to show you. To continue the conversation we started yesterday afternoon." Vicaquirao took a concatenate crystal from his pocket and held it gently in his hand. "First though, I am afraid you will need to take a quick morning nap. The pathway into my world is a maze filled with traps, and I would not want to tempt you to retrace our way."

"But…" Gabriel said, as a cloud of insensibility rolled over his mind. The last thing he felt were his knees buckling and two strong hands taking hold of him.

It could have been a moment later, or it could have been hours, when Gabriel opened his eyes to find Vicaquirao holding him upright.

"We have arrived," Vicaquirao said. Seeing that Gabriel was steady enough to stand on his own, he stepped back. Gabriel looked around. They stood in some sort of jungle.

"Where are we?" Gabriel said, seeing houses and a village through the trunks of the jungle trees.

"The Primary Continuum," Vicaquirao said. At Gabriel's widening eyes, he continued, "but please do not see this as more than an educational excursion. Your freedoms are dependent upon actions, and they can be eliminated as easily as they are granted."

"I get it," Gabriel said with a frown. "Don't try to run."

"Precisely," Vicaquirao said, as he began to walk from the jungle. Gabriel followed him, and in a moment, they walked through a small field of low grass and into the village. It was oddly quite. A mismatched collection of houses, some built of mud bricks, some of wood, some with thatched roofs, and some with roofs of tin, lined the streets of the village. The sun sat well into the sky, but Gabriel saw no people walking the dirt-packed central street. As they walked around the corner of a house, he saw why.

There *were* people in the village. Spread at odd angles along the ground, mangled and disfigured, some with limbs missing and a few with missing heads. Gabriel turned and retched his breakfast into the ditch at the side of the dirt road. Vicaquirao placed a comforting hand on his back. Gabriel shrugged it off and stood up, looking around again. The bodies of the villagers were clearly African. Some were in the road, some in their yards, some had died in an attempt to reach their homes.

"What is this place?" Gabriel said, spitting to clear the taste of vomit from his mouth.

"Rwanda," Vicaquirao said. "A tiny central African country in the spring of 1994. A little after your own time, but I thought it might be instructive to see."

"What happened here?" Gabriel asked.

"Genocide," Vicaquirao said. "In the short course of three months, from April to July, between 800,000 and a million Tutsis will be slaughtered by their Hutu neighbors. Mostly by being hacked to death with machetes."

"Why would they do that?" Gabriel asked, beginning to feel a powerful anger arise in his gut.

"Scarcity of land, ethnic grudges, imbalances of power," Vicaquirao said. "The usual reasons people kill each other."

"But how could the world let it happen?" Gabriel said. "Somebody stops it, right? The United Nations? Somebody."

"Why would you think that?" Vicaquirao said. "Why should people risk their lives, or even the lives of their soldiers, just to stop one tribe on the other side of the world from killing another?"

"Because it's the right thing to do," Gabriel said, feeling the anger rise from his stomach into his chest.

"To you maybe," Vicaquirao said. "And that is exactly why I have brought you here. To see why choices are so important. The people who did the killing were not forced to. They chose to. And their actions have cloaked this village, and villages like it all throughout this country, with dark imprints."

"I suppose you have a concatenate crystal linked to this place," Gabriel said, the anger burning in his chest.

"I would be a fool not to," Vicaquirao said. "But I will bet you that there are also concatenate crystals linked to the imprints of Light here as well. Sense it for yourself. You can feel the imprints here better than anyone can. Dark mixed with Light." Gabriel extended his senses tentatively, fearing what he would encounter. The malignant imprints where just as overwhelming as he had supposed they would be, but there were grace imprints as well. Strong ones.

"You see," Vicaquirao said, "there is always Light with Darkness. Darkness with light. Mothers sacrificing themselves to save their children. Hutu neighbors protecting their Tutsi friends. Right now, in a village not too far away, a Hutu minister is hiding six women in an unused bathroom, risking his life and that of his family. To save women he barely knows. Acts of grace and acts of atrocity side by side."

"So?" Gabriel said, feeling the anger burning in his throat and threatening to burst into his head. "Why show me this? I can't stop it. I can't change it."

"Because you still fail to see the connection between Darkness and Light," Vicaquirao said. "The imprints of Light created when facing Darkness are stronger than imprints of Light otherwise. That is why it takes so long to imprint an object with only the will and the mind. Because Light must balance Darkness, but it is Darkness that drives the universe forward, through action."

"Evil does not determine the course of history," Gabriel said, trying to believe his words.

"Neither do love and compassion," Vicaquirao said.

"I'll take love and compassion over killing and evil any day," Gabriel said, the anger slipping up behind his eyes to become a burning coal in his brain.

"The universe must have both or it stagnates," Vicaquirao said.

"You sound like Apollyon now," Gabriel said. "Creating a twisted philosophy to justify your actions."

"What I am trying to show you is that..." Vicaquirao cut off and looked around. Gabriel didn't need to ask why Vicaquirao had halted mid-sentence. He felt it too. A space-time seal had burst into existence around the entire village. Vicaquirao grabbed Gabriel's arm and pulled him behind a small brick house with a tin roof. Peeking around the corner of the house, they could see black-clad men and women at the far end of the village road. Kumaradevi's mages.

"That is not possible," Vicaquirao said, his eyes squinting in concentration. "Not unless...Yes. I should have seen that." Vicaquirao reached out and grabbed the chain of the amulet around Gabriel's neck and pulled it roughly over his head.

"What's wrong?" Gabriel asked, the anger having dissolved into fear and his voice showing it. Vicaquirao examined the amulet, a grim smile spreading across his face.

"The amulet has a magical trace on it," Vicaquirao said. "It can be used to locate it anywhere in the Primary Continuum. I should have thought of that. I wonder who suggested it to her. Or did she have a flash of intelligence for once?"

"If Kumaradevi is here, what do we do?" Gabriel said, looking around as though there might be an escape route through the jungle.

"The space-time seal will keep us from jumping to another time," Vicaquirao said, "as well as crossing it or jumping within it. But I think at least one of us will be able to escape." Vicaquirao removed his own amulet and handed it to Gabriel. "Put this on."

Gabriel took the amulet and slid the chain over his neck. "I don't understand."

"Always have a plan, and always have a backup plan when that fails," Vicaquirao said. "But always, always, be prepared to improvise. Kumaradevi will be outside the space-time seal. She believes you are here with Apollyon, and she fears meeting him even more than she fears the Council. She will hold the seal while her mages hunt for you. And they will find you."

"You're going to give me back to her!" Gabriel said, the word 'her' making his mouth twist in disgust and fear.

"Of course not," Vicaquirao said. "While an amulet can alter your appearance enough to fool all but a Soul Mage, a True Mage can alter their physical being in ways that cannot be easily detected."

"Like the way Kumaradevi pretended to be Nefferati?" Gabriel said, beginning to see what Vicaquirao's plan might be.

"Who do you think suggested it to her?" Vicaquirao asked as he shimmered briefly. Suddenly Pishara stood before him.

"It was you all along?" Gabriel said, astonished, but realizing how Vicaquirao knew so much about his activities in Kumaradevi's palace. It also occurred to him that Vicaquirao must have been a master at repressing his magical energy to remain undetected for so long. "But she'll know it was you. Pishara vanished when you did."

"There was a body left in the audience chamber," Vicaquirao said as he shimmered and returned to his normal appearance, "sufficiently burned to be identifiable, but unrecognizable. Now for this to work, both you and Apollyon must be seen." Gabriel watched in amazement as Vicaquirao's body began to change shape and size, even his hair growing longer and darker. Moments later, Gabriel was looking at himself.

"You're going back with her?" Gabriel said.

"Of course," Vicaquirao said. "Do you think I would risk letting you fall into her hands twice? It was hard enough to get you away the first time. No, if I cannot influence your choices directly, I am happy to do it from a distance while the Council holds you. Now you must assume the appearance of Apollyon."

Gabriel did as he was told, focusing on the amulet with a clear image of Apollyon in his mind. An image of Apollyon as Gabriel had seen him last in the piazza in Venice. "Good," he heard Vicaquirao say as he opened his eyes.

"But won't the Soul Mages out there in the street see through this?" Gabriel said, looking down at his hands, which now appeared to be Apollyon's hands.

"Not likely," Vicaquirao said. "It takes a moment to see through it, and they will have other things to think about."

"Like what?" Gabriel asked.

"Like me, running up to them and saying I have escaped Apollyon while he was distracted," Vicaquirao said. "And then you will appear and attack them."

"How?" Gabriel said, feeling naked without a talisman and with Dark Mages walking down the street looking to find them at any moment.

"With these," Vicaquirao said, handing Gabriel the concatenate crystal and pulling something shinny from his pocket.

"My pocket watch!" Gabriel said, excitement filling him as he took the watch and the crystal from Vicaquirao.

"Take this as well," Vicaquirao said, handing him the beetle encased in amber. "When you see me with Kumaradevi's mages, you need to attack. Can you shoot lightning from your fingers?"

"Yes," Gabriel said. He had been singed numerous times in his lessons with the Malignant Fire Mage, Malee.

"Good," Vicaquirao said. "It is a signature of his. Attack with all the power you can manage."

"I can't fight twenty or thirty of them," Gabriel said.

"I would not be so sure of that," Vicaquirao said, "but you will not have to. Once they have me, they will signal to Kumaradevi to lift the space-time seal, and they will flee. They have no desire to die fighting Apollyon. They will be happy to have what they think is you and be gone."

"But what will you do once she has you?" Gabriel asked.

"I am touched that you are concerned for my well-being," Vicaquirao said. "You need not worry about me. The important thing is that when you get back to the castle, the very first thing you must do is have Councilman Zhang arrested. He is Kumaradevi's spy. If he has a chance to send a message back to her telling of your return to the castle, things will go very poorly for me. As long as she thinks she already has you, she will not try to capture you again. And I will be free to implement a plan I have been working on for some time." Gabriel could imagine that Vicaquirao had plans within plans ready to unfold at a moment's notice.

"They are almost here. Remember what I have told you. Your choices are of great importance to the Continuum. Good luck." Vicaquirao turned to go and paused, looking back for a second with a devilish smile. "And tell Elizabeth I said hello."

With that Vicaquirao, disguised as Gabriel, dashed to the next house and then the next and then ran into the road, his arms waving at the squad of ten Dark Mages marching down the street checking houses. As Vicaquirao reached the Dark Mages, one of them sent a fireball up into the air.

Taking that as his own signal, Gabriel reached for the magical energy within himself and focused it through the pocket watch and the tainted concatenate crystal. The crystal must have been linked to six other crystals in the Primary Continuum, because it was immensely powerful. Stepping from behind the house and walking into the street, Gabriel spread his arms wide, jets of blue-white lightning leaping from the fingertips of both hands toward the Dark Mages at either end of the street. The mages with Vicaquirao flickered out of existence as they jumped with the false Gabriel.

Turning to the other side of the street, Gabriel focused all of his magical streams of lightning at the remaining mages, careful to make sure that none of the bolts of energy touched any of the buildings. The second group of Dark Mages disappeared as quickly as the first. Letting the lightning from his fingertips cease, Gabriel took the piece of amber from his pocket and focused his time-sense on it. He not only needed to go back to the castle, but back to a time and place where no one would see him except the one person he needed to.

A blackness began to swiftly surround him, and Gabriel had a moment to realize how fortunate he had been, how extremely lucky that Vicaquirao had not thought to remove the amulet Kumaradevi had given him. As the whiteness engulfed him, he had yet another moment to wonder if it had really been a mistake, or whether Vicaquirao was already guiding his choices through some deceptively obscure plan.

And then he stood in Councilwoman Elizabeth's private chamber in the state apartments as she screamed, throwing her cup of tea at him and standing up as he felt himself thrown across the room, striking the wall with a bone-crunching thud.

CHAPTER 22
TEA TIME

Gabriel threw his arms up before his face as the air began to crackle with bolts of lightning. Seeing his hands, he realized what was wrong.

"How dare you come to this place and time!" Elizabeth roared, as the air shimmered around Gabriel and he returned to his normal appearance.

"Gabriel?"

Shocked by the metamorphosis of Gabriel from Apollyon to himself, Elizabeth released all of her magic at once. Gabriel fell to the floor with a thump.

"Hi," he managed to say as he looked up.

"Gabriel," Elizabeth said again as she rushed to him and knelt down to check that he was uninjured. She took his face in her hands. "What are you doing here? How did you get here? What happened? We've been so worried about you."

"It's kind of a long story," Gabriel said, his face breaking into a smile, a feeling of relief washing over him. He was home. He was safe.

"Come," Elizabeth said, helping him to his feet and guiding him around the broken china teacup to a chair. "Have a seat. I'll fetch the others."

"No," Gabriel said, reaching out to grab Elizabeth's arm as she turned toward the door. "Not yet."

"Why not?" Elizabeth said. "What wrong?"

"Councilman Zhang," Gabriel said, looking out the window and seeing the sun well on its way to sunset in the western sky. He must have interrupted Elizabeth's afternoon tea.

"What about Councilman Zhang?" Elizabeth asked, sitting down across from Gabriel.

"He's Kumaradevi's spy," Gabriel said. He wondered how much time had passed here in the castle since his abduction. He had not been sure when he made the jump.

"That's impossible," Elizabeth said. "Who told you this?"

"Vicaquirao," Gabriel said. He watched Elizabeth's eyes go wide at the mention of the name. "He said to tell you hello."

"I'll just bet he did," Elizabeth said, her face hardening into an impenetrable mask. "You had better tell me everything. From the beginning."

Gabriel told her everything. He tried to start at the beginning and follow through in chronological order, but like a Time Mage jumping from era to era, he tended to leap from one part of the story to another related part, sometime later. More than once, he felt himself on the verge of tears as he recounted one or another of the abuses of Kumaradevi and her dark mages.

With Elizabeth's patient questions and a fresh cup of tea, he managed to make it all the way through the recitation of his ordeal. Elizabeth seemed particularly interested in his time with Vicaquirao. She too was suspicious of his amazing good fortune at escaping and the interesting coincidence of Vicaquirao having Gabriel's pocket watch on him at the time.

"Firstly," Elizabeth said, "give me that amulet. Never trust anything that Vicaquirao gives you. And the concatenate crystal. I doubt he would give it up if he really cared about us finding and severing its connected sister crystals." Gabriel handed Elizabeth the concatenate crystal and the amulet from around his neck. She examined both. Standing, she took another amulet from a box on one of her bookshelves and handed it to Gabriel. It was a small glass amulet much like the others with a bright pearlescent pink sheen. Gabriel made a face as he put it on.

"It is a bit girlish, but Sema can fashion you one that is more to your tastes later," Elizabeth said, patting his hand. "For now, wait here. I will lock the door. Do not let anyone in. I will return shortly. In the meantime, help yourself to some apple crumb cake. It's delicious." Elizabeth smiled at him, her bright gray eyes shining with silent assurance of his safely.

As she closed the door, he heard the loud sound of a lock sliding into place. For a moment it reminded him of his tower cell back in Kumaradevi's palace, but he pushed that thought to the back of his mind and reached out to take a piece of apple crumb cake rather than dwell on his memories.

Two pieces of crumb cake and nearly half an hour later, Elizabeth returned. Akikane and Ohin followed her into the room. And another person Gabriel had seen, but not really met.

"Nefferati!" Gabriel said leaping to his feet. "You're alive!"

"No need to sound so surprised," Nefferati said, throwing the door closed as she stepped into the room. "I may be old, but I am not feeble."

"I didn't mean…" Gabriel started to say. "It's just the last time I saw you…I wasn't sure if you would escape."

"Thanks to you I did," Nefferati said with a grin as she wrapped Gabriel in a hug so powerful it made him think he'd been trapped by a bear. "And that sly little Incan we all thought was dead. Can't say I wasn't happy to see him, even if I did think he was a serving girl at the time. He gave me a relic that took me back to the Primary Continuum, but it disintegrated after I used it. Covering his tracks as usual."

"What is this about serving girls?" Ohin said, giving Gabriel a hug.

"It's complicated," Gabriel said.

"Of course, of course," Akikane said as he embraced Gabriel. "You will tell us all about it. Elizabeth has told us about Zhang."

"Who is now residing in the dungeons," Elizabeth said to Gabriel as they all took seats. "He confessed everything."

"After he saw me," Nefferati said with a wicked chuckle. "I've been back and hiding for a month while we tried to figure out who the spy was who had given me away. Zhang was very surprised to see me."

"You showed considerable restraint," Ohin said. "I cannot say I would have done the same."

"Yes, yes," Akikane said, with a chuckle. "You restrained him considerably."

"But why would he do it?" Gabriel asked, looking to Elizabeth for the answer. "Why would he turn against the Council?"

"Because of me," Nefferati said. "He fell in love with a Malignancy Mage, many years ago. A very skilled and beautiful woman. He never forgave me for killing her. Something he and Kumaradevi shared in common. People they loved who died at my hands. Many people share that bond."

"He fell in love with a Malignancy Mage?" Gabriel said, shocked by the idea.

"We have no control over who our heart chooses to love," Elizabeth said, a trace of sadness in her voice.

"So true, so true," Akikane whispered.

"Now tell us what has happened to you," Ohin said, leaning forward with concerned interest.

Gabriel again told the tale of his dual captivity, reliving once more as he did so each moment of the torment, fear, and frustration of the previous two months. It was easier in the second telling, and he managed to recount the events in the same order they had happened in, but it was also exhausting. However, as the fatigue of recalling his capture washed through him, he also felt a sense of relief.

Telling the story restored the inner strength that he had been depleting slowly, day by day, as his internment had worn on. With that strength came an upwelling of anger. Anger at Kumaradevi. Anger at Vicaquirao. Anger at the Council. Anger at the four mages sitting and listening to him speak. By the end of the story, he found it hard to control the anger in his voice.

"You handled yourself very well," Ohin said. "I am extremely proud of you."

"We all are," Elizabeth said, placing her hand on Gabriel's knee. "You seem upset. Maybe you would like to go back to your room?"

"The boy's upset with us," Nefferati said. "He should speak what's on his mind."

"Yes, yes," Akikane said. "The fire of your anger will burn you more than us."

"What Vicaquirao said is right," Gabriel said, his face hot as he spoke. "Everyone is using me or trying to use me. And I'm tired of it. Kumaradevi wants to use me to destroy the Council. Apollyon wants to use me to destroy the Great Barrier. I'm not sure what Vicaquirao wants to use me for, but he admitted he wants to influence my choices. And the Council wants to use me to defeat the Malignancy Mages. Everyone is trying to position me like a chess piece, and I don't want it anymore." Tears brimmed in his eyes and he could not bring himself to look at the others.

"You are right," Elizabeth said. "We are using you."

"Using you before you begin to use them," Nefferati said, with a snort of laughter.

"Just so, just so," Akikane said.

"What do you mean?" Gabriel said.

"What Vicaquirao told you is true," Elizabeth said. "In a few years you will be the most powerful mage that has ever been. At that point it will not matter what the Council wishes, you will be able to do as you please, no matter what our plans."

"Guidance," Akikane said. "Guidance is all we wish for you."

"Like Vicaquirao, we are trying to influence your future choices," Ohin said.

"But you are right," Elizabeth said. "We have not been open about our motives. You are not a chess piece to be played by the Council. However, we are still responsible for you. For now, at least."

"There is another option," Nefferati said. "He could come with me."

"If he chooses," Ohin said.

"If I choose what?" Gabriel asked. "Where are you going?"

"Back to my retreat," Nefferati said. "Someplace a little safer this time."

"What about Apollyon?" Gabriel said. "You were supposed to help find where he's making copies of himself."

"That was how the Council wanted to use me," Nefferati said with a dark smile. "And I have helped them as far as I can."

"Apollyon has cloaked the moment in time where he is making copies of himself too well," Ohin said. "We will have to search on the ground."

"One place at a time," Akikane said, smiling his serene smile. "One place at a time."

"But don't you want to help defeat Apollyon?" Gabriel asked, still staring at Nefferati.

"I cannot say I wouldn't mind seeing him removed from the Continuum," Nefferati said. "But that is not my battle at the moment. I went on my retreat to try to extinguish the anger and the anguish in my heart. But my time as Kumaradevi's plaything and my battle with her at my escape have taught me that I need more time to realize my desires."

"Nefferati's offer is generous," Elizabeth said, seeming sad to admit it. "It does offer you a way out. At least for the time being. And you would be safe. Safer than we can make you here."

"There will be no arrowheads left behind this time," Nefferati said. "No one will know where and when I go except me."

Gabriel thought about it for a moment. It was tempting, the idea of following Nefferati away from all this. Away from the war and Apollyon and Kumaradevi and all the things that made his stomach tighten with the mere thought of them. However, as he looked at Ohin, he realized that it would take him away from other things, as well. Things he had spent months dreaming about and using to keep his spirits up and his will to survive alive. He would have to give up all that he had gained since losing his family. He still mourned the loss of his mother and father and sister and the life he had lived. Would he need to mourn the loss of Ohin and Sema and the others if he accompanied Nefferati?

"What will the Council do about Apollyon?" Gabriel asked.

"Now that you have returned safely to us," Elisabeth said, "we will begin the hunt we postponed when you disappeared."

"You mean you haven't been looking for his bifurcations yet?" Gabriel said, surprised.

"We were devoting all of our resources to finding you," Elizabeth said. "I will give you one guess which Councilman pushed to have our efforts divided to hunt for Apollyon's secret branches of time." Gabriel didn't need to guess.

"Now that you are back," Elizabeth continued, "Ohin and his team will lead the effort to find the place in time where Apollyon is making copies of himself."

"Good," Gabriel said, looking to Ohin. "When do we start?" he added, almost before he knew what he was saying and what it meant.

"Then you have made your choice," Nefferati said.

"You may want to reconsider that choice," Elizabeth said. "While Ohin's team will be leading the search for Apollyon's secret branch of time, you will not be joining them."

"What?" Gabriel said, feeling the anger returning to his gut with lightning speed.

"We have already lost you once," Elizabeth said. "We cannot afford to lose you again."

"So you're going to keep me under a glass jar like some pet insect?" Gabriel said. "I can help."

"I'm sure you can," Elizabeth said, "but the risk is too great. You will continue your training here with Akikane where we can protect you."

"I don't need your protection," Gabriel said, trying to control the emotion in his voice. "I would have escaped Kumaradevi. It would have taken a while, but I would have. I would have escaped Vicaquirao, too. So don't think you can hold me here if I really want to go."

"Gabriel!" Ohin said.

Gabriel looked at Ohin and felt a wave of shame flood over him. "I'm sorry," he said. "But if I'm going to be the one who has to fight them all, I want to learn how to fight, not pretend to fight."

"Very stubborn, very stubborn," Akikane said. "Just what we need."

"You were right, Ohin," Elizabeth said. "He is not at all pleased at the idea of being left out."

"I told you he wouldn't be," Ohin said.

"I could have told you that as soon as we walked in the door," Nefferati said, giving Gabriel a wink only he could see. "You don't survive being Kumaradevi's guest without having a little backbone."

"If the prophecy is true," Gabriel began, "then I will need to learn how to really fight against the Malignancy Mages. I can't just train here. I will need experience. Real experience."

"I agree with Gabriel," Ohin said. "He needs to know what the battle is really like. We can't keep him caged up like some tame tiger and then set him loose in the wild and hope he fares as well as the other feral beasts."

"Yes, yes," Akikane said. "I agree. Let the tiger out of his cage."

"Like you could keep him if he wanted out," Nefferati said with her snort of a laugh.

"You will need more than experience for what lies ahead of you," Elizabeth said. "You will need wisdom." She paused for a moment, but the look on her face left no one tempted to speak. "However, you are correct. You will not gain wisdom without a chance to learn from your mistakes. Especially if the prophecy is true. You may join Ohin's team in their search for Apollyon's secret branch of time."

"Thank you," Gabriel said, the anger draining away as though a plug had been pulled from a tub of water.

"I will accompany them," Akikane said, his eyes holding Gabriel's. Akikane's tone of voice made it clear this was not a suggestion.

"An excellent idea," Elizabeth said.

"Yes, yes," Akikane said. "And Ohin will begin teaching you to increase your magical energy. You should have learned before."

"You can increase your magical energy?" Gabriel said, seeing immediately how that would have helped him in the arena with Kumaradevi's Malignancy Mages.

"Yes," Ohin said. "We usually do not begin training in increasing magical energy until the second or third year of apprenticeship."

"And few who go through the training have much success," Elizabeth said. "It requires a great deal of effort and concentration.

Which is why so few mages, Grace or Malignancy, ever manage much success with it. It's easier to find another concatenate crystal."

"Easy is for fools," Akikane said. "Ohin will teach you. He is a much better teacher than he ever was a pupil." Ohin gave Akikane a sideways glance, and Gabriel suddenly realized that Ohin had once been Akikane's apprentice. It felt weird to think of Ohin as an apprentice.

"So it is decided," Ohin said.

"And we can only hope it is the correct decision," Elizabeth said.

"There's one more thing," Gabriel said, not wanting to speak it aloud, but knowing he needed to. Knowing he needed to know. He looked at Nefferati. "What does the prophecy mean? What am I supposed to do?"

A silence filled the room as the others exchanged looks. "I will speak to the boy alone," Nefferati said finally. It all too closely recalled similar words spoken by a woman he had thought to be Nefferati. Gabriel's stomach clenched involuntarily.

"Are you sure?" Elizabeth asked.

"I made the prophecy," Nefferati said. "I should be the one to tell him about it."

"Just so, just so," Akikane said, getting to his feet and giving Gabriel a smile.

"We'll see you later," Ohin said as he stood. "The team is preparing a special dinner for you."

"It is good to have you back, Gabriel," Elizabeth said, momentarily taking his face in her hands. "Do not do anything foolish to make me regret *my* choice." When the other three mages were gone, Nefferati moved to sit across from Gabriel. He took a sip of the lukewarm tea to cover his nervousness as she stared at him.

"So Vicaquirao told you the words of the prophecy, did he?" Nefferati said.

"Yes," Gabriel said.

"Did he tell you what he thought it meant?" Nefferati asked.

"He seemed to think I would threaten the existence of the entire Continuum," Gabriel said.

"That's one possibility," Nefferati said. "One of many. Prophecy is not like reading the future. Especially when it is a prophecy about things happening outside the normal flow of time in the Primary Continuum." She paused and looked away. Then she bit her lip, an action that Gabriel found a little disconcerting as it seemed so youthful and out of character. When she turned back to him, she stared into his eyes with an intensity that made his breath stop for a moment.

"I am going to tell you something now that I have never uttered to anyone," Nefferati said. "I did not make the prophecy. I found it."

Gabriel was so unsure of the meaning of the words he had just heard that he could not fathom what to say in response. After a moment of silence, Nefferati continued as though Gabriel had found the right words to question her startling statement.

"I was recovering from a battle," Nefferati said. "The one in which I killed Kumaradevi's son. It was a fierce fight with many lives lost on both sides. Nearly my own. I was gravely wounded. Even with the help of two of the best Heart-Tree Mages, Kumaradevi's wrathful curses clung to my body. My recovery was slow. I am told, I was often unconscious and frequently delirious. I remember nothing of that time. Nothing except a dream. A dream I kept having until it seemed that the dream was all there was. A dream of walking in the library and finding a book. A book I could never open.

"Eventually I was well enough to go to the library and I found the book exactly where it had been in my dream. My hands trembled as I held it, afraid to pass in reality where I had been unable to tread in the dream. When I had finally mastered myself and pulled open the cover of the book, a slip of paper fell out. It was a simple piece of folded white paper. On it, written in a slanted English script, was the prophecy."

Gabriel could hear the blood pounding within his ears in the silence that followed Nefferati's words. She held his eyes a moment longer and then looked out the window.

"I have wondered for many years who might come to fulfill those words," she said. "If anyone would come at all. But you have come. You are here. And you can wield imprints of grace and

239

malignancy. And that means the other words of the prophecy may eventually ring true, as well."

"But if you didn't make the prophecy, who did?" Gabriel asked. "And how did it get in that book?"

"I have no idea," Nefferati said, looking back to Gabriel. "I decided it was important for others to know of the prophecy, but the means by which I had come by it were too mysterious to reveal. So I claimed its words as my own."

"It called me the Breaker of Time," Gabriel said, forcing his mouth to speak the words. "And the Destroyer of Worlds. The Dawn of the Endless Night."

"Words," Nefferati said. "Not events that are set in stone. Just words. Prophecy is not destiny. I will give you the best advice I can, and it will take much willpower and much wisdom to follow it. I have tried hard to do this myself. My advice is this — forget the prophecy."

"What?" Gabriel asked, not sure he had heard right.

"Forget you ever heard it or anything about it," Nefferati said. "That is why it was kept from you to begin with. The more you think about it, the more you will second-guess your decisions. Better to forget that you ever heard of a prophecy. Better to let the words slip from your mind like water from an open hand."

Gabriel sat in silence as he thought about what Nefferati had said. Could he forget the prophecy? Could he forget the words he had heard? Could he forget the phrases that pointed to his future, however vague and imprecise? And where, really, had those words come from? Who had written the prophecy? Was its author important if he was to ignore the author's words? They were dark and powerful words. Could they be ignored? Should they be? These thoughts lead him to other dark words he had heard recently.

"Was Vicaquirao right?" Gabriel asked. "Does there need to be darkness for light to exist? Does there need to be evil and malignancy for grace and goodness to thrive?"

"If I thought that evil needed to exist, that anger and hatred were necessary for the universe to function," Nefferati said, "I wouldn't have spent so many years trying to rid my heart of them."

"It almost made sense when he was saying it," Gabriel said.

"I'm sure it made sense to him," Nefferati said. "We all try to twist the facts to suit our needs. I am no exception. There are those who would say that the coming of the Seventh True Mage is too important an event to ignore. That I should give up my search for inner peace and come back to help you fight this war."

"I don't think so," Gabriel said, placing his hand on hers. He thought about his anger and how it felt to defeat the Malignancy Mages in Kumaradevi's arena. "You can't fight out of anger or hatred or revenge or you become those things. You have to fight from another place."

"Just so," Nefferati said. "And when I find that place, I will return. But until that time, I want to give you something." She placed her hands on either side of his head and drew him to her until their foreheads touched. "This is for you and you alone. If you need me. Only you."

A vision filled Gabriel's mind. He saw a long sandy beach, a deeply wooded forest behind it, the waves of the ocean swelling and retreating along the shore. He also saw a house made of stone and wood, set back a good distance from the beach. He knew, without knowing how he knew, where and when this house existed. He knew he could find it with the right relic. He knew this was Nefferati's place of retreat, and she was entrusting him with this secret in case he needed her.

"Thank you," Gabriel said, sitting back in his chair.

"No, thank you," Nefferati said. "For being so understanding of an old woman's heart."

"Can I ask you something else?" Gabriel said, another question tearing at his mind.

"Anything you wish," Nefferati said.

"What did you do with it?" Gabriel asked. "The paper the prophecy was written on?"

"I put it back in the book, and put the book back on the shelf," Nefferati said.

"I won't tell anyone," Gabriel said. He decided this just as he was speaking the words. What good would it do? And what would happen if he did? Was the prophecy any less true for having an unknown author?

"That is up to you," Nefferati said. "I did what I thought was right in the moment. I cannot say I would make the same choice today."

Then another question occurred to Gabriel. "What was the name of the book?"

Nefferati's eyes lit up as she smiled. "*Les Propheties* by Nostradamus."

Gabriel laughed so hard and so suddenly, he almost blew snot out his nose.

"I do not know about you, but I am starving," Nefferati said, chuckling as she stood and pulled Gabriel to his feet. "Elizabeth's afternoon tea breaks only ever left me wanting to have real food in my mouth, not crumbling-apple-whatever." His stomach rumbled in agreement with Nefferati, and Gabriel followed her out of the room and toward dinner. Toward a reunion with his friends. Toward his destiny, whatever it might be.

CHAPTER 23
SEEKING TO SEVER

Cheers greeted Gabriel almost from the moment he entered the Waterloo Chamber for dinner. No sooner had he crossed the threshold of the entrance than the nearest table of mages spotted him and rose to their feet, applauding and shouting their congratulations. Gabriel was so stunned, he stopped dead in his tracks and only moved forward because Nefferati pushed him ahead with a firm hand in the middle of his back. He was thankful for her guidance, because with everyone in the room standing and clapping, he was too short to find the table with his team. Nefferati guided him through the boisterously appreciative crowd to where Ohin stood next to a table with the others. Gabriel had barely reached them when Teresa wrapped her arms around him.

"I'm not letting you out of my sight again!" Teresa yelled above the noise of the crowd. "You can't be trusted on your own."

"I made it home, didn't I?" Gabriel yelled back as he broke into a smile.

"No thanks to us," Teresa said, wiping something from her eye.

"There you are, there you are, you had us worried out of our heads," Marcus said as he gave Gabriel a rough hug. "Got me so out of sorts I'm repeating myself like Akikane." Gabriel saw Akikane raise an eyebrow. Before he could even laugh, Gabriel found himself passed to Sema, who crushed him to her chest so hard he thought her Venetian pendant would leave a permanent imprint on his skull.

"We were all so afraid," Sema said, tears dripping into Gabriel's hair. "We didn't know what could have happened."

"I was okay," Gabriel said as Sema released him. "I had good teachers."

"Damn right he was okay," Ling said as she stepped before him. "He's the toughest one of us." Ling didn't hug him, but gave him a gentle kiss on the cheek instead. She must have seen the flabbergasted look on his face because she frowned before punching him in the arm and smiling. Rajan came next, embracing him like an older brother, quick, but firm, with a tussle of Gabriel's hair.

"It's good to have you back," Rajan grinned. "I knew you'd return."

Others from the castle stopped by the table to give their well wishes, but none so adamantly as his teammates had. After the commotion in the room died down, Gabriel took his place at the table, sitting between Teresa and Rajan. The table sat apart from the others, and was long enough to make room for Nefferati, Akikane and Elizabeth.

As he sat down, a young serving girl filled his glass with cider. She gave Gabriel a huge smile as she poured. Teresa caught the smile and frowned, but Gabriel hardly noticed, distracted by a large bowl of corn chowder another server slid beneath his nose. A salad of fresh spinach, sliced plum tomatoes, cranberries, and walnut-crusted goat cheese followed the soup while the main course consisted of a thick-cut piece of prime rib, garlic-roasted red potatoes, and brazed asparagus. Gabriel was convinced that he could not possibly stuff another bite of food in his mouth when the serving girl placed a coconut cream pie with an almond crust and chocolate drizzle on the table. *Just one piece,* he told himself, but he somehow managed to make room for two.

The conversation was as filling as the meal. It was good to be back among his friends. He had missed them all so much. Teresa's constant wild enthusiasm, Rajan's dry wit, Marcus's wild stories and continual toasts, Ling's foul-mouthed swearing, Sema's mothering frowns, and Ohin's paternal gaze and his clear, deep voice. Near the end of the meal, Gabriel spied Rajan and Teresa exchange the rabbit's foot behind his back.

"Betting whether I'd make it back?" he asked as he pushed the empty pie plate away.

"Don't be silly," Teresa said with a shocked expression. "There was never any doubt about that."

"We were betting on how many pieces of pie you'd manage to put down," Rajan said. "You let me down. I had you for at least three."

"Would it count if I took a piece for later?" Gabriel asked in mock innocence.

"Not hardly," Teresa said. "Besides, I already have the rabbit's foot." She dangled it teasingly in front of Rajan before turning to speak to Ling. Rajan leaned into Gabriel so that only he could hear what the young man had to say.

"It will get easier," Rajan said.

"What will?" Gabriel asked.

"Being the different one," Rajan said. "The odd man out. The special case. It will get easier."

"I hope so," Gabriel said. He wondered if his discomfort at being so different was obvious to the others, as well. It had been something that had been bothering him since he stepped into the room to the cheers of the castle mages. He was happy to be back, but he was nearly as much an outsider here as he had been at Kumaradevi's palace. Here he was accepted, but he was still unlike anyone else. He could touch the power of tainted imprints while none of them could. It was worse than the feeling of difference he had always felt going to school.

With a Jewish father and a Guatemalan mother, he had always stood out in his mostly white, rural school, but here in the castle, everyone looked different, with people from every race and religion and time period in history sitting side by side at the dinner table enjoying a meal together. However, he was different from all of them in a way that none of them could really understand. He could do things they could not. Had done things they could not. Would someday do things that none of them could imagine.

"I was born during the last years of India's fight for independence from Great Britain," Rajan said softly, bringing Gabriel out of his thoughts and back to the table. "It was the mid-1940s, and the country was being torn apart not only by the fight for self-rule, but by clashes between Hindus and Muslims, each afraid the other would gain too much power when India ceased to be a colony. My father was Muslim and my mother was Hindu."

"Like Romeo and Juliet," Gabriel said, remembering his parents' stories of their courtship, the looks they received, and the fights within the families.

"If only it had worked out that well," Rajan said with a weak smile. "My parents were banished from both of their families and forced to flee the city they had grown up in. When I was born, it only complicated matters. Was I a Muslim child or a Hindu child? The other children didn't care until a certain age. And then the opinions of their parents became very important. Independence came in 1948, and the entire country was split into new nations. India proper, for mostly Hindus in the middle, with Pakistan and Bangladesh, for Muslims, on either side. My childhood felt divided, too. I spent a great deal of time either fighting or running from a fight. Fighting Muslims who thought I was a Hindu, and Hindus who thought I was Muslim. It did not help that I was too stubborn to choose.

"I insisted on going to the mosque with my father and attending the temples with my mother. I read the Koran and the Bhagavad-Gita and the other sacred texts of both my faiths. I refused to accept that I had to be one of the other. It felt like having to choose between my father and my mother. As though I would be saying that I loved one more than the other."

"What did you do?" Gabriel asked, seeing Rajan in a way he never had.

"I died," Rajan said calmly. "In a street fight. Fighting because I would not disown part of my heritage."

"But how did it get better?" Gabriel asked, not finding the comfort he thought the story was leading up to.

"It got better because I waited," Rajan said with a genuine smile. "Because I was patient. Because I ended up here. Now I am surrounded by people of every faith, and no one thinks me odd. I've even begun to study and practice faiths I had never heard of. I am becoming something I never knew I could be. Something even my parents would not recognize, maybe would not approve of."

"That sounds familiar," Gabriel said with a rueful sigh.

"Just be who you truly are, Gabriel," Rajan said. "And give it time."

"Well, if I had known it was so easy," Gabriel said, rolling his eyes sarcastically. Rajan threw his head back and laughed, drawing Teresa's attention.

"What's so funny now?" she asked.

"Rajan was just giving me some advice," Gabriel said.

"Oh, that is funny," Teresa said with a wicked grin. Rajan stuck out his tongue at her.

A deep cough from the end of the table brought everyone's eyes to Ohin, who was raising a glass.

"Ah, yes," Marcus said, the first to raise his glass in response. "Another toast is indeed in order. Bad luck to end a meal without a toast."

"Or a sentence, apparently," Sema said, raising her glass of grape juice.

"A simple toast," Ohin said. "To Gabriel's return and the mission ahead."

"Here, here," Marcus said as glasses clinked together.

"Yes, yes. Here, here," Akikane echoed, as everyone took a sip of wine.

"What is our next mission?" Teresa asked as they all placed their glasses back on the table.

Ohin looked toward Elizabeth, who nodded. Suddenly the noise from the dining hall vanished and only the sounds from the table existed. The change was so sharp that Gabriel found himself automatically looking around, a seed of panic growing in his stomach.

"A little trick to keep the conversation private," Elizabeth said with a glance toward Gabriel. "I will leave Ohin to describe the details, but your team will be charged with the mission we were about to begin when Gabriel was taken from us. You will find the place in time where Apollyon is creating copies of himself and sever any branches you find. I doubt even he would be foolish enough to leave all the branches intact after he has taken his doubles from them, but we do not know. Regardless, we will need to ensure that no more branches can be made from that time and place. Akikane will accompany you to help accomplish this. And to further his education, Gabriel will accompany you, as well."

The table erupted in comments, some surprised, but most concerned for Gabriel's well-being. Gabriel remained silent. As much as he wanted to join the shouting, he knew the decision had already been made in his favor. Answering a comment from Ling, Elizabeth said, "He is young, but we put young mages in the field all the time. A necessity of the war. Teresa is only a year older. While I have my reservations, he does need experience that can only be acquired in the field. I think we all know that the revelation of Gabriel as the Seventh True Mage, combined with Apollyon's multiplication of himself, will lead to a massive conflict and likely rather soon. Gabriel will undoubtedly play a central role in this coming battle and if he is not ready, if he has not explored and honed his abilities, he will not be the only one at risk." That thought kept everyone silent as Elizabeth paused. "Ohin, I will leave you to explain the mission to your team."

She stood up to leave the table. Everyone immediately stood. Gabriel was first to his feet. He might still be new to Council and True Mage etiquette, but months at Kumaradevi's table had taught him to rise from his seat at a moment's notice.

"I'll join you," Nefferati said as she rose up and pushed back her chair.

"The sound barrier will remain until one of you crosses it," Elizabeth said with a nod of her head in parting.

"Unless Gabriel can figure out how the trick is done," Nefferati said with a pat on Gabriel's cheek.

As the elder women left, everyone resumed their seats. Gabriel watched them go, realizing that whatever conflict had existed between them had been resolved to a large degree. They seemed now like mother and daughter, walking side by side. He was glad for them. Glad he had played some small part in their reconciliation. Ohin cleared his throat again.

Ohin looked around catching each eye, even Akikane's, before he began. "This will not be an easy mission. As you know, not even Nefferati has been able to locate the place in time where Apollyon is making copies of himself. His magic is too strong for anything less than close examination. We know he was a soldier in Alexander the Great's army."

"Alexander the Terrible, you mean," Sema said under her breath.

"We can assume that Apollyon will want to double himself later in his training, when he is more powerful," Ohin continued. "From what our spies have learned, and what Gabriel has told us from his time with Vicaquirao, Apollyon would likely choose a point somewhere in the last five years of his life while in the timeline. We also know that he is using the power of vast negative imprints to hide his branching of time. We suspect he is creating the bifurcations during one of Alexander the Great's battles.

"We know that Apollyon died in battle in 326 BCE in the battle of Hydaspes in the Punjab of India against Raja Puru. We will start there and work backward. Our mission will be to travel to these battles, examine the evidence on the ground, and locate the point where the bifurcations occur. When we find it, we will sever any branches and seal the spot from further tampering."

"When do we start?" Marcus said, draining the last of his wine.

"We will begin training tomorrow," Ohin said. "A few days. No more. We want to be prepared, but we must move quickly. Gabriel will join us in a day or so, after he has had some time to rest."

"I don't want any time to rest," Gabriel blurted out before he realized he had interrupted Ohin. Ohin gave him a look that seemed a cross between concern and a reprimand. He saw Sema staring at him from across the table and knew she was worried about him, as well. Gabriel didn't care. He didn't want his days filled with idle time. That would only lead to him remembering again and again what he had been through in the past two months. He needed something to keep him focused and thinking about his future, not reliving the horrors of his recent past.

"As you wish," Ohin finally said. "You should all get a good night's sleep. We begin at dawn." Gabriel was glad his was not the only groan to be heard around the table. If he had known his insistence on beginning training with everyone else would mean another early morning, he might have kept his mouth shut.

"To bed, to bed," Akikane said as he pushed he chair back and stood. "I will see you in the morning."

"You're joining us for training?" Gabriel asked as Akikane patted his shoulder.

"Of course, of course," Akikane said with a wide smile. "We must learn to work together. It has been some time since I was a member of a field team."

Akikane's departure broke the barrier that had kept all sound from leaving or reaching the table. Most of the dining hall had emptied out, but the sounds of conversations flooded back to Gabriel's ears. Knowing that Akikane could have easily resumed the barrier, he assumed the elder mage wished to encourage the others to depart for an early bedtime. Curious, Gabriel reached his hand into his pocket and slipped his fingers around the silver pocket watch. Sound waves he knew were a form of energy, but they needed a medium like air to move through. A barrier where the energy of sound waves would be dissipated could be combined with a barrier where the air became thinned to a near vacuum, creating a bubble that sound could not cross.

Everyone stood and said their goodnights, but they all stopped and looked at Gabriel when the sounds from the rest of the dining hall vanished.

"Picked that up pretty quick," Teresa said, cocking her eye at Gabriel.

"I had to try," Gabriel said.

"Yes, you did," Rajan said with a smirk as he extended his open hand past Gabriel's shoulder toward Teresa. She frowned and slapped the rabbit's foot into his open palm. Gabriel hadn't even heard them make a bet. He wondered how many times that rabbit's foot changed hands because of him. More than it paid to worry about, he suspected. He released the barrier to sound as the team walked out of the dining room, wishing him goodnight as they headed to their respective rooms in the different wings of the castle.

Teresa took seriously her commitment not to let him out of her sight and insisted on escorting him to his room.

"You don't need to follow me everywhere," Gabriel said. "I can take care of myself now." It was true, Gabriel felt. As long as he had his pocket watch, he was likely more dangerous than any mage in the castle besides Akikane and Elizabeth. And Nefferati, of course. He had Kumaradevi to thank for that.

"Yes, I'm sure you can," Teresa said as they walked along the hall to his room. "But that doesn't mean you should. If something happens it's always best to make your enemies think you are weaker than you really are."

"And you think they'll believe that if you're my bodyguard," Gabriel said. "You're just a…" he let the sentence fade as he realized it might not be best to finish it.

"A fourteen-year-old girl?" Teresa said. "I'll let you in a little secret that everyone else knows except you."

"Another one?" Gabriel asked.

"I'm not just a pretty face," Teresa said, with a wink, "or just a prodigy at math. I have a natural talent for Fire Magic. More so than most, and most everyone knows it. You won't find a more powerful Fire Mage in the castle. Being seen with me is like being seen with a pack of pit bulls for protection."

"I've always wanted a pit bull," Gabriel said, as he opened the door to his room.

"Woof," Teresa said as she looked inside his room to make sure it was empty. "Remember, bright and early. Don't make me toss you out of bed." She kissed him on the cheek and turned to go.

"I won't," Gabriel said, blushing at Teresa's kiss and wondering why. She always treated him like a brother and she reminded him of his sister, but she was much cuter than his sister and much closer to his own age, and she wasn't really his sister at all, but it didn't matter because they were teammates and…

"Good night," Teresa said, walking down the hall. "Wait until you're in your room to fall asleep."

"Night," Gabriel said as he stepped into his room and closed the door. It was good to be back in his room in the castle. Back someplace he felt safe. Some place familiar. Even if he was alone. And being alone reminded him of all the nights alone in the tower

251

chamber of Kumaradevi's palace. All the nights spent curled in a ball in tears came back to him in a rush. He sat down heavily on the edge of the bed and let the tears come again. This time not out of fear, but from relief. He felt safe at the castle. Surrounded by friends. People he trusted. People he loved. People who loved him. He was back in control of his life.

After a time the tears slowed and stopped, and Gabriel took a deep breath. He felt better than he could remember feeling in a very long time. He changed into his pajamas and climbed into bed. He fell asleep realizing that it was the first night in months that he wasn't planning some escape as his eyes closed.

Morning came much too swiftly, but he woke feeling more rested than he had in ages. He brushed his teeth, showered, and dressed quickly. Teresa knocked on his door a moment later. He smiled and said good morning, trying to forget the thoughts that had flooded his mind the night before when she had kissed him on the cheek. Teresa was even less of a morning person than Gabriel, and she said little as they made their way to the courtyard of the Lower Ward.

The others were there already, Marcus looking like he regretted that fourth glass of wine. They all greeted him good morning and then set about the day's training. For him, training began with a private lesson from Ohin while Akikane drilled the others on how a True Mage could help them in a fight. Ohin and Gabriel walked to a quiet side of the courtyard and sat under a tree.

"This exercise is very simple," Ohin said, settling into a cross-legged position, "but it must be repeated every day for it to be successful."

"Every day for how long?" Gabriel said as he crossed his legs in imitation of Ohin.

"For years," Ohin said. "That is why few mages are able to cultivate and increase their inner magical energy to any great degree. But the greater the energy you have to focus through your talisman, the greater your magic can become."

"Will I be able to do magic without a talisman?" Gabriel asked. It was the only question he was really interested in.

"With a great deal of practice, yes," Ohin said. "But you will never be as powerful without a talisman as you are with one."

"But I may not always have a talisman handy," Gabriel said, remembering all the days in Kumaradevi's palace when he would have done anything to be able to perform magic without a talisman.

"As we have seen," Ohin said. "Now, clear your mind. Settle your thoughts. Watch your breath. Just as you learned." This part of the training was familiar and easy. Well, not easy necessarily, it took a few minutes to get his mind to stop jumping from one thought to the next like some drunken monkey, but eventually he could concentrate clearly on his breathing. While it was easy to still his mind quickly to use magic, keeping it still and focused on his breath was much more difficult.

"Now reach within and sense the flow of your subtle energy," Ohin said. This too was familiar and easy. He did it every time he used magic. "And now as you sense that flow of energy, I want you to imagine it flowing down into you from above, and up into you from below, the two waves of energy meeting at your heart center. Remember, they are not flowing into your physical body. They are flowing into the subtle energy matrix that is expressed as your body. As these two waves of energy meet, they swirl and multiply, flowing back up and down your body, radiating throughout your entire being, every cell, every muscle, every pore, filled with and radiating this energy.

"With each breath in, the energy flows into you from above and below, increasing at your heart center. With each breath out, the energy flows throughout you. If you find a tightness in your chest, pause for a moment and imagine your body dissolving into light. Imagine it as a body of energy-light. Then resume."

Gabriel did as Ohin instructed and felt the energy flowing through him with a power he had never sensed before. Magnified and increased, the energy radiating through him felt pleasing and powerful. And the more smoothly the energy flowed, the more effortlessly he could concentrate his mind, the energy flow and his mind melding together and seeming to become one.

"Now you may relax your mind and let the energy return to normal," Ohin said. A moment later, Gabriel opened his eyes.

"I could feel your energy," Ohin said, "so, I know your practice was successful. Could you feel mine?"

"No," Gabriel said, surprised that he would even be expected to.

"We will try to add that next time," Ohin said. "How did it feel?"

"Powerful," Gabriel said. "Like I had this great clarity."

"Yes," Ohin said. "This practice will help with focusing your mind and eventually with seeing the energy in all things, the interconnectedness of all things through that energy, and ultimately, the lack of separateness of all things."

"But when will I be able to do magic without a talisman?" Gabriel asked.

"The energy feels more powerful than it is," Ohin said. "While even a small amount of practice will yield some increase in the magical effect when using a talisman, it normally takes a few years before the magical energy has been increased enough to use without one."

"I see," Gabriel said. "I don't think I could have kept that concentration for more than a second in a fight."

"Exactly," Ohin said. "But eventually, if you persist, you will be able to. Now it is time for your walk with Sema."

"Thank you for teaching me this" Gabriel said as he and Ohin stood up. He knew it was unusually early in his training for such advanced lessons.

"Thank you for coming back to be taught," Ohin said, placing a firm hand on Gabriel's shoulder. "You are important to us, to me, for many more reasons than the magic you can do."

"I feel the same way," Gabriel said, swallowing hard to keep the ball of emotion in his throat from rising up too far.

Sema greeted him with a wide smile as he approached the others. She broke away from them and guided him on the familiar walk through the grounds. Sema decided that they should continue their daily talks to help Gabriel deal with his time in the hands of Kumaradevi. Now instead of talking about his family or his friends left behind when he died in the bus, they talked mostly about his experiences in the dark palace and what they meant to him. As before, Sema did little of the talking, preferring to ask questions and wait patiently for Gabriel's answers.

After their walk, Gabriel and Sema joined the others to continue their training. They were all impressed with how much he had learned in Kumaradevi's arena, but unlike his Malignancy Mage tutors, they were each more than willing to give him tips and pointers and help him correct mistakes with encouragement.

After lunch, he had a private lesson with Akikane, who began to teach him the basics of how to wield a sword. Gabriel was chagrinned to find that this began with learning stances and postures and the philosophical essentials of Aikido and that flailing around with a wooden blade was frowned upon. Gabriel needed only one frown from Akikane to set him straight. Learning to use a sword was not child's play, and it would not involve playing with swords. Swords were never to be played with. They were not toys, but tools. Tools for concentration in the right hands, and tools for death in the wrong ones. Akikane insisted that Gabriel's hands would know the difference and how to use a sword properly, without bringing harm and causing negative imprints.

The afternoon, and any free time after dinner, was spent learning about Alexander the Great and trying to pinpoint likely battles that Apollyon could use the negative imprints from to increase his magic and hide the branches of time he was creating to copy himself. They studied not only the facts of Alexander's life, but cultures and customs of Macedonia, Greece, and the many lands he conquered. They even learned a few words in Ancient Greek from a Wind Mage named Hestia who had lived a hundred years before Alexander. Many of the team members already spoke a little Greek, but Ohin insisted that everyone have enough words to manage in case things went horribly wrong.

Gabriel struggled to keep all the facts straight. Focusing on just Alexandros, as his name was pronounced in Greek, and what he had done, was much easier. Born in 356 BCE to Philip II, the king of Macedonia, and his fourth wife, Olympia, Alexander was thirteen when the famous philosopher Aristotle became to be his tutor. His father was assassinated in 336 BCE, and Alexander assumed the throne. Shortly thereafter, he began a campaign of conquest through Egypt, Persia, and India. Within ten years, he had defeated all of the major armies of the known world and became the ruler of nearly every land he passed through. In 326 BCE in Hyphasis in India, his troops refused to continue fighting, and he was forced to retreat. He died three years later in 323 BCE after falling ill at a celebration. Those were the bare facts, filled in by a long list of battles in places with names like Granicus, Gaugamela, Tyre, and Issus. Gabriel found himself returning frequently to the timelines in his copy of *The Time Traveler's Pocket Guide to History*.

The training went on like that for five days, practicing magic and combat skills, studying history, and preparing for the long journey. Ohin estimated that it could take as much as a week to thoroughly search each battle, which meant they could be traveling a few months. Of course, they could return to the castle when necessary, but they needed to carry provisions that would allow them to stay away for several days and nights. Apollyon was just as likely to use the imprints of a battle after it was over as while it was taking place.

Rajan and Marcus each carried a tent, one for the men and one for the women, and everyone had bedrolls and backpacks filled with beef jerky, dried fruit, cheese, bread, and water. They also each carried a small first aid kit in the event that Marcus or Akikane were not on hand to help heal injuries. Although Gabriel was making progress learning from Marcus, he was still, thanks to his days in Kumaradevi's arena, much more proficient at creating damage in a body with Heart-Tree Magic than healing it. They also each carried several relics of the time so that if they were separated, Ohin, Akikane, or Gabriel, could get them to another location or back to the castle.

On the morning of the sixth day, they gathered in a corner of the courtyard of the Upper Ward, each appearing as though they were dressed in local ancient Greek clothes. The men were dressed as commoners, with leather sandals, skirts of wool, and loose fitting, short-sleeved cotton shirts. The women wore draping, toga-like dresses that fell off their shoulders and flowed to their ankles. Gabriel found himself trying not to notice Teresa's soft brown shoulders. If she caught him trying not to notice, she gave no sign of it.

Elizabeth arrived to wish them well and send them off with words of inspiration. At least Gabriel hoped they would be words of inspiration. She seemed none-too-happy that morning, although he suspected this was because he was accompanying the team on the mission. He hoped she wouldn't change her mind and try to force him to stay. She could change her mind, but he wasn't about to change his. He saw that Nefferati was with her, as well. He had not seen her since the dinner the first night back and had assumed she had departed for her retreat already. She didn't look very happy, either. Maybe they were back to arguing.

"I wanted to wish you all a successful mission today," Elizabeth said. The silence of the other team members spoke to how rare an occasion it was to receive a sendoff from the head of the Council. "Take care of each other as you take care of business."

"And don't do anything stupid," Nefferati added, looking directly at Gabriel.

"Well, we'll have to change our plans now," Rajan said under his breath. Gabriel wasn't sure if Elizabeth or Nefferati heard him, but they both frowned just the same.

"Well, that's it," Elizabeth said. "Good hunting."

"And good luck," Nefferati said.

"Well said, well said," Akikane said. "Now we go." Akikane touched his sword and smiled as he gave a short wave to Elizabeth and Nefferati, a Greek coin held between his thumb and forefinger. Then the familiar blackness of time travel surrounded them, followed by the whiteness that signaled a jump through space and time.

CHAPTER 24
ALEXANDER THE TERRIBLE

The Chimera Team sat in a circle around a small campfire. Gabriel sat next to Teresa, the Sword of Unmaking lying in the grass beside him. Akikane had entrusted Gabriel to carry the sword both because it would teach him responsibility and because it would mean he had access to a very powerfully imbued artifact if he needed a talisman in the event something went wrong. Gabriel usually wore it slung it over his shoulders with a strap because he was too short yet to wear it at his waist. Teresa had giggled the first time she saw him with it, but no one had said anything.

Rajan and Ohin roasted apples on sticks over the fire. As they rotated the apples in the flames, they played a game of *Go*, the ancient Chinese game of strategy. Players placed small black and white stones at the intersections of cross-hatched lines on a wooden board. The object of the game was to accumulate territory and eliminate your opponent's pieces.

Watching them play, Marcus carefully sliced a roasted apple into sections with a knife, placing the pieces on a small tin camping plate. When he finished cutting, he drizzled honey over the apple slices and sprinkled a little cinnamon over them from a copper tin. Stabbing one of the apple slices with the tip of the knife, he passed the plate to Ling, who grabbed a slice and tossed it in her mouth, her eyes going wide as she spit the apple slice back into her hand, bouncing it up and down.

"Zhǐzé!" Ling exclaimed, blowing on the slice of apple. "That's hot!"

"What'd you expect," Marcus said with a laugh. "It's a roasted apple. They tend to be warm."

"You could have warned me," Ling said as she took a wary bite from the slice of roasted apple and passed the plate to Sema, who carefully took a piece with her fingers.

"I'll blow on the next ones to cool them down for you," Marcus said as he grinned and bit into the apple slice skewered by the tip of his knife blade.

"It's interesting how much Apollyon and Alexander resemble each other," Gabriel said, blowing on a piece of roasted apple as he passed the plate to Akikane. They had been watching the two on battlefield after battlefield for several weeks now and Gabriel had noticed how much Cyril, as Apollyon was called then, modeled himself on his leader, Alexander. The two even looked a little alike.

"He's a little more dangerous than Alexander the Great," Ling mumbled, apple in her mouth. "And his copies of himself are a more dangerous army than Alexander ever hoped to command."

"Can he really manage to get the copies of himself to follow with the same devotion of his mages?" Rajan asked as he stared into the fire. "Will his philosophy of power work as well on a group of copies as it does on other Malignancy Mages?" They had repeatedly debated this question around the evening campfires.

Every night the same questions came up and they went through them again. Ohin promoted it as a means of looking for pieces of information and ideas they may have missed. They all knew that once they found and severed the branches of time Apollyon was using to create copies of himself, it would only signal the beginning of a new battle, not the end of the war.

"It's hardly a philosophy," Sema said.

"Balderdash is more like it," Marcus added as he sliced another apple.

"Let's look at it again for weaknesses," Ohin said. He always encouraged them to look for weaknesses as part of creating a long-term strategy. He and Akikane had begun insisting that they play games like *Go* and *Chess* to develop their sense of strategy. Rajan had added *Chaturanga*, the Indian precursor to chess that up to four people could play. Ohin placed another white stone on the *Go* board and looked up. "Gabriel, why don't you summarize Apollyon's philosophy for us?"

"Do we need to go through it again?" Teresa asked, licking honey from her fingers.

"Of course, of course," Akikane said. "Each time we look at the puzzle, more pieces will begin to fit together." He smiled at Gabriel as he took another bite of roasted apple.

"Right," Gabriel said as he swallowed a chunk of apple. He had heard and recited the philosophy before. "Apollyon's basic philosophy is that mages exist to rule over non-mages, and in particular to rule the whole of the Primary Continuum and use it for their glory. Or for his glory, since he wants to rule the mages. He seems influenced by the late 19th century German philosopher, Fredrick Nietzsche, and his idea of an Übermensch, or Over Man, or Super Man. Essentially, the strong are strong for a reason, and they should rule the weak. And the strongest should rule them all."

"A bit of a condensation," Rajan said.

"I thought I was supposed to be brief," Gabriel said. "Apollyon believes he can become something that has never existed, someone more powerful than anyone in all of history." Gabriel paused for a moment as he realized that thought was similar to something Vicaquirao had told him about himself. Gabriel was something that had never existed and was destined to become more powerful than anyone in or out of history. How was he similar to Apollyon? Was that what Vicaquirao had been hinting at? It was unsettling to consider.

He pushed the thought aside as he continued, hoping the others had not noticed his pause in speech. "Anyway, Apollyon believes that mages should unite under his leadership and rule the people of all the alternate realities and that they should break The Great Barrier in 2012 so they can rule the future. And I remember something now. Vicaquirao was reading a book by Nietzsche when he had me captive at that cabin. It may have been coincidence, but maybe not. Maybe Apollyon got his philosophy in part from Vicaquirao."

"Or maybe that's what the slippery devil wants us to think," Sema said.

"Maybe," Ohin said. "But good to know. This is why we go through it again and again."

"Yes, yes," Akikane said. "Little pieces that help reveal the whole."

"Assuming we're not seeing exactly what Vicaquirao wants us to see," Ling said.

"Very possible, very possible," Akikane said with his usual smile.

"Instructive for us," Rajan said, "that Nietzsche also wrote *He who fights against monsters should see to it that he does not become a monster in the process. And when you stare persistently into an abyss, the abyss also stares into you.*"

"I've seen the abyss," Teresa said. "It's overrated."

"What else?" Sema asked, looking at Gabriel as she began a game of chess with Teresa.

"Apollyon wants to rule over the Grace Mages, as well," Gabriel said, taking another piece of apple to cover the discomfort of the thought. "He believes that Grace Mages are essential to the balance of the universe, but they must be subservient to the Malignancy Mages, similar to Vicaquirao's idea that dark and light must balance each other. Except Apollyon doesn't believe in balance. He believes that balance creates stagnation, and that only from destruction can new creativity arise."

"Bad complexity theory," Teresa said, moving a white pawn. "Too much stability and structure, and your system is too rigid to allow creativity. You need just enough chaos to stay on the edge of creativity, but too much and everything falls apart. He's not looking to create new levels of complexity, he looking to destroy and dominate what there is."

"Exactly what I was going to say," Gabriel said, grinning at Teresa.

"That raises the question then," Rajan said, "do we need someone like Apollyon to add chaos to our system?"

"Not bloody likely," Marcus said.

"There's plenty of chaos in the Continuum without his help," Ling said.

"Or the opposite question," Gabriel said. The others looked at him quizzically.

"Just so, just so," Akikane said, smiling at Gabriel again.

"What do you mean?" Sema asked.

"Is the Council too rigid, too stable, to be creative enough to defeat the Malignancy Mages?" Gabriel asked. It wasn't a question he really wanted an answer to.

"Good question," Ohin said.

"We'd better bloody well hope not," Marcus said.

"But there's a better question," Teresa said.

"I didn't want to ask it," Gabriel said.

"What question?" Ling said.

"Are we too rigid to be creative enough to defeat Apollyon?" Gabriel said.

"Exactly, exactly," Akikane said. "Can we use the chaos he causes to creatively defeat him?" Everyone was silent for a moment, their eyes meeting over the flames of the fire.

"I think we can," Gabriel said. He wasn't entirely sure he believed it, but he knew someone needed to say it and since he had posed the question, it seemed like his responsibility.

"Good answer, Gabriel," Sema said with a nod of her head.

"And a good answer to end on," Ohin said. "Who would like to entertain us tonight?"

"Oh, I've got something," Marcus said, gently using his tongue to remove the honey from the tip of his knife. Every night they traded turns around the campfire, reciting poetry and telling stories. Ohin would play his wooden flute, and Rajan would do magic tricks. Not real magic, but tricks of sleight-of-hand. Teresa found it terribly amusing and ironic. She often entertained by doing wildly complicated mathematical computations in her head. Rajan usually protested that they had no way of knowing if she was giving the right answer or not, since she was the only math genius present. Teresa would chide Rajan that it wasn't her fault he couldn't count beyond ten without taking his shoes off.

"This evening," Marcus began as he took a sip from a wineskin to clear his throat, "I thought we might enjoy a little Shakespeare. A little something to stir the hearts in the face of our obstacles. A little speech from Henry the Fifth, I'm sure you've heard once or twice." Marcus stood before the fire and coughed once before he began to recite.

"If we are mark'd to die, we are enow
To do our country loss; and if to live,
The fewer men, the greater share of honour.
God's will! I pray thee, wish not one man more.
By Jove, I am not covetous for gold,
Nor care I who doth feed upon my cost;
It yearns me not if men my garments wear;
Such outward things dwell not in my desires:
But if it be a sin to covet honour,
I am the most offending soul alive."

As Gabriel listened to Marcus reciting the words, playing out the part of Henry the Fifth inspiring his troops, his thoughts turned back to Apollyon, as they always did. The Malignant True Mage was likely placing the copies of himself at different moments in history where the great atrocities that took place would give him more combined power than any mage had ever held. Linked together, he and his army of copies might hold sufficient power to break through The Great Barrier of Probability that kept Time Mages from moving any further into the future than October 28, 2012 CE.

He had probably created several dozen copies already. How could they defeat dozens of versions of Apollyon linked together through time? *One at a time,* he thought to himself. *Slowly, slowly,* as Akikane was fond of saying about his training. And how far could that training take him? And how fast? And as he gained mastery of all six magics, and as he gained more power than any mage had held before, would that power tempt him the way it so obviously tempted Apollyon? He had to hope not, but how could he know?

He was on a path to becoming something he might not even recognize as himself when he was finished. How could he remain true to who he was? He knew he would not truly know until it was too late to change what he had become. Gabriel returned his attention to Marcus, hoping to forget his questions for a few moments.

"We few, we happy few, we band of brothers;
For he today that sheds his blood with me
Shall be my brother; be he ne'er so vile,
This day shall gentle his condition:
And gentlemen in England now a-bed
Shall think themselves accursed they were not here,
And hold their manhoods cheap whiles any speaks
That fought with us upon Saint Crispin's day."

Those seated around the campfire burst into applause as Marcus finished reciting.

The bald man blushed and bowed slightly.

"Wonderful," Sema said as Marcus sat beside her.

"It's the words, not the man who speaks them," Marcus said, grabbing the wineskin and taking a quick swig.

"It's the man who speaks them that gives them life," Sema corrected.

"Thank you," Marcus said, patting Sema's hand. "Who's next?" he asked as he turned to the others around the fire.

"Flute, flute, flute," Teresa began to chant as she clapped her hands. Rajan copied her first and the others quickly joined in, even Akikane. Gabriel noticed that it was Ohin's turn to seem embarrassed as he pulled his wooded flute from his leather satchel and settled in to play.

"Any requests?" Ohin said, licking his lips as he settled the mouthpiece on them.

"*The Girl I Left Behind Me*," Marcus called.

"Maybe we can convince Ling to sing," Rajan said, poking Ling.

"I hardly know the words," Ling demurred.

"Balderdash," Marcus said. "You never forget anything. You're like an elephant without a trunk."

"Isn't she though?" Teresa teased.

"Oh, all right," Ling said, clearing her throat as Ohin began the tune. Ling waited for the intro and then began to sing in a voice so sweet and lush that it had taken Gabriel completely by surprise the first time he had heard it weeks ago. There were many things that he had imagined Ling being able to do, but singing Irish folk songs was not one of them.

"I'm lonesome since I crossed the hill,
And o'er the moorland sedgy
Such heavy thoughts my heart do fill,
Since parting with my Betsey
I seek for one as fair and gay,
But find none to remind me
How sweet the hours I passed away,
With the girl I left behind me."

By the second verse, Marcus had joined her, his resonant baritone balancing Ling's clear soprano. Soon the others joined in, and Gabriel added his voice, stumbling over the words he only vaguely remembered from when Marcus had taught them the lyrics the week before. He laughed and looked up at the stars glittering in the night sky above. He wished this moment would last, but he knew they would soon be asleep, each taking turns with the watch, waking in the morning to observe yet another battle, searching again for the moment where Apollyon was breaking the Continuum to serve his vile plans. But there under the stars, sitting around the campfire with his friends and teammates, he laughed and sang and tried not to think.

CHAPTER 25
BATTLE FATIGUE

The morning brought battle.

It was a battle much like the others Gabriel had witnessed: violent, bloody, and loud, filled with the cries of men and horses and even elephants, in combat and in death. This one was the Battle of Gaugamela against Darius III of Persia in October of 331 BCE, in what would eventually be known as northern Iraq in Gabriel's time. Darius III had aligned his archers, cavalry, war chariots, infantry, and elephants against Alexander's smaller number of cavalry and infantry, the Persian king holding the advantage in numbers by nearly two to one.

However, Alexander was nothing if not a brilliant battlefield strategist. Darius III lined his forces up along the battlefield, taking the central position, as was Persian tradition for the king. Meanwhile, Alexander broke his force into two units, allowing him to attack the Persian line at two points, eventually breaking through it and causing the Persian forces to flee, King Darius III among the first to leave the battlefield in haste. The battle lasted only a couple of hours. Far less than other battles Gabriel had seen.

Gabriel and the rest of the team watched the battle and the aftermath from a safe distance on a nearby hill, lying close to the ground and viewing the action through binoculars. Ling had assured Gabriel, as wild as it sounded, that she could have used the force of gravity to bend the light coming from the battlefield in much the way the lenses of the binoculars did, and allow them to see it all with great precision. But that sort of magic would have drawn attention from Apollyon if he showed himself, so the team made do with traditional optics.

Teresa had come up with the ingenious notion of taking black nylon stockings and stretching them over the lens of the binoculars

266

to keep them from reflecting light to anyone on the battlefield. Stretched tight, they only slightly hindered the resolution of an image at a distance. The stockings didn't eliminate the glare completely, but reduced it enough to make daytime observation a little more clandestine, particularly when the sun was low and shading the lens with one's hand was no longer possible.

They observed the battlefield all day, through the fighting and well afterward. Ohin and Akikane were both of the opinion that Apollyon would likely wait until after a battle to seize all of the negative imprints generated by the fighting to use in creating the magic that would hide the bifurcations he was making to copy himself. While the magic would hide the bifurcations at a distance in time, Ohin felt certain that if they were physically close enough when Apollyon created his new branches of reality, he, Gabriel and Akikane would be able to sense it. So, they continued to watch as Alexander's troops took prisoners and camped as night fell, waiting for something to happen, waiting for one of the True Mages or the Time Mage to sense something.

The watching centered mostly on Apollyon himself, on the soldier Cyril, as he was known then. They took turns keeping him under surveillance, making sure there were at least two pairs of eyes on him at all times.

Gabriel was watching with Teresa, his guard dog, as he had taken to thinking of her. They lay on another hill near the Macedonian camp as Apollyon and his fellow captains celebrated around a fire below. The men drank and sang and cheered their leader. As Gabriel watched, it reminded him in small ways of the nights around the campfire with his teammates. Only he could never imagine his friends celebrating at the deaths of so many. Thousands and thousands of people dead so Alexander's empire could keep growing. After weeks of witnessing horrible battles, Gabriel did not laugh when Sema referred to him as Alexander the Terrible. He could not fathom why such a talented and charismatic man devoted himself to expanding his power at any cost. Apparently, Apollyon understood.

As the men celebrated, a fight started. Gabriel wasn't certain who had started the fight, he had been daydreaming a bit, but Cyril, the man who would become Apollyon, was at the center of it with another man, another captain. The two lunged at each other, grappling and punching, the other man trying to wrestle Apollyon to the ground. Gabriel felt something then. A prickling sensation that filled his mind and reverberated against his time-sense. Little needles poking into his pincushion-brain. He knew that sensation. Someone nearby was warping the fabric of space-time to travel to this moment. Not just one someone. It was like a series of tiny lacerations made and sealed in moments. Dozens of them. So many that Gabriel lost count.

He felt more than saw Ohin and Akikane joining him and Teresa on the crest of the hill.

"You felt it?" Ohin asked, lifting a pair of binoculars to his eyes.

"How could I not?" Gabriel said.

"Felt what?" Teresa asked and then gasped to indicate that she realized what, adding, "Apollyon is fighting with another soldier."

"I see, I see," Akikane said as he looked through another set of binoculars at the fight in the campsite below. "It is as you suspected, Ohin."

"Yes," Ohin said.

While they watched, Cyril, the man who would become Apollyon, was thrown to the ground and knocked insensible as the other man swung a rock into his head. As Cyril fell to the ground unconscious, Gabriel felt something else, something that made his time-sense swirl and his gut wrench.

The fabric of space-time twisted upon itself again and again. He had felt something similar when he had created the branch of alternate realty he used to save Ling back in Venice. This was oddly far less intense, like listening to sounds that had been muffled by cotton in his ears. As though the layers upon layers of alternate reality being ripped away from the Primary Continuum were a dream and not something happening right in that moment. Gabriel knew it was the masking effect of Apollyon's magic that made it so hard to discern what was happening to the fabric of the Continuum.

Gabriel could feel some of the branches of time ceasing to exist even as others burst into existence. He dropped the binoculars and looked around the campsite, straining to see any evidence of Apollyon. He could find none. Apollyon was as well hidden as Gabriel and his teammates. He was probably closer to the action, closer to where the soldiers still fought among themselves, and where Cyril lay unconscious. Gabriel looked through the binoculars again. The man who had struck down Cyril was now fighting with another man.

The twisting of reality that Gabriel sensed abruptly stopped. The moment of bifurcations had passed. He felt the prickling sensation again, only once this time, and then there was only the camp of Alexander's men below, his captains fighting around the unconscious form of Cyril.

Gabriel put the binoculars down. Teresa stared at him. "What just happened?" she asked.

"We have found the moment and place where Apollyon is copying himself," Ohin said.

"Yes, yes," Akikane said. "Ohin thought it would be at a moment that Apollyon wanted to change. A moment he had thought about for years and wanted to make different."

"Like losing a fight to a man he considered to be beneath him," Gabriel said, replaying in his mind the scene had just witnessed.

"Exactly," Ohin said. "I'm sure in almost all of the alternate realities created, Cyril arises to defeat the man he was fighting."

"How many time-jumps did you sense at the end?' Akikane asked.

"Just one," Gabriel said. "I assume it's one of the Apollyons leaving after using magic to hide where the branches are being made." Gabriel had tried to probe that magic, but could find no clear trace of it even as he felt for it. It was like trying to catch the wind in your hand.

"Probably you are right," Ohin said. "We wait."

"For what?" Teresa asked.

"In case there is a second Apollyon around here waiting for someone to find what he's been doing," Gabriel said.

So they waited. For an hour. Just when Ohin looked like he was going to give the go ahead to move, Gabriel felt the familiar tickling of his time-sense that indicated another time-jump being made.

"Wise we waited," Ohin said.

"Another one?" Teresa asked. She clearly didn't like not being able to sense what was happening the way Gabriel and the older men could.

"Yes, yes," Akikane said. "All clear now. We hope. I will go." Gabriel felt the prickling of his time-sense again, and Akikane was suddenly gone.

"Where did he go?" Gabriel asked.

"We need half of a relic to link us to that moment in space-time when the branches were made," Ohin said, gesturing back to the camp of Alexander's men.

Gabriel picked up the binoculars and scanned the campsite until he found what he was looking for, the form of an unconscious Cyril still lying on the ground, apparently asleep. He had been pulled closer to the fire by one of his men, but left to slumber. Akikane knelt down next to him. No one stopped him or even noticed him. He must have felt it safe to use magic to conceal himself. A quick flash of metal in the firelight and Akikane held a lock of Cyril's hair in his hand. A moment later, Akikane knelt beside Gabriel.

"What is that for?" Gabriel asked, pointing to the lock of hair that Akikane was placing in a pocket of his clothes.

"Dis-phased non-local quantum entanglement," Teresa said with a grin.

"Yes, yes," Akikane said. "To link us to the moment we need and the person in particular."

"We should get back to the others," Ohin said, beginning to slide down the backside of the hill toward the rest of the team. Gabriel and Teresa followed Ohin down the hill, Akikane bringing up the rear. When they reached the others, Sema was the first to see the looks on their faces.

"Have you found it?" Sema asked, standing to greet them.

"Yes," Ohin said. "Strike the camp as fast as you can. We leave in five minutes."

"My prayers are answered," Marcus said as he began stuffing his belongings into his backpack. "No more long nights on hard ground. My aching back thanks you."

"My ears thank you," Rajan said as he began to pack up the tent. "No more listening to Marcus complaining about his back."

"And no more listening to you complain about the food," Teresa said as she snuffed out the fire with a wave of her hand.

"Hurry, everyone," Ohin said as he grabbed his own backpack and checked it. Gabriel helped Rajan with the tents and then made sure he had everything in his own backpack. Within minutes, the campsite was packed with no trace of them having been there beyond a small fire. Rajan then used his Earth Magic to make the ashes of the fire disappear into the soil, erasing the last sign of their presence.

"Eyes on the ground," Ohin said and everyone paused and took a moment to scan the surrounding area for anything they might have accidentally left behind. It would be inexcusable to leave something behind like a lighter or a pair of binoculars that might result in an alternate reality being created when they were found. "Are we good to go?" Ohin asked. Everyone voiced their affirmation. "Good. Gather close. Akikane will take us to someplace far away near the moment we need."

"Yes, yes," Akikane said, holding up a small animal bone he had taken from his robes. "Off we go." As Gabriel stepped closer to Sema and Teresa, the blackness he knew so well began to surround them followed by the whiteness that faded to reveal a rocky plateau and a wide, incredibly tall canyon rising around them. Gabriel instinctively shielded his eyes from the harsh glare of the sun directly above in the sky. He knew this place. Not from being there, but from pictures.

"The Grand Canyon," he said aloud as he focused on the amulet at his neck and resumed the appearance of wearing his normal cotton tunic and pants. The others did the same.

"Just so, just so," Akikane said. "Same moment, other side of the world."

"We want to be far enough away from the moment of the branching so that Apollyon will have less chance of knowing we are here at all," Ohin said. He stepped toward the river that flowed along the canyon floor, as it had for millennia. "Spread out. Defensive positions. We don't know what to expect, but we should expect something." The team moved to take defensive positions in a circle around Akikane, each facing outward. Ohin took a place by the river so that he could see far down each end of the canyon. Gabriel started walking toward the defensive circle, but Akikane placed a hand on his shoulder.

"No, no," Akikane said. "You are with me. You have the blade. The Sword of Unmaking. We will need that."

"Right," Gabriel said, turning back toward Akikane. Gabriel unsheathed the sword over his shoulder, handing it to Akikane, blade parallel to the ground and aimed back behind himself, the handle pointing forward, as he had been taught. Akikane took the blade in one hand as he pulled the locket of Apollyon's hair from the pocket of his kimono.

"Ready, ready," Akikane said. "The moment is almost here. Almost. Almost." Gabriel reached out with his time-sense to the locket of hair and found he could feel the moment of the branching drawing nearer, as though he were back in the Macedonian campsite with Apollyon and the other soldier. If he focused his mind just right, he could almost see what was happening on the other side of the world in the middle of the ancient Persian Empire right at that moment. And it was close. So close. So very close. And then he felt it.

The twist in the fabric of space-time, curling and coiling, and then he felt a wall of magical power radiating from Akikane, more intense than Gabriel had imagined possible. He had never felt power like that so close. Gabriel realized that Akikane must have mastered the art of cultivating magical energy within himself because it was like being next to a furnace whose energy was being magnified and amplified by the Grace imprints of the Sword of Unmaking.

Gabriel extended his time-sense to slow the moment and perceived, through the locket of hair, a portal of potentiality, a slender thread trailing off from the Primary Continuum. It was similar to what he had felt back in Venice when Akikane had severed the branch of time Gabriel created to save Ling. However, this was more like a tangle of threads wildly woven and knotted around each other. More a portal of portals, each leading to a different, but similar place. Gabriel could feel Akikane wielding the power within himself and the sword into a fine razor-thin blast of energy, slicing through the multiple tendrils of possibility, closing the portals with a single cut. A cut that not only severed, but also cauterized, sealing that moment and place from any further branching. Gabriel was stunned by the intensity of the power needed to seal a tear in the fabric of space-time like Akikane had just done, making that moment unchangeable.

Then there was only silence and the sound of the river swiftly rushing through the canyon floor. The branches of time had been severed from the Primary Continuum. They did not exist anymore. In all likelihood, the people in them no longer existed, either. Gabriel hoped that they did. Somehow. In some frame of possibility. It seemed unfair that billions of people in these alternate worlds should have to cease to exist in order to save the Primary Continuum from Apollyon. There was no way to know for certain. So, Gabriel decided to hope.

"Done, done," Akikane said, visibly relaxing and taking a deep breath. The severing had required a great deal of magical energy, and Gabriel was certain that Akikane was even now immersing himself in the meditative practice that would allow him to restore it more quickly.

"Good," Marcus said. "I think a pint of ale is in order."

Gabriel began to laugh with the others, but stopped when he felt it. Just like before, only not at all cloaked by magic: the sensation of multiple time-jumps being made nearly simultaneously. And quick on the heels of that sensation, a feeling he knew all too well, a jabbing at his time-sense that instantly made him think of Kumaradevi's arena and the Dark Mages.

"Run!" he shouted in unison with Ohin. "A space-time shield!"

As he looked up around the canyon, he saw them. Too many to count in one glance, but at least twelve men. All the same. All Apollyon.

"Flee! Flee!" Akikane said as he thrust the Sword of Unmaking into Gabriel's hands. Gabriel had agreed earlier, weeks ago, that if Apollyon found them, he would run. He would not try to stay and fight. Gabriel had agreed only because he knew that Apollyon would have little interest in fighting the others if it meant missing a chance to catch him. But he could not flee as Akikane had instructed. The space-time seal Apollyon held on the canyon prevented him from jumping away through either time or space.

Fireballs streaked through the air even as the walls of the canyon rumbled and threatened to crash down. Gabriel saw Teresa running toward him, casting fireballs and blinding blue arcs of lightning and whirling vortexes of white-hot energy at two of the Apollyons on the canyon above. They raised their hands and the flames and electric arcs rebounded toward Teresa. Gabriel had no time to think, but did not really need to. He raised the sword and the balls of flame and lightning flew harmlessly into the river. He could not jump out of the negative space-time field the circle of Apollyons held in place, he could tell it was too strong to break through easily, but he could jump within it.

He jumped to Teresa's side even as the first man called Apollyon raised his hand. Gabriel grabbed Teresa and jumped through space again, appearing behind a large rock outcropping.

"You're supposed to run," she nearly yelled at him.

"The space-time seal prevents any jumps out," Gabriel said. "Stay here."

"Wait!" Teresa said, but Gabriel was already gone, disappearing from her side and reappearing on the far side of the river. His only hope was to draw the fire from the Apollyons above toward himself and away from his teammates. He looked around and tried to follow what was happening. It had only been a few seconds since the appearance of the Twelve Apollyons. Twelve that were linked to at least twenty more throughout time, channeling the power of innumerable negative imprints into the circle above.

Across the river, Ohin had drawn a sword and was jumping through space, grabbing teammates and placing them safely at the edges of the canyon. Akikane was battling with one of the Apollyons at the top of the canyon wall above. Suddenly he vanished and appeared a moment later in front of another Apollyon, his sword imbedded in the stomach of the man he stood before. The Apollyons above all roared in pain at the same moment, a moment in which the space-time seal they held flickered and waned. Gabriel did not wait. He knew that the faster he traveled away the sooner the others would be safe. Concentrating on the sword, using it as relic, he jumped. Blackness surrounded him, followed quickly by the familiar flood of white light.

Even as the whiteness faded, he reached in his pocket to grab another relic. This time a coin from ancient Rome. He barely had time to look down on the sight of the medieval Japanese fishing village before the blackness flowed around him again. As it came, he saw all twelve of the Apollyons surround him, and he felt them attempt to create a space-time seal. But it was too late. He was gone.

As the whiteness faded, he looked upon the Coliseum in Rome, first or second century, he guessed as he jumped again. He saw fewer Apollyons this time. When the whiteness began to fade, he still saw the Coliseum, only this time in ruins, hundreds of years later. His fingers were already in his pocket and holding a pottery shard, the blackness enveloping him as he spotted six Apollyons. As the whiteness faded to reveal the Great Pyramid of Egypt, still under construction, his hand clutched a small stone statue of a man with a sword, and the blackness surrounded him again. He spotted only three Apollyons this time. Whiteness evaporated as Gabriel stood in the middle of an expansive Chinese Palace of wood and stone. He didn't know when it was, and didn't care. His hand grasped the last object in his pocket and the blackness followed swiftly, the lone face of a single Apollyon dissolving before his eyes.

CHAPTER 26
ANGEL OF DESTRUCTION

Gabriel stood in a forest, snow floating down through the still air, adding to the thick layer that was already on the ground, the afternoon sky dense with grey clouds. Between the trees, men in snow covered uniforms huddled in foxholes dug deep into the cold, hard earth. He knew where he was. He jumped again. Not through time, but through space, further into the woods. Further from the place in time he had leapt to.

Standing in the snow up to his knees, he looked back through the trees to the spot where he had been only a moment before. He saw nothing. He was tempted to jump again. Another time. Another place. Maybe even back to the castle.

He looked down at his hands, the Sword of Unmaking in his right and the pocket watch in his left. He had not intended to use the pocket watch, but it had been the last object he could try. And this battlefield in Western Germany was safer than somewhere along the timeline where his Grandfather might be even closer. At least here, he could hide and catch his breath for a moment. Looking back where he had been, he saw nothing appear. No one. Apollyon had not been able to follow him here.

He let out a sigh of relief even as he sensed the space-time seal come into existence, even as he heard the voice behind him.

"Very clever," Apollyon said.

Gabriel felt an icy chill run up his back as his stomach cramped with fear. He wanted to spin and throw the sword at Apollyon. He wanted to run. He wanted to scream out for help. He made himself swallow his fears instead. He remembered all those days in the arena facing the Kumaradevi's *Light* Mages. Apollyon was just the same. More powerful. More dangerous. But just the same.

He wrapped the chain of the pocket watch around his left hand and then joined it to the right hand around the hilt of the Japanese sword. He still held the magical energy of them as firmly as he had before, but as he reached out to try and touch the negative imprints of the World War Two battlefield, he discovered they were already held. By Apollyon. Gabriel slowly turned around.

"You did not learn that lesson well enough the first time I see," Apollyon said, his handsome face breaking into a satisfied smile. "You bring me to a place with dark imprints like handing me a gift and only think to try and hold them yourself as an afterthought. I will teach you the advantage of taking all that is presented to you when facing an opponent."

"Which one are you?" Gabriel said, hoping to stall for time. Time for something he could only hope would happen, because it was the only thing he could think might allow him to escape.

"It does not matter," Apollyon said. "We are all one now. We see with three dozen pairs of eyes. Think with three dozen minds. We are becoming something that has never been before. We are becoming the sum of all mages. The sum of all time. You could have seen through the eyes of your double had you left that branch of time you created intact. You would have had a taste of what it means to become something more than merely human. More than a mere mage."

"So you're not the original," Gabriel said. "I didn't think so."

"I tell you it does not matter," Apollyon said.

"I'll bet it matters to him," Gabriel said. Where was it? It must happen soon. He hoped it happened soon.

"Spread doubt and uncertainty in the enemy," Apollyon said, smiling again, but with more of an effort. "You learned much in your short time with my old master."

"He had very nice things to say about you," Gabriel said.

"And why should he not?" Apollyon asked.

"He is still upset that you tried to kill him," Gabriel said.

"It is his own burden to put down, not mine," Apollyon said. "The past is past. I am about the future."

"Controlling the future, you mean," Gabriel said.

"I fear you have gotten a warped perspective of me from those you have been keeping company with," Apollyon said. "Why don't you put down the sword and we will speak. Like men. It will be a pleasant change, I am sure, being spoken to like an adult rather than a child."

"Your turn to sow doubt and uncertainty?" Gabriel asked, keeping the sword held high, the point of its shaft aimed at Apollyon's heart.

"As you will," Apollyon said. "You cannot hope to defeat me. I am simply too powerful for you. Too powerful by far. And you cannot escape the time-seal I have set around us. But I believe it will be better for both of us if you come with me willingly."

"How do you plan to manage that?" Gabriel asked. "Going to threaten me with torturing versions of my parents?"

"Crude tactics are often required for dealing with crude people," Apollyon said, his smile returning as he opened his hands and spread them wide. "I am suggesting that we talk."

"Talk all you want," Gabriel said. "I promise to listen to you as closely as I did to Kumaradevi."

"I was thinking of someplace a little more comfortable," Apollyon said. "A little warmer."

"I feel very comfortable right here," Gabriel said, shaking his head to free it of the accumulation of snow that had been building up on his hair. He hoped it happened soon. It had to. How long could he stall?

"Then let me put my case before you and allow you to decide," Apollyon said. "Like an adult."

"You're going to give me a choice?" Gabriel asked.

"Of course," Apollyon said. "The end result will be the same, but you will have a choice along the way." Gabriel gritted his teeth at that. Always people making his choices for him.

"So tell me how we can rule the universe together and what a great pleasure it will be for me to serve you," Gabriel said, lacing his voice with as much sarcasm as he could muster past the fear. If it didn't happen soon, he was good and truly trapped.

"Not the universe," Apollyon said, his smile fading at being mocked. "Merely the Primary Continuum of this world. And whatever that may lead to after The Great Barrier has been eliminated."

"Maybe it's there for a reason," Gabriel said. "Like a fence around the hen house to keep the wolves out."

"Or a pointless impediment to a great man's destiny," Apollyon said.

"You know a great man, do you?" Gabriel said. Seeing how completely Apollyon's plastic smile had faded, he wondered if he had pushed the sarcasm too far.

"I will not be mocked by a boy," Apollyon said, his voice deepening in anger.

"Why not?" Gabriel asked. "Everyone else mocks you." That had definitely been too much. Too far. Why did he always have to say what he really wanted to say at times like this? Maybe he had said it for all the times he had wanted to speak what was really on his mind with Kumaradevi.

"I could make you serve me and you would never even know it was not your heart's greatest desire," he heard Apollyon say in his mind.

"And how weak would that make your powers of persuasion?" Gabriel thought back. *"How weak would that prove your grand philosophy to be?"* That had clearly been too far to push his luck. He could see the anger in Apollyon's eyes now and the quickness of his breath. For all his cool exterior, no doubt learned by studying Vicaquirao at close range, Apollyon was just as hot tempered and susceptible to anger as he had been when he lost that fight in Alexander the Great's campsite while he was still known as Cyril. Gabriel wondered if he could use that weakness. If the thing he was hoping for happened, maybe he could.

"Ah," Apollyon said, "you see a truly brilliant philosophy requires a truly brilliant mind to comprehend it."

"So who's the brilliant person who explained it to you?" Gabriel said. It had to happen soon. If he kept egging Apollyon on and it didn't happen…He didn't want to think about that.

"I will explain it to you," Apollyon said, ignoring Gabriel's taunt. "In simple language for a simple boy." Gabriel noticed that any pretense at flattery had vanished. "Life is composed of two manners of people: leaders and followers. Even the leaders follow other leaders. Eventually, you find that everyone follows one leader. Or does if that leader has the vision to claim that place of leadership. If that leader can hold that position. And a true leader must be more than his followers. He must attain more. He must accomplish more. He must become what has never been. He must become more than he thought himself capable of being. And those who follow him, those who lead under him, they too will accomplish great things. And the greatness of these accomplishments will be the proof that their position as leaders is justified. And the followers shall take their proper place in supporting the leader."

"So what about the people who don't want to follow?" Gabriel asked. "What about the people who want a different leader? Or who want more than one leader?"

"They will be swept aside as obsolete obstructions," Apollyon said. "The bringing of a new order requires the destruction of the old order. Chaos must reign for truly new forms, truly new beings, to arise."

"And what if your chaos destroys everything that exists while this great leader is creating his new order of being?" Gabriel asked. He thought he could hear something. Something faint, but it might be what he needed.

"There is a power beyond chaos," Apollyon said, a fire in his voice and his eyes. "A power that drives the heart of the universe as it churns out the history of the Continuum. It is a power that can be awoken and grasped and bent to submission. A power outside time. A power beyond life and death. An eternal force that can be commanded to create, as well as destroy." This part of Apollyon's philosophy was new to Gabriel. He wasn't sure if he was talking about some evil power, some dark demon or devil, or if he was talking about some supreme being beyond human understanding. But it didn't matter. He heard the sound now. Clearly. A high-pitched sound. The one he had hoped for. Now all he needed was the time to use it.

"You sound like you're saying you want to use the power of God to rule the Primary Continuum," Gabriel said.

"Not God in the limited and infantile sense you use the word," Apollyon said, with apparent annoyance.

"Well, that's good," Gabriel said. "You only want to use some nameless eternal universal power for your own selfish satisfaction. For a moment, I was afraid you'd really gone crazy."

"Enough," Apollyon shouted, as much from anger as to be heard above the sound that now filled the air. The sound of mortar shells falling. "This place will not be safe soon. We must go. You may come willingly or I will take you by force. You cannot resist me."

"I like your idea of there being one supreme leader," Gabriel said. "A supreme person becoming what others can't. I am the Seventh True Mage, after all. I'll tell you what, you agree to serve me as the supreme leader and I'll go with you."

"You have mocked me for the last time," Apollyon said, raising his hand, his mouth tight with the anger he was barely holding in check.

"I hope so," Gabriel said, flicking the point of the sword to aim through the trees, creating a field of invisible energy above the men in the foxholes he had appeared next to only minutes before. The mortar shells exploded in the air right where he had hoped they would. Right above the men he knew to be his Grandfather and his fellow soldiers. It was what he had been hoping for. An opportunity to create what he needed to escape. And Gabriel felt it. The fabric of space-time splintering like a brittle piece of ice, a new branch of reality breaking away from the Primary Continuum. A reality where the men in those foxholes all lived. An alternate reality that he and Apollyon now stood in, as well.

Apollyon laughed as Gabriel aimed sword at him again. "You stupid, sentimental little child. You've created a bifurcation. The very thing the Council has been trying to avoid for centuries. What kind of training have they been giving you? Can't you feel it? You're not in the Primary Continuum anymore."

"I know," Gabriel said as the blackness swirled around him. "And a bifurcation is the only thing that can break a powerful space-time seal." Whiteness became everything and he stood again in the forest, the mortars falling as they had before, just at the moment the new branch of reality had been made, just after the moment he and Apollyon had broken off from the Primary Continuum. He had not doubled back on his personal timeline, so there would be no copies of him or Apollyon. Both had slipped seamlessly into the new branch of reality.

Even as he appeared in the Primary Continuum, Gabriel grasped for all the imprints of the battlefield, embracing both the tainted negative imprints and the Grace-filled positive imprints, adding them to the power he wielded in the Sword of Unmaking, and focusing all of the magical power on that slender thread of frayed reality leading to a new world, that slim portal to an alternate version of history. An alternate history Apollyon was trapped in. Gabriel's head swam with the power of those imprints and he tightened his stomach against the instinctual retching that arose from holding so much tainted power. He focused all of the magical energy he possessed into severing that thin thread of reality.

The magical energy was enormous, amplified through the imprints of the pocket watch and the Sword of Unmaking and the battlefield where he stood. The portal to the other reality began to close, the thread nearly sliced through, when he felt something push back. The portal seemed to hold. The thread did not shear away. And the power behind it was more than he had ever imagined was possible. Apollyon was pushing back from the other side of the branch of reality, trying to keep Gabriel from severing it. The thread was too weak to allow Apollyon to jump to the same moment of time and space that Gabriel inhabited at that instant, but he was still connected to all the magical energy of the copies of himself.

Gabriel tensed and tried to summon up more magical energy from within using the breathing and energy exercises he had been practicing every day with Ohin. He felt the energy swell in his heart center and radiate down his arms into the Sword of Unmaking. He was holding Apollyon, but he did not know how long he could last. If the thread of reality gained any more stability, Apollyon might be fully connected with his many twins, who might be able to locate Gabriel in this place and moment in time.

This place and time really was a single moment. Gabriel noticed the silence around him. The mortar shells hung suspended in mid-flight and some in mid-explosion. He and Apollyon were suspending time in that moment of the bifurcation's creation. Gabriel didn't know how long he could sustain it. He was mustering all the energy he could from within himself. Without more imprints of some kind to focus that energy, it was only a matter of time before Apollyon overwhelmed him. Apollyon was at the disadvantage, in that he needed far more magical energy to re-establish the alternate branch of reality that Gabriel struggled to sever, but he also had far more energy at his disposal than Gabriel.

Trying to break a part of his mind away to think, to plan, to search out a possible source of more imprints, Gabriel struggled to maintain and concentrate the magical energy at just the right spot, just the right moment. No matter what he considered, nothing seemed plausible. There were no imprints left for him to claim. Even if he could release the energy directed at severing the branch of reality that Apollyon was trapped in and tried to jump through time, there was a good chance that Apollyon would follow him. And his wrath was not something Gabriel wanted to see any more of than he already had.

He almost thought he could hear Apollyon's screams of anger from the other side of the reality portal. Gabriel screamed himself then, in exhaustion and frustration. He would not allow Apollyon to take him and use him as a weapon for his conquest, to become some puppet with a sword. He would not be taken prisoner again. That was the plan that he kept coming back to. He could turn the sword on himself before Apollyon could stop him. If Gabriel was fast enough, Apollyon would not be able to save him no matter how strong his magic might be.

It was a feeble plan, and one that felt like surrender. But better to end his own life than risk it being used to kill and destroy others, especially those he had grown to love and care for. And what would they say? What would Ohin or Sema or Akikane or any of the others tell him to do? Or his family. His mother and father and sister, who he had lost as surely as if they had died. He thought about the last moment that he had seen them. The feel of his mother's lips on his forehead. The smell of lilacs from her favorite perfume. His father's strong arms around him. The weight of his father's hand on his shoulder as they said goodbye that last time. Would they agree with his plan? Would it matter? Would any of it matter? He was already dead to them. He would be right back where he had started. Where he had ended.

There at the bottom of the river, trapped in the bus, the water filling his lungs. He would be right back at the moment of his death. He had faced it once. He could face it again. The loss of all he loved. He could make that choice. Just like he had chosen to dive back into the water, back down to the bus where he had drowned. Like he had chosen to risk his life to save others. Like he had died risking his life to save others.

Why hadn't he seen it before?

The yell that filled his throat now was not a howl of frustration, but the roar of triumph. Gabriel reached for the imprints he had found, the imprints of Grace that had been with him ever since he had given his life to save others beneath the water of that river. He had never considered them. The actions of a person left imprints on themselves, as well as the objects they used. The power of the Grace imprints from willingly risking and giving his life to save others in that bus were far more powerful than the imprints of the pocket watch or the Sword of Unmaking. More powerful because they were closer to the source. They were part of his very being. He claimed hold of them and used them to redouble his focus on the magical energy aimed at the slim thread still tying the alternate reality with Apollyon in it to the Primary Continuum.

Gabriel was surprised at the power of the imprints he held within himself. He would not have been able to access them without first using a talisman, but now that he held them, they increased his magical strength considerably. The thread of the alternate reality ceased to exist even as he concentrated his will upon it.

Then it was gone and he was alone in the forest of bare trees, the mortars falling through the snow-filled air and exploding in the clearing. Apollyon, the one he had confronted at least, had been eliminated from existence, trapped in an alternate reality that most likely had collapsed into nothingness the moment its connection to the Primary Continuum had been severed.

Gabriel took a deep breath and looked around. He reached in his pocket and pulled out the fossil of the beetle suspended in amber. He thought a moment about what he had just done. He had created an alternate world and severed it to save himself. The second time he had created an alternate reality and ended it. *Destroyer of Worlds indeed*, he thought, as he resheathed the Sword of Unmaking. He looked at the piece of amber in his hand and then turned his head away, toward the battlefield clearing. Toward the foxholes. Toward his grandfather. Nearly without thinking, he jumped through space, coming to stand at the edge of the foxhole where he knew his grandfather was.

Mortar shells still rained down from the sky, exploding throughout the clearing and the forest. Men shouted orders and screamed in pain. Gabriel cast a web of Soul Magic around himself that would make him invisible to anyone nearby. Then he did what he knew he did not entirely want to do. He stepped forward and looked into the foxhole.

He recognized his grandfather from photos of when he was a young man. Blood covered his uniform and he held that same dented pocket watch Gabriel grasped in his own hand. Little to nothing remained of his friend's body. The look of terror and anguish on his grandfather's face stabbed into Gabriel's heart and made him gasp. He had wanted to see his grandfather, but he did not want to see him like this — in unimaginable pain and with no way to comfort him.

He could do nothing. Except shed a tear. And leave.

Clasping the chunk of amber in his hand, he focused his magical energy through the pocket watch and the all-encompassing blackness of time travel followed swiftly.

CHAPTER 27
HOME

Whiteness faded like gauze pulled from Gabriel's eyes to reveal that he stood in the northernmost edge of the courtyard of the Upper Ward of the Castle. That was where they had all agreed they would return if something went wrong. He had tried to return to a time equal in days and hours since the last time they had all been there. He stood facing the state apartments. Spinning around, he heard the voices even before he saw the faces.

Then a streaking cannonball of black hair struck him and he was lying on his back on the ground.

"Don't you ever do that again!" Teresa shouted as she sat on top of him, an angry angel of protection. "How am I supposed to guard you if you run away from me?"

"I was trying to protect *you*," Gabriel said, the wind starting to come back to his lungs. "That was the plan. For me to run."

"But I was supposed to go with you," Teresa said, tears in her eyes. "What if something had happened? What if you needed me to back you up?"

"Something did happen," Gabriel said. "And I'll always want you to back me up. But sometimes we have to face things alone. Now can I get up? I think you broke a rib."

"Sorry," Teresa said, her eyes darting away. "I got carried away. Thanks for trying to protect me." She said and kissed him on the cheek before she rolled away and stood up. Gabriel found a sudden need to avert his eyes.

"Anytime," he said, trying to not to think about the kiss on the cheek. "Thanks for trying to protect me too."

"She was a little worried," Rajan said, stepping up and extending a hand to help Gabriel to his feet.

"You don't say," Gabriel said, accepting a brotherly hug from Rajan.

"We were all a little worried," Ohin said.

"More than worried," Ling said.

"Yes, yes," Akikane said. "Very concerned."

"What happened to you?" Sema asked, stepping close and inspecting him with her hands, turning him this way and that to see if there were any marks or bruises. "Why is your hair wet? Is that snow?"

"Don't tell me you've been sledding while the rest of us were running for our lives?" Marcus said clamping a hand on Gabriel's shoulder.

"How did you get away?" Gabriel asked.

"Most of them disappeared after you did," Teresa said. "We thought for sure with that many of them they would catch you."

"And then we fought and ran as best we could," Ling said. "Each of them is as powerful as Akikane."

"Much more, much more," Akikane said. "We were very concerned."

"As soon as the space-time seal was broken, we fled," Ohin said. "We jumped in groups. I took Sema and Ling while Akikane took Marcus, Teresa, and Rajan. After a few jumps, they seemed to give up."

"Very odd, very odd," Akikane said. "I expected them to chase us farther."

"What about you?" Ohin said. "How far did they chase you?"

"I kept switching relics and using different time frames like you told me," Gabriel said. "By the time I ran out and used the pocket watch only one followed me."

The questions all came at the same moment.

"You met with one?"

"Did you fight him?"

"Where were you?"

"How did you get away?"

Gabriel looked around and realized he would have to tell them what he had done. "I used the pocket watch to take me to the battle of the Hürtgen Forest during World War Two in Western Germany in January of 1945," Gabriel began. "It's where my grandfather was given the watch by a friend who saved his life. It was a copy of Apollyon who followed me. Just one."

Gabriel recounted what had happened. The conversation. The mortar shells. The alternate branch of time he created. Trapping Apollyon in the branch and severing it from the Primary Continuum. Using the imprints from his near death in the bus that seemed like so long ago. He finished to a profound and prolonged silence. He could not tell from their eyes or the looks on their faces what they were thinking. Only Akikane was smiling.

"Well done, well done," Akikane finally said, his smile radiant. "I think the Sword of Unmaking has a new master now."

"No," Gabriel said, trying to figure out what he wanted to say next.

"Yes, yes," Akikane said. "The Sword of Unmaking is yours now. But you will need to learn how to wield it. How to master it. I will teach you."

"Thank you," Gabriel said, his hand unconsciously sliding to touch the tip of the sword sheath hanging below his back. "Will I need to go before the Council? For creating an alternate branch of time."

"Are you totally daft, lad?" Marcus said, bursting out in laughter, quickly joined by the rest of the team. "You just destroyed a Malignancy Mage with the power of thirty some copies of himself at his disposal. You'll be bloody lucky they don't try to make you a member of the Council."

"No, no," Akikane said, in mock seriousness. "You do not want that."

"You aren't in any trouble," Ohin said, embracing Gabriel quickly and then holding him by the shoulders. "You did the only thing that could have been done, and you did it very well."

"We're all very proud of you," Sema said, kissing Gabriel on the forehead.

"Very proud," Ling said, punching his arm.

"And happy you're back," Teresa added, extending her hand toward Rajan, who frowned.

"More happy than you know," Rajan said, passing Teresa the rabbit's foot.

"Happy indeed," Marcus said, extending his hand toward Teresa, who frowned herself now, before handing him the rabbit's foot. Marcus grinned.

"What was the bet this time?" Gabriel said, his eyes widening in surprise.

"Some bets you can't know unless you join the wager," Teresa said.

"Those are the rules," Rajan said.

"And never bet against a highwayman," Marcus said. "That's the first rule. Now, this," he said, holding up rabbit's foot, "and Gabriel's return, call for something special. And I've got a bottle of Spanish port I've been saving for a unique occasion."

"How do you manage to turn every triumph into an excuse for drinking?" Sema said as they all began to walk back to toward the castle proper.

"Sobriety and success are mutually exclusive in my view," Marcus said. "Besides, port is a fine way to end a victory dinner."

"I don't know if we can call this a full victory," Ohin said, stroking his chin and sounding a little more serious than the others.

"No, no," Akikane said. "But every battle counts toward winning the war."

"Victory or not," Rajan said, "it's still time for dinner."

"And how do you turn everything into an excuse to eat?" Teresa teased.

"Because I'm hungry," Rajan said. "Besides, a victory dinner means dancing, and we know how you feel about that."

"Right!" Teresa said, suddenly as excited about dinner as Marcus and Rajan combined. "I claim the first dance with our hero of the day." Teresa grabbed Gabriel's arm and held it high.

"What!" Gabriel exclaimed as the others laughed. "Dancing? I'm no hero. And I can't dance."

"Neither can she," Rajan said.

"Coming from the one who trips over his own feet, that's a compliment," Teresa said.

"I'm sure you dance wonderfully," Sema said.

"I'll take the second dance," Ling added.

"But," Gabriel said, "I really can't dance."

"You don't want to dance with me?" Teresa said with a fake pout.

"No," Gabriel said, his face flushed. "Of course I'd dance with you if I knew how to dance, but I don't, so…"

"Gabriel," Ohin said with a wide smile. "Let me give you some advice as tutor to apprentice. Stop while you're ahead." The team laughed again and Gabriel laughed with them as they walked toward the state apartments.

"I'll dance," Gabriel said, "but we need two more people."

"What kind of dance is this?" Marcus asked. "A cotillion?"

"Not for dancing," Gabriel answered. "For baseball. You need nine for a team. We already have seven. We just need two more people. And another team to play against."

"Only one more, only one more," Akikane said. "Baseball is sublime. Particularly the peanuts."

"And hotdogs," Rajan added.

"And let's not forget the ale," Marcus quipped.

"Beer," Rajan said. "Lager, not ale."

"Close enough," Marcus replied.

"You want to start a baseball team?" Teresa asked her voice rising in incredulity.

"Sure," Gabriel said. "There's plenty of room for a baseball diamond beyond the north wall of the castle. And it'll be good for team morale."

"Not a bad idea," Ohin said.

"I call catcher," Ling said.

"First base," Rajan added.

"What sort of game is this?" Sema asked.

"It's like cricket," Marcus said.

"Hardly," Rajan said.

"They both use a ball and a bat," Marcus said. "How different can they be?"

"I think we may need to review the rules," Gabriel said.

"You can explain them over dinner," Teresa said. "But get this straight right now, we're not starting a football team. I don't look good in shoulder pads." Gabriel laughed and followed the others toward the Waterloo Chamber and dinner.

The dinner that night was as appetizing as usual, the conversation and the company as warm and filling as the meal. The small sip of port made his head light, but helped him quit worrying about where he placed his feet while he danced, first with Teresa, then with Ling, then with Sema, and before he knew it, learning a waltz with Councilwoman Elizabeth to teach him. It was a night that went on and on, seeming to stretch time out and spread a few hours over days.

When he finally lay in bed that night, his head spinning from the dancing, looking up at the stars through the window, Gabriel wondered, as he often did when staring at the stars, what the future would bring. What his future would bring. There would be other missions surely. He wasn't certain what they would be, but he could think of several. Stopping Apollyon and his copies from destroying The Great Barrier for one. Saving an entire alternate world from the crushing rule of the cruel and despotic Kumaradevi for another. And Vicaquirao was out there somewhere, plotting and scheming, creating plans within plans like booby-trapped Russian matryoshka dolls, hoping to control Gabriel's destiny from a distance. There was a lot of work left to do in saving the Continuum. And he'd need some sleep if he was going to be ready to train for it.

He fell asleep dreaming of dancing and stars and Windsor Castle and swords and magic and time travel and hoping that for once, he could finally sleep in.

6463465R00160

Made in the USA
San Bernardino, CA
09 December 2013